Everything I Knew

PETER GOLDSWORTHY

Everything I Knew

A novel

HAMISH HAMILTON
an imprint of
PENGUIN BOOKS

HAMISH HAMILTON

Published by the Penguin Group
Penguin Group (Australia)
250 Camberwell Road, Camberwell, Victoria 3124, Australia
(a division of Pearson Australia Group Pty Ltd)
Penguin Group (USA) Inc.
375 Hudson Street, New York, New York 10014, USA
Penguin Group (Canada)
90 Eglinton Avenue East, Suite 700, Toronto, Canada ON M4P 2Y3
(a division of Pearson Penguin Canada Inc.)
Penguin Books Ltd
80 Strand, London WC2R 0RL England
Penguin Ireland
25 St Stephen's Green, Dublin 2, Ireland
(a division of Penguin Books Ltd)
Penguin Books India Pvt Ltd
11 Community Centre, Panchsheel Park, New Delhi – 110 017, India
Penguin Group (NZ)
67 Apollo Drive, Rosedale, North Shore 0632, New Zealand
(a division of Pearson New Zealand Ltd)
Penguin Books (South Africa) (Pty) Ltd
24 Sturdee Avenue, Rosebank, Johannesburg 2196, South Africa

Penguin Books Ltd, Registered Offices: 80 Strand, London, WC2R 0RL, England

First published by Penguin Group (Australia), 2008

1 3 5 7 9 10 8 6 4 2

Text copyright © Peter Goldsworthy 2008

The moral right of the author has been asserted

Design by John Canty © Penguin Group (Australia)
Cover photography: Photolibrary
Author photograph by Nicholas Purcell
Typeset in 12/16 Adobe Garamond by Post Pre-press Group, Brisbane, Queensland
Printed and bound in Australia by McPherson's Printing Group, Maryborough, Victoria

National Library of Australia
Cataloguing-in-Publication data:

Goldsworthy, Peter, 1951–
Everything I knew/Peter Goldsworthy
9780241015339 (pbk.)

A823.3

penguin.com.au

Contents

Before *1*

During *23*

term one *25*
term two *98*
term three *217*

After *261*

Acknowledgements 297

Before

I

Universe, Milky Way, Solar System, Earth, Australia, South Australia, Penola, Church Street, 26. It's December 1963, and I spend the first week of the summer holidays writing my galactic address on everything I own. I write it backwards, which offers an easier pathway home if anything finds itself lost, especially in another galaxy. I'm thirteen years old and I'm going to Mars, perhaps as soon as the end of the holidays. I flip my new 28-inch Super Elliott upside down and carve the sequence into the rough rawhide underbelly of the saddle with my sheath-knife, although if that beautiful, lighter-than-air machine – a reward for finishing primary school as top boy – loves me as much as I love it, it will surely come freewheeling home riderless whenever I whistle, even from Mars.

I am so happy that happiness escapes my notice. Happiness is a default state, a given, like the town I was born in, the family I was born into. Like the mind I am growing into, the brain I am slowly beginning to fill.

Summer is another given, a recurring given. Billy Currie is also a given; we have been best friends since he first moved to town, a lifetime – a child's lifetime, without remembered beginning or imagined end – ago. Call it an arranged best-friendship, a match made by proximity and limited opportunity, like most from childhood. We shared a desk through primary school. We go to the same church; Reverend Riddoch sponsored both Currie families when they were relocated from the mission years before. We play in the same Caledonian band; me on pipes, Billy on kettle. We both have stick-thin bodies with big, difficult-to-balance heads, and even bigger mouths that are forever getting us into trouble.

We are both expected to get into trouble; me because I have a cop for a father, Billy because he's an Abo.

He inherits my broken-down 26-inch Malvern Star that Christmas, after a difficult bargaining process between the dads. Mine sees himself as some sort of local Protector of Aborigines and offers the old bike for free; Jacko Currie, a proud, prickly man who works plenty of overtime at the sawmill, and once knocked out the East Gambier full-back during a grand final for calling him a curly worm, doesn't want charity. Somehow a price is agreed on; a clutch of pound notes goes one way and the bike the other in a terse, wordless ceremony outside the courthouse. I overhear the missing words later that night, a muffled whispering behind my parents' bedroom door. *Not as if they don't need the money. You'd think they'd be grateful. You've done so much for those people, Jim.*

In our boy-world, both bikes are common boy-property. Centaurs of bicycle and boy-flesh, we ride everywhere that summer, ride to the ends of the known world, or at least to the ends of our endurance, whichever comes first.

We spend long mornings digging for buried treasure in the dump south of town, and long afternoons losing ourselves in the cool, dense-packed pine forests to the east and west. On the hottest January days, bare-chested and barefoot, but with thick, stiff caps of Brylcreem fixed to our heads, we cycle north to the flooded limestone quarries and sinkholes beyond the vineyards. Our given corner of the universe, the South-East of South Australia, Earth, Solar System, sits on a thousand-square-mile slab of porous limestone, a great artesian sponge so sodden with rain that even in summer the water is pressed upwards and outwards into swamps and springs and creeklets by the sheer wet weight of itself. We, on the other hand, are utterly weightless as we dive and swim in those vast limestone rooms; we might be flying, in a different kind of sky. The sunlight falls unobstructed through the deep, clear water as if through air; the rocky floors and walls are as lime-white and dazzling as a beach. Even twenty feet down the light still hurts our eyes, and the underwater world of yabbie-infested crevices and tiny freshwater fish is as vivid to the senses as the *National Geographic* pictorials in Doc McKenzie's waiting room. Legend has it that horses, cattle, tractors, and even entire picnicking families have fallen through the thin limestone crust and vanished into this watery world (it has happened to friends of most of my parents' friends), but we dive for the sunken treasure of horse skulls and human remains in vain.

On the long haul back to town, waterlogged, bladders bursting, we stop frequently to piss among the vines and eat the ripening grapes. My parents are total abstainers and have never touched a drop, but talk proudly enough to outsiders of the special flavour of the local claret and the famed *terra rossa* soil that produces it. Nicking a bottle from Redman's packing shed one afternoon, I can't see what the fuss is about; the taste surely owes less to the soil than to the copious boy-piss foaming about the vine roots.

I prefer sweet sherry, which I keep stashed with the rest of my contraband in a battered leather suitcase on the roof of our house.

I'm seldom at home that summer and when I am, I'm more often on the house than in it. Ours is a two-humped camel in a street of the one-humped; the valley of flaking corrugated iron between the high twin gables is my crow's nest and sanctuary. That leather treasure-chest is stuffed with plenty more common boy-property: Dad's police-issue binoculars, Billy's slug gun, old war comics, copies of *Astounding Science Fiction* and *Amazing Stories,* cigarettes. Waiting for Billy after breakfast, I like to lie on my belly on the warm iron slope and pick sparrows out of trees with slugs, or sprawl flat on my back on the corrugated valley floor and read and brood and dream.

More usually Billy has arrived before breakfast and we are already miles away. Once or twice we camp out in the depths of the forest, if only to terrify ourselves, but there are no rabbits there, and rabbits are our subsistence crop, worth four bob a brace at Jeffrey's Butchery. Farmers everywhere welcome us, direct us to the best warrens and campsites. Short, sweet nights these, at the end of long, exhausting days. After setting our traps we light a fire, lay out our blanket-rolls and smoke pilfered tailor-mades – Craven A, Rothmans, Peter Stuyvesant – or pungent rollies of newspaper and palm-crumbled stringy-bark. Probably the first freshly skinned rabbit is already roasting on a wonky twig-spit between us, and with luck there will be something to drink, perhaps a bottle of Autumn Brown sweet sherry bought from Billy's oldest brother, Neville, or filched from his Uncle Possum, who subsists on it as if it were pungent brown mother's milk. More traps are springing shut in the darkness about us, more rabbits crying to be released, if only from pain, but very soon we will have eaten too much meat and drunk too much sherry to move, or even to stay awake.

'Tell another story,' Billy might mumble across this sleepy twilight zone. 'Tell me the one about going back in time and rooting Sophia Loren.'

'It's set in the future, remember? I bring her *forward* in time.'

'Same diff. You still *shag* her. Tell it again. Or tell the one about the really flat planet where people grow wheels instead of feet. Four wheels —'

'Two wheels. The people are a kind of centaur – half-man, half-bike. The animals have four wheels.'

'Maybe the people should have one wheel, Robbie. So they're standin' up. Like unicycles.'

'Pig's arse! Whose story is it?'

'Yours. Tell it again.'

I am always happy to tell it again, I am happy to tell all my stories again, although usually one of us will be asleep before I finish.

'What if we're not in the same class at high school?' he shakes me awake to ask on another night towards the end of summer.

For the moment, giddy and barely sensible, I can't move. What's the time? Halfway to morning, and then some. The fire is almost dead, the moon and stars all shifted and strange.

'My sister told me they done this test on the first day. Last year. Next day they put everyone in a different class.'

'Go back to sleep, Billy.'

'*Can't* sleep. What we gonna do if we're in a different class?'

'We won't be in a different class.'

He rolls over onto my swag and jams a headlock on me; he might be as skinny as me, and much shorter, but somehow he's much stronger. 'You'll be in the *brainy* class for sure.'

'Your sister got into the brainy class,' I remind him.

'She's a brain! Like Neville. That's why we got sent here.' His grip is vicelike. 'Only had primary school on the mission. Wish we'd never left.'

He has been in this half-maudlin, half-violent state many times before; sweet sherry especially can get him started on everything that might go wrong with his life, or has gone wrong since leaving the Coorong and an idyllic childhood of swan-egging and fishing and messing about in boats.

'Let go, bugger ya! You're brainy enough. You know more than me about lots of stuff.'

'I'm *dumb*, Robbie. Everyone knows I'm dumb. I'll be in the dumb class. What stuff?'

'That tiger snake we killed at the dump,' I remember. 'You knew how to skin it.'

Open sesame; he releases the headlock. 'Course I knew. We used to eat 'em back on the mission.'

I don't fully believe him. That is, I believe that a Currie uncle or cousin probably ate a snake, somewhere, Dreamtimes back – but not Billy. He hadn't wanted to eat our tiger snake.

'What'd they taste like?'

'Like fish. Mullet. A bit muddy.'

'I grabbed a king brown by the tail once,' I tell him.

He doesn't really believe that either, but we don't have to believe each other, especially this late at night. The story is the thing, whether set in the amazing future or the even more astounding past, and now he needs to hear the rest.

Soon enough he has listened himself back to sleep, but I can't follow. My neck hurts a little – Billy's affectionate violence often leaves me sore. And although the giddiness of the sherry has faded, nausea remains. I slip out of my blanket-roll, take a long purifying piss into the night, then grab my torch and knife and wander off to check the traps. Rabbits might be a plague but they are still God's creatures, according to my old man. They shouldn't be left to suffer. Or left (*his* old man was a Scot, after all) to work their two-bob carcass free, or drag a ten-bob trap down a burrow. Less hunter than gatherer tonight, I twist two rabbit necks, slit open their bellies by torchlight, and fling the guts between my legs far out into the darkness. A four-bob night already; I don't bother resetting the traps. My share of the spoils will buy second-hand copies of *Astounding Science Fiction*, or bottles of Spirits of Salts and bags of zinc dust for making astounding explosions in the stables at the back of the house. I have no idea what Billy will spend his pocket-money on. *Superman* comics. Slippery Sam iceblocks. Sweet brown mother's milk for the town drunk.

I empty the last of the sherry into my big chipped enamel mug and stoke up the fire. High school is suddenly no more than a few days away. Will we end up in the same class, or even – the root cause of his panic, I see now – in the same friendship? Time will tell; far more pressing that night is the promise of high school itself, growing closer with each less small hour. I am restless for change. Primary school bored me; the oldest in my class by accident of birth date, I found the work too easy – and found it all too easy to play up, play the smart-aleck.

Billy sleeps on; I stir the embers and pick over the rabbit bones and sip at the sweet sherry, alone in my default happiness, in my default corner of the big default Universe. Penola, South Australia might be the width of a paddock or the width of a galaxy away – no matter. In the morning our bicycles will find their way home easily enough, bed-rolls and skinned carcasses and rattling traps strapped to their wheel-racks, the two of us half asleep in the saddle, our long morning shadows pacing us, neck and neck, flat shadow-centaurs of boy-flesh and steel tubing and spinning wheels made one.

2

Every year of childhood is a year of first times and fresh discoveries, but by the end of primary school everything that is first and fresh has begun to feel – for the first time – like a rite of passage.

Those rites are marked by standard-version adult liturgy – *You shaving yet, young feller? What's the weather like up there?* Plus (water off a duck's back) *Maybe you'll act more maturely now, sonny-jim.* But I need no ritual noises from adults to notice the passing of milestones, or at least to sense – being something of a dreamer and futurist, time-travelling back and forth in my head – that in years to come I will think back on them as milestones.

I am fast approaching giraffe-height – a human crane, a skin-and-bone gantry, if less mechanically coordinated. My hands and feet have grown too far from my body, too quickly; I have lost a feel for where they are in space and time. I fumble cutlery, drop crockery, bump into table edges and doorframes; there are small but crucial delays in locating my extremities when even basic motor skills are planned. Everything seems so far away. Lying flat on my back I search for my toes on the southern horizon and envy the dinosaurs; an extra brain down there would come in handy.

More centrally placed body parts also seem out of control. A moustache of dark fluff has appeared beneath my nose, and another moustache, or perhaps more of a raised eyebrow, above my cock. The first moustache is much joked about, especially by my mother; the existence of the second, shorter and curlier, I manage to keep to myself for some months, all the while trying vainly to comb it straight.

About this time, the first hairline crack appears in my perfect soprano voice, a get-out-of-church-choir-free pass, at least until the pot breaks completely. About this time, also, my first pair of long pants. My first 45rpm disc, 'She Loves You', priced at two and six at Dalziel's store but free of charge at five-finger discount, and best played with the backing of cracked-pot vocals.

My first sheath-knife. I sharpen the mirror-bright blade nightly, and although its sworn sole purpose is to skin rabbits I wear it everywhere, even, turned inwards, inside my new long pants to church on Sundays.

Next comes my first wet dream, the 'nocturnal emission' my mother chooses to mention, in passing, across the tea table at the end of a long washing day – a low-key, nudge-and-wink rite of passage.

These standard boy-milestones unsurprising to everyone, of course, except me.

My first daytime emission surprises me as I pore over a picture of the voluptuous Sophia Loren on the front cover of *Women's Weekly*.

'So where is it, Robbie?'

'Where's what?'

'Mrs Dalziel said you picked up the *Weekly* for me.'

'Um. I dropped it in a puddle.'

This is less a lie than an exaggeration; a small puddle dropped in it. A private ceremony only, this: I cremate the sticky pages in the oil-drum incinerator out the back while she hurries off up Church Street to buy another copy.

Soon after that comes first love, although it seems doomed from the start since Miss Loren is thirty-ish, and married, and living in Rome, Italy, Earth, and I am thirteen and although available and living on Earth, my hometown – Penola, Australia – is as far from hers as it is possible to be without leaving our shared planet.

Then I nick the next edition of the *Weekly* from Dalziel's and stumble across my first photo of Carlo Ponti. I imagined her husband would be stiff competition. I read women's magazines for their stories too, trying to understand what romantic women want. A man, it seems, can never be too tall or dark or brooding. So what is Miss Loren doing with this fat bald dwarf? My heart leaps at the sight of him. I am still in with a chance. I've been dealt back into the game. For my fourteenth birthday I order a duffle coat to go with my long pants, a pair of desert boots, and my first safety razor. I comb extra Brylcreem through my hair until it's as hard and shiny as metal. I might not be dark but I'm tall, and I know how to dress to kill. When our paths finally cross, hopefully before the end of the year, I plan to look my best for Miss Loren.

About this time, too, the Facts of Life chat. Doc McKenzie is invited to address the boys' confirmation class in the Caledonian Hall one Tuesday night. A lifetime bachelor with a food-flecked beard and a befuddled, mumbling manner, his nose is buried in a battered copy of *Astounding Science Fiction* as we straggle in – a man after, or perhaps before, my own dreamy heart. Astounding science-fiction magazines of all types jostle with the *National Geographics* in his waiting room; he goes nowhere without a copy jammed in a pocket of his big, loose-fitting tweed jacket. He has been known to read a page or two during difficult deliveries and almost miss the birth.

Eventually he stares up at us from beneath his bushy eyebrows, blinking as if we are Martians ourselves. Having never been of this world, how can he speak of worldly things? He keeps a town-famous collection of anatomical specimens in pickling jars on the shelves of his consulting room; he has brought a boxful along tonight. From time to time he points at some severed body part so bleached and unrecognisable that it might have been pulled from the wreckage of a flying saucer, and mutters a word or two in a language that might also be Martian: *Foetus, vas deferens, uterus, testis.*

'An interesting if little known scientific fact,' he is still mumbling in his beard as we leave, 'the Bartholin's glands of the sexually aroused female human vulva produce the ester trimethylamine, the same molecule that gives fish its characteristic odour . . .'

'The birds and the bees,' my father reports to my mother that night behind their bedroom door, 'and the fish.'

3

That summer is also a time of last things. Cleaning the gutters, Dad finds his missing binoculars, and the suitcase, and the stash of war comics hidden inside. Having fought in that war, he refuses ever to speak of it; he spills the entire collection into the oil-drum without a word, douses it in kerosene and tosses in a match. Billy's slug gun is handed back to Jacko Currie in another terse, wordless ceremony. The crude comics I sketched myself on butcher's paper (frame after frame of Billy and me fighting off hordes of evil Japs) are spared, but for how long? The big pepper tree outside the primary-school hall offers a safer hideout. I know every fork and crevice of that ancient tree; Billy and I like to shimmy up after pipe-band practice for a smoke or drink. Perched birdlike on a branch, he once famously pulled down his shorts and dropped a condor-sized shit onto the grass far below; I nearly fell out of the tree after it, I was laughing so hard. A high triple fork is our preferred eyrie; a nearby possum hole offers a safe hiding place for contraband.

I stash my comics there the next day, then immediately forget about them. War comics are history now; for some time I've been reading stories without pictures, stories set in the future, not the past. A copy of *Astounding Science Fiction* nicked from the doctor's waiting room got me started; now a small alp of pulp magazines is hidden under my bed: *Galaxy, Fantasy & SF, Amazing Stories, Analog, Alien Worlds*. Some I even paid for. When I run out of science fiction to read I write my own, setting my stories down on paper for the first time. War stories of a kind, perhaps, but with Billy and me turned loose in outer space instead of Japan or Germany. The villains are aliens now, although more likely to be little yellow men than green, and not beyond screaming some war-criminal pidgin of *Banzai!* and *Schnell!* and *For the Emperor!* and *Heil, Hitler!* as they wave their ray guns.

'When I was a wee child I spake as a child, I understood as a child, I thought as a child,' Reverend Riddoch lectures the confirmation class the next Tuesday night. 'But when I became a man I put away wee childish things.'

His long gaunt nose and fierce, tufted eyebrows have the look of a Scottish sea-captain, or perhaps a Scottish breed of dog. His terrier eyes aren't aimed my way as he speaks, or at Billy, but he is talking at us, clearly enough, as he has often talked at us – the class rascals, the designated troublemakers – in the past. For once in my short life I agree with him.

I hurry home and take down the model Spitfires and Zeroes and Messerschmitt 109s suspended by fishing line above my bed and pack them away. (My father – who resembles a British bulldog more than a Highland terrier – worships all things finely engineered, and permitted those.) My bag of marbles, bulging with precious agates and cat's eyes and a single big chipped tombowler, also goes into the bottom drawer; the chemistry set that was my Grade Seven school prize is my new favourite toy.

My chemistry set, and my equally dangerous pen.

4

It's the year one million AD and the sun has gone supernova, boiling the oceans from the Earth and leaving only a crust of baked salt. The dazzle of that flat white surface can be seen from light-years away, as bright as a white dwarf star itself. On its great saltpans, wheels offer a clear evolutionary advantage, from six-wheeled ants to eight-wheeled spiders and upwards. The biggest herbivores are the size of steamrollers: brontosaurs on wheels. Gentle creatures unless provoked, they defend themselves by rolling their predators flat.

Their one weakness is a wide turning circle. Their two-wheeled predators, all sabre teeth and tiger fur, can easily cut inside. Of course it's suicide for them to nip at the heels of their lumbering prey – fox terriers attacking the tyres of a Mack truck – but the soft, cartilaginous crankshaft of the dinosaurs, and the bone and gristle of their differential joints offer a vulnerable underbelly.

Nineteen sixty-four, late January, late afternoon, High School Eve. The story has been sitting unfinished in my head for weeks. I'm riding no-hands across town clutching the last sackful of summer rabbits to my lap when inspiration strikes. Of course! The intelligent life-form in one million AD must be a kind of unicycle. *Homo unicyclis.* Have I read the idea somewhere before? Van Vogt? Asimov? I don't think so. I conjure up the footwear of my single-wheeled beings – lace-up leather tyres – but figuring out the biology of the wheels has me stumped. I brake and dismount and stare into the gleaming spokes of my machine. How to get fragile veins and nerves through an axle joint? A live, growing wheel will need a blood supply, will need nerve endings, will need to feel touch, heat, pain. As I shoulder the hessian sack and walk away, inspiration strikes again: the human shoulder joint is *almost* a wheel. I drop the sack and flap my long arms wildly, rotating them at speed to test the limits of their sockets.

'Trying to fly, Master Burns?'

An all too familiar voice tugs me back to the present, but which present? Primary school, a year before? Plump, plain Miss Burke stands before me as she has stood before me a thousand times, wearing a half-amused, half-exasperated look on her face. 'Did you achieve liftoff?' she asks.

No, not school; she has a glass of red wine in her hand. I'm in the doorway of the teachers' house on Arthur Street, looking in as she looks out.

'I must say you've shot up over summer, Master Burns.' She turns and aims her next words back into the house. 'Miss Hammond! Come and inspect the rabbitoh. Tell me if he reminds you of anyone.'

Her housemate, plumper and prettier, but also well past thirty according to my mother, appears at her side, cigarette in hand. 'A giraffe, Miss Burke?'

They giggle together, Tweedledum and Tweedledee, wearing the same permed hairstyle and thick cladding of face powder and dressed identically, or at least in each other's clothes.

'Think insect likeness, Miss Hammond, not mammal.'

'That Beatle person, Miss Burke! The one called Paul.'

Flush-faced and a little unsteady on highish heels, they swap the wineglass and the cigarette; inhale, imbibe, swap back.

'A mop of hair and the world would be your oyster, Master Burns,' Miss Burke tells me.

I hoist my sack back on my shoulder. 'Paul McCartney looks like a *girl*, Miss.'

'I think he looks like a nice young man. What say you, Miss Hammond?'

'Indeedy-doody, Miss Burke. Most presentable. Unlike the other three. How much do we owe this week, Master Burns?'

'Two bob, Miss.'

They also share a taste for rabbit stew. Miss Hammond blows a wobbly smoke-ring over my shoulder as her companion fishes in her purse. 'And where is Ringo today?'

'Sorry, Miss?'

'Your partner in crime. Don't you think young Billy looks a little like Ringo Starr, Miss Burke?'

'A rather *swarthy* Ringo, Miss Hammond. Ringo with a touch of the tar-brush. Did you tell the rabbitoh that we'll require two bunnies next week?'

'All in good time, Miss Burke. The rabbitoh might not have heard that we have a new lodger joining us. The improbably named Miss Pamela Peach.'

They giggle at the sound of it, spluttering smoke and wine.

'No doubt the rabbitoh will come across our new colleague next week, Miss Hammond.'

'Do you think the rabbitoh is *ready* for high school?'

'He must prepare himself for the challenge, Miss Hammond. Miss Pamela Peach,' she smirks at the name again, 'might not be as tolerant as some.'

'Do I detect a wistful tone, Miss Burke? Is it possible that you might miss the little rascal?'

'Just thank your lucky stars, my dear, that boys don't do Domestic Science. The mind boggles at what the rabbitoh might get up to in *your* class. Exploding cupcakes. Anzac biscuits that levitate above the world like flying saucers.'

'You look like Ringo Starr,' I tell Billy the moment he arrives after breakfast the next morning.

'Do *not!*'

'Do so.' Ringo Starr in a neat high-school uniform, straddling a 26-inch Malvern Star. Ringo Starr with a dark brooding face, jutting brow-ridge, and a flattened, unbreakable nose.

Of course I know Billy is a half-caste, whatever that means. It seems to mean he isn't a full-blood, which means even less, even though people speak the words somehow upper-case, as if they are proper nouns. It means he is part-Aborigine, but so are his mum and dad. So what does 'part' mean? Not half, after all? What does Aborigine mean? Aborigine: the word has always sounded unnatural to my ear, and even somehow unpleasant, musically. Does it belong in the English language? Abo is a more natural fit in the mouth, a word with the feel of a nickname. Davo. Tommo. Jacko.

Being called half-caste or Abo never bothered Jacko Currie, but he always saw red at 'curly worm'.

'You don't use that kind of language to an Abo,' Dad explained mysteriously.

Because Abos eat curly worms? Because they used to eat curly worms but don't any more? Because they eat curly snakes? Billy had no more idea than me.

Another Saturday, his old man walked off the field mid-game when the ump called him Jacky Jacky.

Dad's version? 'Must have got out the wrong side of bed.'

He'd opposed the assimilation of the Curries at first – 'The town's not ready for it' – but changed his tune the first night Jacko, Possum, and Billy's brother Neville showed up at football training. Two Border League premierships later, he was all for the Curries, as many as the deep back-pockets of the showground oval could hold. 'Got any aunties who can kick a footy, Billy-boy? Got any sisters?'

Mum took longer to convince. 'I don't think those people live very hygienically,' she declared, changing the sheets of the spare bed after Billy came to stay the first time. My sheets looked dirtier than his, but her mind was made up. 'Someone should teach that boy to wash.'

'Someone should teach him to box,' Dad told her. 'It's in his blood. Look at the head. Born to take a punch.'

My father often tried to lace toy gloves onto my reluctant fists, but I refused to spar with him, or to hit anything that might hit back, including the wide-swinging punching-bag suspended from a beam in the stables. Nor could I lift the weights he urged on me. He claimed to have been skinny himself as a boy, but I didn't believe him. When he ran a tape-measure around my chest and biceps I had the feeling he'd like to lay me out on his workbench and repair me, turn my beanpole-frame into oak.

Turn a girl into a boy? Miss Burke isn't the first to tell me I look like Paul McCartney's little brother – but I worry more that I look like his sister. If my pretty-boy face makes Dad anxious, he never mentions it. Billy has even less meat on the bones of his kite-frame than me, but at least he has an Abo's squashed face.

'You half-caste boys are made for the ring,' Dad nagged at him over the occasional weekend meal. 'You got the best of both worlds.'

Billy looked past him, looked away, said nothing. He was born with that flat, boxer's face, not beaten into it. Like me he had no interest in boxing, or any other source of pain.

Nor did my mother, on my behalf. 'Remember he's the policeman's son, Jim.'

'All the more reason to learn to look after himself, Mother.'

'And get himself into even more trouble?'

'He needs the discipline.'

'But he's so slightly built. There's a rough element in some of those boys from the forest towns.'

'A boxing club will keep 'em off the streets. Be good for Billy's mob too. Stop 'em going walkabout.'

His own fists are weapons of last resort. In his Senior Constable days he carried a truncheon in a secret pocket sewn into his trouser seams, but never had cause to use it. His police-issue Browning .38 has been taken from the office safe just twice in his working life, once to shoot a sick dog and once a horse tangled in a fence. His cuffs also never leave the safe; he prides himself on Come Quietly methods. Speak softly and carry a big fist. He is known to have left the occasional drunk with a black eye, but even the most disorderly still seem to respect him in the morning, including those who spend time in the holding cells in the backyard. The cells could as easily be two brick shithouses, a Ladies and Gents, if always used as two Gents. They are seldom locked. The regulars, like Uncle Possum, or the Skinner brothers from Nangwarry who spend a night or two in the cells each month working off unpaid fines, are allowed out in daylight hours to rake the gravel drive or trim the lawn edges. Work makes free? Not for Mum, who cooks the prisoners' food (the same three square meals a day that we eat; the Department pays an allowance for this), and does their washing, which in the case of the Skinners is no task for weak stomachs. Nor is emptying and hosing out their slop pails, an occasional punishment for me far worse than any belting. None of the prisoners ever hightails it over the back fence. Uncle Possum especially prefers to dry out with the comforts of a Sunday roast and mint sauce and even my dad's repetitive jokes: 'You still here, Poss? Thought you'd gone walkabout.'

Earth, Penola, Church Street, our first day of high school. 'No more walkabout,' he tells Billy, who looks past him, looks away, says nothing. We sit astride our bikes, impatient to set off, while he aims his ancient box Brownie at us. This is an important ceremony, the formal passing of another milestone. Our long summer walkabout is over, and all the long years before it. Here we are: less Paul McCartney and Ringo Starr than Tom Sawyer and Huck Finn, shoehorned into long pants and strangled by school ties, bike clips handcuffing our legs, the weight of extra Brylcreem as heavy on our heads as the caps of some fancy city school.

'You knuckle down in class, young Billy,' Dad says, staring down into the viewfinder. 'Nose to the grindstone. No more high jinks. You follow your brother Neville's example. He's a credit to his people. You too, sonny-jim. Say Kraft cheese, boys.'

'Don't forget,' Mum calls after us from the front porch, 'I want to hear all about this new teacher from the city. The young glamour-puss everyone is talking about.'

During

term one

Penola High, Cameron Street, Room 1A, February 1964, our second
day of school. She enters our classroom and our lives with a quickstepping, marionette jerkiness. Is it the absurdly high heels? Even
perched on these she is tiny, shorter than most of us, and probably
not much older. Not that anyone could mistake her for a student.
A tight red skivvy moulds the small symmetrical breasts within;
her tight black pants are stretched even tighter by a kind of stirrup
tucked beneath her feet inside those dangerous shoes.

'Ski pants,' Anne Hunter whispers across the aisle, awed.

All of us are awed. She is the smallest woman we have ever
seen, yet so perfectly proportioned she seems more doll-like than
human. *Is* she human? I wonder. Does she have a navel? Navels are
the proof, according to a recent astounding story. Her dark hair
is yanked back into a roll as tight as a grenade, accentuating her
slender neck and elf-like face: a face too dainty, surely, to frame
such huge eyes and high cheekbones. Yet that tiny, perfect face is

expressionless, an impassive robot's mask. I watch for further proof: will she – will *it* – blink?

'Audrey Hepburn,' Anne Hunter whispers.

'A cyborg duplicate,' I whisper back.

Anne smiles, uncertainly; she smiles at everything I say, especially when she doesn't understand it.

'A robot, stupid.'

A robot with stage fright. A half-smile is frozen on its face; it licks its lips, opens its mouth as if to say something, closes it again. Licks again. We wait, mesmerised. Long seconds tick by. Someone titters, then someone else; perhaps it's me. Is the robot going to speak at *all*? It glances about for help, then seizes a stick of chalk and by sheer act of will clacks the words MISS PEACH across the blackboard, forcefully. Having got two words out by hand, it now seems able to produce a few more by mouth: 'Good morning, IA.'

A chorus of incoherent mumbles: 'Good morning, Miss Peach.'

The fixed half-smile becomes three-quarters, and almost human. 'It's your first week at high school, IA – but it's also mine. If *you* feel a little nervous, spare a thought for me.'

Rehearsed robot words, but several of the girls smile back reassuringly; her own smile (yes, her – definitely human now) brightens even more in response. 'Let's all try saying good morning again. One more time with feeling?'

Whatever this means goes over our heads as she waves her stick of chalk like a baton, 'Ready? Good *morning*, IA.'

A few more voices give the correct reply, at proper volume. Mine isn't among them.

'*Much* better, IA. Sit please, and I'll call the roll.'

What follows is less the premeditation of a schoolroom of boys than the instincts of a school of piranha, acting with one mind. The noise of our seating is deafening: a deliberate, prolonged clattering and scraping of metal chair-legs back and forth on the wooden floor, the legs of my chair loudest among them.

Anne Hunter turns on me, horrified. 'But she's *beautiful, Robbie!*'

Astonishment more than horror on Miss Peach's elf-face. 'I think we might do that again, IA.' Another tentative smile. 'One more time – with *less* feeling. Everyone stand, please.'

The clatter of our rising is even more deafening than our sitting. Head and shoulders above my classmates, I watch her recoil as if struck, then stand frozen again. Do robots weep? Asimov has nothing to say on the subject, but tears might be another proof. Blood certainly is, and I can smell blood in the water. Something in this beautifully perfect creature begs to be made ugly. Or something vulnerable begs to be hurt.

She is trying hard to be less vulnerable. 'You are *high*-school students now, IA. *And* you are the top stream.' Her ballerina's face is comically stern, her bluster forced – another page of actor's lines not yet properly rehearsed. 'But if you insist on behaving like infants, I will gladly treat you like infants. So: we're going to do it yet again. Boys remain standing. Girls, all together – sit.'

The girls' chairs might be hovercraft on cushions of air, their sitting a breeze rustling through leaves.

'I hope you were paying attention, boys. Because now it's your turn. Wait!' A few chairs have begun to scrape. 'You are going to do it differently. Each of you will tell me your name, one by one. Then and *only* then will you sit. Name?'

'Brian Bell, Miss.'

'Sit please, Brian.'

A lucky first choice. 'Tinker' Bell, the headmaster's son and class swot, seats himself as quietly as the girl he half is. Relieved, Miss

Peach high-steps down the first aisle on her high-heels, and one by one, each larrikin meekly follows suit.

'Name?'

'Robert Burns, Miss.'

A flicker of interest as she stares up into my eyes. 'Ah, yes. The rabbitoh.' A smile. 'You have a famous name, Robert.'

I plan to *make* it famous, I almost tell her. Famous for me. She looks even younger and smaller staring up at me at close quarters. At least it's not a famous fruit, I want to tell her. Unlike every other woman in town, she wears no makeup, apart from lipstick; her unpowdered face might be a girl student's after all. I feel an urge to give her a push, to unbalance her from those high, grown-up heels.

'Do you write poetry too, Robert?'

'No, Miss.'

'He writes stories, Miss,' Anne Hunter pipes up.

'Really? What sort of stories?'

'War stories,' Anne answers for me. 'And comics.'

I am less interested in correcting out-of-date information than studying Miss Peach. She holds the chalk baton in her left hand; a tiny watch encircles her bird-thin right wrist. Made in America, I think to myself. Left-hand drive. Not only a robot, but an imported model.

She is still smiling, wanting to be friends. 'You can sit now, Robert.'

What comes over me? A need to be noticed more, to stand out in her big, Audrey Hepburn eyes? A need to be noticed less, or at least differently – to escape the millstone of my ridiculous name? Or just the need to unbalance her again, to find out what she is made of? I collapse my giraffe-frame with deliberate awkwardness into a scraping, clattering seat; Anne Hunter turns once more, open-mouthed not so much at my rascal nature – a given – as at the fact that our teacher's delicate beauty has again failed to protect her.

'Miss Burke warned me that you were the class clown, Robert.'

'The chair slipped, Miss.'

The other boys snigger, emboldened.

'I was so looking forward to my first morning here, Robert. My first morning as a teacher. It meant a lot to me. Clearly you don't have the sensitivity to understand that, but do you think you might be able to make this at *all* easier for me?'

I hold my ground. 'What's the magic word?'

She also holds hers. 'Wait outside, Burns. I'll deal with you later. Just make sure you stand in the porch where I can keep an eye on you.' She pauses, then adds a sarcastic, '*Please.*'

No titters this time. The fish school has turned, and is mouthing bubbles at me. *Fair go, Robbie. She's beautiful. It's her first time.*

I overhear the remainder of that lesson from the porch, some of it ('I'd like to thank the *rest* of you for your cooperation . . .') clearly meant to be overheard.

'As your class teacher, I'll be taking you for three subjects this year. All of you will be with me for English and Latin and Modern History, some also for Ancient History . . .'

An odd thing: as I stand there I begin to enjoy the sound of her voice, as if, disembodied, it can be itself, a soothing contralto unencumbered by doll-clothes and elf-face and jerky robot movements.

'The boys from all first-year classes will do Woodwork together with Mr Bailey, and the girls . . .' a pause here '. . . the curiously named subject of Domestic Science, with Miss Hammond.'

Time passes; her voice dispenses its balm, its music more important than its content.

'. . . people call Latin a dead language. But it is *very* much alive. Excuse me while I kick off these ridiculous heels. Normally I never wear them. But I thought – my first day with you, something formal perhaps? That's better. Many of our English words come from Latin. You will find they sound familiar . . .'

The February day is heating up outside, the sun beating down on the tin roof of the porch. I have slept restlessly the night before, the enclosed heat is another balm, and soon my eyes are heavy-lidded.

'*Femina*, for one. Can anyone guess what *femina* might mean in English?'

'Feminine?'

'Close, Anne. It's a feminine noun. In fact, it means woman. *Familia*?'

'Family?'

'Of course. Now a tricky one. Does anyone know what *rex* means?'

Tinker Bell's voice: 'Dog, Miss?'

His stupidity jerks my sleepy eyes open; my mouth follows. 'King!' I shout from the porch.

Silence inside, then Miss Peach's voice: 'Would you care to rejoin us, Robert?' Another, shorter silence. 'Please?'

She keeps talking to the class as I walk in, not wanting to pay me too much attention. '*Rex, regis*, masculine, third. A problem word for the Romans, "king". A problem for the Roman republic, as we will discover in Ancient History. But this is Latin . . .'

On stockinged feet she is even shorter, but more at ease. Less robotic? She pads to the board and begins chalking up more of these half-familiar, quarter-English words. *Lux.* 'Anyone? No, it's not a brand of soap, David.' *Crux.* My arm as usual first in the air: 'Cross!' At last a cursory nod my way as she talks on. 'From which, clearly, the verb "to crucify". We will be discussing the slaves' rebellion under Spartacus in a few weeks. No doubt you have all seen the Hollywood version.' Her chalk keeps clacking. *Anser.* 'If you think "answer" is the answer you are a goose. But geese are also important in the history of Rome. I hope later in the year we might read a little Tacitus together. In the original Latin.'

Original Latin words cover the board, and soon we are copying them into our exercise books. Soon after that the lunchtime siren sounds, releasing us. I try to sneak past her desk in the crush, but she is waiting to pounce. 'A word, Robert.'

A pale manila file sits open before her. Mine?

'Is there anything you'd like to say to me, Robert?'

Standard, before-sentencing liturgy. I supply the standard response: 'I'm sorry, Miss.'

'Then why?'

'Don't know, Miss.'

More liturgy: 'I don't want us to get off to a bad start.'

Without an audience, there seems no need for further tomfoolery. 'Me neither, Miss.'

'*Nor do I,*' she says, which at first I take to be an odd agreement, then realise is a correction.

'Nor do I, Miss.'

She shakes a cigarette from a pack – Kool, I note – and lights up.

'Can I have one, Miss?'

A smile twitches at the corner of her mouth; she exhales a cloud of sharp, mentholated smoke sideways from the same corner. 'Given your test scores,' she says, bending over my file, 'I'm expecting big things from you.'

I stare down into the coiled energy of her tight bun of hair. Her neck is arched like a swan's; the word 'alabaster' comes to me, perhaps from the pages of a women's magazine. Her small size seems to concentrate and magnify her beauty, intensifying it. When she looks up her large eyes are startlingly vivid. 'A fresh beginning then, Robert?'

'Thank you, Miss.'

I stand there for a moment longer, confused. Audrey Hepburn isn't my type – too skinny, too flat-chested. But I like being alone with her duplicate; I relish the odd intimacy of being rebuked by it. I feel calmed by its nearness in ways I can't explain and barely recognise, consciously. Consciously I am still fighting the urge to reach over and pull the pins from that hair, let the grenade explode.

'Is there anything else you'd like to say?'

'Me?'

'I can't see anyone else in the classroom, Robert.'

'No, Miss.'

'Then run along and join your friends. Oh, one other thing. I'd like very much to read some of those war stories of yours sometime.'

'I don't write *war* stories, Miss!'

'What do you write?'

'Different stories. You wouldn't like them.'

'Perhaps you could allow me to be the judge of that. If you wanted to, of course.'

I don't want to. I don't write stories for girls. Dismissed into the sunshine, I move through their seated lunch-groups, their dumb, gossipy chatter. '. . . so beautifully *presented* . . .' '. . . stirrup pants . . .' '. . . fab *hair*do . . .' '. . . Vespa scooter . . .' '. . . Audrey in *Roman Holiday* . . .'

The boys are further out, munching sandwiches on the run, already tossing around a balding tennis ball. I'd left early for school that second morning to avoid Billy; it's time to face the music.

'She chucked you out!' he says as I join the circle.

'She's a bitch,' I tell him.

'Told ya!' He grins, vindicated. 'You shoulda listened!'

'Shoulda. Might end up in your class after all.'

The grin vanishes. 'Pig's arse. You don't *want* to be in my class.'

The ball stops moving; the circle of boys waits, expectant.

'You want to be in *her* class.'

What's he talking about? 'Bloody do not.'

'Bloody *do*.'

'She's got a scooter,' someone changes the subject. 'You seen her scooter, Billy?'

What scooter? The only place I've seen scooters are in Rome, Italy, under the ample backside of Sophia Loren. The slightly fat backside, it strikes me for the first time.

'Course I've seen it,' Billy says. 'Rides round town like Lady Muck. Like she's got a *carrot* jammed up her arse.'

'Miss Carrot!' someone shouts, and the ball starts moving again amid laughter. 'Miss Banana,' someone else yells, which seems hysterical. 'Good morning, Miss Pineapple,' I join in.

'It ain't funny!' Billy shouts us down. 'She crosses the road when she sees my mob coming, Robbie! Stuck up bitch! What you want to be in *her* bloody class for?'

Murmurs of agreement around the circle; all eyes on me.

'It ain't my fault,' I say.

'Well, it sure the hell ain't mine!'

'Whaddya want me to do, Billy? Flunk the test?'

'Why not, bugger ya? I couldn't do any better!'

The ball stops moving again. 'You coulda flunked the test, Robbie,' someone says.

'He's your best friend,' from another.

'*See!*' Billy spits the word at me. 'Told ya! You coulda done worse!'

'And you coulda tried harder!' I shout back. 'You're just dumb! You're just a . . . a dumb curly worm!'

The words surprise me as much as they do him. I stand frozen as he steps forward, enraged, and punches me, once, in the soft pit of my stomach. I am winded more than hurt, but gasping less for air than for thoughts, as if he has also winded my brain. The others watch open-mouthed as he dances about, shaking his wrist. 'Ow! That hurt!' Aware he is acting girlish, he turns on me again. 'And you can keep your *fucking* bike! I'm getting a *fucking* new one!'

The violent strangeness of the word stuns me, stuns all of us; the tennis ball starts travelling again from hand to hand as if to give us something to do, something to save us from having to speak. 'Bloody' has seen us through primary school; is it time to put away childish adjectives? Having spat out the new manly word, Billy at least feels better, or emptied for the moment of anger.

'I got no *friends* in 1C, Robbie,' he says more quietly.

A dumb thing to say in front of his new classmates; I try to help him out. 'I've got no friends in 1A.'

'You got that fat pig Anne Hunter. She *loves* you!'

'She *doesn't* love me.' The ball is in my hand; I hurl it at him with all my strength, bouncing it hard off his squashed head.

'Brandy!' I shout.

The game's afoot. Boys helter-skelter across the oval. I am already on the far side by the time Billy retrieves the ball and begins chasing down his first victim. Simple rules: as each boy is branded by the ball, he joins the growing gang of hunters. I am good at this game, a crafty fox staying ahead of a baying pack, always among the last to be caught. There are patterns to be found in the swirl of ball and boys and shifting alliances; I seem able to predict the flow of the game, to see just a little into the future – a few seconds is more than enough. What I lack in speed and coordination, I more than make up for in short-term clairvoyance. I *know* where the ball will be, although not this ball, today, as it is plucked from midair by the bear-paw of Merv Bailey, Deputy Head, Woodwork Master, and Vice-captain of the mighty Eagles.

'I thought I made it clear yesterday that brandy is out of bounds at high school, you boys!'

'Whisky too, sir?'

He glares about him, a big, box-shaped man with a big box head. His face, roughed up by years of football, worked over at some length, wears a permanent scowl, as if keen to get its own back on someone. On anyone. 'There's one in every pack – Burns, isn't it?'

'Yes, sir.'

'You the Sarge's boy, Burns?'

'Yes, sir.'

'Hard to believe.' He eyes my beanpole frame sceptically. 'Your old man's built like a brick shithouse, but you – you'd have to run around in the shower to get wet.'

Relieved laughter all about; the day's scapegoat has been found.

'What do you think your old man would make of you acting the fool, Burns?'

'I don't think there's a law against it, sir.'

He steps closer, seizes me by the ear, twists it hard and stares into my eyes. 'You playing funny buggers with me? Listen carefully, you skinny weed, because I'm only going to say this once. It's Miss Peach's first year out of teachers' college, and if I hear of you giving her a hard time again, you'll answer to me personally, got it? And I don't care *who* your old man is.' He pockets the bald tennis ball, turns away, then turns back. 'Oh – and Burns.'

'Sir?'

'You related to the singer in that band? The one who looks like a girl?'

2

My parents are both big people, although their bignesses are of different kinds. Dad is the more pear-shaped, but there is plenty of veteran footballer muscle packed beneath the paunch; he's a pear with a tough, fibrous core. Mum is as square in shape as every other mother in town, all fleshy arms, fat-puckered thighs, and giant squashy breasts. A recent milestone: overnight her wobbling flesh has become revolting to me.

She taught me to read early, mostly by trapping me in the folds of that flesh each night and reading aloud to me. At me. Poetry came first – my namesake's second only to Mother Goose – then a nightly chapter from whatever Reader's Digest condensed book had thumped onto the front doorstep that month. *East of Eden. Cry, the Beloved Country. The Dam Busters.* Hard to believe now that I tolerated this, that I liked to squeeze handfuls of her, liked the way her soft bits would ooze ticklishly between my fingers like half-deflated balloons. Hard to believe, also, that I once found that great square bulk useful to hide behind, a kind of family sandwich-filling, a buffer between me and Dad.

'I don't want to have to tell your *father* when he gets home, Robbie.'

'Your father doesn't need to know *this* time. Just don't let it happen again.'

In fact my father did have to know, whether he wanted to or not. Another recent milestone: the realisation that she has always loaded the gun, he has merely fired the bullets, and if she is still useful to hide behind, it is mostly from her, the nagging woman around the corner of herself.

'Where *are* you, Robbie? Come out where I can see you!'

People often say that she is good for him. He's a man of few words, but her chattiness has the power to drag more out of him. He's a man of few songs, too, but when she sits at the piano, finger-noodling through the latest show tune – 'Gonna Wash That Man Right Out of My Hair' – she can sometimes even drag a chorus out of him. Whenever he gives me a dressing-down it always sounds like a chorus, sung more in duty than in anger. After the standard liturgy – 'Larceny is a serious charge, sonny-jim. It might be just a magazine, but I've seen kids put under Welfare for less' – I might even catch the corner of a wry smile as he turns away. 'Boyish high jinks,' he argues my case to her behind the bedroom door. Boyish high spirits. Larking about.

He uses the same words after I accidentally fumigate the house with rotten-egg gas and we have to take a room in the pub for the night. She wants my new chemistry set confiscated; he carries it out to his workshed instead, and clears a bench-end for me among the battered copies of *Popular Mechanics* and piles of machine parts and broken-down gadgets. The odd condensed book can be glimpsed here, also – slipped under his nose by Mum – but he never reads them. This dark, cluttered cave – the old Mounted Police stables – is his refuge; his spare evenings are spent thumbing the magazines and trying to piece his machines back together. Disassembled gearboxes, starter motors and carburettors are spilled across the bench, but also more domestic mechanisms: broken toasters, cameras, clocks. Clockwork trains. Bicycles. Tricycles. Sunbeam mixmasters, valve wirelesses. I can't recall a single appliance getting out of there in one piece; fixing gadgets was always less important to Dad than understanding how they worked.

Like father, like son? My chemical investigations are also more pure than applied; I have soon made several involuntary attempts on my own life. Boyish high jinks? Chemistry is not an ideal hobby for an overgrown troublemaker with butter-fingers; too much can go wrong too easily. I displace hydrogen gas from various acids and detonate it with a match, distill pure alcohol and drink it, sublimate liquid bromine, the most beautiful of elements, a kind of translucent ruby-mercury, and stare, filled with awe, as its violet vapour corrodes everything it touches, including my lungs.

Soon I will stumble on the alchemists' secret and transmute lead into gold. Meanwhile Doc McKenzie is summoned to raise me from the dead on a weekly basis; sensing a kindred spirit, careless of consequence, more at home with ideas than with people, he takes a shine to me.

'Deep breath, young Lucifer. Hold. Had a backyard laboratory myself your age. Breathe out. Got up to all kinds of mischief. In again. Cough. Ever made rotten-egg gas?'

Kids' stuff, I want to tell him. I can produce stinks of any kind on demand. The choke of burning sulphur, the bleachy pool-smell of chlorine, the nose-paralysing shock of ammonia. I refine phosphorus, which stinks like garlic, and acetone, which stinks like glue. I pack copper tubes with a solid-fuel mix of zinc dust and sulphur, hammer one end shut, attach nose capsules improvised from jam tins, and launch crews of highly trained beetles into shallow orbit, around two hundred feet. The beetles always crawl happily out of the wreckage; my own survival is less certain.

'Close shave, young Lucifer. Had a few myself at your age. Hold still. The eye drops might sting.'

'Ouch!'

'What's this on your desk? Latest *Galaxy*? Seem to have misplaced mine. Mind if I borrow it? Haven't quite finished. Blink.

Good piece by Van Vogt. Blink again. New slant on time travel.'

My ears prick up; time travel is very much on my mind. I have hopes – on some far distant day – of persuading Sophia Loren to travel forward in time to meet an older, darker, more brooding me. But how to pull it off? Time travel is only possible at or near the speed of light, and nothing travels at the speed of light – except, well, *light*. A flashbulb pops in my head: since light includes radio and ultraviolet waves and X-rays, might it be possible to send a radio message back in time? A warning, perhaps? But of what? The story begins to flesh itself out in my head. *Dear Miss Loren, first the bad news. You will get lung cancer next week. The good news is you can be saved, by a lung transplant here in the future. This may sound like science fiction, but next week you will know I tell the truth. I will send further instructions then. Yours faithfully.*

'Beautiful machine, the eye,' says Doc McKenzie as he bandages mine. 'Evolved separately several times, of course. Shut tight now. Insects, fish, mammals – all found the eye independently. Evolution tries out most ideas sooner or later. Except wheels. Always wondered why wheels never evolved. I'll remove the pad tomorrow.'

I rip off the pad and reach for my pen as soon as he has left. *Dear Sophia, so now you know – but you also know there is hope. A new lung will be waiting for you if you will agree to have your body frozen for twenty years. As you lie there like a sleeping beauty in a thicket of ice crystals, it will seem no more than a night's sleep . . .*

The technical details need fleshing out here. Not so much the lung transplant stuff – the world's first kidney transplant is still very much in the news – as the body freezing. The next morning I experiment by sealing live moths in paper envelopes in the freezer. Thawed in sunlight hours later, they feebly flap a wing once or twice, but never regain full moth-consciousness. Water expands when it freezes, ice crystals rupture the brain cells; if you wake at all, you wake as jelly.

My own sleep that night seems to last for twenty years. Adrift in a delirium of worry, out of sight of daylight in every direction, my dream-story seems feverishly real. I lie on my bed in a cold sweat, terrified things might go wrong. Miss Loren might choose to die in the present, with a short fat man at her side. A power blackout might thaw her out prematurely, leaving her with a jellied brain and the IQ of a moth.

Only with dawn do I stop tossing and turning. At worst she will be brain-dead, but so what? She was dying anyway. Her voluptuous, wasp-waisted body might still be in working order. And the best case? I imagine waking my sleeping beauty with a kiss, yes, but lying in the safe harbour of morning, my cock as hard and heavy as an anchor, a kiss is only the beginning.

3

Miss Hepburn, not Miss Loren, is the talk of the town. Sightings are compared, conversations tallied, rumours checked for consistency. Small talk abhors a vacuum; with the football season still months away, and the steady summer weather offering no scope for speculation, the diminutive Miss Peach soon fills the conversational space, less a topic than an expanding universe of gossip. Her city-slick beauty, her exotic clothes and shoes – 'Holly Golightly in *Breakfast at Tiffany's*.' Her hairdo – 'Remember *Love in the Afternoon*?' Her smoking – '*Breakfast at Tiffany's*' again. Her choice of groceries and cuts of meat, why she prefers claret to moselle and moselle to beer, why she rides a 'Continental' scooter – 'The Vespa in *Roman Holiday*.' And especially her likeliest suitors in the district: the key issues are debated across school desks and shop counters, church steps and pub bars and petrol bowsers.

And kitchen tables. 'How was school today, Robbie?'

'Good. What's for tea?'

'Curried sausages. This Miss Peach of yours. What's she like?'

'I dunno. All right, sort of. A bit stuck-up. What's for dessert?'

'Stewed pears and chocolate custard.' She turns to my father. 'Have you seen her, Jim? I must say I'm surprised they let her wear those tight slacks to school.'

'Can't see much harm in it, Mother.'

'They're hardly flattering on a woman. And they say she smokes like a chimney. A very modern miss.'

Idea for a story: Frockworld, a planet on which every woman is compelled by law to wear frocks. A young woman wears slacks and is immediately tried and burnt at the stake. By the end of the year the whole world is wearing slacks. I take a mouthful of sausage; the idea is going nowhere. We already live on that planet.

'. . . and painfully thin, don't you think, Jim?'

'Can't say I've noticed, Mother. Course I like a bit of meat on a woman meself.'

Me too, I want to add. If in different places. 'She'd have to run around in the shower to get wet,' I say, and they both chuckle indulgently.

'As for that scooter she gads about on. Who does she think she is, Audrey Hepburn in *Roman Holiday*?'

The scooter. Perched in the pepper tree on Arthur Street, weary of pinging slugs off the roofs of passing cars, I focus the reclaimed binoculars on the object, parked in the Tweedle-twins' driveway three doors away. What is it? A toytown version of Constable Hicks' police-issue BSA? A girl's motorbike, lacking, like a girl's pushbike, a manly cross-strut between the legs? Unfamiliarity makes it ugly to me, or at least ungainly. The colour is a sissy sky-blue, the alien words *Vespa Sportique* are raised in chrome letters on the leg guard. The wheels are squat and comically fat, like toy tractor wheels, or wheeled versions of big floppy clown shoes. Mental note: a new, half-intelligent species for Wheelworld, Vespa the Clown.

'Robbie! Answer me! I know you're up there, fuck ya!'

Useless to pretend otherwise; my bike is leaning against the trunk. 'So what if I am?'

Billy is at my side within seconds, an agile possum leaping up through branches. 'Watcha doing?'

Has he forgotten he hit me the week before? Has he not noticed I've been avoiding him since? 'Nothing.'

'You spying on Lady Muck?'

'Course not.' I put the binoculars to my eyes again. 'Just look-ing at the scooter.'

'Give me a look.'

'*Ssh*,' I hiss, as a familiar white EK Holden pulls up opposite her house. 'Jesus!'

'What? Let me see.'

I ignore him as the car door opens and the driver steps out. 'Shit! It's my old man. What's *he* doing there?'

The same thing as his son, apparently, as he squats on his haunches before the scooter, muttering to himself. I can't hear a word of course, but know his repertoire well enough to guess. *Where do you wind it up?*

Billy is whispering, 'Give me a look.'

'Find your own binoculars.'

'Then find your own slug gun!' he says, and slings it over his shoulder.

Below us, Dad is testing the squeeze of the handbrake. His lips move again; binoculars trained on his mouth I take another stab.

A bit of give in the cable. He twists the throttle, lifts the seat and peers into the cavity beneath, unable to leave the thing alone. He glances up and down the street; is he thinking of wheeling it home and hoisting it up onto his bench? Too late. Here is Miss Peach, stepping from the house carrying a string shopping bag.

Something wrong, Sergeant?

Another guess, but near enough, surely. Dad, flustered, thrusts out a paw. *Miss Peach, isn't it? Sergeant Burns.*

'I'm taking the sweet sherry too,' Billy threatens.

She shakes the proffered hand, smiling. *Pleased to meet you.* Her red lips are easier to read than his inarticulate slit, but his mouth is moving more than usual.

Nice-looking piece of machinery. Not my cup of tea – but nice lines. Like a . . . a young filly. Where does this come from? His mouth or mine? *Bit of give in the rear brakeline. Causing any trouble?*

Billy has fossicked a cigarette from the possum hole and lit up; the smoking seems to calm him. 'You want to go rabbiting tonight?'

'Maybe.'

Miss Peach is straddling the seat now. *It's been very reliable, Sergeant.*

Jim. Please. We don't stand on ceremony round these parts.

A short silence. He looks at his feet, shuffles them, looks up and speaks more seriously. Now I understand: they are talking about me. Have they been talking about me all along?

You teach my boy – Robbie. He can be a handful.

A conspiratorial smile on her elf-face. I give my imagination free rein. *I have high hopes for him, Jim. He's a special boy.*

I crawl out along a branch to get a better view. What next? Will she say too much? Tell stories out of class? I am straining now for literalness, not invention. I twiddle the focus knob, as if it might make her words appear magically in the air, like cartoon speech-balloons.

These stories he writes — the war stories — I'm hoping he'll show me some of his work.

He frowns, puzzled. *War stories?* Three slow syllables, correctly lip-read, surely.

Billy tosses his butt out of the tree. 'What's so bloody interesting?'

Another awkward standoff below. Her body language is easier to read than her lips; she realises she has said too much. His glance shifts back to her scooter and he begins talking again, rapidly. Perhaps it goes something like this: *You have any trouble, I'd be happy to take a bo-peep. Bit of a hobby of mine.* I hadn't known this man of few words could offer up so many. *Workshop out back. The old stables. Pretty well set up. Everything that opens and shuts . . .*

A ridiculous urge: to turn the binoculars around and put them to my mouth and lip-read words at her, beam some kind of magnified warning directly into her brain. *Don't let him anywhere near it! Keep your scooter, your toaster, your fountain pen out of his hands at all costs.*

A last smile fills her small face, a last few words animate her lips — *Kind of you to offer, Jim* — then she turns the key in the ignition, kick-starts the pedal. Nothing happens. Has he managed to cripple the Vespa merely by the laying on of hands? No: on the third attempt the engine sputters into life.

She pulls out from the verge with a textbook hand signal as the local Police Sergeant stands in the middle of the dirt road and watches her putter away, watches her all the way to the Church Street corner, although it's surely the exotic machine underneath he is watching, not the exotic machine on top.

Billy's voice in my ear again: 'What time shall I come round?'

'What are you talking about?'

'Rabbiting, stupid. Tonight.'

'Can't tonight.'

'But you *said*.' Incredulity gives way to anger. 'What you gonna do instead? Sit up here and watch *her* all night? You are, aren't ya! Why don't you just knock on her door and ask her for a root! Like your old man!'

My turn for anger. 'That's bullshit!' I shout. 'And you know it! That's *not* what he was doing.' I give him an almighty shove; he loses his balance, tumbles backwards, but manages to grab the branch behind and lower himself, cat-footed, possum-handed, away from me.

'Jesus, Robbie! You coulda *killed* me!'

'You got what you deserved. Why did you say that? About my old man!'

He drops the last few feet to the ground, grabs his bike and straddles it before answering. 'Because it's true. They all want to root her.' His eyes are full of tears now, if partly tears of rage. 'Fuck you, Robbie! I thought we was friends.'

I look up and down the street, alarmed. Doors are being opened, curtains twitched aside. I shrink back invisibly among the ferny leaves and pepper berries as Billy pedals away, slug gun slung over his shoulder, still in full cry. 'You're no friend!'

Is what he said about Miss Peach true? Do all the men in town want to root her? It's probably true about Big Merv, I realise. But Dad? By the time I reach home I'm more amused than angry. He's more likely to root her Vespa.

'I hear you've been writing war stories, sonny-jim,' he remarks over tea, confirming some of my lip-reading.

'Who says?'

'A little bird.'

'Wars between worlds, Dad.'

'What's that supposed to mean?'

'Wars set in the future. Wars with aliens.'

'Uh-huh,' he murmurs, easily satisfied. 'Had a look at the Vespa today, Mother.'

'It looks dangerous to me, Jim. Shouldn't be allowed on the roads.'

'Can't see much harm in it. Pass the sauce? Roadworthy enough. Put-put engine. Wouldn't mind getting it up on the workbench. A few gremlins need sorting out.'

'Let me guess, Prince Charming. You offered?'

'Seemed the decent thing to do. Make the lass feel welcome.'

'How gallant.' She laughs, a little harshly. 'From what I hear, all the men in town have been falling over each other to make her feel welcome.'

'Now, Mother. You know it wasn't like that.'

'Perhaps you could sort out my toaster first, Jim Burns. It's been sitting on that bench of yours for weeks.'

4

In the year 2064 a lone time-traveller – me – is sent back in time to change history. My secret mission? To prevent the birth of a key historical figure and thereby change the world for the better.

A war story? Of a sort, although lacking Panzer tanks and samurai swords. It also lacks, although I fail to notice this at the time, Billy. I have other things on my mind. My chosen method of assassination, for one.

The technical details are as sketchy as ever. I've heard whisperings behind closed doors about knitting needles and wire coathangers, but can find nothing on the subject in the *Britannica*. I pick Doc McKenzie's brains one Saturday morning after a rocket launch goes wrong, but his mumblings about perforations and septicaemia go largely unheard as he jabs a tetanus shot into my skinny arm. He takes down a couple of pickling jars from his shelves and I stare, mesmerised, at the pale baby-monsters within – but there is no help there. In the end I make it up as I write, just as I make up the method of speed-of-light time-travel. My first destination is the village of Braunau, Austria, 1897 (date and place from the *Britannica*), where I abort the third pregnancy of a certain Frau Schickelgruber (ibid.) by injecting a not-yet-invented drug.

Mission accomplished, I return to the present and find – what? That nothing has changed. There has still been a Second World War. Millions of Jews have still been gassed, apparently the same ones. Millions of soldiers and civilians have still died. The only difference: the name Hitler no longer appears in the history books. *Heil Goebbels! Sieg Heil!*

Plan B. Back I travel into the past again and inject the pregnant Mutter Goebbels with my abortion drug. The only ripple-on effect in the present? *Heil Goering! Sieg Heil!* If there is a moral in all this, I haven't a clue what it is. Morals are for Aesop's fables; I am just having fun, making fictional mischief.

I am having a lot of fun during a Latin lesson – scribbling myself back in time again to abort the inventor of the gas Zyklon B – when my exercise book is whipped out from under my pen.

'If you can't do schoolwork during school hours, Robert Burns, you can stay behind after school and finish it.'

Anne Hunter turns and glares, but I am watching Miss Peach, standing at the window now, reading my confiscated story. She turns a page and gasps, covers her mouth with her hand, turns my way. I immediately look down. When next I risk a glance she is sitting at her desk, fountain pen in hand, scribbling. What can she be doing? Taking notes? The home siren sounds, the rest of the class files out. I stand at her desk, awaiting sentence, while she shakes out a Kool from her pack and lights up.

'Can I have one, Miss?'

A smooth jet of smoke. 'I have to admit it's imaginative, Robert. Highly imaginative. I just wish you'd apply the same dedication to your lessons.'

She slides the story across the desk. I stare dumbfounded at the vivid ticks – her trademark purple ink – and crossings-out and spelling corrections that deface the pages. She *marked* it?

'It's one view of history.' She sets down her cigarette in the ashtray and turns and tugs two thick black paperbacks from the bookshelf behind her. 'You should read these. Tolstoy has some interesting things to say on the subject.'

Those twin tomes – *War and Peace* – look as forbidding as bibles. And who is Tolstoy? Did he fight on our side or Hitler's?

'Like you,' she says, 'Tolstoy believed the engine of history has its own irresistible inertia.'

Like who? I write by instinct, making it up as I go. Whatever she means is beyond my fourteen-year-old brain, but I don't mind being spoken to this way. As an equal? As if I am an equal, perhaps, because clearly I'm not. I haven't been offered a cigarette, for one thing.

'I don't necessarily agree with Tolstoy. Or even,' a small smile, 'with you. I think people count as individuals. People do make a difference. We're not helpless, Robert – not victims of huge social forces.'

My eyes stray back to the desk as she prattles on. Which of those big black bibles is *War*? I might – just might, I make no promises – try that one first.

5

By the Friday morning of the second week every girl in class is wearing her hair in a tight back-roll – a chignon, Anne Hunter calls it.
So, still, is Miss Peach, although everything else she wears changes
daily. Today's lipstick is more pillar-box red than ruby; today's tight
green slacks are cut off at calf height, and she walks more easily in
shoes that look like ballet slippers. Ballet-paws. A striped scarf is
knotted casually around her neck; tomorrow night at the drive-in
every girl will be sporting an exact copy.

'Good morning, IA.'

'GOOD MORNING, MISS PEACH.'

A fulsome chorus and a smooth seating, as has been the case
all week. I take more care with my own chair. The vulnerability I
wanted to damage I now want to protect, even as she has grown
less vulnerable and more confident with each lesson.

John Shaw Neilson, she chalks up on the board. Then turns.
'Does this name mean anything to anyone?'

'Are those Capri pants, Miss?'

'This is a poetry lesson, Anne, not Domestic Science.'

No further hands in the air; she shakes her head with mock
disbelief. 'A prophet in his own land! He is *your* poet. Born here,
in this very town – your town – in 1872.'

Anne tries to re-ingratiate herself. 'Did he know Adam Lindsay
Gordon, Miss?'

'Most probably not, since Gordon committed suicide in 1870.'
If this is a joke, it's over before we notice. 'Of course, Neilson was a
much better and more original writer than Gordon. A more modern
sensibility. And much, *much* richer in feeling. Although he could
also be playful.'

Perhaps I am not so much hearing this word for word

as imaginatively lip-reading again; I am more interested in watching than listening as she begins to pace excitedly about.

'I was introduced to Shaw Neilson by a friend of mine —'

'You *met* him, Miss?'

'Not in the flesh, Anne, since he died before I was born.' The joke brings a few titters second time round. 'I mean I was introduced to his poetry by a friend. Who is a very fine poet himself.'

'A boyfriend, Miss?' I pipe up for no particular reason.

'Of course not.' She stops pacing, looking slightly startled. 'My friend is a professor,' she adds, as if this somehow proves the point. 'I plan to show you some of his poems later in the term.'

'What's his name, Miss?'

'Shall I spell it for you, Robert?' A pause. 'No? We're talking about Shaw Neilson today, so if we could move on – with your permission? Take out *Australian Poets Speak*, please class. There's a poem in the book I hope will speak to many of you – a poem about a bush childhood, about the richness of childhood experiences.' She aims her chalk-baton at me. 'Since you have so much to say, Robert, and since it's a poem your famous namesake would be proud of, perhaps you could read it for us. Page twenty-one.'

'*You* read it, Miss,' Anne Hunter pipes up, help from an unexpected quarter.

For once I am quick to agree with my rival. 'Yes, Miss. You know it best. Please.'

She smiles, easier to flatter now that her first-day nerves have passed. She assumes a dancer's position: duck-footed, one knee slightly behind and bent. '"The Poor, Poor Country",' she enunciates, pauses, looks about. We look back, curious: she doesn't have a book in her hand. Is she going to read the poem or dance it?

Oh 'twas a poor country, in Autumn it was bare,
The only green was the cutting grass and the sheep found
    little there.
Oh, the thin wheat and the brown oats were never two foot
    high,
But down in the poor country no pauper was I.

   She begins to move about again as she speaks, not so much dancing as pacing, unable to keep still, as if in the grip of strong emotions.

I waded out to the swan's nest – at night I heard them sing,
I stood amazed at the pelican, and crowned him for a king;
I saw the black duck in the reeds, and the spoonbill in the
    sky,
And in that poor country no pauper was I.

   I'd blame her ballet slippers for her restlessness if I hadn't already sensed it was the poetry. The words seem to pour out of her, following their own rhythm; the sentences heel and toe, dragging her along lockstep with them.

The mountain-ducks down in the dark made many a hollow
    sound,
I saw in sleep the Bunyip creep from the waters underground.
I found the plovers' island home, and they fought most valiantly.
And the poor, poor country made no pauper of me.

   The class is spellbound, and me with it. Sissy poetry, I want to think it, but goosebumps climb the length of my spine each time she recites the refrain. *In that poor country no pauper was I.*

The siren for the end of class sounds, deafeningly.

'Shall I stop?'

Several voices. 'No, Miss.' 'Don't stop.' 'Read more.'

> My riches all went into dreams that never yet came home,
> They touched upon the wild cherries and the slabs of
>   honeycomb,
> They were not of the desolate brood that men can sell or
>   buy,
> Down in that poor country no pauper was I.

She repeats the last line in a barely audible whisper. '"Down in that poor country no pauper was I."'

Outside, other classes are pouring into the yard for morning recess; in ours, no one stirs. What is the source of this spell? The music of the poem, or its effect on her? She plucks a handkerchief from her shirt-sleeve and dabs at the corner of her eye. 'I'm sorry,' she says, smiling through glistening eyes. 'Poetry sometimes does this to me.'

'I felt it too,' Anne Hunter whispers.

'Me too,' from several of the other girls.

Me too, but I'm already past it now, and not about to admit it in public.

'Neilson led a lonely life. There is always a sense of . . . loss in his work. A melancholy at its heart.'

'He never married, Miss?'

'He loved a much younger woman for a time. A girl, really. Not much older than you, Anne.'

'*My* age?'

'You find that shocking? Most women – girls – would have been married off at your age in the past. We'll be studying

Shakespeare's *Romeo and Juliet* next term. That was Juliet's age. Twelve. Thirteen.'

'*Twelve?*' Incredulous glances around the class.

'It's been the normal age in human history. It still is, in most parts of the world. Where women are still treated as chattels.'

'But you couldn't even have babies,' Anne Hunter says.

Miss Peach smiles indulgently. 'We might continue this discussion next lesson. If you remember nothing else from today, remember this: words can do more than just tell a story, or transmit information from point A, a page in a book, to point B, your head. Words also have other properties. Magical properties. Musical properties.'

'Do you know all his poems by heart, Miss?'

'Not all of them, Robert.' Another smile. 'My friend Geoffrey – Professor Barry – thinks we should always read poems aloud, and always memorise them. I agree. That is what is special about poetry, its memorability. The professor says poems have little burrs, like rhythm and rhyme, that make them stick in the head. But some poems stick in the mind – and heart – more than others.'

Those two prickly words – Geoffrey Barry – have stuck in my head. The high-pitched scream of recess-time voices outside seems momentarily louder; the spell is broken.

'Are you going to the hospital fête tomorrow, Miss?'

'I'm afraid not, Susan. I'm going away for the weekend.'

'On the Vespa?'

'I'm catching the morning train to Adelaide.' She glances at her watch, as if even now, a full day before, there's a chance she might miss it.

No one has yet made a move for the door. 'You won't be here on Monday?'

'I'm coming back on the Sunday train.'

Surprised glances around the class; this is unheard of. An entire day in the train one way, another whole day coming back – for a single Saturday night in the city? She sits down, then bounces straight up out of the seat, as if worried she might get stuck there for the weekend.

'Are you staying with your friend, Miss?' I ask as she gathers her books together.

'What friend?'

'The professor. Geoffrey.'

Where does this come from? Inspired guesswork? Trouble-making instincts?

'Of course not, you silly boy!'

Her sharp reaction silences me, silences us. I have learnt plenty this morning, despite myself – about John Shaw Neilson, about Miss Peach – but here is the first inkling of a lesson she might have learnt: that every word she utters in class, however trivial, will stick in our heads and be filed away for later use.

'I'm staying with my mother,' she adds, more calmly.

'It's a long way to go to see your mum,' Anne says.

In my mouth those words would have been edged with sarcasm; in hers they are meant literally, and kindly.

'She misses me,' Miss Peach says simply. 'And I like trains. I can read on the train. Think.' She smiles wryly, back in control of herself if not, yet, the class. 'I can watch the poor, poor country slide by.'

She stashes her books into her briefcase and dismisses us, or perhaps dismisses herself, for she hurries from the room ahead of the throng as if tomorrow's Bluebird is already waiting at the station. I have a new story to show her, but it's too late. I watch the others file out after her, regretting I hadn't scraped my chair more loudly today, or said something outrageous enough to earn another detention, hers as much as mine.

6

In the year 1964 the city is still 265 miles away: five hours of motion sickness by car, ten shillings and ten hours of smooth riding by train. Decimal currency is still two years off, centimetres and kilometres miles away in space and time. A round pound – a quid – is my mother's weekly housekeeping; sixpence – a zac – the sum total of my pocket-money. A weekend rabbit or two goes a long way in this bargain-basement world. If it can't be stolen, *Women's Weekly* costs a shilling, *Astounding Science Fiction* likewise. A bottle of Autumn Brown sweet sherry from the pub is two and six, but our middleman – Uncle Possum – always takes a commission, in kind more often than cash. In 1964 the Curries are still not allowed to buy liquor by law, but Possum, an ex-serviceman who fought in Korea, has exemption from the Blackfellers' Act. On Saturday nights the law sometimes turns a blind eye; if the Eagles win, Dad slips out of the clubrooms early so that Jacko and Neville can celebrate with Possum and the rest of the team.

More weights and measures: sixpence worth of licorice allsorts comes in a paper bag so bulky it takes two hands to handle. I am paid the grand sum of a guinea – one pound, one shilling – from the *Weekly's* Teen Lift-Out for a letter I write on the joys of chemistry as a hobby. I am permitted to spend it on yet more chemicals for my backyard laboratory, mail-ordered from Selby's Chemical Supplies in the city.

Do my parents realise what sort of dangerous alchemy is being boxed up in Adelaide and freighted down on the night train? Concentrated sulphuric and nitric acids, hazard-coloured oxides, deadly azure-blue or cobalt-blue sulphates, reels of magnesium-flare ribbon, conical glass flasks and rubber bungs, spirit burners, asbestos mats, glass tubing by the yard. Various other dangerous substances – packets of zinc dust and sulphur powder for rocket fuel; bags of ammonium nitrate, garden and gunpowder fertiliser – can be bought, or sometimes nicked, from the hardware store. I love the way these dark materials can be relied upon to make violent magic. And when it doesn't work, it doesn't work for a reason. The future can be predicted in my back-shed laboratory according to precise formulae, at least in the short term, its zodiac the periodic table. Of course there are unplanned explosions, unintended poisonings, but such malefic conjunctions of the chemical elements can also, eventually, be predicted.

That Friday night I sublimate nitrous oxide – laughing gas – for the first time, bubbling the vapour through a flask of water to dissolve any poisonous byproducts – nitric oxide, nitrogen dioxide – then filling a series of balloons with the pure gas. Balloons have two advantages: ease of inhalation, and less danger of back-compressing the hot, explosive ammonium nitrate at the other end of the makeshift apparatus. No laughter comes my way as I suck on the rubbery teats of those balloons, but I feel plenty mellow by bedtime. And plenty pleased with myself, in a mellow sort of way. Is my euphoria due to breathing the sweet fumes or the triumph of making them? Ample time to muse on this; time has slowed down. Time has ground to a complete halt. But how can this be? Surely time is as predictable as all else in the given world? Time is the very basis of predictability; time is its measure, its clock; time makes the world, the solar system, the universe, run on, well, *time*. If time is as elastic as a party balloon, what of the other givens, the other universal constants? The invincible sequence of chemical processes that has produced this magical gas, for one.

The planet is wobbling a little on its axis, the laws of nature are looking more than a little unnatural, possibly even illegal. Can those wobbly laws be appealed? Repealed? Jerked to my feet by this profound thought, I find my mellow brain and marshmallow legs can support me no further than a few yards. Toppling backwards onto the lawn outside the stables, I lie flat on my back, unable to move further, lost in contemplation of the high, shivering stars.

'You doin' all right, Robbie?'

A voice from where? Outer space? The grille window of the holding cell on the far side of the rosebed?

'Robbie! You hear me, boy? Billy in there with ya?'

I try to rise; the planet keeps me glued flat to its surface. I can feel its great mass pressed up against me. I seem stuck fast, unable even to lift an arm free of that giant toffee-apple, Earth.

My words are slow and slurred. 'Who turned up the gravity?'

'You boys gotta get off that sweet sherry,' the voice says.

I am more interested in getting up off the planet. My thoughts are coming slowly, but that at least is for the good; there will be time to think things through, an entire added lifetime of time. Here comes one now: why should things always fall downwards when dropped? At eye level with the raked gravel path, I reach for a fistful of stones, raise my heavy hand and begin releasing them into the atmosphere, one by one, as if they are tiny birds, as if one larrikin pebble, with a little luck, might choose to drop upwards, or sideways, instead of down.

'You need a hand out there, boy?'

'S'alright, Possum. You'd better stay in there.'

My legs are beginning to work again. I push myself upright and wobble back into the shed, fill a last balloon with gas from the still, somehow remember to turn off the spirit burner, and head for bed. Mum is sitting at her ancient Singer in the kitchen, pedalling; Dad is nowhere in sight. 'Night,' I murmur, sneaking past with the balloon. Possum is right; taking small sips of gas, I resolve to swear off sweet sherry for ever. My heavy lids slide shut, but as I lie there in a swoony, gas-addled state, stranded between wakefulness and sleep, a story comes to me, complete, in technicolour.

It turns out that the little green men of Mars are a very happy species. They never let their size or colour get them down; in fact they find it a hoot. Green dwarves, they tease each other. Green *niggers*, they laugh uproariously. Everything is funny to the Martians – plague, blizzards, mars-quakes, death – for the simple reason that on Mars the atmosphere is three parts oxygen, seven parts laughing gas.

Inspired, I switch on my rabbiting torch, rustle up pen and paper, and start scribbling. Why such a contented species should want to conquer planet Earth isn't an issue; I am reading *War of the Worlds* at the time – much better than *War and Peace* – and nick the plot to advance mine. In brief: the invasion starts well but soon goes wrong. Breathing an atmosphere of plain nitrogen and oxygen instead of nitrous oxide, the invaders begin to feel depressed. Within days they forget how to laugh. We Earthlings have our little jokes to get us through the day, the Martians don't get jokes. Living in a naturally amusing atmosphere, they've never needed them. The end comes quickly: without their drug, the invaders are so overcome by despair that they commit hara-kiri with their ceremonial Martian sheath-knives, en masse.

Which is roughly what I feel like doing myself the next morning, hung over and headachy, limbs semi-paralysed, struggling even to raise my head from the pillow – until I remember that it's Saturday morning and I've promised to walk Miss Peach to the station. That is, I've promised myself; as I pull on my desert boots and duffle coat and hurriedly comb Brylcreem through my hair, she has as yet no idea of her great good fortune.

7

Nine-twenty on the big station clock. My bike clatters to the ground behind me as I sprint up under the wide eaves and onto the platform, gasping for breath. No sign of my quarry among the waiting passengers. My head still throbs; I've eaten nothing. My tongue has grown a pelt of fur overnight; each breath – separate molecules of nitrogen and oxygen today – rasps painfully against it, seems almost to ruffle the fur. I jog back out onto the road and squint up Arthur Street. The sun is terribly bright, my eyes ache.

A figure in a blue frock and a mass of fluffy hair is struggling along the road with a large suitcase some distance off, but there is no sign of Miss Peach. I check Clarke Street in both directions. No sign there either. The woman in blue is finding the going heavy, stopping every few yards to set down her luggage. Miss Peach doesn't wear frocks; she can't be Miss Peach.

Until she is, and I sprint the remaining distance between us. 'Let me carry that, Miss.'

Resting on her case with her back to me, she jumps slightly. 'Robert – where did you come from?'

'The station, Miss. I'll take the case.'

'Well, thank you. I should have worn more sensible shoes.'

I recognise the high-heels from that first day of school, but not much else. The grenade pinned to her head has finally exploded, becoming a loosened bob, a compact swirl that kicks outwards just above her shoulders. She is wearing perfume for the first time – my stomach lurches as its chemistry does its work – as dislocating as nitrous oxide, as sweet as sherry.

She produces a pack of Kool from somewhere, lights up, exhales. 'I *was* promised a lift. God knows where he's got to.'

He? I grab her bulging case and stagger along in her wake,

wondering less who the pronoun belongs to than what is in the luggage. Books? Bricks? The Vespa scooter?

She half turns, as if reading my mind. 'I'm sorry, Robert. Packing makes me anxious. I can never decide what to leave behind.'

I set down the load, change hands, stagger on again after those slightly wobbling heels and swirling hair.

'Do you live nearby, Robert?'

Another change of hands. 'At the police station, Miss.'

'Oh, of course. Silly me.'

'I'm here to collect a parcel from the train,' I dissemble, before she reads my mind more deeply. She gives no indication that she hears, let alone cares. She is glancing at her watch again, wanting to be somewhere else.

'Chemicals. For my laboratory.'

A small smile this time. 'I hear you are very good at Science, Robert. Try not to drag the case, please.'

'Yes, Miss.'

An alarming thought: perhaps everything she owns is squeezed inside. 'You *are* coming back, aren't you Miss?'

Her laugh, from some distance ahead. 'Of course, Robert.'

I heave the case up in both arms and stagger after her, in perfumed seventh heaven despite her luggage being filled with bricks. Of course my cock is stiffening; there is something thrilling in carrying her bag. Gallantry? Intimacy with things she is intimate with?

'I like your frock, Miss. And your shoes.'

'Thank you, Robert. I'm not really a frock kind of girl, but some people seem to think they suit me. As for the shoes – might as well have Chinese foot-binding.'

'I like your hairdo too.'

One bird-hand flutters up, prods. 'All Miss Hammond's work. A Domestic Science extravaganza. It took for ever. The things we let ourselves be talked into! I drew the line at wearing war paint.'

The friction of each step is squeezing my cramped cock ever more tightly, but I'm not about to stop. The last fifty yards to the station have become some kind of test, a trial of strength, a proof of manhood. Her perfume helps, its scent now mixed with mentholated tobacco smoke – an invisible, trailing scarf that might as well be a noose around my neck, dragging me in her wake.

'Have you caught the Bluebird before, Miss?'

'I came down on the bus.'

'No comparison. The Bluebird is . . . a beautiful piece of machinery.'

'Strange words to use about a train, Robert.'

My father's words. More follow. 'The 250-class has twin V-6 diesels, 300 horsepower. Dad took me to the workshops last Christmas. In the city. They were fitting the engines.'

'That must have been riveting. Can you hurry?'

'Top speed of seventy miles per hour. *Much* faster than the old Red Hens.'

'You country boys certainly know your trains.'

A faint double blast of an air-horn from the southern end of town: the Bluebird crossing the old Kalangadoo road.

'Will someone meet you in Adelaide, Miss?'

'I hope so. I don't know how I'll manage otherwise.' She smiles again at the sight of me struggling along with her case. 'Perhaps I'd better take you with me. My very own native bearer.'

'Will the poet be there?'

'Who?'

'The professor. Geoffrey.'

For the first time I have her complete attention, this time without the slightest hint of amusement. 'Professor Barry and I share a literary friendship, Robert. Nothing more.'

She tosses away her half-smoked cigarette and stalks on, nylons swishing, blue hem twitching violently. At the station archway she turns and says, 'He's a married man. Of course he's not going to meet me.'

Why not? Another married man is arriving to see her off, skidding the only VW Beetle in town into the verge of the gravel drive and jumping out, his thick face flushed, his scowling expression for once contrite. 'Sorry, Pam! I know I said eight-thirty. Had to drop Rita at the fête. Got away as soon as I could.'

Her tone is cool. 'Water under the bridge, Merv. Luckily Robert here stepped into the breach.'

Big Merv looks my way without enthusiasm. He reaches across me for the handle of the case. 'I'll take it from here, Burns.'

'I've got it, sir,' I insist, clinging on.

A tug of war between the powerful Eagles centre-halfback and a just-turned-fourteen stick insect can only end one way. I let go before I am dragged into the station by my enemy, who effortlessly heaves the case up onto a broad shoulder.

'Strewth, Pam! Who you got in here? Your grandmother?'

'The Vespa,' I say, and am rewarded with a smile from Miss Peach.

'Thank you, Sir Knight. You were most gallant.' She stands on tiptoe and plants a kiss on my cheek, followed by a sly wink. 'Which is more than I can say for some.'

My pulse flares, thrilled to receive these crumbs – the thanks, the secret wink, but especially the slight, soft pressure of her lips against my face. Is there lipstick on my cheek? I hope so. Somewhere signals are clanging, and sure enough, here comes the familiar blue-and-silver caterpillar of the Bluebird with its flat, oddly impassive face. Should I follow her up onto the platform and blow a return kiss? A better idea: resisting the temptation to let down a tyre on the Beetle – to let down two tyres, vengeance also owed for the schoolyard humiliation of the week before – I retrieve my bike and pedal north, parallel to the tracks, at speed. Another blast of an air-horn as I reach the Robe road crossing. Looking down the line, I can just make out Big Merv standing on the platform, waving. I wait beneath the clanging signals, straddling my bike, a centaur dangerously close to a train track. Too close? No closer than on those numerous evenings perched as a young child on my father's shoulders, watching – *worshipping* – the big new 900-class freight locomotives thundering through. 'Feel the suction!' he would shout up to me as I swayed there precariously. 'Feel that bloody suction, sonny-jim!'

Down-track, the Bluebird is gaining speed, its robot face all hazard-orange cowcatcher chin and recessed silver door-nose between two big square glass eyes. The driver's smaller face floats like a pupil inside the left-hand window; the right-hand eye is sightless. The air-horn blasts again, and more urgently again, warning me to roll my bike back, to pull away, but I am too excited, my cock squeezed now against the hard saddle, the train only adding to the weird thrill as it bears down on me, closer, closer, the driver shaking his fist angrily.

Then nothing but streaming chrome-and-blue metal and thundering wheels and clanging signals and rushing air. No sign of Miss Peach in the windows flashing by above; her seat must be on the far side. Just as suddenly the rear-end face of the receding train is looking back at me, as inscrutable as the front face, stupidly unaware of the precious passenger nestled inside, and the erection I am fondling in my pocket.

The toot of a car horn close behind almost jolts me over my handlebars. 'Don't be filthy, Burns!'

Where has *he* come from?

'You dirty little bugger!' he shouts, and beeps his horn again,

and then again, in time, for some reason, with his words. 'You –
beep – filthy – *beep* – little – *beep* – pervert!' The beeps stop as he
jumps out of his car, but not the shouting. 'If I catch you near her
out of school hours again, I'll thrash you within an inch of your
life! Understand?'

I pedal around the car, keeping it between us. 'Come back here
when I'm talking to you, you insect!' He breaks into a trot but I
am pedalling away now, standing high in the saddle, head down,
looking back at him through my armpit. If I am shamed, it is only
because I've been caught. I feel no guilt as I ride on, just a growing,
seething anger as the Beetle reverses in another spray of gravel, turns
and accelerates after me.

The primary-school oval is a block away, the gate locked, the
Beetle close behind. I dismount and toss my bike over the fence
in one adrenaline-fuelled movement, jump after it, give Merv the
two-fingered, up-yours salute, and set off, riding straight across the
turf. He is out of his car again, hurdling the low fence with surprising ease for such a big man and sprinting my way, fast. Have I
miscalculated? On the old Malvern Star he might have caught me;
the gap is closing until I reach full speed and suddenly the task is
beyond him. Bent double on the cricket pitch, hands on knees, he
can only watch as I ride triumphantly out through the open gate
opposite. I brake and turn, smirking back at him.

'Fuck off, yourself!' And he can surely lip-read even if he
can't hear. Is it my first time with the high-school word? I like the
liberating taste of it. I use it again as I ride home, and again and
again, emptying out the anger, shouting myself empty, pleasurably.
'Fuck off, you dirty, filthy bastard!' 'If I ever catch *you* near her, I'll
fucking kill *you*!'

The possibility that he might be waiting for me at home doesn't
enter my mind. Somehow I know he will say nothing to my father.

My powers of clairvoyance are growing daily, if still not fully understood, and I sense that his wife Rita will take a dim view of his early-morning luggage chivalry. I might not have thought this thought yet, but I already know it. I have grown up in the back half of a police station after all; the scattered cogs and wirings of the great machine of the adult world, scavenged from hints and nudges and whispers, eavesdropped through closed bedroom doors and barred cell windows, lie spread across the workbench of my head, needing only to be fitted together.

8

I love all machines, all things fitted and turned, bored and re-bored, wired, welded, bolted, riveted and greased. I love the mechanical lower half of my fleet centaur-self; I groom its rigid limbs and oil its moving parts ceaselessly. I love the Liebig condenser I fit together on my end of the workbench, a machine of glass whose only moving parts are heat and vapour and the steady drip-drip of distillate. What is a chemical molecule if not a very small machine, a tiny machine part? What are my backyard experiments if not fitting those parts together, making the molecular machinery purr? And what is a chemical equation but a logic machine? $2Zn + 2HCl = H_2\uparrow + 2ZnCl$. $2H_2 + O_2 + match = 2H_2O + BOOM!$

I spend the weekend among such purring gadgetry and suddenly it's Monday morning, Modern History, and she is back from the city. The frock and loosened hair have gone. She wears the same tight green Capri pants and ballet slippers she wore the Friday before; her hair is drawn into the familiar French roll, a scarf is knotted around her neck.

The past is a foreign country, she chalks across the blackboard. *They do things differently there.* She turns, smiling. 'Does anyone know where this quote comes from? No? A clue: it's from a novel.'

I check my timetable. Modern History, definitely. English comes later in the day. Anne Hunter's hand is in the air, the usual lone pine above the shrubbery of heads. '*The Robe*, Miss?'

Why this is a stupid answer I have no idea, but Miss Peach's amused 'Not even warm' gladdens my heart.

'Anyone else? No? Finding the source is your homework for tonight. For now, write the words down in your exercise books, and think about them as we explore the country of the past together. It will be our epigraph. How many of you have fathers who served in the war?'

A forest of hands this time, including those who only wish their fathers had.

'I think,' Miss Peach speaks across the waving treetops, 'that the world before the war was a *very* different country. Hands down, please. None of you were born then, and I was only born during the war —'

'What year, Miss?'

'None of your business, Robert. Of course it wasn't the first time everything had been changed by a war. This term we will be studying the First World War, the Great War, 1914 to 1918 . . .'

History, after all. Now we are getting somewhere.

'*Don't* write that down, Robert. History is more than names and dates and places. Any woman and her dog can parrot the kings and queens of England, or the dates of famous battles, but history is about people, the foreign people of the foreign countries of the past.' She has commenced her pacing about now, her baton of chalk beating rhythmically, as if conducting her words. 'How can we truly know what they were like – their ideas, their beliefs, their habits of mind? Some say we can't. The people of the past are too different.

But I think that reading their poetry is one way. Poetry, to me, is the closest we can get to the way another person thinks – the closest, that is, in words. Reading a poem is like reading a mind.'

Her thoughts seem to jerk about as much as her hands and her swivelling steps. She chalks this last up on the board too; we dutifully copy it down. *Reading a poem is like reading a mind.*

'We don't just read that other mind, we *become* it, if only for a moment. Its rhythms and rhymes and thoughts capture us, hold us with it in a kind of lockstep. Professor Barry has written a poem which compares poems to magic shoes, red dancing shoes. When we read a poem – put a poem on – it traps us, holds us. Do you know the old fairytale *The Red Shoes*?'

A few hands in the air, all girls, all ignored. What has happened to Modern History again? Her new idea seems to excite her as much as anything she has said; her own dancing shoes keep her moving restlessly about as she talks on.

'Today I want us to look at two poems. Brian, could you pass out these copies? The first was written by a very good poet before the Great War, the second by another poet – a very great poet – towards the end. Both were soldiers, both died during the war. But it's hard to imagine two more different poems, two more different minds. Brian, would you read the first?'

'Me, Miss?'

'Of course you. Stand up, please.'

'"The Soldier",' he enunciates carefully. 'All of it, Miss?'

'It's only a sonnet,' she says, which must mean yes, whatever else it might mean.

'"If I should die, think only this of me",' he begins, and Miss Peach stops pacing about and tilts her head to listen. '"That there's some corner of a foreign field/That is forever England."'

Vaguely familiar words from Anzac Day dawn services. The

returned men of both wars (my returned dad never among them) standing at attention in the Soldiers' Memorial Park, we schoolkids in ranks behind them, a lone bugle goose-bumping our spines, a cold autumn wind snapping at the flag.

'"There shall be in that rich earth a richer dust concealed . . ."' Tinker Bell burbles on, but I have eyes only for the stilled Miss Peach. Her eyes are closed, but she seems to have an expression of distaste on her face.

'". . . Under an English Heaven,"' Tinker finishes.

Silence.

'Powerful words,' Miss Peach says, rousing. 'And very patriotic. Was anyone else moved by those noble sentiments?'

A forest of arms in the air.

'*Sieg heil*,' she says, as if quoting from some war comic. 'Rupert Brooke would be proud of you,' she adds, equally mysteriously.

Her gaze flits about the thicket of raised arms before alighting on me, sitting at the back with my arms folded.

'Ah! A dissenter.' Another mysterious word; I will check it in the dictionary later. 'We'll talk more about the poem in a few minutes, and what Samuel Johnson has to say about patriotism.' Something in the way she speaks this last word, as if handling it with tongs, surprises me – the same tone she has used when speaking of Domestic Science. 'And perhaps also about dissent. But first I want us to hear the next poem – another very famous, but very different, poem.' Her wandering gaze finds me again. 'You can do the honours, Robert. You write war stories; let's see if Wilfred Owen can unlock your warrior heart.'

Every face is turned my way; there will be no rescue this week. I unfold my long frame up out of my seat. 'All of it, Miss?' I parrot Tinker Bell.

A few guffaws at his expense; a stern glance from Miss Peach.

'"What passing bells for these who die as cattle,"' I begin, all too aware of Miss Peach in the corner of my eye, stilled again, eyes closed, her trance-state less surprising but still unsettling, her fine nostrils flared as if she is inhaling the words rather than hearing them. '"Only the monstrous anger of the guns . . ."'

Her eyes stay shut after I've finished, her lashes seem to be glistening.

'Are you all right, Miss?'

She rouses herself. 'I'm fine, Anne.' She offers a half-smile, retracts it. 'Well, no – I suppose I'm not fine. Which . . .' she plucks a handkerchief from her sleeve and dabs at her eyes, 'is a good example of what I was talking about. How poetry has the power to take over our thoughts.'

My kind of lesson, after all. Half science fiction, half zombie flick.

She licks her lips as if on the point of saying more, but the siren sounds for the end of the lesson, a rude trumpet blast which seems to jar her back into a more businesslike manner, and all too soon we are filing out for lunch.

Woodwork next. As I absentmindedly shave wood curls from a lump of four-by-two, I can see only those wet lashes. I don't believe her for a moment; words alone cannot have such power. There must be something else, something personal.

'*With* the grain, Burns!' Big Merv seizes my hand-plane; he has been on my back all lesson. 'If you can't listen, at least watch and learn. You waste this bit of wood, you won't get another. You think it grows on *trees?*'

He reverses the timber in my vice and runs the plane smoothly over its surface, but this is less a demonstration than an excuse for him to hiss, bent over his work, for my ears only, 'Don't think I've forgotten the weekend, you little perve!'

I reverse the timber again as soon as he walks away, and concentrate hard for the rest of the lesson on ruining the wood.

Miss Peach is back for the last lesson, Latin, dry-eyed and restless again, a petite centurion leading us on a forced march across a dozen pages of basic sentences. *The farmer rides the horse. The sailor rows the ship. The soldier throws the spear.* When the home siren sounds she continues speaking through it, as if wanting to make up for lost time.

'*Hasta, hastae*, feminine, first. Strange that the word for spear should be feminine in gender, isn't it? Homework for tonight: think about the genders of the nouns on your list, and what that gender might mean. Or even if it means anything. War – *bellum* – is neuter. Soldier – *miles* – masculine . . .'

I sit down at the kitchen table after tea that night and rewrite my abortion story instead. *Once upon a time there will be a future in which time-travel into the past is possible . . .*

It's the year 1943 and a secret agent from the future – me – materialises at midnight inside the Keswick army barracks in Adelaide, armed only with an HB pencil and a rubber eraser. His mission? To tamper with recruitment rosters so that a soldier who would otherwise die in New Guinea is given a desk posting at home. Why I choose to give him the rank of captain or the surname Pear is not immediately clear to me, but feels right.

I leave the story on her desk the following morning. Individuals *can* make a difference, I am prepared to concede – up to a point. A difference to other individuals. And to the bigger picture? I've given this some thought since our chat. Nothing important can be changed in history – nothing, in short, *historical*. Captain Pear might not be fighting by their side now, but the heroic Australian diggers still turn back the yellow hordes at Kokoda. I still grow up speaking English, not Japanese. I have found nothing in Tolstoy's

War to convince me otherwise, at least not in the fifty-odd pages I managed to get through before tossing the book aside. I'm prepared to defend these ideas – ideas I didn't know I was writing about until she pointed them out – but I'm not prepared for the peculiar smile she gives me as she sets the story aside after reading it through. The mix of kindness and sadness on her face is as incomprehensible to me then as it is indescribable now.

Nor am I prepared for the way she lightly squeezes my shoulder as she walks past during a Latin test later that morning.

She, too, bends and whispers something for my ears only. 'Thank you, Robbie. My father was only a corporal. And he was killed in North Africa, not New Guinea – but it's a beautiful thought.'

9

Words flow out of me that year as easily as words flow in, as if one displaces the other, as if the tip of my pencil is the chattering needle of one of those complicated machines that record brain waves directly and smoothly onto paper. What is a science-fiction story but another kind of machine? A machine for testing ideas, an experimental prototype. As with a chemical experiment, the parts fit neatly together, the whole device *gets* somewhere, all on the smell of a hypothetical thought. And if that somewhere is more smoke and mirrors than flame and noise, it's all part of the fun.

My days pass in a flurry of such stories, scribbled into exercise books before breakfast and during lessons and between after-school detentions and after-dinner homework. My weekly test results – Woodwork aside – are the best ever. If I play the fool less, it is more a pragmatic than a moral choice: to gain Miss Peach's attention more durably. The perfect scores I had hitherto achieved only in Arithmetic and Science are now commonplace in Latin and History and English. I can decline and conjugate my way through Giles' *Latin Grammar* blindfolded, recite Wilfred Owen's collected works backwards. I know what a sonnet is; I can measure poems by the meter. I can name the chief imports and exports of all the British, German and French colonies before the First World War. Of course I can quote the exact death tolls at Gallipolli, Ypres, on the Marne and on the Somme, nation by nation; more importantly, I know the history behind such arithmetic. To please Miss Peach I pick up *War and Peace* again, and this time finish it. That is, finish scanning it; I skip the interminable essays and banquets and balls embedded among the action scenes. As expected, I find peace less interesting than war, but I am eager to impress and if I don't read every word I read every second. In every second paragraph. And feel a definite sense of elation – part relief, part half-deserved achieve-ment – when I find my way out of the maze of Tolstoy's sentences by torchlight late one night. *It is necessary to renounce a freedom that does not exist, and to recognize a dependence of which we are not personally conscious.*

I close the book, re-enter the nearer world. Rain is clattering on the tin roof, unnoticed till now. What Tolstoy meant a hundred years before I have no idea, but I can't wait to tell Miss Peach I've finished. I am half conscious of my growing dependence on her, if not ready, yet, to renounce an individual free will that I am certain does exist. I climb out of bed, sit at my desk, and begin to create my own maze of sentences by torchlight.

I continue to flood her with these clever, nutty stories; she continues to drown me – to drown all of us – in poetry. English lessons are taught through poetry, history through poetry, and although we are not yet chanting Catullus in Latin, she uses various rhyming tricks to help us remember irregular verbs.

'Rhythm and rhyme make things stick in our heads,' she lectures. 'Our brains are formed that way. That's why you will remember your favourite nursery rhymes all your lives.'

Weekends are a struggle. That second Friday taught her an important lesson: keep your cards close to your tightly sweatered chest. These are your students, not your friends. Anything you say may be taken down and used in evidence against you later. 'You going to the cricket tomorrow, Miss?' 'Only if I'm picked in the team.' 'You going to the drive-in, Miss?' 'What's a drive-in?' 'What church do you go to, Miss?' 'Reformed Hindu.' Is it my feverish imagination or does her smile light on me at such times, as if only the two of us are capable of sharing these private jokes and deflections?

I look up 'dissenter' and decide she has a thick streak of it herself.

Every Friday night and Saturday morning I investigate the comings and goings at the station. If she fails to board the Bluebird I check her house. If the Vespa is parked in the drive I sit high in the pepper tree, smoking and waiting, binoculars in hand. Usually I see nothing but Miss Burke and Miss Hammond, coming with shopping bags and going with tennis racquets. Or Big Merv in the front yard next door, shirt off, muscles flexed, taking all morning to mow his postage stamp of lawn while keeping one eye on the Vespa himself. The slug gun would come in handy; I squeeze an imaginary trigger, although he is well out of range. I am loath to reveal myself. I hide my bike behind the hall; I make myself invisible if Billy rides by. Around noon I patrol Church Street on foot, pressing my nose to shop windows, loitering by the trading table. Late in the afternoon I slow-bikeride behind the cars that surround the cricket pitch, snooping through rear windows.

She is nowhere to be seen, not even at the drive-in on

Saturday nights. *Birdman of Alcatraz* and *Charade* come and go; I stake out the kiosk at intermission, check out the likely cars. I'm not allowed to see *The Guns of Navarone* – 'A *war* flick, sonny-jim? They haven't a clue what it was like' – but it doesn't sound like her kind of picture either.

Where is she? When she appears each Monday morning, where has she been? 'Did you have a nice weekend, Miss?' 'A lovely weekend, thank you Anne. Turn to page thirty-five of *Legamus*, please.' 'You went to the city, Miss?' 'This is a Latin lesson, Robbie – not Geography.' 'What are you doing for Easter, Miss? Are you going away?' 'From the top, everyone together. Caesar's speech to the Gauls.'

What will *I* do for Easter? For suddenly it's Maundy Thursday and school's out, and Miss Peach is puttering homewards on her Vespa, having given nothing away. I pedal after her, clamber up the pepper tree and watch with a sinking heart as Big Merv loads her heavy case – I know it by sight – beneath the front bonnet of his rear-engined Beetle. His wife watches from the porch of their red-brick house, her red-brick face expressionless. I train my binoculars on her mouth, but can read nothing on those thin, pursed lips.

A moment's panic: are Miss Peach and Big Merv spending Easter together? The faint air-horn of the Bluebird dispels this ridiculous thought. Climbing higher, I locate its glassy eyes and orange chin a mile or two to the south, just beyond the cemetery. Will she make the station on time? I hope not. Big Merv shouts something; Miss Peach appears on her front porch in her blue frock and exploded hair, closely followed by the Tweedle-twins, each with a cigarette in one hand, wineglass in the other. Waves and blown kisses all round, the thin-lipped Mrs Merv merges back into her brick house, the Beetle reverses out and chuggles up Arthur Street towards the station. I would leap down and follow, but for some reason the Tweedle-twins are taking a slow stroll along the street in my direction. Worse still:

they stop and sit on the bench beneath the tree, sipping at their wine, sucking at their fags. Miss Burke tilts her head back and exhales upwards into the leaves and berries.

'So many admirers, so little time, eh Miss Hammond?' she says loudly.

'Places to go, sugar daddies to meet,' her companion replies, and they chuckle together.

'Is "meet" the apposite verb, do you think, Miss Hammond? My impression of the beautifully presented Miss Peach was that her pants were on fire – pardon the expression.'

'The elegantly attired Miss Peach is never backwards in being forward, Miss Burke. Would you agree, Master Burns?'

I freeze. Are my ears playing tricks?

'Master Burns? You *are* roosting on your nest today?'

They are guessing, surely. I am well hidden. My bike is behind the hall.

'You've been up there a long time, Master Burns. Perhaps hatching an egg?'

'The nesting habits of the Lesser Perve, Miss Burke. Are those police-issue field glasses perchance, Master Burns?'

Still I keep my mouth shut. Eye contact has not been made.

'I'm afraid you've been abandoned for the weekend, Master Burns. The exotic Miss Peach has bigger, um, *birds* to catch. Was that your impression too, Miss Hammond?'

'The highly strung Miss Peach couldn't seem to get out of this shithole fast enough, Miss Burke.'

They chortle, as amused as ever with themselves.

'No one to spy on but little old us,' Miss Burke says. 'What a let-down.'

Miss Hammond stubs out her cigarette and inspects her empty packet. 'Master Burns? Might I trouble you for a fag?'

Silence has become pointless. 'I don't smoke, Miss.'

An arch look between them. 'The rabbitoh must think we came down in the last shower, Miss Hammond.'

'A little something to top up our glasses while you're there, rabbitoh. No doubt you have something drinkable in your larder?'

I take a deep breath, fish my sack of treasures out of the possum hole, and begin the slow climb down.

'Well, ho, ho, ho!' Miss Burke says. 'Look who's coming down the chimney!'

'A little early this year,' from Miss Hammond. 'But we have both been *very* good girls.'

They find this the most hilarious thing yet said; they are still spluttering away as they rummage in the hessian sack. Miss Hammond fishes out a crumpled pack of Craven A and turns up her nose. 'I thought at the very least you would be smoking Kool, Master Burns.'

She straightens a bent cigarette, lights it, passes it to her companion, straightens another.

'I understand sales of Kool cigarettes have gone through the roof in the district, Miss Burke.'

'Country folk are so impressionable, Miss Hammond.'

'She's gone to the city for Easter, Miss?' I get in as they continue rummaging.

'We should definitely confiscate this,' Miss Burke announces, and stands a half-full bottle of Autumn Brown on the bench between them.

'Perhaps we should taste the contraband first, Miss Burke? Who knows what it might be doing to the brain of the precocious Master Burns. Let alone his faithful offsider.'

'Where is Sancho Panza this afternoon, Master Burns? Throwing rocks on someone else's roof? He's been making an awful nuisance of himself round these parts lately.'

Miss Burke fishes out the binoculars and trains them on her own house. 'Remind me to keep the bedroom curtains open at all times, Miss Hammond. I would hate to disappoint any keen birdwatchers.'

Her companion is waving an exercise book in my face. 'Aha! And what have we here? A diary?'

'A novel, Miss.'

'A diary by any other name, Master Burns. Let me guess, a young boy has a crush on his perfectly groomed but highly strung teacher, and spies on her through her bedroom window each night? Would the plot of your, um, *Bildungsroman* bear any resemblance to that?'

'No, Miss. It's set on a planet in the future.'

'A planet on which a little green boy has a crush on his little green teacher?'

She tosses the exercise book my way with a smoky laugh and the two of them rise from the bench and walk away, taking my bottle of Autumn Brown with them.

10

Good Friday. Time and rabbits to kill, money to pocket, space again for my best friend in my life. Our gruffness on the church steps in the morning – 'Going rabbiting this arvo. Wanna come?' 'Spose. Not much else to do' – dissolves soon enough in the familiar physicality of cycling, setting traps, gathering firewood. The Easter bunny is roasting on a spit by sunset, its heirs and relatives already skinned and gutted and stuffed inside a sack hanging from the nearest stringybark.

After we've exhausted such jokes and eaten the last Easter eggs that will ever be delivered, talk stalls, and we sit stirring hot coals and sipping sweet sherry in silence until Billy can bring himself to mention Miss Peach.

'She told my old man I smashed her front window.'

'Why would she tell him that?'

'She hates my guts.'

'Pig's.'

'She saw me chuck the rock, Robbie.'

'You chucked a rock through her window? You didn't tell me!'

'I ain't seen you! I'm telling you now.'

'Why did you do it?'

'Cos I hate her guts.'

Tranquil with sherry and fire-warmth I am only mildly provoked. 'She hates Big Merv's guts.'

'Bull! He's probably rooting her already. He rooted the others.'

'Bull*shit*. How do you know?'

'My brother saw 'em. At the footy club.'

'*Both* of them?'

'Miss Burke. In the change rooms. He was lying on his back on the bench. She was sittin' on him. Bouncin' up and down on him.'

We splutter sherry and half-cooked fragments of Easter bunny into the fire at the picturing of it.

'What was the rest of the team doing? Watching?'

'Playing, stupid. It was the middle of the game. He hurt his knee. Limped off. Neville says she was all red in the face. And bawling.'

'Bawling? Why was she bawling?'

'I dunno. Maybe it hurt.'

This mystifies me. 'Why was she *sitting* on him? You have to lie down to root.'

'Dogs don't. And what about horses?'

'They're animals, stupid. They've got four legs.'

'Ya can do it all kinds of ways, Robbie. Neville's got this book of pictures . . .'

I have eyes only for the picture in my head: Big Merv flat on his back, a bawling Miss Burke bouncing up and down on him. It makes no sense. The fact that I am becoming aroused thinking about it makes even less sense. Does my cock know something I don't? Schoolyard phrases remembered less for meaning than music find their way into our mouths. 'He shoved his tool right up her!' I shout. 'Bangs like a shithouse door in a gale!' Billy shouts back.

The nonsensical words feel as thrilling to blurt into the air as farts once were. Thrilling also the feel of the erect cock – mine – which I spring loose from my shorts and begin to squeeze rhythmically.

'Whatcha doing?' Billy says. He turns his torch on it and shouts, 'What's *that*?'

Have we drunk too much sherry? It's my cock, certainly – as absurdly long and skinny as the rest of me – but I also seem to be looking down at it for the first time, as if from outer space, or through the wrong end of a telescope. What is this alien body part *for*? It juts out into the torchlight, going nowhere and doing nothing, less useful tool than useless extra limb.

'You've seen it before,' I tell him.

'Not like that.'

'It's just a stiffy. Ain't you seen a stiffy before?'

'Course I have,' he says unconvincingly.

I turn my torch on his groin. 'Get yours out.'

He yanks down his shorts and spreads his thighs; we compare my stiff state with his flaccid slug by torchlight.

'Mine just looks long cos yours is short,' I say.

'Pig's arse! Mine's like everyone else's. And why are ya *milking* yours?'

'It feels good. You squeeze it.'

'Are you nuts? I'm not gunna squeeze your cock!'

'What ya scared of? It might bite?'

He stares at the pale knob-head with its pink mouth-slit and giggles. 'It might. Looks like a snake!' He reaches across and prods the head of the thing cautiously. 'Needs a couple of eyes.'

I pluck a piece of warm charcoal from the margins of the fire with one hand, grip my stiff cock firmly with the other, and sketch two rough cartoon eyes on each side of the head.

'Frill-neck lizard!' I shout, laughing.

'Nah – a fish!' Billy bends and blows fish-bubbles at that moist fish-mouth. 'A fucking great eel!' he shouts, and we splutter more sherry and rabbit meat over each other.

'We used to catch 'em back on the mission,' he says. 'We was always fishing. Short-fin eel. Bream. Murray cod. You shoulda seen this cod Neville caught once. A fuckin' submarine!'

I refill my mug and flop onto my back and begin to squeeze my fish more forcefully. Billy's reminiscences peter out; he watches me intently, then shines his torch again into his own groin. 'Fuck!' he says, surprised. His own dick is beginning to swell, a pale inner head emerging from a dark fold of foreskin.

'It's pink!' I tell him. 'Pink on the inside! It looks like a bloody *dog's* dick!'

'Yours looks like a *giraffe's*,' he says, and we laugh drunkenly, flat on our backs now, those stiff, different animal dicks aimed vertically at the night sky.

'Auntie Dulcie reckons your tool is the same size as your foot. You can tell by the shoe size.'

'Why would you want to tell?'

'I dunno. I'm just saying. That's what I heard her telling Uncle Poss.'

Up on our backsides again, facing each other, we measure our feet against each other's cocks.

'Told ya, Robbie!' he says, then presses the sole of his foot against my cock, rolling it against my belly. 'You still want me to squeeze it? I wouldn't mind.'

A wave of pleasure washes through me. 'Spose,' I say.

His small hand is less expert than mine, but when I shut my eyes it is Miss Peach's even smaller hand. It's her face and body in my head. I surrender to the waves of pleasure, drown in them, seeing her as vividly as I have ever seen her.

'Jesus, Robbie! It *slagged* on me.'

I open my eyes. Billy is turning his hand this way and that, inspecting it by torchlight.

'That's what comes out, stupid. Milk yours.'

'You fucking milk it! You reckon ya know so much about it. I did yours.'

I shine my torch on his odd, half-caste cock: dark on the outside, pale on the inside. A few minutes ago I would have gladly squeezed it, now it looks – my mother's word pops into my head – unhygienic. Not that he needs help as stares across at me and begins squeezing. He rolls onto his back, arching up into those squeezings, and grunts repeatedly. 'Jesus! *Jesus!*'

One last loud grunt and he rolls towards the fire, facing away from me, knees to chest, as if hiding himself. I crawl up over him and aim my torch into his groin. His hands cover his dick, I push them aside. 'You've slagged on your*self*, Billy.'

He shoves me away. 'Get off! What are ya, a fucking *poofter?*'

We lie in silence, gathering our drunken thoughts, mystified and embarrassed. Somewhere the dull snap of a trap and the cry of a rabbit. Needing an escape, we yank up our shorts, grab our torches, and stumble off into the night to slit the throat of another

Easter bunny. Then stumble back to our bed-rolls and sleep. We are both too hung-over in the morning to mention what happened. The ride home into a stiff westerly blows any conversation away before it begins; at the edge of town we nod goodbye and ride off with our separate embarrassments.

By Easter Monday I've checked the length of my skinny eel-cock many times with my school ruler. The length of my feet, heel to toe, likewise. A terrifying thought: adults are forever telling me that I haven't stopped growing, that I'm shooting up, caught in a growth spurt. What if my cock stretches even more as I elongate, thinning out like a strand of chewed gum? It might be a less obvious deformity than Billy's squashed nose, or Anne Hunter's stick-out ears, but I know it is there, a shame waiting to happen, a trouser snake that Miss Peach will never want to see, let alone touch. Let alone (the notion more nonsensical each time I imagine it) have shoved up her.

I take a cold shower every morning, emerging shivering and goose-bumpy but with my cock shrunk as small as a baby's bootie. This incredible shrinking manhood never lasts long enough; warmed up, it is soon itself again, more overlong earthworm than eel or snake. Self-consciousness seems to make it even longer; might it be possible, I wonder, to have surgery to make it shorter? I will ask Doc McKenzie the next time he is called to the house for an emergency. I have plenty of ideas that can all too easily end in emergencies.

11

It's the year 2064 and all human diseases have been cured and everyone can live for ever — with one catch. Lung cancer can only be cured by transplanting lungs from a dead donor. And since no

one in the year 2064 is dying of anything except lung cancer, there
are no lungs available.

I begin the story in Woodwork class, scribbling on draughtsman's
paper with carpenter's lead while my classmates measure up slabs
of pine for our first-term projects, breadboards for Mother's Day.
I finish the story the same day, in Algebra. In brief: when a drug
that cures lung cancer is finally discovered it proves so expensive – a
million Earth-credits per patient – that only the filthy rich can
afford it. And the masses? They have the opiates of religious faith,
but since immortality in the future is very much in *this* life, here
on Earth, the churches have long since fallen on hard times. Their
traditional sticks and carrots – heaven and hell – have no meaning,
except for the victims of lung cancer. Before long, the last surviving
churches have been turned into giant casinos in which a few lucky
cancer victims gamble their way to a million Earth-credits and win
eternal life at the expense of the unlucky.

I set the story aside at lunchtime, pleased. Geography next, an
hour of Headmaster Bell droning on about river deltas and alluvial
floodplains, to the constant jingling accompaniment of keys in his
trouser pocket. Time passes far too slowly. When I take up my story
again in Latin I find that time has passed even more slowly in the
future; living for ever has not quite turned out as promised.

It's the year 3064 and the Immortal Ones are bored out of their
brains. New churches begin to spring up, holding out the promise
of eternal death. Around me the rest of the class is taking dictation
from Miss Peach; I am taking dictation from myself. Ideas tumble
out. There are sects whose sacraments are bullfighting, car racing,
cliff climbing, big-game hunting with sheath-knives. There are
churches which train members of their congregation as gladiators,
pitting them against each other in a ring fenced with pews till death
doth them part. The Eastern Orthodox Church survives with a holy

sacrament of vodka and Russian roulette; onion domes resound with the noise of gunshots, the splatter of brains. I laugh out loud at the final twist: these new churches, dedicated to gambling for death, soon put the casino churches, wagering against death, out of business. For as people begin to die again, especially of gunshot wounds to the head, there are plenty of lungs to go round.

Back in the present, every face is turned my way. Miss Peach eyes me suspiciously: what's so funny about second-declension nouns? She holds me back after the lesson; I stand before her desk as she reads through the confiscated story, pausing to scribble something purple here and there. At last she lifts her ballerina's head and gives me a look of worried puzzlement.

'I don't quite know what to say, Robbie.'

'You don't like it, Miss?'

'"Like" is hardly the word.' A pause. 'Are you happy, Robbie?' Her eyes search my face; what is she looking for? 'If there's ever anything you'd like to tell me, anything at all – any problem you want to discuss – it would be between us.'

My turn for puzzlement. 'What sort of thing, Miss?'

'Problems with, well, girls. Or at home. It must be difficult to have a policeman for a father. To grow up in that environment. You must be exposed to, um, things that other children aren't . . .'

Where has this come from? Another planet? 'What about the story, Miss Peach?'

A shrug. 'You're an enigma, Robert Burns.'

Another word to look up, but it sounds more positive. 'So you did like it?'

'I'm . . . disturbed by it. I don't think I'll forget it in a hurry. But I'm not ready to talk about it now. I need time to digest it.' A half-smile. 'Perhaps you should go. Your friends will be waiting.'

ENIGMA *1. Somebody or something puzzling, or inexplicable.*

2. A riddle. She is the enigma, I decide when I arrive at school the next morning and find three closely typed sheets of paper sitting on my desk.

The Church of Orthodox Roulette. It looks like my story, but with a new title and fewer pages. As my classmates unpack their bags, I read on bewildered, picking out the bare bones of my story among the corrections and deletions. I find it hard to concentrate on the lesson that follows – the Versailles Treaty, the League of Nations – but Miss Peach doesn't seem to notice. The smile on her face is as wide as it has ever been when I approach her desk afterwards. Whether she is pleased with me or with herself is hard to tell.

'I typed it up, Robbie. What do you think? Do you like it?'

'I'm not sure that "like" is the word, Miss.'

A tinkle of laughter. *'Touché!'*

'Sorry, Miss?'

'A hit, Robbie. A very palpable hit.' English words, but she might still be speaking French. 'I've typed it up because you can't possibly submit it to a publisher in a school exercise book.'

Not so much French now as Martian. Or some language in which recognisable words have unrecognisable meanings. Note for a story: in the year 2064 the Earth's magnetic field flips and the meanings of words change into their opposites overnight.

'My friend Geoffrey edits a little poetry magazine. *Black Swan of Trespass.* I think this might be suitable.'

My thoughts are yanked back to 1964. 'You mean he might *publish* it?'

'I can't promise anything, but yes. Perhaps. It's very inventive.'

'It's not a poem, Miss.'

'It's a kind of poetry. The ideas behind it are poetic. It's difficult poetry, depressing poetry – but somehow very true. What do you think of the new title?'

'Not sure, Miss.'

'Trust me.'

I more than trust her, much more. But if she is to love me in return, she needs to love my stories, which somehow feel part of me, anatomically, even after they've left my brain. Like my other distant extremities – toes, fingers – they are also sensitive to pain.

'Geoffrey would tell you that titles are important, Robbie. You need to grab the attention of the reader. Seize him by the eyes. And it's not an easy story. It's a dark story. It needs all the help it can get.'

'But it's *my* story, Miss.'

A playful laugh. 'Are you always this stubborn? Tell you what – I'll offer Geoffrey both versions, yours and mine, and he can decide. What do you say?'

Silence while I mull this over.

'If I see him during the holidays I can give them to him personally.'

'You're going away again, Miss?'

'Of course.'

'The whole week?'

'Nothing to keep me here,' she says, careless of my feelings. 'If he likes it I'll send you a postcard. Deal?' No answer is required as she slides a small stack of paperbacks across the desk. 'Your holiday reading. Since you like inventing dystopias, here's some food for thought. I'd start with the Huxley. Then the Orwell. Leave the Samuel Butler till last.'

12

I tail the Vespa to the Royal Oak after school on the last Friday of term. Miss Peach parks and enters; I keep watch high in my corrugated valley across the road. Time passes. I fire short bursts at passing semitrailers with an imaginary Bren gun. I take aim at the parked Vespa but can't bring myself to squeeze even an imaginary trigger. At six o'clock she emerges, a little flushed in the face, climbs on and putters off in the direction of home.

An hour later I am at the station as the Bluebird pulls in; she isn't. I ride back past her house, sight the Vespa, park my bike behind the hall and my backside in the pepper tree. No sign of life in any windows. Billy rides by after an hour or so, stands high on his pedals to look for my bike, rides on. I smoke a couple of cigarettes and scribble a line or two till hunger and darkness drive me homewards.

Unable to sleep at first, I wake late in the morning and have to race to the station, pedalling furiously, to check the train. Still no sign of Miss Peach, but here are Miss Burke and Miss Hammond, bulging out of their best frocks as they lug bulging suitcases along the platform. Their four plump breasts precede them, shaped into jutting cones today as if by giant pencil-sharpeners.

'Master Burns! How kind of you to see us off.'

'Just here to collect a parcel, Miss Burke. You off to the city?'

'We're off *any*where,' from Miss Hammond.

'On the first stage out of town,' the other adds.

Their chuckling allows me to get a word in. 'Miss Peach isn't with you?'

They roll their eyes at each other. 'Ah – the mystery of Miss Peach. Can you shed any light on the matter, Miss Burke?'

'You refer to the strange comings and goings in the depths of night, Miss Hammond? The tall dark stranger at the door?'

'Or was it a short bald stranger? It was too dark to tell.'

I leave them snickering together, clamber back on my bike and ride off to check the house. No sign of the Vespa. I knock on the front door anyway, just in case. No answer. A golden opportunity; my pulse quickens. I walk around and try the back door: locked, an affront I take personally. Who locks their back door? And why? The bedroom windows along the side of the house are likewise shut and latched. City habits? I feel insulted now on behalf of the entire town, on behalf of country folk all over the state. I also feel frustrated; I *have* to get inside. I can't risk trying the front windows in full view of the street; the high toilet window, shielded from Big Merv's house by a hedge, offers the best chance. I tug the metal garbage bin beneath it, climb up, and with the tip of my sheath-knife ease the six glass louvres free from their brackets, one by one.

Task complete, I squirm head first through the sharp-edged aperture. The house might be empty but still my heart pounds. Not much light inside; I swim carefully down through the gloom, feeling my way over cistern and bowl, taking my weight on trembling arms. Upright on trembling legs, I inch open the toilet door and take a peep. Little to see out in the dim hallway but plenty to feel inside me: fearful excitement, thrilled curiosity. I like this edge-of-the-precipice feeling. I've sought it out many times before, standing at the lip of a flooded quarry with the water level too far below, or on the ridge of my roof-valley, tempted to jump, to see if maybe, just once, gravity might relinquish its hold on me. I've jumped today; where have I landed?

My eyes adjust: kitchen at one end of the hallway, front door at the other, four closed doors between, two on each side. Vague idea for a story: *Bear and the Three Goldilocks*. Which bedroom is Just Right? Contrary to the rules of story suspense, her door is the first I open. How do I know it's her room? Simple: I've seen nothing like it before. Richly patterned rugs cover the floor; cushions that seem made of that same rug material, doubled over and thickly stuffed, surround the fireplace and cover much of the bed. The double bed! But only married people have double beds. And princesses in children's stories. A Persian rug also hangs, weirdly, from one wall; framed paintings cover two others. The curtains are drawn, but my eyes are thirsty for even the dimmest details. The paintings are mostly what my mother likes to call modern art; I call them badly coloured-in shapes from a Geometry primer. A row of half-melted candles wedged into wine bottles lines the mantelpiece. Peculiar wicker baskets encase most of these; runnels of dried wax encrust their sides like eruptions of lava. A box of Redheads sits at one end; wanting to see more, I light three candles with one match, four with a second. Candlelight seems safer than opening the curtains. A portable gramophone sits on a small desk between two framed photographs. In the nearest, Miss Peach's eyes and high cheekbones stare out from an older, plumper face – her mother's, presumably. A younger man in army uniform and slouch-hat and corporal's stripes is profiled in the other.

A pine dresser with a hinged mirror is draped in scarves and covered with such a variety of coloured glass bottles it might be a secret laboratory, or alchemist's cave. Makeshift bookshelves line the wall either side of the fireplace: pine boards supported at each end on blocks of local white limestone and stacked all the way to the ceiling. Some of the names on the thicker books are now familiar – Tolstoy, Huxley, Orwell – but most aren't. The topmost shelves are filled with much slimmer volumes, numerous *Selected Poems* by someone called Faber, others with offbeat titles that catch my eye and stick in my head, if only because they don't make sense. *Once Bitten, Twice Bitten. His Thoughts Made Pockets. The Drunken Boat.* Only one name – common to four of the slimmest volumes – makes sense: Geoffrey Barry. I prise the slimmest of these – *A Little Nightmare Music* – free from the grip of its neighbours. No photograph of the poet, which disappoints me, but I read through a short Note

on the Author: 'Emeritus Professor of English at the University
of Adelaide . . . Fourth volume . . . Widely esteemed . . . Married
with three children . . .' No age or birth year is given. I imagine an
absentminded Doc McKenzie-type with a food-flecked beard and
perhaps food-flecked eyebrows.

The handwritten inscription on the title page doesn't help. 'For
the Teacher's Pet. Toujours, G. xxx.'

I flick to a random page with an incomprehensible heading:
'*Et Tu, Brute Force*'. The lines beneath offer no illumination.

> Nothing earths us more than pain,
> Or ties us to the world of things,
> Among which things this body,
> Willing torturer's accomplice,
> Torturer's apprentice . . .

Is it a poem or a list of contents? I flip back a few pages: no,
there is a separate contents page, which makes just as much sense.
Baffled, I squeeze the book back into the tight grip of its fellows.
The lower shelves are devoted to LP records, stacked in piles, face
up. No 45s in sight: roll over Beatles, here are Beethoven, Bach and
Brahms, names which I know belong to a world called Classical
Music, but of which I know nothing else. The topmost sleeve is
empty: *Last Quartets, Volume I*. A corner inscription on the cover
in a now familiar hand: 'Our splendid journey continues. Toujours,
G. xxx.' My journey, too, continues; the missing disc is quickly
located on the turntable. I switch on the power and lift across the
stylus.

A sawing of fiddles erupts, deafeningly; Miss Peach likes her
music loud. I lift the needle off before the neighbours, one neighbour in particular, come banging on the door.

The mystery of the double bed. As usual, my cock has a better understanding – a crowbar jammed in a vice. My entire body feels jammed in a vice; I kick free of my sandals, strip off my shirt and pants and cast them aside. I pull open the wardrobe door and step in among her clothes instead. Somehow it seems both the obvious thing to do and still the most surprising. Familiar outfits rustle about me thrillingly: blouses, ski pants and Capri pants folded neatly over wooden coathangers, the blue frock she wore at Easter. Everything I have ever seen her wear is here, so what can she have taken with her? The enclosed space smells powerfully of her perfume; even naked I still feel constrained, under pressure, about to explode. My bare soles trample about on a small hill of rough-edged shoes; the rising pressure in my cock feels as painful as a boil, and whatever bursts out of me, sperm or pus or both, needs no helping hand.

I stand there on trembling legs, surprised again, if only by the urgency of it all. The pus has vanished into the dark reaches of the wardrobe, hopefully as far as Narnia. I allow myself to topple backwards onto the mattress, recovering. She has stripped the sheets but those big, plush Arabian Nights cushions still smell of her, and my cock stirs slightly again.

My stomach is also stirring, more strongly. I roll off the bed and head for the kitchen, still naked and half tumescent. The fridge has been emptied for the holidays; there's nothing on the shelves but a half-full flagon of Coonawarra claret. I unscrew the cap, take a small swig, a larger swig, then pluck a mug from the dish rack and fill it to the brim. Plenty of tinned food in the pantry cupboard; I open a large can of Rosella spaghetti and spoon it down cold, follow it up with a can of baked beans, then explore the rest of the house, naked.

A further mystery: a double bed in the second bedroom also, but no bed in the third at all, just two identical roll-desks. My heart warms towards the Tweedle-twins; how decent of them to give up one of their bedrooms – and one of their big double beds – to make room for Miss Peach. And share a bed themselves. Each mouthful of wine adds to the warmth in my chest, but the rest of me is goose-pimpling now with the cold. I carry the flagon and wine mug back to Miss Peach's bed, plucking another of the professor's skinny books from the shelves en route, and lie there propped among her exotic cushions, sipping wine. The poetry this time is also easier to sip.

> In the Beginning
> God toppled the first
> Domino,
> Then left the room
> To play with other toys,
> For ever.

No title. Just a handful of lines, a dozen-odd words. A sprinkle of islands in a square white sea. A similar archipelago on the next page.

> When I die
> And go to Hell,
> Promise me
> You'll come as well.

At least it rhymes. I read on, but find no more that do; perhaps it was an accident. He's not a poet and he doesn't know it? I've finished the flagon off and almost finished the book before the increasing weight of my eyelids drags the rest of me down with them into sleep.

What time is it when I wake? Where *am* I when I wake? Ball-bearings are clattering loudly on the roof of the house and even more loudly on the roof of my aching skull. My mouth is all cockroach. Am I in hell? No, heaven. Miss Peach's bed. The candles are out, the room in darkness, but her faint perfume fixes the time and place. Rain is falling outside, with nightfall not far behind. Have I slept all afternoon? There is no time to waste if I want to make it home in time for tea: Saturday night, oxtail stew, my favourite.

13

Rain is still drumming on the roof the next day, and the next: the first steady rains of the year. Another childhood given, water. Ours might be the driest continent on Earth, but Earth is the wettest planet in the solar system, and rain has to fall somewhere. Where there is water there is grass, and where there is grass, life. The poor, poor country? No paupers are we. Great flocks of water birds cover the swamps and dams like downy quilts; the lush wet pastures are covered with fat wet cattle. The rain spills its heavy coins over the roofs and trees; all about us the land is flowing with milk and money, with meat and wheat and lucerne and wool and wine.

Ours is a world thickly buttered. A world, in short, in clover.

And still the rain falls. The limestone underworld is a water-logged sponge; the water runs from the back of the sodden Earth as if from a duck's back, overspilling sinkholes, pooling into swamps, ponds, billabongs and lakes, until the town might be an island kingdom, cut off from the rest of the country by rising sea levels. On that island, a smaller island: by Monday I am sealed inside the house. Dairy cattle might flourish in wet pastures, but not the rust-prone hindquarters of a centaur. My roof-valley is flooded; I sit at the kitchen table and think and write. Dad has been out all night in his police-issue oilskins; there are any number of bogged cars and overturned tractors, cattle break-outs and snakes seeking the higher ground of farmhouse kitchens and bedrooms. There is a drowning at Saw-pit Swamp, a fatal head-on on the old Kalangadoo road. The network of channels dug decades before to drain the marshy land — hundreds of miles of open drains all the way to the sea — can't cope. The railway and the Naracoorte road are cut by rising waters at Mosquito Creek, above Bool Lagoon.

'Those woodwork lessons could come in useful, sonny-jim,' Dad shouts, shaking himself down on the porch like a Bool Lagoon duck. 'Might need to get started on an ark.'

Wordwork is easier. An ark of words? An ark for Miss Peach and me and no one else. A few animals, perhaps, admitted in pairs, two by two. Rabbits. Chooks. Sheep, cattle, ducks. As the rain drums against the tin roof, cascades over gutters, chortles in the downpipes, such thoughts are displaced, as always, into words, which spill out of my head like a kind of liquid themselves.

In the year 4064 the icecaps have melted and the world is entirely covered by water. The seven seas have become one Great Sea; all the Earth's landscapes — her Grand Canyon and Himalayas and Sahara Desert — are now miles underwater. Not so much as a reef peeps above sea level anywhere. The fierce light of the nova-sun penetrates into the very depths; even a hundred miles down, the ocean floor is as dazzlingly bright as a beach on a summer's day.

Is there life down there? Of course. Kelp pastures, coral gardens, grazing sea mammals, giant yabbies. Intelligent life? We humans have long since evolved into mermen and mermaids, complete with gills and webbed hands and fishtails and a queer musical language of dolphin-squeaks and sonar-pings.

All this I create on the first day. On the second, I read back and see that it is good, but there can be no rest; I pick up my pen and scribble on. More dominoes to topple? The professor's poem comes back to me, and this time I manage a smile. The most valuable commodity in the galaxy – titanium ore – is discovered beneath the ocean floor; soon afterwards aliens arrive from the evil planet Morg to mine it. To get to the ore they have to drain the oceans, but to where? There is no land; the only possibility is to pump the waters into outer space. How? A plan is hatched to speed up the planet's rotation by simultaneously detonating a hundred nuclear torpedoes against the submerged Mt Everest, all from the same westerly direction. Spun eastwards like a top, the planet throws its ocean off into outer space like a dog shaking itself dry after a bath.

The few mermen who cling on are kept in big glass aquariums in a zoo on the newly dry planet. This zoo, or theme park, is called Waterworld. The titanium miners from Morg visit on their lunch breaks, eating seafood sandwiches and watching the last of the natives doing tricks: arfing and balancing balls and leaping out of the water to grab sardines in their mouths.

Sealed in his mother's warm kitchen, the all-seeing Creator of Waterworld scribbles on. The hero of his story is a tall skinny merboy who has survived inside a wobbling globule of water that now slowly orbits the planet, along with a zillion other blobs and droplets and misty water-wisps. For the time being there is enough dissolved oxygen in these globules to breathe, and enough fish to eat; other mermen and women have survived in other blobs. The hero realises that if all the scattered drops and globs can be made to aggregate together into one great ball, floating about in space, its gravity will drag it back to Earth. The survivors begin using their flippers to sweep the water together like shatterings of quicksilver. There is no time to waste, the trapped oxygen won't last for ever. As the main blob grows, gravity takes over, mopping up the scattered waters as it rolls across space like a giant orbiting snowball.

I've seen the ending coming for hours; on the last page of my story it arrives with a rush. The water reaches critical mass – a giant quivering moon, a jelly planet itself – and down it comes out of orbit, smacking onto the dry surface of Earth with a *whoomf* to end all *whoomfs*, and washing away all the titanium mines and aquariums and Morglings.

The End, I write, and sit there pleased as punch, hoping that Miss Peach will also be pleased. Outside it is hailing again; I venture out to scoop up a cupful, but as I sit by the warm stove sucking cold hailstones I begin to feel less pleased. The story has a flaw. The temperature in outer space is subzero, the globules of water will freeze, there can be no survivors.

I fetch more wood from the porch and stoke up the fire, fetch a fresh exercise book from my bedroom and begin again.

Waterworld, Mark II. This time the Morglings stop the rotation of the planet dead and the oceans keep moving, a giant tide sliding off out into space where it instantly freezes. All this prophesied by my dreamy hero; months before, he dug a huge cave deep beneath the seafloor, an underground cistern so many cubits wide and so many cubits long sealed off from the rest of the ocean. Into this ark of water he takes two of every fish and mollusc and dolphin; he also takes a wife, the smaller but older mermaid who was his school teacher. His excavations are widely mocked, but on the day the planet stands still he and his dainty wife are the sole survivors. With the oceans gone, the fierce sun beats down, the seabed is soon a desert littered with the bones of fish and whales and mermen. The Morglings restart the rotation of the planet, but they have miscalculated the specific gravity of water in its frozen state. The orbit of the space-ice begins to wobble, pieces start to fall out of the sky, snowflakes at first, then hailstones, then blocks of ice the size of cars, and finally, after many days, giant, all-crushing bergs the size of mountains.

After forty days and forty nights my hero sends a flying fish out of the cave; it returns with seaweed in its mouth, and the hero and his petite merwife know that it is safe to come out.

On planet Earth, Penola, the rain falls for seven days and seven nights. Every morning I chop and stack firewood in the stables, but it's too cold for chemistry and I soon return to the kitchen and my seat near the big woodstove, the warm heart of the house. Between chapters there might be flour to sift, eggbeaters or cake spoons to lick clean, linen to help fold. From time to time I fire up the stove and flick water droplets onto the hot metal top. The smallest bounce off instantly as vapour, the heavier last seconds, wobbling frictionless on a cushion of their own steam until vanishing point. How long can each tiny hovercraft survive; how far will it travel? I set new records daily. Time passes. My stories write themselves frictionlessly onto the page; other people's stories – amazing and astounding stories by Isaac Asimov and Arthur C. Clarke and Ray Bradbury and Harlan Ellison and A. E. van Vogt – lift themselves just as frictionlessly into my head.

I dip into Miss Peach's stack of holiday reading but find the first book slow going. DYSTOPIA n. 1. *An imaginary world in which everything is as bad as it can possibly be.* What did she mean? Life in *Brave New World* is perfect. Sex, happy drugs, more sex, 'pneumatic' women, another word to look up, but not right now. I toss the book aside and sit gazing through the open vents of the stove into the inferno, poking the odd escaping spider or cricket back inside. I imagine I'm gazing instead down some volcanic vent into the fiery heart of the planet itself, the great shifting mass of molten lava that is – amazing, astounding thought – no more than a mile or two beneath my feet.

In the year 5064, I write, a race of cruel aliens drills a series of giant plugholes through the seafloor of planet Water, and drains the single encircling ocean down into the molten magma at the centre of the world, where it vanishes for ever in hot steam, hot air . . .

term two

I

The rain stops falling on the last afternoon of the school holidays, in the last hour of holiday light. A stiff westerly soon shoves the quilt of cloud aside; the world, uncovered, shivers all night. I set out for school early, shivering myself as I pedal through ground-hugging mist and frost-covered fields, but warmed inside by the sight of the Vespa in the teachers' car park. I feel an absurd gratitude towards it: the machine I once thought underpowered and ugly and unfashionable now strikes me as singular and stylishly unconventional.

Where its stylish, singular owner has been all week no longer matters, only that she is safely back. I stand at my desk grinning like an idiot as she enters the classroom. The winter term has brought a wardrobe to match: ribbed wool jumper, tight-fitting tartan slacks, elastic-sided boots. Audrey Hepburn in *Roman Holiday*? No, Pamela Peach as herself. I wait, still beaming, for a nod or smile of acknowledgement.

'Sit down, 1A,' she orders tersely instead.

We sit, disconcerted. Is a frosty manner also part of her winter wardrobe? She makes no eye contact at all as she reads the roll – not with me, not with anyone. Has something happened over the holidays? A death in the family? Has Big Merv been bad-mouthing me again in the staffroom? The three-high stack of exercise books on her desk – my *Planet Water* series – goes unnoticed. Once written for Billy and me, my stories are for her eyes only now, written as gifts. That she ignores these gifts disturbs me most of all. I find it hard to concentrate on the lesson: Shaw Neilson again, but a more wintry side of him also.

> Unholy wenches
> Lie sweet and clean,
> In the cool, cool country,
> Under the green.

I don't remember which of us recites these lines; I only remember Miss Peach staring blankly out of the window as if feeling the pull of the cold earth herself.

> The little brown wench
> And the holy and lean
> Are all good citizens
> Under the green.

'A word, Robert,' she says curtly as the class files out.

'About the stories?'

'Hmm?' Her glance strays to the stack of exercise books for the first time. 'No. Something more serious.' She pauses, takes a deep breath. 'What I am going to say must remain between us – understood?'

'Yes, Miss Peach.'

Another deep breath. 'Someone broke into our house during the holidays.'

My heart drops a thousand feet inside my chest. 'How do you know?'

She gives me an odd glance. 'A strange question, Robert. You know as soon as you walk in the door. Things don't *feel* right. The wine flagon was . . . lower.' A small, hollow laugh. 'The toilet seat was up.'

My heart bangs on. 'Was anything stolen?'

'A tin of baked beans.' Another small laugh. 'It's more my *privacy*, Robert.' She examines my face, as if deciding whether to say more. 'Sharing a house isn't easy. Especially with . . .' She checks herself. 'Let's just say, my room is my sanctuary.'

The pounding of my heart slows. She doesn't seem to suspect me. Why should she? I am innocent, or at least I feel innocent. I didn't *break* into her house. I replaced the unbroken louvres as I found them. I stole nothing, or at least took nothing from the premises. Technically. Every single baked bean was eaten in the house, and probably digested there. I even returned the wine, in a way. That's why the toilet seat was up.

'My candles were burnt down.'

'You have candles, Miss?'

'A burglar who eats baked beans by candlelight! I don't know whether to laugh or cry.' Her mobile face seems to be attempting both at once. 'I'm not naturally suspicious by nature, Robert. But it had to be someone small enough to squeeze through the toilet window.' My heart plummets again as she gives me a sideways glance. 'It's a *very* small window. I wondered if you might know something about it?'

'Me?' My puzzlement looks genuine because it is partly

genuine. I believe I've done nothing much wrong. I half believe I wasn't even in her house.

'I'm not suggesting for one moment you might be involved personally. Just that you might have, well, heard of someone who was.'

I open my mouth to speak; she holds up a hand. 'Hear me out, Robbie. I'm not one to judge people by the colour of their skin. Or jump to conclusions. And I know it's asking a lot to expect you to tell tales. Especially on a friend.'

Should I have seen this coming? Am I too worried about saving my own pink skin? 'Billy isn't my friend any more.'

'I like to think *I'm* your friend, so I'm going to ask you *as* a friend: is there anything you feel you can tell me? Anything at all?'

I want to tell her whatever she wants to hear. 'He *might* have done it, Miss,' I venture, which is true in the sense that he has done similar things in the past. He smashed her window once. He's capable of doing it. He bears her enough malice to do it. 'But I'm pretty sure he wouldn't.'

'I think I understand what you're saying, Robbie. And you don't need to say more. In some ways your loyalty is to be commended.'

'No. I mean, I really don't think he did it. I *know* he didn't do it.'

'Of course.' A pause. 'If it's any consolation, I don't intend to take the matter further. He's been making a nuisance of himself – the window, rocks on the roof. The girls want to involve the police –' a small smile – 'your father, but I'm not so sure. God knows, those people are disadvantaged enough. And the main damage was to my pride. I thought, if I could just have a quiet talk to him . . .' Another deep breath, another wan smile. 'I'm sorry to give you the third degree, Robbie. I was told you and Billy are as thick as thieves.'

She smiles. 'Not the best choice of words, perhaps.' Her glance falls again on the exercise books on her table; her smile brightens. '*Three* stories today?'

'Three *novels*. But all set on the same planet.'

'A trilogy! You *have* been busy during the holidays. I'll take them home to read.'

'Any news from the professor, Miss? About the other story?'

'Not yet. You'll be the first to know. Now, one other thing. Something less, um, unpleasant. I'm starting a club this term. For the senior students mostly – those with an interest in the arts.'

'In painting?'

'The arts in general. Music, poetry, film. Also politics, philosophy. Ideas, in a general sense. I'm thinking of calling it the Lyceum Club. What do you think?'

I try to look knowledgeable.

'I hope Professor Barry will be able to travel down and read to us later in the year. We'll be meeting in the library. The first Wednesday evening of every month.'

An instant calculation. 'This Wednesday?'

'If the film arrives.' Her first full smile of the day, the break-in forgotten for the moment. 'I thought we'd start with film.'

That stand-alone word again. Film. Is she planning a photography class? Do we bring our box Brownies?

'I managed to get my hands on a print of *The Bicycle Thief*. It's one of my favourite films.'

The penny drops. 'A *picture*, Miss?'

She nods. 'An Italian picture. *Cinéma vérité*. I don't think it's ever been shown here.'

'Is Sophia Loren in it?'

Another cheekbone to cheekbone smile. 'De Sica prefers to use ordinary people as actors. People off the streets. Shall I pencil your name in for the Lyceum Club?'

My heart is in my mouth: she's inviting *me*? 'You said senior students.'

'I showed the headmaster one of your, ah, novels.' A smaller, teasing smile. 'He agreed we could make an exception in your case. *I* think you're ready for it. I hope you don't mind.'

I mind in the best possible way; my mind feels nothing but elation. That she has been thinking about me – thinking about me, in particular, when I wasn't there – is all *I* can think about as I roost in the pepper tree that afternoon. No sign of her coming or going, but I don't much care. I bounce a couple of stones off Big Merv's roof for the sheer joy of it, wolf down a bag of licorice allsorts, then head home.

LYCEUM n. *a lecture-room or meeting-room in ancient Athens.* I set the Concise Oxford aside and mull this over. Did her friend Geoffrey come up with the name? I wish she had asked me sooner, I would have come up with something better. Is it too late to change? I make a mental list to put to her – the Shaw Neilson Club, the Tolstoy Club – names I know will curry favour. The Isaac Asimov Club. A long shot, but who knows? Curried sausages for tea, Dad's Monday-night favourite, but no sign of him.

'Police business,' Mum says brusquely, and plonks a heaped plate on the table before me.

She picks silently at her own smaller heap as I eat. What's going on? Police business is no great secret in our house. Adult-only details might be discussed behind bedroom doors, but she is too naturally chatty not to drop hints.

'Can I have another helping?'

'Your father hasn't eaten. He'll be back any minute.'

'Where is he?'

She meets my eyes for the first time that night and the words seem to explode out of her. 'None of your business!' She stares back into her food, then lifts her face again. 'If you must know, he's serving a summons. So he won't be long.'

I stare at her angry face, astonished. A summons? Is that all? Her chin quivers, her lips twitch; clearly it isn't all. 'I need to ask you something, Robbie. Your father wanted to wait till he got home, but I won't. I can't. Did you know about it?'

'About what?'

'About Billy! You weren't with him, were you?'

'When?'

'When he broke into the teachers' house. Over on Arthur Street.'

'No,' I answer instantly, and truthfully. 'Of course I wasn't with him.'

Relief softens and loosens her face, like a pillow plumping itself out. 'I knew it! I told your father. You've got into some scrapes, but you wouldn't go that far.'

I mop uncomfortably at an already clean plate with a crust of bread. 'When did it happen?'

'No one seems sure. Sometime during the school holidays.'

'It rained all holidays, Mum. I was home. Sitting right here. You *know* I wasn't with Billy.'

Crunch of tyres on gravel outside, the thud of a car door. 'This is hard on your father, Robbie. He's bent over backwards for the Curries. He's taken that boy under his wing.' She rises from the table and begins fussing at the stove. 'Against my better judgement at times.'

His face is as impassive as ever as he walks through the door. 'Something smells good, Mother.'

She sets another plate heaped with rice and curry on the table. 'How did it go?'

'Not easy.' He glances my way, briefly, as he sits. 'The suspect in question denies the charge, of course.'

'I've told Robbie already, Jim.'

He gives her a stern look. 'It's a police matter, Mother. You shouldn't have done that.'

'Of course I should have. Anyway, he knew nothing about it.'

This is not what I claimed and I don't want to be held to it. His eyes search my face. 'That true?'

'I haven't seen Billy for ages. Anyway, how do you know he did it? He *wouldn't* do that.'

His face relaxes. 'Good on you for sticking up for him. I'd expect nothing less. Fact is, he's let us all down.'

'He ate a can of baked beans!' I blurt out. 'So what? He was probably hungry.'

His smile vanishes. 'Whoa there. Let's take a step back. First you tell me he didn't do it, then you tell me he ate a can of beans. Anything else you want to say?'

'I know he didn't *take* anything.'

'It's breaking and entering. With larceny. The law is very clear. And I take it very, *very* seriously.' His eyes begin searching my face again. 'I want you to choose your words carefully. Were you with him or not?'

'Of course he wasn't. I told you —'

'That's enough, Mother. Answer the question, boy.'

'Course I wasn't with him. But I *might* have been. If it hadn't been raining.'

'So how do you know about the baked beans?'

'I might have let a few details slip,' Mum lies.

'Mother!' he growls. 'I'm waiting,' he says to me. 'What else did Billy tell you?'

'Nothing!' I'm indignant now. 'Miss Peach told me. Today. At school.'

'See!' from Mum. 'Can we stop the third degree now?'

'Sorry, sonny-jim. Had to ask.' He forks up more sausage and chews thoughtfully. 'Funny one, that Miss Peach,' he remarks to Mum.

'You're telling me?'

'Didn't want to lodge a complaint. Wants to keep it quiet. It's the other two kicking up the fuss.'

'So they should,' she says.

'And why was she telling muggins here all about it if she wanted to keep it quiet?'

'She wanted me to dob in Billy,' I say. 'Same as you.'

'And did you?'

'Course not. I mean he might *want* to do it. He hates her guts. But he would have told me!'

'You can defend him till the cows come home, son. He did it all right. Written all over his guilty dial.' He looks up at Mum. 'Couldn't tell Jacko that, of course. Had him jumping up and down like a cut snake. Thought for a moment he was going to plant one on me.' He rubs his chin, perhaps imagining a bruise that might have been.

'What happens now?' Mum asks.

He gives her a warning glance. 'Not in front of the boy. Any more rice?'

Dessert is served instead – Golden Syrup roly-poly, my Monday-night favourite, although barely noticed today. We eat in silence, my feelings noisy inside me. An odd mix: frustration, apprehension. Guilt? For what? Spooning down a tin of cold baked beans? A few swigs of wine? Lying? I've told no lies, except by omission, which doesn't count. And Billy? I feel more indignant towards Billy than guilty about him. I stuck up for him but he's getting us both into trouble. I didn't betray him. Is betrayal the word if he didn't do it?

But he's done worse. We've both done worse. Burning the old slab shepherd's hut on the Casterton road to the ground. Changing the names and years on gravestones in the cemetery with stolen Texta pens. Secretly pissing on the Reverend Ridddoch's toothbrush in the bathroom on a youth camp in Robe. Wolfing down a tin of beans didn't add up to much on this charge sheet.

'Homework,' I excuse myself as soon as I can, then lurk outside the closed kitchen door, listening.

'If it was one of the forestry kids, I'd just give him a hiding. But it'll be hard to keep the Abo Protection Board out of this one.'

'Perhaps that's what the boy needs, Jim?'

'Dunno. They take a hard line on these half-caste kids running wild. Could mean a spell in the boys' home.'

'They'd take him away?' She seems to regret her earlier anger. 'Bit steep, isn't it? For a can of baked beans? Like something out of *Oliver Twist*.'

'Might be better off under Children's Welfare. Jacko reckons it's nothing to do with the Protection Board. He's not an official Abo any more. Got a fucking dog licence.'

'Language, Jim.'

'*His* language, Mother. I need to check the police manual. Bit hazy on the new Blackfellers' Act. Exemption certificates might be on the way out. Course, Welfare might still send the boy away.'

'I know he's no angel, Jim. And he's not the best influence on Robbie. But – really. What if it had been Robbie? No wonder Jacko is jumping up and down.'

'Best thing all round would be to leave it in his hands. He's a hard nut, Jacko – but he's fair. But there's been a complaint. It's in the pipeline. Got to follow procedures.'

Silence.

'Should have got the boxing club up and running. Always

meant to. Had hopes for the boy, Mother. He's a good kid underneath. And you're right. Robbie's no angel, either.'

2

Riding head down through sprinkling rain I don't see him till too late, coming out of nowhere, cutting in front of me. I brake hard, but the centaurs clash heads, or is it hooves, and I'm trapped, my front wheel firmly wedged against the gutter.

'Jesus, Billy! What you *doing*?'

His face is wet, his sodden school jumper and trousers plastered tightly to his thin body. 'Waiting for you!'

'In the rain?'

'Your old man didn't *tell* you?'

'About what?'

He scrutinises my face. 'You know what! Shit, Robbie, he was gonna arrest me!'

'He wasn't gonna arrest you. It was just a summons.'

'So you do know!'

'I told him you didn't do it, if you must know. Move your bloody bike. We're gonna be late for school.'

'You tell him *why*?'

'Why what?'

'Why you know I didn't bloody do it!'

I manage to reverse my wheel, free it from his obstruction. 'We're getting wet, Billy.' In fact the rain has stopped as I push out into the road again and ride away.

'I know who done it, Robbie!' he calls after me.

'Pig's!'

I pedal hard, not wanting to hear who did it, but he draws

level again, pedalling even harder. 'I saw you come out! I was up the tree.'

My heart stops but my feet keep pedalling, my thoughts racing. 'Pig's *arse*! You saw nothing, it was too dark. But so what if I was? You gonna tell my old man?'

He shoots me a look of contempt. 'Course not. You think I'd dob?'

Silence again, apart from the squeaking of our pedals and the hiss of tyres on wet bitumen.

'I got to go to court next week.' A pause, his tone now more pleading. 'You wouldn't let them put me in a home, would ya Robbie?'

'They can't. Your old man's got a dog licence. Anyway, they got no proof.'

'That's what Dad reckons.'

'He doesn't think you did it?'

'He got stuck into me, but believed me in the end.'

I pedal on, mulling this over. 'Nothin' will happen, Billy. Anyway, what did you do? Eat a canned of baked beans. So what?'

His turn to think things over. 'Is that all I done?'

'You pissed on her toothbrush,' I tell him. An inspired lie; his rain-glazed face breaks into a grin.

'Did ya, Robbie? Like that time with Riddoch? She must have used it, mustn't she? Stupid cow! I wished you'd told me. Why don't you tell me what you're doing no more?' And he laughs for the first time, and laughs again, often, all the way to school. 'I woulda come with you. Why didn't you tell me? I woulda *shat* on her toothbrush. You heard about her stupid club?'

Everyone has heard about the club. Wednesday morning, over breakfast, I decapitate my second boiled egg with extra care. 'You wouldn't like the film, Mum.'

'So you keep saying.'

'Is Sophia Loren in it?' Dad asks without lifting his eyes from the morning paper.

An easy answer at last. 'It's made with ordinary people. Not real actors.'

'Don't you want me to come, Robbie?' from Mum, again.

'Of course I want you to come. If you *want*. But the club is for the Leaving students. And Intermediate. And *their* parents. She just asked me specially.'

'She must think highly of you, Robbie.'

'I spose. I don't want to go myself. Probably be dead boring.'

'Well, I think I will come. She has her city airs and graces, but we need some cultural life in the district. Adam Lindsay Gordon came from these parts, after all.'

'And John Shaw Neilson,' I add, unheard.

'It's time I met this Miss Peach of yours. Made up my own mind. Never see her about on weekends. What church does she go to?'

'Don't know, Mum.'

'Heard plenty *about* her. Good and bad.' She gives my father a glance. 'Of course, your father is putty in her hands – like every other man in town. He'd love to join her little club.'

'Footy training tonight, Mother. Committee meeting afterwards. Any more bacon?'

'You've got hollow legs, Jim Burns. Here's your lunch, Robbie. You seeing anything of that Billy Currie at school?'

'No, Mum,' I say truthfully.

'Your father wants you to keep your distance. Till it's all sorted out. Isn't that right, Jim?'

'Innocent till proven guilty, Mother.'

'I'm not judging the boy. Just saying we should be careful. I bet Miss Fancy Pants hasn't asked *him* to join her club.'

At school the break-in might never have happened; Miss Peach paces about excitedly all day, a cat on a hot tin roof. 'Don't forget tonight, Robbie,' she reminds me repeatedly.

There is no sign of her as I dawdle into the school library later that night, keeping some distance between myself and my mother. No sign of Billy either; I've successfully avoided him all week, but dread another ambush. A picture screen has been set up at one end of the room, the school's projector on a tripod at the other; twenty or so chairs fill the space between. The staffroom urn chuggles on a trestle table, a gleaming gasometer towering above a neat township of cakes and scones. Mum slips her suburb of flat buttered pikelets in among them; I maintain a low, flat profile myself, pretending I don't know her. Doc McKenzie sits off to one side, his unkempt beard at an angle to the bookshelves as he checks spines in the science-fiction section. What's *he* doing here? Is *The Bicycle Thief* a sci-fi picture? I think about joining him, decide against – too hard to escape when Miss Peach arrives.

Which she still hasn't. A group of older girls huddles about the only other boys, two prefects, both too senior to talk to me, and both clearly dragged along by girlfriends. Other girls have dragged along their mothers, the older women still dressed, like their daughters, in the Miss Peach summer style, if less flatter-ingly: tight buns of hair clamped to big square heads, stirrup pants stretched about heifer rumps, swollen ankles bulging from tiny slipper-shoes. The boys are dressed like me: duffle coats, desert boots, heads waterproofed by thickly Brylcreemed hair. The headmaster – Eric 'Jingle' Bell – is there with his wife; an uncharacteristically jovial Big Merv without his. Shouldn't he be at footy training? I keep a weather eye on his whereabouts; I need to keep a safe distance. Mrs Bell, a loud, energetic woman, has also adopted the chignon and slacks; only my mother and the

Tweedle-twins have held out, she in woollen winter sacking, they in tweedle-twinsets and stiff perms.

'The ubiquitous Master Burns,' Miss Burke exclaims as I slip past. 'You are an *aficionado*, perhaps, of neo-realist Italian cinema?'

Her offsider snickers. 'Very *simpatico* styling of the hair, Master Burns. Very *La Dolce Vita*.'

Miss Burke flutters her eyelids, a mock swoon. 'Miss Hammond, *please* don't remind me. The divine Marcello.'

Their flushed cheeks are as red as the wine in their chipped blue teacups. I hide myself behind the prefects, not actually part of their group but hoping to appear so.

A snarl across a shoulder: 'Piss off, Burns.'

Mum is chatting with the Bells. I orbit on towards the door, planning to hide outside in the darkness of deep space until Miss Peach arrives, but Big Merv is there before me, his meaty right arm barring my exit.

'You wouldn't be sneaking outside for a smoke, would you, Burns?'

'I don't smoke, sir.'

His tough, squashed face leans closer and, disconcertingly, winks. 'Then what filthy habit are you planning to indulge?' His cheeks are redder than usual, his breath beery. 'You're here to broaden your mind, sunshine, not any other part of your anatomy. If you get my drift.' He chortles, and punches me playfully on the arm. 'Don't look so terrified. I was your age once.'

Playful for him, painful for me. Are they *all* as pissed as newts? Too much six o'clock swill at the Royal Oak? I look past him for help. Where is Miss Peach?

He reads my mind. 'She seems to think there's hope for you, Burns. You're lucky to have her in your corner. I hope you won't let her down.'

'No, sir.'

'I still have my eye on you. And your dusky friend. Been wondering if there's an Italian picture called *The Baked Bean Thief*.'

My blood freezes, but the corner of his mouth begins to twitch, the sign of another joke trying to break out. 'These little, ah, *novels* of yours she tells us about in the staff room – I hope they're better constructed than your breadboards.' He hoots, hugely amused with himself. 'I'm not one to bear a grudge, Burns. We all make mistakes. If you've turned over a new leaf as she seems to think, I'll feed you a bit of slack. No hard feelings?'

He offers his bear-paw; I am about to shake it when he whips it away. 'Perhaps not,' he says, 'if you've been doing what I think you've been doing with that hand.'

His laughter absorbs him so completely I escape under its cover back into the library. Where to next? Line of least resistance. Doc McKenzie nods vaguely as I plonk down next to him, and goes on reading. His battered black bag sits at his side. Has he wandered in by accident on his way to a house call? But here at last is Miss Peach, rushing through the door with two big flat metal canisters under her arms. 'I'm *so* sorry everyone! The Bluebird was late.'

No one cares as she stands before us beaming, in a rainspangled beret and fur-trimmed coat.

'Audrey Hepburn in *Charade*,' a girl breathes as Big Merv gallantly relieves her of the film canisters.

'We have her for History,' from another.

'We have her for History *and* Latin.'

I have her for *every*thing, I want to trump them. She's my class teacher.

Doc McKenzie plucks a fountain pen from his coat pocket and begins to scribble notes in the margin of the book. *The Time Machine*. What is he writing? Corrections? Advice? A warning to the time-traveller? His hand is illegible: a doctor's code, Leonardo handwriting meant to be read in a mirror. I crane his way, trying to decipher it; he leans unconsciously away from me, as if protecting schoolwork from a cheat.

Mum eases her bulk into the chair next to mine. 'Doctor,' she nods across me, but he fails to respond. The Head is on his feet out front, jingling keys and loose change and welcoming those 'hardy souls' who have 'braved the elements for the sake of culture', praising 'the energy and vision of our very own Miss Peach', who brings 'a breath of fresh air' and 'a touch of city sophistication' to 'our neck of the backwoods'.

Divested of coat and beret – '*Black* stockings,' come the awed whispers, and '*Polo* neck' – Miss Peach stands at his side, embarrassed but glowing. I am glowing with her, glowing inside as if I've been praised myself, as if, weirdly, *we* have been praised as a couple.

'And so without further ado –' a last jangle of his pocket casta- net – 'I hand you over to the woman of the moment.'

'*Buona sera,*' she begins. '*Signori e signore*. That's Italian for good evening, ladies and gentlemen.' Chuckles, beaming faces, one tentative *buona sera* in return. 'Welcome, *mi amici*, to the first of what I hope will be many Wednesday-night journeys we will take together.' Already she is pacing back and forth, swivelling dancer- style. 'To whet your appetites before we start, a preview of coming attractions. I plan a philosophy discussion next month, starting with the Greeks. Perhaps dialogue in the Socratic style; this is the Lyceum Club, after all.'

A winning smile, a few tentative smiles in return. 'We might look at some of the new abstract expressionist painting from America the following month; I'm trying to get my hands on some slides. I also hope to offer a poetry reading this term by the distinguished Australian poet Geoffrey Barry, but tonight, to get the ball rolling,

I want to share with you one of my *very* favourite films: Vittorio De Sica's *The Bicycle Thief*. I look forward to a fruitful discussion afterwards, and a splendid supper of course – thank you, ladies.' Another winning smile. 'I think Mr Bailey is ready with the projector. Merv? And perhaps someone could get the lights?'

I leap to my feet but Jingle Bell beats me to it. Total darkness, then a scratchy, flickering countdown on the screen – 3, 2, 1, 0 – and the film is launched.

'It's in *Italian*,' Mum blurts out.

As words of similar astonishment bounce up and down the rows, Miss Peach jumps to her feet and inserts herself into the brightness of the screen. 'I'm sorry, everyone, I should have warned you: the film has English subtitles.' Images of Rome splash across her body, and for a moment her shadowed silhouette might be another actor on the screen. Audrey Hepburn in *The Bicycle Thief*. 'Subtitles may feel a little strange at first, but they grow on you. Besides, the story tells itself, visually. It's very economical with language.'

Her shadow sits, vanishing from the screen, the whisperings subside. Doc McKenzie has his pocket torch out now, reading in its narrow beam, but no one seems to mind. Within minutes the promised miracle happens: as if the switchboard of my brain has been somehow reconnected, eye plug to ear socket, the actors are now speaking English, if with cartoon Dago accents.

By the end I can't recall reading a single word, except the very last. *FIN.*

'Lights, please.'

She repeats the command before I take notice. Is Mr Bell asleep? As the lights come on she is already on her feet, pacing excitedly about. 'Now, I know better than to stand too long between country folk and a country supper, but would anyone like to start the discussion?'

Silence. Her gaze moves about as restlessly as her feet, cajoling, seeking help. 'It only needs one brave person to break the ice.'

'It's a very, ah, slow picture, isn't it?' from the Head, helpfully.

'I think that's part of its magic, Mr Bell. I like to think of film in musical terms. Like a symphony, a film must build a mood.'

'An awfully bleak mood.' Mrs Bell comes to her husband's aid.

'Life in Europe after the war *was* very bleak, Mrs Bell.'

She glances about for more questions. This time my mother, never lost for words, supplies one. 'Perhaps it would help if it were in colour, Miss Peach.'

She stops in her tracks, an incredulous look on her face. 'I can't begin to *imagine* it in colour,' she says with some vehemence. 'The whole essence of *cinéma vérité* – the character revealed in these people's faces, their impoverished backgrounds – would be utterly *lost* in colour.'

Silence again, everyone now too awed or too scared to say a word. I glance at Mum's reddening face, gratified. 'Well I never!' she mutters to herself. Doc McKenzie is still scribbling away by torchlight – has he not noticed the lights are on? I nudge him; he grunts but scribbles on.

Miss Peach resumes her caged-animal pacing. 'But I'm saying too much, as usual. Has anyone else anything to say?'

I want to help out, but with what? Some disparagement of those broken-down Italian bikes I wouldn't be seen dead on? Something clever about mechanical centaurs? I stick up a hand.

'Robert?'

'The scene where the mother takes her linen to the money lender, and he stacks it in a great cupboard full of other people's linen – is that what you meant when you said the story tells itself, visually?'

'Exactly! A *very* intelligent question.' A lucky question, but I beam back at her, proud of my luck. 'A picture tells a thousand words. Things don't have to be spelt out. It's an important lesson, especially perhaps for . . . a budding novelist. That scene at the pawnbroker's is my favourite, it stabs me through the heart every time I watch it. And it needs no dialogue at all.' A friendly smile at my mother. 'In Italian or English.'

Mum's pursed-lipped judgement as we head for the supper table – 'A very *confident* young miss, isn't she?' – can no more dent my euphoria than the gossipings of the Tweedle-twins, washing down thickly buttered pikelets with more cupfuls of flagon wine.

'Our Miss Peach certainly knows how to make an entrance, Miss Burke.'

'Always pays to keep them waiting, Miss Hammond.'

'Even the doctor! What on earth is he doing here? Has he so much as noticed a woman before?'

'A little bird tells me Miss Peach is a frequent visitor to his rooms. Women's problems, Miss Hammond.'

'Such a sensitive constitution, Miss Burke. May we help you, Master Burns – or are you just eavesdropping?'

I move on. 'Piss off, teacher's pet!' from a prefect keeps me moving. *War of the Worlds* has been abandoned, open, spine up, on the doctor's chair; I sit down and turn it over. Another entire novel seems to have been scribbled in its margins, but I can decipher none of the doctor's exotic script. It might be Cyrillic, it might be Arabic. Which gives me another idea: to invent – design? – a Martian alphabet. I glance up at the swarm of bodies around the urn, their conversation a blended, unintelligible buzz. What might the writing system of a species of, say, intelligent insects look like? I imagine a few letters, sharply angular, sticklike. But isn't that our human alphabet? Ants crawling across a page. Bent insect-legs. Stick antennae.

'Can I trust you to carry these to the staffroom for me, Robbie?'

A teasing smile on Miss Peach's face as she stands before me with a tray of teacups. Behind her the crowd has thinned out. Mum is chatting with the Bells, Big Merv is folding away the projector screen. I jam *War of the Worlds* back onto its shelf and take the tray.

'Lead on, Macduff. I'll follow with the plates.'

I've already filled the staffroom sink with water – anything to curry favour – when she materialises with another tray. 'It was such a success, don't you think, Robbie? So many people! I'd hoped for a dozen; there must have been, oh, thirty.'

I keep the number I counted – twenty-three – to myself.

'I'll wash, you dry,' she says, and hands me a tea towel, pushing me aside with a playful nudge of her hips.

As we work she chatters on, still glowing. 'Everyone seemed so pleased. Don't you think? And . . . stimulated.'

She smells pleasantly of sweat and perfume. *I* am stimulated, standing there towelling the blue teacups, leaning slightly forward so that she won't notice the bulge in my shorts.

She is more interested in my hair. 'You should grow it a little longer, Robbie. Perhaps try a mop-top. It would really suit you.'

She has downed a cup or two of wine, yes, but is mostly drunk on the success of her club. Still talking, she tugs the plug from the sink and strips off her rubber gloves. 'And what was the doctor doing there? He's such an eccentric. But a real dear. You know, I think the town is just starved of culture.'

She shakes out a Kool, lights up, blows a wobbly, unravelling smoke-ring into the empty staffroom.

I hang the last cup from its hook. 'Can I have one, Miss?'

A tolerant smile. 'Don't push your luck. Truth is, I pulled you in here for a reason.'

I look at her shining face, her wide smile, and my heart lurches. What reason? To tell me she feels the same way about me? 'It's about your friend. Billy. I've talked the two girls round. They're going to withdraw the complaint.'

For the second time that night my blood freezes. 'Do they suspect someone else?'

A puzzled look. 'No, Robbie. Why would they? There's no one else.'

Am I more relieved for him or for myself? 'I never thought he did it, I knew he didn't!'

The words burst out of me, surprising both of us. She takes a step back, then smiles. 'Good for you, Robbie. I like someone who sticks up for what he believes in. But that's not the reason we're withdrawing the complaint. I felt . . . well, how *difficult* it must have been for him. An Aboriginal boy. Coming to a strange town. Leaving the mission. Everyone he knew.'

'His family came with him.'

'One thing if you go on writing, Robbie. Your ideas are wonderful. Brilliant. But a novelist needs to understand the human heart.' Another smile. ' Though I'm sure that will come – with time.'

'I understand my heart, Miss Peach.'

She stubs out her cigarette. 'His father came to see us.'

'Jacko?'

'He wanted to know why we blamed Billy. He said it wasn't Billy. Of course he doesn't want to believe it was his son. He's a loyal father. He said he knows Billy isn't an angel. He knows the two of you have got up to a lot of high jinks.'

'He talked about me?'

'Your ears would have been burning. He said your friendship has been very important for Billy. A big influence.' A wry smile. 'For good *and* bad.' She lights another cigarette, examines my face, exhales. 'I'm teasing you, Robbie. He meant mostly good. You helped Billy adjust, he said. Assimilate. You've been a good friend. Helped him with his schoolwork.'

Relief mixed with indignation. I *did* his schoolwork, day after day, and his homework, night after night. 'He didn't get into IA, Miss.'

'Was it a fair test? For someone like Billy? Someone without, oh, the advantages we take for granted? His life has been awfully difficult.'

His life has never struck me as even slightly difficult, but this time I keep my thoughts to myself.

'I wondered. What if I took him under my wing a little?' That winning smile. '*Our* wing. Yours and mine. Would he enjoy the Lyceum Club, do you think? Or some novels? Which reminds me, have you started *Anna Karenina*?'

'Robbie?' My mother's voice from the door. My mother's bulk blocking the door. 'Are you done?'

Miss Peach turns. 'Mrs Burns – I borrowed him for a few minutes. He's been such a help. I don't think we've formally met.'

My mother stays where she is. 'Joan, please. I should thank you for organising this evening, Miss Peach.'

'Pam.'

'We'll have to agree to disagree about pictures in foreign languages.' A smile, to make her point. 'If you're finished with him, Robbie should be getting home. It is a school night.'

'I hope you did your homework before you came, Robbie,' Miss Peach says, unruffled.

'He always does his homework, Miss Peach. I see to that. If you'll excuse us?'

Miss Peach's smile is her most winning yet. '*Si certo!*' she says. More Italian follows us out the door. '*Ciao, Roberto. Arrivederci, signora.*'

'No shrinking violet, *that* one,' Mum mutters as we drive home, more to herself than to me. Again, a block later: 'Talk about bunging on the side. And those *pants* she wears.' Another pause. 'Glad Rita Bailey wasn't there to see Merv make a complete ass of himself.' By the time we reach home she has talked herself around a little. 'Have to admit, she's got energy . . . Queer taste in pictures . . . What do Misses Burke and Hammond make of her? She of them, for that matter. Love to be a fly on the wall in that establishment.'

Me too, is my last thought as I fall asleep. Especially on her bedroom wall.

3

A week passes. Then another, identical to the first: too-short days of Latin and History and English; long, restless afternoons of tree-sitting and avoiding Billy; lonely weekends of writing stories to show the missing person when she returns from the city. A month passes, and the Beatles are also visiting Adelaide; I peer at the crowd photographs in the Sunday paper over my father's shoulder – 'Hysteria, sonny-jim. Pure hysteria' – hoping to spot her face among the others that line the streets, three hundred thousand strong. 'Did you see the Beatles last weekend, Miss?' 'I prefer Beethoven, Anne.' 'They sang "Roll Over Beethoven", Miss. At Centennial Hall. My cousin told me. It was their biggest crowd ever. In the whole world . . .' 'Just pass out the essay topics, please Anne.'

Another month. The Fab Four have come and gone; the rain has gone and come.

It's the year 2064 again and everyone can live for ever. Unless they have lung cancer, in which case they need a new pair of lungs . . . Trapped in a church pew, bored out of my brain as the Reverend

Riddoch drones on, I see what my story lacked first time round: a father would always donate his own lungs to save his son. I find a pencil stub in my pocket and begin scribbling ideas inside the cover of the nearest hymn book. *For he so loved his only begotten son, that he gave his lungs that he should not perish, but have everlasting life* . . .

'Robbie! That's church property! Lucky your father isn't here!'

The property is snatched out of my grasp but I scribble on in my head. Other possibilities leap to mind. Why choose a father? Why not a brother? A loyal, faithful friend? My lost stash of war comics was full of sacrifice, soldiers giving their lives for others on the battlefield. *Traveller, tell the Spartans that here we lie, obedient to their law.*

I avoid Billy after church under cover of rain. Safe home again, I open a fresh exercise book and begin to collect my teeming thoughts. Dad arrives back from an assault in Nangwarry in time for the Sunday roast; I set down my pencil to eat but pick it up again immediately afterwards. I write all afternoon. I write about a boy who gives his lungs so that his beautiful young teacher might live. He gives this precious gift anonymously, but after his death she discovers his identity and never forgets him for as long as she lives. Which is to say for ever.

'I can't help worrying, Robbie. Are you *sure* you'll be all right on your own?'

'Course he's sure. It's just a weekend, Mother.'

Sunday night. I sit at the rickety card table in front of the lounge-room fire, writing. Rainsqualls rattle the roof and windows, Dad crouches over the fireplace toasting slices of bread on a fork. His night to cook, his only night. And Mum? Her night of rest, flat on her back on the lounge, recovering from the rigours of church organ duties, Sunday roast duties.

'If you don't want us to go, Robbie, just say so. Of course, it would disappoint your father. It means a lot to your father.'

A low mutter from the fireplace: 'Means sweet FA to your father.'

'You had a wonderful time last year, Jim.'

'*You* had a wonderful time. Seen one police ball, seen 'em all.'

'I *have* made a new frock especially. But if you say the word, Robbie, we won't go.'

I want them to go. I want them to leave right now. I want to finish my story in peace and quiet. But it's time to eat and I put aside my book and set out the plates, and butter and quarter the toast while the cook slices fritz and white pudding. Sunday nights we eat on the card table by the open fire, one thick slice of sausage per toast-quarter, thickly smothered with tomato sauce.

'If we go we'll be back on Sunday night, Robbie. I'll leave sandwiches for your lunch. Mutton stew for Saturday tea. Just heat it up. Can you do that?'

'Of course he can do that, Mother.'

'Don't let us down, Robbie. Your father and I agree you've been more responsible lately. We want to trust you. Jim?'

'No monkey business, sonny-jim. Or you'll answer to me.' He pauses, gives me a wink. 'And I'll be answering to your mother. Pass the sauce.'

In the year 2064 everyone is finally happy. No one is hungry or poor or sick; there are no wars, there is no crime. But people are bored witless again, living happily ever after. Nothing but good news in the papers. No weather to discuss – the towns are enclosed in great air-conditioned domes. The police, especially, are bored; they have nothing to do. Then a young cop decides to *commit* crimes, to steal handbags in broad daylight, to break into houses and leave obvious clues, to crash cars. People begin to have a spring in their step again, are animated, full of beans. Uncertainty adds zest to their lives – the pepper of danger, of random luck. Soon the police – all police – are being paid to commit crimes as part of their official duties.

'You hear a word I said, Robbie?' Mum is saying. 'Constable Hicks will be manning the front desk on Saturday morning. Any other problems, ring him at Nangwarry station.'

'Life-and-death problems only, sonny-jim,' Dad adds, banging the palm of his hand against the base of the upended sauce bottle. 'Any more dead horse, Mother?'

'Don't ask me. *Your* night to cook, remember? Don't forget to take out a tray for Possum. And an extra blanket.'

'Do I feed the prisoners while you're away?' I ask.

'I won't arrest anyone next week. If I do we'll take them with us to the ball. You hungry, Mother?'

'Perhaps a small slice. There's one other matter your father wants to talk to you about. Jim?'

A blank look. 'Mother?'

'Billy Currie. He might be officially off the hook, but we all know he did it.'

'That's not the way the law sees it, Mother.'

'Well, I don't want him coming around while we're away. Give him an inch and he'll take a mile. Your precious Miss Peach might have a soft spot for him, but she'll learn soon enough.' With Billy now safe from being sent away, my mother has resumed her attacks. 'I can't *believe* she withdrew the complaint . . .'

I fill my mouth with sausage and toast and sauce and my head with thoughts of the weekend to come as she prattles on. I don't want Billy around either. I want the time and space to myself, but how to keep him away? I owe him for keeping his mouth shut, but don't want to be endlessly reminded of it.

I manage to avoid him on the way to school next morning,

after which Miss Peach's first words put him out of my head.

'I have some *very* exciting news, 1A. Professor Barry will be visiting Penola later in the week.' She stands before us smiling; she looks more tranquil, more still than I have seen her before. 'It's a marvellous opportunity to meet a real poet. Professor Barry – Geoffrey – will be giving readings of his poems to a special meeting of the Lyceum Club on Friday night. But he's also promised to come and talk to you in the classroom, personally.'

What lesson follows? History? English? She doles out the day's prescribed dose of curriculum at snail's pace, and when she speaks her heart clearly isn't in it. Her head is altogether elsewhere as she forgets her train of thought mid-sentence, or sits gazing out of the window as we work.

'A word, Robbie?' she murmurs as the others file out for recess. 'Geoffrey is keen to meet you. He's very enthusiastic about your stories.'

'I like his poetry too, Miss Peach.'

Surprise on her face. 'I didn't think I'd shown you any.'

'I read some in the, um, library.'

Surprise gives way to puzzlement. 'Which book?'

'*A Little Nightmare Music.*'

'I didn't think the library had a copy,' she says, then shrugs. 'We can talk about his poetry later. I have a small favour to ask. I'd like you to meet the Bluebird with me. If that's all right with your mother.'

'Of course it's all right with her.'

'Just make sure you ask.' A teasing smile. 'And make sure you do your homework first.'

'I'll do it straight after school, Miss.'

'Thursday night then,' she says, and turns away to the window, dreamily.

Her tranquil state lasts until Wednesday; she arrives on Thursday morning fidgety and restless again. By lunchtime she is once more a cat on a hot tin roof, glancing at her watch, willing the hours to pass, sitting down in her seat then immediately bouncing out of it again, as if the evening train might have arrived at noon. I get most of my homework done during lessons, under the desk, but her constant movement is a distraction. 'Seven o'clock,' she reminds me at home time, and is out the door before I have begun to pack my bag.

Dad is at the football club, Mum about to leave for the CWA. I wolf down a small alp of mashed potato and a landslide of lamb chops and am at the station by six-thirty. A dark, deserted platform; have I got the time wrong? Has the track been washed out again?

A match flares at the far end of the platform, fades; a glowing cigarette tip remains, and a small dark figure in the shadows.

'Robbie?' the figure calls, in the voice of Miss Peach. 'Over here.'

Her clothes are unchanged from school but her hair is looser beneath her beret, shaken free by the day's restlessness perhaps. The scent of her perfume is especially strong, as if this also is being flung about by her movement.

'Can I have one, Miss?'

A routine between us now; a raised, half-amused eyebrow, a standard answer. 'What would your father say?'

'I won't tell him if you won't.'

She hesitates, then for the first time – a huge milestone, this – offers me the packet. Kool might be a despised, girl's brand, but I am more than happy to be one of the girls tonight.

'If you tell anyone, Robbie,' she says, striking a match, 'I'll have to kill you.'

Our heads lean together; a whiff of perfume and wine-breath, then tobacco smoke drowns everything.

A shout from the other end of the platform. 'Hey – what the hell's going on down there? You kids smoking?'

Miss Peach plucks the cigarette out of my mouth as Blue McPherson waddles our way, his wild thatch of red hair untamed by his stationmaster's cap. 'What would your old man say, young Burns? I don't want to be the one —' He stops in his tracks, open-mouthed. 'Miss Peach? Sorry. Thought he was here with that rascal Billy Currie. Thick as thieves, those two.'

She seems untroubled that he should have mistaken her for a boy. 'We're just waiting to meet the train, Mr McPherson. Everything's under control.'

His glance moves from the cigarette between her lips to the cigarette between her fingers and back to her face. Holding his gaze, unruffled, she removes the cigarette from her mouth, tosses it away and replaces it with the other.

I almost laugh out loud; Blue struggles for words. 'Ah. She's running a bit late tonight.'

A look of pain crosses her face. 'How late?'

'Hard to say. Slow going up Bool Lagoon way. Water on the line. Half an hour?'

'Shit.' Her whisper is barely audible, a faint hiss of breath, and for a moment I can't believe my ears. Neither can Blue. He backs away, his gaze falling on me. 'You mind your manners, young Burns,' he says gruffly, as if the word must have been an act of ventriloquism, then turns on his heels and flees.

'You didn't hear that,' she says, handing back my cigarette. She lights another for herself and stalks away in the other direction, puffing smoke like a locomotive pulling out. I hesitate, then follow, catching her as she skips down the platform ramp and onto the road. She hurries on, barely noticing me, two quick-time ballet steps for each loping stride of mine. My cigarette feels sticky on my lips – her lipstick, a first kiss, if at one remove. At the corner of Bright Street she stops, tosses her butt away and shakes the next from the packet.

'Stay close to me tonight, Robbie,' she says mysteriously. She lights up and sucks deeply before continuing. 'What I mean is, I don't want you to leave me alone with him.'

More mystery.

'It could be dangerous.' She exhales a long jet of smoke; her intensity seems to dissipate with its release and she gives a little snorted laugh. 'I'm sorry. You must be wondering what the hell I'm talking about. I mean to say, you're my chaperone tonight, so stay close. All right?'

'All right,' I say. 'Pam.'

Another snort, more smoke than laughter this time. 'Not *that* close, Master Burns.'

A far-off air-horn, very faint, but loud enough to startle her. 'We'd better be getting back.'

'Plenty of time,' I say, but she is already quickstepping up the road.

I follow. Cars jostling for parking space outside the station now; scattered gatherings of people on the platform, some with baggage, some without. I know all the faces, all of them know mine. If they don't know Miss Peach they clearly know of her, and want to know more: all eyes are on my tiny elegant companion in her beret and boots. *She's with me!* I want to shout, standing tall at her side. *She wants me to stay close!* The blast of the air-horn deafeningly close itself, and here comes the Bluebird, its inscrutable face sliding by, the thundering hooves of two hundred and fifty diesel-fed horses following. Miss Peach on tiptoe scanning the passing windows. A hiss of airbrakes, doors opening, passengers stepping out.

'There he is, Robbie.' She waves an arm. 'Geoffrey! Over here!'

Is she addressing the tall man in the felt hat and overcoat at the far end of the platform, bent over a match-flare? My heart sinks. I'd hoped for Carlo Ponti, not Gregory Peck. I follow, staying close, as Miss Peach walks towards him, rapidly at first, then slowing, and finally halting, as if she too is a little uncertain as to his identity.

'Geoffrey,' she says lamely.

He doffs his hat with a weary smile, gives a small, ironic bow, replaces the hat. 'Blithe spirit,' he murmurs through a cloud of smoke.

His eyes have a bruised, rubbed look around the rims and are deeply sunken, as if rubbed so hard they've been pressed back into the sockets. His lined, weatherbeaten face is still handsome enough – or once was handsome, at least. The head of hair, briefly revealed, is silver-grey but thick. How old is he? Older than her, certainly. Older than her father, possibly. If her father were still alive.

She thrusts out a tiny paw. 'So here we are.'

He examines it through those tired eyes. Dark, brooding eyes. 'After a day on the train I'd hoped for more than a handshake, blithe spirit.'

A port-wine voice, if a little hoarse. Miss Peach glances nervously around, then darts forward, plants a quick bird-peck on his cheek, steps back. 'Welcome to Clochemerle.'

He turns his dark gaze on me. 'And who might this be? The town crier?'

'This is Robbie. Robert Burns. I sent you some of his work, remember? Robbie, this is Professor Barry.'

A loud whistle. Further along the platform Blue McPherson stands under the single light, his red hair the only remaining colour in the night. He blows his whistle again, a Redhead match bursting into a flame of noise. An answering burst from the air-horn and the train begins to slide away. The professor sways slightly, as if he is still on board, then takes a steadying sideways step. Those sunken eyes are bloodshot, I see for the first time.

'You're much younger than I imagined, Burns. Your poems – "Coming through the Rye", "Auld Lang Syne" – seem works of great maturity.'

An obliging laugh from Miss Peach. 'The science-fiction stories, Geoffrey. Remember?'

He takes another drag on his cigarette, watches me through smoke-narrowed eyes. 'Quirky compositions. Can't say I've read them all. I took the liberty of posting a couple to a friend in London. As a personal favour to your, ah, muse here.' He speaks slowly, like someone used to being listened to. 'Vic Gollancz knows the science-fiction caper like the back of his hand. I imagine he's reading your deathless prose even as we speak.'

Miss Peach beams. 'Isn't that wonderful, Robbie? Oh Geoffrey – that's *so* like you. So generous. Isn't it, Robbie?'

The professor shrugs. 'No skin off my nose. If nothing else, Vic can tell your protégé he's wasting his time. Shall we hail a chariot?'

'It's a one-cab town, Geoffrey. It left five minutes ago.'

'You expect me to ride pillion on the wasp?'

'I expect you to walk. Robbie will carry your bag.'

That half-wry, half-weary grin. 'Shanks's pony then,' he says. 'Might I offer you my arm? Or would that be too *risqué* for the good burghers of Clochemerle?'

She glances about. The platform is empty now, apart from Blue McPherson, watching us while pretending not to.

'What the heck,' she says, and slips her arm through his. 'They all know you're coming anyway. Everyone knows everything in this town.'

I pick up his bag and follow, keeping close as per instructions, eyeballing Blue on the way out. Thick as thieves, indeed!

'Your digs are nearby, country mouse?' the professor asks.

'I've booked you a room at the pub.'

He glances at her, his hat-shadowed face even harder to read. 'If that's your decision.'

She lowers her voice, but not below the acuteness of teenage hearing. 'I'm not ready yet, Geoffrey. For that.'

'You seemed more than ready last weekend.'

'I'd had too much to drink last weekend.'

He lifts his head and barks a hoarse mock-order. 'Double Scotches all round, barkeep!'

'Keep your voice down, *please*,' she urges, but smiling. 'It's a small town, Geoffrey.'

'It's a small life. And each of us only has one of them. *Carpe diem.*'

'Have you told *her* that?'

Silence for a dozen paces.

'Have you told her anything?'

'Hinted. These things take time. You know that.'

She shoots a warning glance at me over her shoulder, I drop back a pace, they stroll on, arm in arm, a tall dark brooding man and his delicate ballerina daughter.

'I've written you a poem,' she murmurs tentatively.

'With a thumbnail dipped in tar?' he says.

If I dislike him at first sight it's less for anything he says, most of which is over my head, than for his tone – teasing, perhaps, but a weary, harsh teasing.

'Will you read it?'

That she writes poems at all is news to me; I feel more than a little miffed.

'Of course, blithe spirit. Of course. Have you cast a cold eye on *my* new manuscript?'

'I've read it all, twice. Oh Geoffrey, I loved it. Just loved it. Your best work yet. I can't wait to talk about it with you.'

I can't see her face but her tone of voice is all relief, all smiles. Does lip-reading have a bringing-up-the-rear version? Back-of-the-head reading? 'Can I expect an exam at the end of it, Professor?'

'You can take an oral.'

She turns to him, a frozen smile in profile, then giggles – a high-pitched girlish sound that I've never heard from her before. 'Geoffrey Barry!'

The odd couple turns the corner into Church Street, still arm in arm. I have no trouble keeping up, the professor's bag is as light as a feather. What's in it? Is that a muffled clinking? Port wine to lubricate the voice? Autumn Brown mother's milk? Or just a spare belt buckle?

'I tossed off a couple more odes on the train. Ode to an Exit Sign. Ode to a Luggage Rack.'

'I love your odes to the mundane. I can't wait to hear them.'

'Then lead me to a low bar, country mouse, and we'll talk literature till closing time. Or till you've had too much to drink, whichever comes first.'

Another girl-giggle. 'It's after closing time, city mouse.'

'For a bona fide traveller? Eating a bona fide meal?'

'The fish and chip shop is open,' I pipe up.

'Ah,' he says, without turning. 'The native bearer. I was rather afraid we'd lost contact with you.'

'Geoffrey,' she warns again. 'You promised to be on your best behaviour.'

'When the cat's away,' he murmurs.

The warmth in her voice fades. 'How *is* Margaret?'

'Margaret is Margaret. She almost jumped aboard the train at the last minute.'

Miss Peach turns to him, incredulous. 'She came to see you off?'

'She misses me when I travel. She gets very lonely.'

She cuts him short. 'Here we are. The Clochemerle village inn.'

We push in through the frosted-glass doors of the front bar of the Oak. The stink of stale beer is overpowering, although the bar is empty apart from Mrs Fergusson, the licensee's wife, mopping up after the six o'clock swill. A stout woman in a headscarf and pinafore, she looks up at us, down at the bag in my hand, nods towards another door. We push through to find an unmanned reception desk at the foot of a steep, carpeted staircase.

The professor bangs his palm down on the bell. Nothing happens, he bangs again. 'Looks like I might be sleeping on your couch after all, blithe spirit.'

Miss Peach steps forward and bangs the bell herself. Mrs Fergusson, red-faced and sweating, barges through the door, stalks past us with a glare, sends a foghorn shout upstairs. 'Harry! Guests!'

No answer. She glowers at us again, as if Harry's absence is our fault. 'Har-*ry*! Some of us down here have work to do!' Still no answer. She focuses her fierce gaze on the professor. 'You after a room?'

'A booking in the name of Barry,' Miss Peach puts in politely.

Mrs Fergusson wipes her hands theatrically on her pinafore and lifts open the ledger. 'Surname?'

The professor takes off his hat, a battered felt marsupial that has seen better days. As has, I see in the better light, the wrinkled suit. 'Barry,' he says.

'*Sur*name,' she repeats.

He runs a hand through his thick mane of silver hair. 'Barry *is* the surname, my good woman.'

'Professor Geoffrey Barry,' Miss Peach says. 'The distinguished poet.'

The stout older woman looks the petite younger woman up and down, unimpressed. 'You that new teacher at the high school? The young thing they're all talking about?'

Miss Peach offers her best smile. 'Pamela Peach.'

The older woman remains unimpressed. A key is tossed onto the desk, the breakfast hours recited staccato.

'Any chance of a little something tonight?' Miss Peach asks. 'The professor has been travelling all day.'

'The bona fide professor,' he adds, and gives me a wink.

'Bit late for a meal,' she tells him. 'But then we don't get a lot of *distinguished poets* here. I'll ask the lord and master. If and when I find him.' She saves a parting shot for Miss Peach – 'No visitors allowed in the rooms after ten p.m.' – and pushes her way back through the doors of the empty bar.

'Colourful local identity,' the professor murmurs. He reaches for his bag. 'I can manage from here, Burns.' He turns to Miss Peach. 'Coming up for a nightcap? Before curfew?'

'I'll wait for you in the ladies' lounge,' she says, 'with Robbie.'

His sunken eyes and tired face are hard to read. 'Then I'll see both of you in the lounge. If I make it down again.'

I follow her through a maze of dark, wood-panelled walls and frosted-glass windows into the empty lounge; she plants herself at the nearest table. For a time she seems lost in thought, then seems to remember me and rouses herself. 'It's *very* exciting news about Victor Gollancz. Wasn't that a lovely gesture?'

'I suppose.'

'Of course we mustn't get our hopes up too high, but who knows?' No answer is required as she presses on. 'He's a generous man, Robbie. He's given me so much of his valuable time over the years. So much of his *mind*.' She pauses, leans closer. 'First impressions can be misleading. He, um, drinks a little too much when he's bored.' An overly bright smile. 'Don't we all. But I love listening to him. It's like a window into that wonderful mind.' She stands up abruptly. 'Speaking of drinking, I might just poke my head into the bar and see what I can rustle up.'

The moment she pushes out through one door, the professor pushes in through another, as if in the pictures. 'Ah,' he says. 'The shadow.'

'Miss Peach asked me to stay.'

'And you took her at her word?' Is it the brighter light of the lounge, or are his cheeks flushed? 'Did it occur to you that she might have meant the exact opposite?'

I sit puzzled. But willing to listen and learn from that wonderful mind. Especially on the subject of Miss Peach.

'A trap for young players, Burns.' He cranes his head, looking about. 'Who do you have to kill to get a drink around here?'

'Miss Peach went to look,' I say, but here she is back again, followed closely by the grumpy Mrs Fergusson.

'Beauty and the Beast,' the professor says, slightly too loudly.

'*What* did you say?' from the grump.

'I'm in the mood for a feast.'

I suppress a laugh, warming to him a little despite myself.

'And a drink,' he continues. 'A bottle of champagne. Two glasses. And something for our young friend. A wee dram of Scotch, Rabbie?'

'Sweet sherry?'

Mrs Fergusson snorts. 'You're a minor, sunshine. And your old man has been riding us ever since we took over the licence. Does he even know you're here?'

This astonishes me. I hardly know her, she knows everything about me.

'Robbie will have a lemon squash,' Miss Peach says.

'*I'll* have a sweet sherry,' the professor adds, and gives me another wink. Perhaps he is warming to me in return.

'As well as the champagne? You think I came down in the last shower?'

'A sweet-sherry chaser,' he tells her.

She glances from him to me and back again, then shrugs. 'It's on your head. Two and six.'

'Put it on my room tab.'

'Cash only for drinks. Too many fly-by-nighters.'

The professor affects astonishment. 'Do I look like a fly-by-nighter?'

'No offence, but you can never tell. Two and six.'

He turns to Miss Peach. 'I have no coin of the realm about my person, blithe spirit. Squandered en route, I'm afraid.'

'My shout,' she says, reaching into her handbag.

'A loan,' he tells her. 'I must insist. Until the bank throws open its vault to me at first light.' He produces a silver hipflask from an inside pocket of his jacket and empties it into a teacup. 'If I could trouble you for a top-up, my good woman. Irish, if you have no Scotch. Metho if you have neither.' He flourishes the flask in the direction of our grumpy, reluctant waitress.

Miss Peach giggles. It crosses my mind I might sell him a flask of my best backyard moonshine in the morning.

'And a simple country repast for my good self and my boon companions.'

The more he drinks, the more nonsense he talks. He'd struck me as the laconic type at the station, the strong and silent type. Mrs Fergusson snatches the flask from him. 'Bangers and mash?'

The professor opens his mouth but Miss Peach gets in first. 'For three,' she says, and smiles. 'If it's not too much trouble.'

'No bloody trouble at all. If I can find the chief cook and bottle washer.' She turns on her heels and stalks off.

'Don't think I don't know what you're up to,' Miss Peach says. 'You're doing your best to get thrown out.'

His dark eyes crinkle above a crooked smile. His teeth – a slight shock – are yellow. 'By gad, Holmes, you've seen straight through my dastardly scheme yet again.'

She titters, laughing too easily at his tomfoolery. 'Well, don't expect me to take you in.'

'No room at the inn?'

'None.'

'Not even the honeymoon suite?'

He rests his hand on hers; she shakes it off but giggles again, irritatingly. They are still bantering when a champagne bottle and two glasses are plonked on the table a few minutes later.

'The sherry?' the professor reminds the grim-faced Mrs Fergusson.

She ignores him. 'Any sign of His Lordship?' she asks instead, then turns and pushes back out through the swing doors without waiting for an answer. 'Har-*ry*!'

'Last seen heading for the hills in a cloud of dust,' the professor murmurs. 'And who could blame him?'

He pops the bottle and fills the glasses, draining his before Miss Peach has touched hers. 'Never eat on an empty stomach,' he remarks in my direction, refilling his glass. This time he raises it before drinking. 'A toast. To Clochemerle. Gateway to the south. Home of the mighty Eagles. Birthplace of the bard. Speaking of whom, I would like to pay homage. How full is my dance card tomorrow?'

'What time can you start?'

'At whatever time that busy old fool, the unruly sun, doth call on us.'

'You have lunch with the headmaster in the staffroom. My English class straight afterwards. But come early, I'll show you around. The Lyceum Club meets at seven. The rest of the afternoon is free.'

'Ah. Then I can expect a tour of the birthplace?'

She smiles and shakes her head. 'I can't get away from school before four. I could give Robbie an early minute. If you need a guide. Or want company.'

He briefly aims his crooked grin at me, then back at her. 'I think I can manage.'

The glass of sherry arrives, closely followed by food: the usual alps of mash, log-piles of felled sausages. The professor raises his glass again, to Miss Peach. 'A Book of Verses beneath the Bough, a Jug of Wine, a Plate of Mash – and Thou.'

Another of his weird poems? Her own delicate face is beginning to flush. 'You don't think you should slow down, Geoffrey?'

'Tomorrow we work, tonight we play.' He slides the sweet sherry in its etched glass across the table to me. 'Put that lemonade aside, laddie, and drink a real woman's drink.'

'Geoffrey – he's a minor. *And* I'm his teacher. I can't give my students alcohol.'

'You didn't.' He forks a thick slice of sausage into his mouth. 'I did.' He swallows, examines me. 'I must say you have a disconcertingly familiar look about you, Burns.'

I wash down my lump of mash with a swig of sherry. 'People say I look like Paul McCartney.'

'You have a doppelganger! Can't say I know the cove. Is he a local? Centre-half-forward for the mighty Eagles, perchance? Vice-president of Lions?'

Miss Peach giggles again and taps me playfully on the arm. 'He's such a wag, Robbie.'

'Hard work, but someone's got to do it.' He shovels in the last of his mash. We've both finished our meals, she has barely touched hers.

'Shall I eat yours, Miss Peach?' I offer, which seems to irk him for some reason.

'Have you no home to go to, laddie? No errands to run, no farm chores? No *milch* cows to bring in?'

'Miss Peach asked me to stay,' I remind him.

'And we must always do what Miss Peach commands.' He gives her a sardonic glance. 'She who must be obeyed. We cross Miss Peach at our peril, Burns. We travel enormous distances. Sleep in lonely hotel rooms. All in the faint hope of being granted a glance. A kind word in the shell-like. Or – heaven forbid! – a kiss.'

Her smile has become a little fixed. 'You were going to show me some poems, Geoffrey.'

'All in the fullness of time, blithe spirit. Meanwhile, where has the *sommeliere* secreted herself?'

He rises from his chair, walks with a slight stagger towards the door, thrusts his head through and shouts: 'Lady Macbeth! Another round of your finest paint-stripper, *s'il vous plaît.*'

Miss Peach gives me a nervous smile; the professor stumbles back, but collapses into his chair safely enough.

'It's been a long day,' she says. 'You must be very tired, Geoffrey. And it's a big day tomorrow. We should let you get to bed.'

'The night is young,' he says. His eye falls on my half-full sherry glass; he reaches across for it. 'I think I paid for that, laddie.'

'Miss Peach paid for it,' I remind him, moving it out of his reach.

He grins. 'I do believe I'm beginning to take a shine to you, young Burns.'

The red-faced, middle-aged man who appears in the door

might be a twin of the mop lady. In fact it's her husband, Harry, the missing publican. 'Time to lock up, folks.'

'Hear it not, Duncan,' the professor mutters darkly in my direction. 'For it is a knell.' He turns to Harry. 'One for the road, sirrah?'

Harry hands him the hipflask. 'That's for the road, sport.' Then, looking at me: 'And don't you go telling your old man you were here, young feller. I don't need any more grief.'

I'm beginning to think I need a secret identity, like Batman. The professor unscrews the flask, sniffs, takes a swig. 'Ah! The second-best brandy.'

'If it was second-best it wouldn't set you back five bob, mate.'

Miss Peach fumbles in her purse again, her smile gone, her expression troubled. 'Will you see me home, Robbie?'

'*I'll* see you home,' the professor says, and half-rises, only to fall back into his chair again.

'I'm seeing *you* to bed,' the publican says, taking his arm.

The professor shakes himself free. 'Take your hands *off* of me, mate! As they say in the classics.'

The publican laughs. 'Let yourselves out, folks. Don't worry 'bout our friend here. If he plays up I'll sool the Lady Wife onto him. And you don't mess with her.'

'Unhand me, sirrah,' the professor shouts as he is bundled towards the door. 'Or by God I'll come at you.'

'Sleep well, Geoffrey,' Miss Peach calls after him anxiously. 'You'll feel better in the morning.'

He doesn't seem to hear. 'I have places to go, people to meet!' he shouts. 'Birthplaces to visit! Shrines! The Shrine of the Virgin Teacher! The shrine of shining Miss Virtue there!'

But Miss Virtue is pushing out through another door, with me in hot pursuit. The professor's voice echoes after us as she hurries ahead down the dark-panelled labyrinth: '"When shall we three meet again? In thunder, lightning, or in rain? When the hurlyburly's done, when the battle's lost and won!"' One last door and we are on the street, walking away in silence. Walking half the way home in silence.

'He's not usually like that, Robbie,' she murmurs eventually. More walking, more silence, then: 'I wouldn't want you to get the wrong impression.'

She slips her arm inside mine, clings to me slightly. 'The poor darling. It's been a long day. And he has such a sensitive temperament. He must be exhausted.'

We turn a corner. 'He has a special gift, Robbie. But that means he has special needs.'

Still I say nothing.

'I don't think Margaret – Mrs Barry – has ever understood that. Not that I want to say anything against her. I've always liked her well enough personally.'

I sneak a glance at her face as we pass beneath a streetlight, confirming what I have sensed: tears glisten on her cheeks. She dabs discreetly; by the time we reach her front gate she is composed enough to smile.

'Thank you, Prince Charming, for seeing me home. And especially for being my chaperone. If he'd had one less drink, or I'd had one more . . .' She covers her tracks with an even brighter smile.

'Are you in love with him, Miss?'

Her smile vanishes, but perhaps my words surprise me even more than her. How could I say anything so ridiculous?

'Of *course* not,' she says emphatically. A pause, a rethink. 'And I'm not going to love him. I don't want to love him.' A frown has replaced her smile. 'Not that it's any of your business.' She composes herself. 'But why should you care about any of this?' Stretching up on tiptoe, she presses her lips to my cheek. 'You'll see a different side of him tomorrow. The real Geoffrey Barry. Now hurry off home. Or your dad will have a search party out for you.'

The door opens, she steps into its dark vertical mouth, it closes, swallowing her from sight. I turn away and wander a little aimlessly homewards. Her answer to my dumb question reassures me; how could there be anything between them? They're Beauty and the Beast. Chalk and cheese. Age and youth. I can still feel the touch of her lips, a far more tender kiss than the bird-peck she offered the professor at the station.

I glance up as I walk home past the darkened Oak. In the great stone bulk of the building one small window is lit, upstairs, but I have no idea if it is the professor's room or the room of Lord Harry and his fearsome Lady Wife, or maybe the Gents, in which a disorderly drunk is chucking his guts up.

4

Imagine a world swimming in alcohol, a planet on which the lakes and rivers are pure alcohol, the icecaps frozen alcohol, the oceans salty sea-alcohol – a world in which it rains alcohol. Imagine a colder world, necessarily (melting point of ethyl alcohol, minus 179 degrees fahrenheit), but picture swimming on that planet. Envisage being a fish.

Farfetched? Not to me. At fourteen I am the full bottle on alcohol. Molecular weight, specific gravity, chemical structure – I can recite its properties backwards. In the backyard stables, such knowledge is more than theoretical. I've lived its effects, I know how to make the stuff. Hooch. Moonshine. Firewater. Countless times I've watched the clear pure droplets condense out of their cloudy steam in my glass still. The beautiful simplicity of the molecule – C_2H_5OH, not much more complex than water itself – intrigues me. Why shouldn't an entire planet, given certain conditions, be awash with the stuff?

Even more intriguing is its effect on the brain. On my brain. How can such a simple substance work such magic? More mysteriously, why? To the high priests of the planet Wineworld, it seems too much of a coincidence, it seems a gift from God. A proof of God: a rain that falls from heaven. The rain that falls in heaven.

In the year 5064 a skinny, elongated boy-genius discovers that alcohol comes not from God but from aliens; it is a gift, yes, but with strings attached. Wineworld is a giant product-testing site, one of a system of laboratory planets peopled with human guinea pigs on whom dangerous items are tested. Humans, it turns out, make the best guinea pigs in the universe, better than rats, better than monkeys, better even than guinea pigs.

'Not now, Robbie,' Miss Peach says. 'I'm busy.'

Lunchtime, Friday, my exercise book on her desk, unopened.

'Did you like the title?' I persist.

'Where *is* that impossible man?'

'You didn't like it?'

She manages to make eye contact momentarily. 'Of course I liked it.'

'What did you like about it?'

'Hmm?' She glances at her watch, glances back at me, glances down at the title of the story: *God the Sherry, God the Port, and God the Methylated Spirit*.

'I like its . . . its irreverence. Can we talk about this later? Please. I've other things on my mind.'

She rises abruptly and walks to the rain-streaked window. Penola, planet Earth – nothing but water falling from the sky. She stares out hopefully, but no one will be walking in that product, or testing it for dangerous side effects like pneumonia. 'If he misses English, perhaps he'll make it in time for History.'

'Shall I go and look for him, Miss Peach?'

She glances at me, startled. 'In this?' Her eyes hold mine for a moment, then she takes a deep breath, walks back to her desk and picks up my story. 'The title *is* intriguing, Robbie. I think that's what I like most about your stories. They . . . they surprise me. They take nothing for granted. They surprise me but at the same time they seem somehow . . . inevitable. It's a nice paradox.' A tentative smile. 'Are your parents religious?'

'Presbyterian.'

'Do you show them your stories?'

'They wouldn't understand them.'

'Geoffrey and I often talk about religion. Long into the night.' She checks herself. 'I mean, with mutual friends. Over a meal. He's like you in some ways, Robbie. A restless mind. Nothing is sacred. I think the war made him like that. Made him ask questions. Doubt everything he'd been taught.' A smile of real warmth now; talking about him seems to makes her happier. 'It's cost him, of course. Friendships, prizes. He's made a lot of enemies by telling the truth, asking the hard questions. But that's why he's a great poet, Robbie – people don't realise how great. Oh, he'll tell you there are mysteries. His poetry is full of the mysteries of the world.' She is speaking rapturously now, as if by quoting the absent poet she has conjured him into the room, and he is speaking his own words himself. 'Why is there something instead of nothing? What is this mysterious thing we each wake up *inside* every morning, this thing we live in, called consciousness? This first thing we *know*?' She looks at me triumphantly, then her smile slowly fades. He isn't there after all. 'I'm sorry, Robbie. I must sound like a schoolgirl. He can put it so much better.'

'I could make it back before the next lesson,' I say, returning to the mystery that matters. 'I'm sure I can find him.'

'I don't think finding him will pose a problem.' She opens the exercise book and reads the first lines. 'Tell me, why are so many of your stories about drowned worlds?'

'Don't know, Miss.'

'Really?' she murmurs. She reads on, then reaches for her pen and scribbles in the margin. 'You've no shortage of ideas, Robbie, but your style can be a little . . . abrupt. You might take a leaf from the content of these stories and try to make your style more fluid. I'll make some suggestions.' Her eyes stray to the window again. 'Leave it with me. Run along now. You must be starving.'

Outside, a slow steady drizzle. The flooded quadrangle is deserted; lunches are being consumed under shelter, out of sight. The rain draws a useful veil behind me as I sneak my bike out of the bike shed. I button my school blazer tightly around me, duck my head and pedal out into the weather, water-resistant hair first. Is it the ceaseless rain that drowns my imaginary worlds? The real world is as waterlogged as any I could invent, a sodden landscape in which the town floats like a self-contained island. Or is it the sweet sherry that my sodden mind occasionally drowns in? The sweet sherry and the hundred-proof moonshine. The sweet sherry, the moonshine, and the laughing gas.

Sodden through myself by the time I reach the pub, I ride up onto the shelter of the wide verandah and press my nose to the window. The transparent lettering – FRONT BAR – etched into the opaque frosting offers various odd-shaped spy holes. A few morning regulars prop up the bar, but no sign of the irregular professor. Behind the bar Harry is filling a stem-glass with red wine. Who might that be for? I lean the centaur against the wall and shove my wet head through the big swing door.

He sits hunched over a table by the fireplace, writing in a note-book. A cigarette is smoking itself in an ashtray at one elbow, an empty glass sits at the other. Harry swaps it for the full one.

'Professor,' I hiss, then again, more loudly. 'Professor!'

Every face in the bar turns my way except his, lost in work.

'Outside, sport,' Harry tells me.

'I need to talk to the professor.'

'Then wait in the ladies' lounge.'

'Fair go, Harry,' a regular pipes up. 'The boy's as wet as a shag.'

'A bona fide drowned rat,' from another. 'Give him something to warm him up.'

'A sweet sherry?' I say.

The general laughter seems to rouse the professor. He glances up, takes a drag on his cigarette, examines me through narrowed eyes. His tired face looks even older this morning; those eyes are what my father likes to call pissholes in snow, though none of us – probably no one in the entire district – has ever seen snow.

'Get in here by the fire, lad,' someone else is saying.

It blazes in the big corner-grate. I slip out of my soaked school blazer and crouch in its warmth near the professor's table. Still he doesn't speak to me. He writes on, I squat there shivering. After a time he closes his eyes and rubs his temples wearily, as if something annoys him. Perhaps it's the chattering of my teeth.

'Give the boy wonder a shot of triple malt, Sir Harry,' he says.

'Told you last night, Prof. His old man gives me enough grief.'

'Then give *me* one. In fact, give me two.'

'You got the necessaries?'

'I'll be in receipt of a small honorarium this evening. For services rendered.'

I shiver on; the professor sets down his pen, finishes his

cigarette. The shot-glasses arrive, he hands me one. 'This'll warm the cockles.'

I glance towards Harry, who is busy pulling more beers. The professor gives a mocking laugh. 'What Sir Harry pretends not to see he pretends not to know about.' He raises his glass. 'Here's to coming through the rye.'

I choke down the fierce, eye-watering heat of the whisky, then luxuriate in the slow creep of warmth through my chest.

The professor watches, mildly amused. 'So spill the beans, young Quatermain. You bear a message stick from She Who Must Be Obeyed?'

He seems sober today, his speech slow and measured, but its sense still resists me.

'You're supposed to be at school,' I tell him.

'I haven't finished drinking breakfast yet.'

The others watch from the bar, sipping at their own breakfasts.

'She's very upset,' I say.

'She who must be assuaged.' He rubs his temples again. 'Has she taught you the derivation of the word "hysteria"?' he says mysteriously. 'No? Classical origins. From the Greek *hysteros* – womb.'

'What shall I tell her?'

'Whatever she wants to bloody hear!' The momentary flare of anger is quickly swallowed in a crooked smile. 'Safest course with hysterics. Also known as women.' A pause. 'Also known as prick-teasers.'

'She said if you're late you can take us for History.'

Another tired laugh. 'You're too young for history, Burns. Or maybe history is too old for you. Cigarette?'

I take the cigarette – a Camel – wait in vain for a light, strike a match myself. He is more interested in his wine, which he lifts, examines, sets down again. 'Enough hair of the dog for one day. Which history?'

'We're studying the First World War.'

'I thought your province was the future, not the past. Tomorrowland. Fantasyland.'

'Miss Peach says we can't predict the future without understanding the past.'

A snort. 'Wonder who she nicked that from. What else has she taught you?'

'Mostly she reads poetry at us.'

'Cry havoc and let slip the dogs of art. Use the ashtray, young Burns. Which poets?'

'Some that hate war, some that like it. She wants us to make up our own minds.'

'There's a good reason for that,' he says. 'A very good reason.' He shakes his head, exasperated. 'She can't make up her own bloody mind. About *anything*.'

Silence. I want to stick up for her but don't know what to say.

'A brilliant career ahead of her, Burns. Doctoral scholarship. Oxford beckoning – I still have clout there. And she throws it all away and flees into exile.'

'So she made up her mind about that,' I say.

He eyes me again through those narrow eyes, the faintest of smiles playing about his mouth. 'I like you, Burns. Wise beyond your years. Beyond anyone's, for that matter. Another cigarette?'

'I have to get back. What shall I tell her?'

He lifts his glass once more. 'That I need to finish breakfast.'

'So you're coming?'

A last, bent smile. 'You forge ahead on your trusty steed, brave scout. Search out the terrain. Bring the good news from Ghent to Aix.'

I pull on my hot wet blazer and stand there by the fire, steaming, waiting for further reassurance. He shakes out another Camel and sticks it in my mouth. 'Alert me with smoke signals, paleface, if the coast is clear. Hysteria-wise.'

'Have you got an umbrella?' I mumble between clenched lips as he strikes a match.

'I'll follow. But don't look back, or the sacred bond of trust between us will be broken.'

He turns away and picks up his pen as though he needs to write these last mysterious words down. I step out into Wetworld again, glowing inside from the whisky, taking great sucks of the cigarette before the rain extinguishes it. I can't wait to tell Miss Peach my quest has succeeded, and the frigid needles of rain now feel invigorating. Perhaps she will show the professor my new story after the lesson. I like him, I like the things he says, even if I don't understand half of them. I wish I could talk like that. I wish I could write like that. A stray thought: is Miss Peach right? Do I need a fluid style to do my drowned worlds justice? My mind feels liquid enough, but perhaps can't yet find a liquid expression to match.

I halt under a tree at the school turn-off and look back along Church Street. No sign of him. What to do next? Wait? Go back? But he promised. Distantly, the blast of the school siren; lunchtime is over. I wait a few more minutes then pedal onwards reluctantly, rack my bike, and slip very late and wet into class.

'I am so disappointed,' Miss Peach is telling the others. 'I can't tell you how disappointed. I know you've all been waiting weeks for this moment, IA – as have I. But the professor is unwell.' Her reddened eyes find mine, skid past. 'He sends his apologies. He hopes to make it some time this afternoon. Perhaps in time for History. So. If you'll take out your Shakespeare . . .'

She talks us absentmindedly through act one, scene one,

allocates parts. Hands shoot up, mine and Anne Hunter's among them. 'The first scene is boys only, Anne. Your turn will come. I'm saving Juliet for you.'

'Who will be Romeo, Miss?'

'Um, I thought perhaps Robbie —' A chorus of wolf-whistles and hoots go up in the class; the nape of Anne's neck, a few inches from my nose, turns scarlet. Miss Peach seems not to notice. As the first stumbling lines are read, her interest is still in the rain-streaked window, or – whenever footsteps pass outside – the doorway. Even the laughter in the class as various boys read on – 'Draw thy tool, sir!' 'My naked weapon is out; quarrel, I will back thee!' – fails to rouse her.

'What does it mean, Miss? "I bite my thumb at thee, sir!"'

'Hmm? What's that, Brian?'

Between scenes she apologises again – 'Like all artists, the pro-fessor can be a bit temperamental' – and invites everyone, 'Your parents too,' to hear him at the Lyceum Club that night.

The lesson ends; real Italian history – the rise of Musso-lini – replaces imagined Italian history, but her distracted state remains unchanged. 'Please come tonight,' she begs as we file out at home-time. She shoots a final glance at the rain-swept window, as if her plea is aimed more at the missing poet than at us. 'Please come.'

I come. Mum is busy packing for tomorrow's train: 'Do you mind if I miss the club, Robbie?' Dad drops me at the school gate – 'You can't ride in this weather' – and I sprint through the wet to find the library empty. Am I early? I check my watch: ten minutes late. Am I in the right place? The door is open, the lights are on, an array of chairs has been set out in front of the lectern. The sole sign of life is the chuggling urn, its red thermostat winking some kind of robot-morse at me. I uncover my supper plate and choose the thickest slice of jubilee cake. Half past seven on the wall clock. I've eaten the second- and third-thickest slices before there is movement outside: car lights sweeping the rain-blurred window, the splutter of an engine that could only be a Beetle. Doors slam, voices approach – human voices – and the Tweedle-twins burst in through the door, shaking their matching umbrellas.

Miss Burke scans the empty room gleefully. 'Big turnout, Miss Hammond!'

'Miss Peach will be *so* disappointed,' the other gloats. Her glance falls on me. 'The loyal Master Burns! Single-handedly holding the fort.'

'If you're the urn monitor, Master Burns, you might like to answer its call of distress.'

I bend and examine the controls as Merv Bailey enters, clutching a flagon of red wine, shaking his head ruefully. '*My Fair Lady* at the drive-in. I warned her there was a clash.'

'It's not too late to make the main feature, Merv,' Miss Burke says, and smirks at Miss Hammond behind his back. 'But you won't see much in this rain.'

The three of them gather around the urn as if to warm themselves, the big man pouring wine, the plump, frocked-up women eyeing the single plate of supper.

'Bought cake,' I pass on Mum's apology. 'She was too busy packing.'

'Beggars can't be choosers, Master Burns,' Miss Hammond says, and seizes a slice. 'Would you agree, Miss Burke?'

Her companion's mouth is already full. 'Indeedy-doody, Miss Hammond. Indeedy-doody in spades. Better bought cake than none.'

'Packing for whence, might we ask, Master Burns?'

'The police ball. In the city. They're catching the morning train.'

'The sheriff is leaving on the noon train to go dancing? At the very moment the hard-drinking poet arrives in town?'

Miss Hammond gives a mock swoon. 'Miss Burke – don't remind me! Gary Cooper in *High Noon!*'

Doc McKenzie sidles in, nods vaguely, heads straight for the sci-fi shelves. I stand to one side, keeping an eye on the door and an ear on the conversation around the urn.

'P'raps I should check the Oak,' Merv says.

'Oh, I wouldn't dream of doing that. Would you, Miss Hammond?'

'Lift no rocks, Miss Burke, find no centipedes.'

'What *are* you two talking about?'

The women exchange arch glances. 'Perhaps the distinguished professor requires a special . . . *inducement* to leave his hotel room.'

'In my experience those inducements can take time, Miss Hammond. Would you agree?' And they both explode into cake-crumbed laughter.

'Now, ladies!' Big Merv growls, but the two take this less as a warning than an invitation for more of their gossipy double act.

'Would you say that depended on the size of the task at hand, Miss Burke?'

'The task *in* hand, perhaps, Miss Hammond.'

'Ssh!' Merv hisses, for standing in the door is the professor himself, hatted and overcoated, with Miss Peach close at his side, beret on head, umbrella dripping. She looks crestfallen at the small turnout, he curls his lip.

'The rain must be holding people up,' Miss Peach tells him, setting down her umbrella. 'We'll give the stragglers a few minutes more. Come and meet my friends.'

Have they walked from the pub? The professor's overcoat is sodden; despite the hat his face is varnished with rain. He removes both and tosses them on a chair; names are exchanged, hands shaken.

'Something to drink, Professor?' Miss Burke asks.

'Perhaps afterwards, Geoffrey,' Miss Peach suggests.

Miss Hammond gives her offsider a wink. 'And what will you be reading from tonight, Professor? Your latest slim volume?'

He looks from one to the other, amused. 'Any requests?'

'Ah – Adam Lindsay Gordon?' Merv puts in.

The professor gives one of his harsh laughs. 'The *horse* poet?'

Incredulity on Merv's broad, lumpy face. 'You don't like Gordon's poetry?'

'Killed himself and who could blame him? It's depressing enough having to read his guff – imagine having to write it!'

'He's buried in Westminster Abbey,' Merv says defiantly.

'Well, that should keep him from writing anything else. I think I will have that drink, ladies. Looks like we're in for a long night.'

Merv stiffens. Miss Burke steps deftly between the men and pours the wine, smiling sweetly.

'Do you think Adam Lindsay Gordon wrote so badly because of the demon drink?' she asks, simpering. Her offsider chokes a laugh, but she presses on. 'I understand it's a problem many artistic types have struggled with.'

The professor drains his cup of wine, unfazed. 'Not just poets, ladies, but the criminal classes in general. Pickpockets, standover men, swindlers – schoolteachers.'

'Um, perhaps we might all sit down,' Miss Peach says as he fills and drains a second cup, 'and get started.'

The doctor is already seated, scribbling margin notes in another library book. I join him. The professor refills and sits in the middle of the front row; the three mutineers remain clumped around the urn at the back.

'A small crowd,' Miss Peach says from the lectern, smiling her brightest smile yet, 'but discerning. It's my pleasure to introduce our distinguished guest tonight. Professor Geoffrey Barry, who holds the Chair in English at the University of Adelaide, is currently editing the *Oxford History of Australian Literature* —'

'Does Australia *have* a literature, Miss Burke?' comes a hoarse whisper behind me.

'As against the professor having a history, Miss Hammond?'

Miss Peach ignores their snickering. 'Tonight, he is wearing his other hat as one of this country's finest poets. His most recent collection is *A Little Nightmare Music*,' she holds up the familiar slim volume, 'but I know Geoffrey has been working on some new poems and I'm hoping we might persuade him to share them with us. So without further ado . . .'

He rises and faces the empty ranks of chairs. 'In fact,' he says, 'not. My recent works can be rather . . . difficult. Hermetic. At first hearing. To readers unfamiliar with the currents in contemporary world poetry.'

'Up yours too,' I think I hear one of the misses whisper.

'So I thought I might read something more accessible.' He sways a little, takes a large sip from his cup as if to add more ballast.

'Two-pot screamer,' Merv mutters, and the ladies snicker again.

'I like to get the feel of an audience,' the professor says, looking over my head at the snickerers. 'To pitch a reading at their mental level. So with your kind permission . . .'

He takes the silence as permission.

'The owl and the pussycat went to sea,' he begins, 'in a beautiful pea-green boat . . .'

Miss Peach looks around, her smile fixed. She catches my eye, looks away towards the mutterings by the urn.

'You're reading a bloody nursery rhyme!' Big Merv says loudly.

'Ah, so they do teach the teachers *some*thing these days,' the professor says.

'I'm beginning to take exception to your attitude, mate.'

'A thousand pardons, effendi. But on what grounds could you possibly take exception? Adam Lindsay Gordon, for Christ's sake. Pig ignorance is grounds for humility, not for anger.'

Merv takes a step forward, enraged. 'Just who the hell do you think you are, mate?'

'Um, can I have three guesses? Mate?'

'What the fuck are you *talking* about?'

'Who the hell I think I am. A tricky question. I hadn't taken you for an existentialist. Sartre gives several answers, but I have never been convinced.'

A titter from one of the misses. 'I might warm to the man yet, Miss Burke. Gives as good as he gets.'

Big Merv is standing in front of the lectern now, a short thickset man shouting at a tall dark one. 'What would you say if I asked you to name the last three Magarey Medallists, Professor bloody Einstein?'

A mock-pensive look in return. 'That's a hard one, Professor Merleau-Ponty. Is it something to do with the quaint folk custom in these here parts of kicking an inflated pig's bladder around a paddock on a Saturday arvo?'

Miss Peach is on her feet now, between the two. 'Please, Geoffrey. Merv. Can we continue the reading?'

'No we bloody can't!' Big Merv explodes. 'What do you see in this . . . this *poser*? You're worth a thousand of him!' He turns his anger on the professor again. 'You're not fit to lick her feet!'

'Now, there's an idea,' the professor murmurs.

'You . . . *arsehole*. Too hung over to show up at school today!

And back on the turps tonight! There's only one thing you came down here for, sport, and we all know what that is!'

'Merv,' Miss Peach begs, 'stop it! Please!'

Silence. The big man stares at her for a long moment, a defiant, overgrown five-year-old, then reluctantly clamps his mouth shut.

Tag-team whispers at the back of the room. 'Well, that was a declaration, Miss Hammond.' 'The pot calling the kettle black, Miss Burke.'

'You can do better than him,' the pot tells Miss Peach, more calmly.

'We share a *literary* friendship, Merv. Nothing more. Not that it's any of your business.'

The pot turns back to the kettle. 'If you were any kind of man, you'd stop playing your little games with her.'

The professor smiles his crooked, wry smile. '"Oh, beware, my lord, of jealousy. It is the green-eyed monster which doth mock the meat it feeds on." As for games,' he turns to Miss Peach, 'I think we know who's toying with whom, don't we, blithe spirit?'

He walks steadily enough, if very slowly, to the trestle, pours another cupful of wine, drains it – 'One for the road' – retrieves his coat and hat and walks just as slowly and steadily out the door.

The silence is louder than ever. Big Merv refills his own cup, perhaps for want of something safe to do with his fists, the two misses share arched glances and pursed mouths, the doctor has gone back to reading as if nothing seen or heard in the present is as astounding as the world to come in the future.

Miss Peach just stands there looking vacant, lost for words.

'I didn't start it,' Merv tells her, a five-year-old again.

She finds her tongue. 'You didn't exactly help.'

'The professor *was* rather discourteous, Pam,' from Miss Burke. 'He *is* a guest in our town.'

'He's *my* guest,' Miss Peach says, staring back like a defiant five-year-old herself, before grabbing her coat and umbrella. 'But so stubborn! He'll catch pneumonia out there.'

'Shall we stay behind and help you clean up?' Miss Hammond calls after her simperingly, but Miss Peach is already out the door. I hesitate, then repossess my mother's empty cake plate and head out after her.

They are through the school gate, the tall dark figure of the professor walking steadily through the drizzling rain, tiny Miss Peach stumbling in her high-heeled boots a pace behind, struggling to hold the umbrella over them both.

'You didn't exactly help, Geoffrey,' she repeats.

'Pearls before swine,' he mutters.

'Those swine are my friends.'

'With friends like those . . .'

'You all right, Miss?' I ask, coming abreast.

She turns towards me, turns on me. 'Robbie, what on earth? Of course I'm all right. Go away! Go *home*.'

'I'm going home. This is the way.'

'Look at you! You're drenched. Go back inside, out of the rain. Merv will give you a lift. Or someone.'

'What about you, Miss?'

She stops in her tracks and glares. 'You are *not* to spy on me, understood? This is none of your business!'

The professor has stalked on, more steadily and purposefully now, as though the frigid rain is sobering him quickly, washing the booze out of him. She turns and runs after him with her raised umbrella. 'Geoffrey! Wait!'

I follow, keeping my distance. At the Church Street corner he turns and they stand facing each other beneath the umbrella; I merge my sapling body with the trunk of the nearest pine.

'*I'm* the one playing games?' he asks with some force.

'Ignore him, Geoffrey.'

'I don't give a fig about him, I'm talking about you. Wasting yourself down here! Squandering yourself on these bumpkins! Come back to the city, country mouse. End this absurd exile.'

'You know I can't.'

'Why not? You've made your point.'

He turns his head aside and sneezes violently, then again. The force of the second explosion bends him double; Miss Peach offers a supportive arm. 'We must get you out of those wet things. Come on. It's not far. You can have a hot bath and dry out by the fire.'

'Your bath?'

'My bath. Just don't go getting any ideas.'

'No ideas but in things. One such thing being a little something to soothe the throat.'

'You've had enough.'

'A church mouse!' It's hard to read his face in the darkness but I sense he is smiling. 'And if I swear off the demon drink? What might be my reward?'

She leans up and kisses him on the mouth, briefly. 'We'll see. But I do want to hear those new poems.'

'Promises,' he says, and they move on again, his arm around her waist now, she holding the shared umbrella. I follow them up Arthur Street, protected only by the smaller umbrella of my oiled hair, until they turn into her driveway and disappear inside the house. I am wet through and shivering uncontrollably, a shag on a planet-sized rock. I seek shelter beneath the pepper tree for a time, but there are too many holes in that giant umbrella and I can see nothing in the house, and at last I dash for home.

5

Dad is on his hands and knees in the kitchen, poking about with a screwdriver beneath the Singer. Mum sits above him with a foot on the heavy wrought-iron treadle, making her own last-minute mechanical repairs to an elaborate ballgown.

'Pedal now, Mother. Stop. And again.'

Open suitcases everywhere; she must be in a panic to allow him anywhere near her precious machine.

'Losing traction in the drive-belt. Might need to get it up on the bench.'

'Over my dead body, Jim Burns.'

She is too distracted to notice my drenched state. I sit quietly by the stove and sip hot cocoa while they tinker and bicker and tinker; when I am warmed up, inside and out, I sneak off to bed. Rain falls all night, I hear every drop. My sleepless thoughts are of Miss Peach – who else? – and for once I agree with Big Merv. She could do better. Much better. She could, for instance, wait for me . . .

Someone else is shaking me awake. 'Better pull on some clothes, Robbie. If you're coming to see us off.'

I carry Dad's battered case through the lightly sprinkling rain. He carries Mum's heavier one, she a basket of provisions for the journey and an unequally shared umbrella. Of course I've tagged along mostly in the hope of seeing Miss Peach. The professor is also due to leave this morning; will she see him off?

The waiting room is empty, the rain-slicked platform deserted. We sit in silence until the Bluebird rounds the bend, horn blasting, and Miss Burke and Miss Hammond totter out of the ticket office with a cumbersome array of black brollies, brown suitcases and white beauty cases.

'Better lend your teachers a hand, sonny-jim.'

'They're not my teachers, Dad.'

'I won't ask you again.'

'Master Burns,' Miss Burke pants, out of breath. 'How positively gallant. Careful with my beauty case.'

'Weekend in Adelaide, Miss?'

'Fleeing the scene of the crime, Master Burns. Don't drag that, please.'

'Who would have believed, Miss Hammond? Such a *fragrant* young woman, throwing herself at the feet of such a . . . such a . . .'

'Now, now, Miss Burke. Our houseguest did spend the night on the lounge. As far as we can tell. The great man is after all too ill to travel.'

They giggle themselves up onto the train; I struggle behind with their bags.

'I trust you will keep an eye on someone we all know and love, Master Burns.'

If my face turns red it's only with the effort of heaving their cases up onto the overhead racks. Miss Burke has her purse open; she presses a shilling into my palm.

'Don't spend it all at once, Master Burns. Regard it as an advance. We wish to engage the services of your detective agency for the weekend.'

'We expect your report on our desks at nine sharp Monday morning. In duplicate.'

'Think of it as homework. Would it qualify as English home-work, Miss Hammond – or biology?'

A warning blast from the air-horn. Their cackles chase me back through the carriage to my parents' seats, where I manage to evade my mother's fleshy embrace but can't escape my father's wood-sawing handshake: hard down, slow back, hard down, slow back.

'Just remember what I said, sonny-jim. Keep out of the stables. I've padlocked the door, just in case.'

'It's not that we don't trust you,' Mum adds.

I haven't been in the stables for weeks – my experiments take place mostly on paper now and always with the same ingredients, a highly combustible mix of thinking and ink – but it immediately sounds like a good idea. A second blast on the air-horn; the carriage jerks, jerks again, and begins moving, slowly. The platform is moving in the other direction. I jump from the open door, misjudging the speed, stumble, regain my footing. Am I becoming coordinated at last?

'Don't worry, I won't burn the house down!' I shout, but my mother's anxious face has slipped from view. The amused faces of Misses Tweedledum and Tweedledee follow; lastly comes the impassive rear face of the train, its sightless eyes, its inscrutable expression. Fuck you too, Bluebird.

Bikeless, I walk out of the station into the drizzle. Where to first? Where else? The Vespa is parked in the drive, the house blinds drawn. Is she inside? Is he? Should I knock? Merv Bailey is pushing his hand-mower around his front yard. Mowing in the rain? I slip behind a tree and watch for a time. He only has eyes for the house next door; he fails to notice me as he mows the same smooth wet patch of billiard-felt lawn again and again.

No need to break in for the time being, Merv can keep watch. I hurry home and force the back window of the stables instead, not so much squeezing as pouring my long-drink-of-water body through the aperture. Gloom inside, the big shed is a dark magician's cave. Long time no see, chemical friends. I splash spirits of salts into a flask and drop in a handful of granulated zinc. Parrot science: the bits and pieces of metal fizz and bubble and thrash around in their acid bath like tiny glittering piranhas.

I toss in a match – more parrot chemistry – there's a familiar *whoomf,* a sheet of flame. The adrenaline rush is all too mild and all too brief. My dissatisfaction seems to settle on the fact that I knew what was going to happen. Parrot know-how. For the first time it strikes me that the natural state of all these old friends, these rainbow-coloured powders and dangerous liquids, is stability; that even the most explosive gases are, in some sense, inert. That is, the future is inert. For all its explosions and poisonings, my backyard laboratory is a tame and predictable place, it can hold no real surprises. I haven't set out to displace hydrogen gas hoping the method would work, I knew it would work. It always works. The surprise would be if it didn't.

And the rest of my life, by extension? Was I not merely doing things that others had done already? Passing milestones passed by countless others? Was everything I'd done to this point predictable?

Not my stories, perhaps. Curious how those word experiments never quite turn out as intended. Thinking on this, I feel reckless again, ready for anything. I ransack my cluttered shelves, looking for inspiration, or trouble, or an explosive mix of both. I unscrew the wick-lid of my spirit lamp and sip the hundred-proof firewater inside. Mouth burning, I take down various jars of bright powders, unstopper their tight lids and sniff. No, *snort* – a pioneer of this technique, perhaps the inventor of this technique, unheard of before. I dab pinches against the tip of my tongue, force myself to swallow their bitterness or saltiness or strange, suspicious sweetness. What next? Laughing gas? I reach for the nitric acid and immerse myself in the preparations.

'Robbie!' a familiar voice wakes me. 'You home?'

Billy's face in the window frame; I seem to be looking up at it, from the floor.

'Down here,' I mumble.

He waves a half-empty bottle of Autumn Brown. 'Possum drank the top half.'

'The best half.' I am groggy, but able to complete the routine.

'Whatcha doing?'

'Made some laughing gas.'

'What's laughing gas?'

'Like when you go to the dentist.'

'Never been to the dentist,' he says, and why would he with those big gleaming Abo teeth? 'Open the bloody door.'

'Can't. S'locked.'

'Take the sherry,' he says. 'I'll climb through.'

I push myself upright on difficult rubber feet. 'Nah. I'll climb out.'

How long had I been lying there, time-travelling? An entire afternoon, in suspended animation? I fall out more than climb through the window; Billy helps me to my feet, supports me inside the house. I lie on the lounge while he polishes off his sherry and talks excitedly about the weekend ahead. Not even listening to both my Beatles 45s on the gramophone, both sides, several times each, at maximum volume, can rouse me from my stupor. Billy, naked now apart from his underpants, ransacks the house for more to drink.

'Must be *something* around,' he mutters to himself, but my parents have not renounced abstinence since his last visit.

He returns with a plate of cold mutton chops instead. 'You go to that dumb club last night?'

'I think so,' I say, guessing. Time has become elastic.

'That bitch Peach asked *me* to come,' he says.

'She asked everyone to come,' I remember. 'But no one did.'

'She called me out of class and asked me specially.'

This sounds so unlikely it focuses my attention a little. 'She feels sorry for you,' I come out with.

'What the fuck ya talking about?'

'The break-in, stupid. She knows you did it. But she doesn't blame you.'

'I *didn't* fucking do it!'

Haven't I thought this through before? Why must I think it through again? 'But you might have. So you need help either way.'

'You're talking bullshit! I was never coming to her stupid club. Never! Neville reckons it's a club for poofters.'

My head is clearing. 'Yeah? Try and tell that to Big Merv.'

Why is he stripped to his underpants? It's pouring again outside; isn't he feeezing? He takes another cold chop and gnaws at the tough meat. 'Got any good stories to tell, Robbie?'

'Too buggered.'

'Neville told me this dirty story . . .'

When I next open my eyes he is sitting on the edge of the lounge dangling a chop over me. 'You want one?'

A wave of nausea. 'Bed,' I mutter, and somehow raise myself and stagger to my bedroom, where I topple fully dressed onto the mattress and travel on that soft time-machine a little further into the future. How far? Far enough to enter a strange twilight zone in which Billy is lying next to me, propped on an elbow.

'Spare bed's over there,' I mumble.

His speech is a little slurred, but his gaze – fixed on me, purposeful – anything but. 'I thought you'd tell some stories.'

My heavy lids slide shut again. 'Go to bed.'

'At least you can say goodnight.'

'Night,' I murmur into the darkness of my head.

'*Properly*, Robbie.'

'What d'ya mean, properly?'

'You know. Kiss me goodnight.'

This flings my eyelids back open. 'You can't kiss me goodnight!'

'Why not? Why shouldn't best friends kiss each other? Sometimes. Special times.'

There seems no point in answering such stupidity.

'I ain't seen you for so long, Robbie.' His words sound even more slurred, his voice thick with sherry. Or is it – the sharp thought forces its way into my dull head – choking with emotion?

'You see me at school.'

'Yeah, with others. Sort of. You never talk to me no more.' He sniffs, sniffs again. Emotion, definitely; he's close to tears. Tears with – his voice rising now – an edge of anger. 'I stuck up for you! I woulda gone to the boys' home. I woulda gone to *jail.* You're me best friend! My only friend. But you never want to do nothing.'

'We'll go rabbiting next weekend,' I say, to shut him up. 'Now go to bed. Your bed.'

He doesn't move. 'I been thinking about Easter.'

'What about Easter?'

'You know – that time.'

I roll away to face the wall. 'Go to sleep.'

'The time we played with our dicks.'

His naked body is oppressively close to mine in the narrow single bed. 'I need to sleep, Billy,' I say, fully awake.

'I been thinking about it, Robbie.' Silence, then: 'I been thinking about your tool.' He moves closer, pins me against the wall. 'Can I see it again?'

'Piss off! Course you can't.'

'Why not? What's the harm in just looking?'

'I don't *feel* like it, that's why.'

'What're you fuckin' afraid of, Robbie? You too chicken to show me? Chicken!'

I'm chicken about nothing. I roll onto my back and slide down my pants.

Billy stares, mesmerised. 'Can I kiss it?'

His words are so nonsensical he has to repeat them before I register any meaning at all. 'Are you nuts? Why would you want to kiss a *cock*? Kiss your own fucking cock!'

'I tried,' he slurs. 'I couldn't reach.' He rolls over on top of me. 'Why can't best friends kiss each other's cocks? You let me *pull* it last time! Same diff. Let me suck it!'

'Fuck off,' I say, and at last find the strength to shove him away. Feeble with booze, he rolls off the bed and tumbles onto the floor. Silence for a time, then comes the sound of a soft, drunken sobbing, then almost immediately an even softer snoring.

What time is it? I step carefully over the body of my former best friend and stick my head out the door. Ten to nine on the hall clock. He has passed the baton of wakefulness to me, and perhaps also – my cock stirring a little between my legs – the baton of sexual curiosity. Free now of nausea, I polish off the last mutton chop then push out through the back door and climb onto my bike. No police in town tonight, no need for lights. Where to first? I ride across the road. The locked front bar of the Oak is in darkness; vaguely human shapes seem to be moving behind the lit, frosted windows of the ladies' lounge, but when I find a patch of clear glass and peer through I see only empty tables. I merge back with my centaur half and ride on. The fish and chip shop is shut, as is the Golden Fleece roadhouse. Saturday night in the small smoke of a country town – everyone is either at the football club or the drive-in.

The Vespa is parked in the drive, the house is in darkness. I hide my bike and shimmy up the pepper tree, light a cigarette, wait, watch, think things through. Merv's house is also in darkness. The mower still stands in the middle of the front lawn but there is no sign of him. Nothing moves, anywhere. I finish my smoke, drop to the ground, cross the road and knock on her front door. No answer. I look about, then sneak around the side. The back door is wide open; either she is getting used to country habits or was too keyed up to remember to shut it. Too keyed up to lock up – the beginnings of a poem?

'Hullo?' I call through the flyscreen door. 'Anyone home?'

Still no answer. I step through, then freeze in my tracks as the door clacks shut behind me, noisily. No sign of life. Dark as pitch in the back half of the house; should I risk turning on a light? Not yet. My eyes slowly adjust, I feel my way along the passage, heart thumping. The blinds in her bedroom are up, the room bathed in the faint glow of a streetlight. The bed is made, everything seems in place. I ease the blind down, night falls for the second time. Should I light a candle? If so, to what end? To pry? Again, to what end? What am I looking for? What am I doing in her room at all? Part of me wants to vamoose from the house, pronto; part of me wants to stay, relishing the thrill. This mental civil war is still raging within when the sound of footsteps and voices on the front porch startles me. A key turns in the lock; this second shock of adrenaline seems to clear my head. No time to make the back door and no place to hide. Except . . . I drop to my belly and roll beneath the bed as the front door opens.

'. . . I have to *live* here, Geoffrey. And it will be all over town by morning.' Miss Peach's voice. The hall light comes on, her high-heels and stockinged legs appear outside the bedroom door. Wedged beneath the bed I can see nothing above knee-height.

'Relax, country mouse. He's a publican. A man of the world. If he thinks I spent last night in your bed, so what?'

A pair of brown brogues steps onto the small theatre-stage framed by doorjambs and bed. The professor's battered suitcase is lowered to the hall floor. I breathe more easily. If I can't see the actors, they surely can't see me.

'It's not him I'm thinking about.'

'The Lady Wife?'

Her feet kick off their high-heeled shoes impatiently. 'Thanking you for not having to make your bed this morning? I mean, was that *necessary?*'

'You added fuel to the fire, blithe spirit. Insisting I was ill. Insisting I slept on the sofa. She didn't believe that for a moment.'

'You *did* sleep on the sofa!'

'I could have used some company.'

Silence. The toes of his brown shoes face her stockinged toes, an inch apart, her feet now up on tiptoes. The small mime of feet clear even to me: she is kissing him.

Her feet step back. 'Just don't go getting any ideas. You still smell like a brewery.'

'Haven't touched a drop since last night! Poet's honour.'

'What kind of salute is that?'

'The poet's salute. Up yours.' The tinkle of her laughter; encouraged, he goes on. 'But I wouldn't say no to a small nightcap.'

'I'll make a pot of tea.'

'What is this? The Country Women's Temperance Association?'

Her feet step out of frame, stage left. 'Make yourself comfortable,' she calls back.

His brown shoes turned my way now. 'In the *boudoir?*'

'In the *lounge!*'

'Again? I hardly slept a wink.'

'You can sleep in the girls' bed tonight.'

But the brogues take a step towards me, into her bedroom; the light is switched on. More easy-to-read leg language: he is looking around the room, taking it all in. 'I approve!'

An answering shout from the kitchen: 'Of what?'

'The Byzantine decor.'

'Are you in my bedroom, Geoffrey Barry?'

He is muttering what sounds like another of his poems to himself. '"An aged man is but a paltry thing/A tattered coat upon a stick, unless/Soul clap its hands and sing."'

His shoes vanish upwards, the bedsprings groan, the mattress sags, but not enough to crush me. '*You* sleep in the girls' bed,' he shouts, 'I'm very comfortable here.' He drops his voice and speaks more poetry to himself: '"And therefore I have sailed the seas and come/To the holy city of Byzantium."'

Footsteps pad along the passage; her bare feet appear in the door. 'The *lounge*, I said, Geoffrey.'

'We don't always mean what we say, church mouse.' The bed-room light goes out, he gives a theatrical sigh, the mattress rises, yielding him up. '"Consume my heart away; sick with desire/And fastened to a dying animal/It knows not what it is".' His shod feet follow her stockings across the hall and into the lounge room.

The stage is still narrow – squared off by two doorways – but deeper; he is in full view as he folds his tall frame down onto the sofa on the far side of the lounge. For a moment his dark eyes seem to be looking straight back at me across that room and the intervening hall. Am I sprung? I worm my snake-body further back beneath the bed, but the bedroom is in darkness and soon enough he looks away.

Miss Peach leans into the frame with a cup and saucer, then out again. 'You mustn't rush me, Geoffrey. You know I want to be, well . . . *with* you.'

'Mixed messages, blithe spirit. You invite me down for the weekend, then drag your protégé everywhere with you like some boy-scout honour guard.'

She laughs uncertainly; I bristle.

'Do you think you're being fair to him?' he asks.

'Fair to him? What do you mean?'

'I mean, you might have given the boy genius a little too much encouragement.'

'He's my student, Geoffrey. Unlike some, I don't take advantage of my students.'

'My mistake. Of course. You only take advantage of your teachers.'

Her hand appears in frame with a jug. 'That's not how I remember it. Milk?'

'Please. So you do remember that night?'

'Say when.'

'When. I was beginning to think you'd completely forgotten.'

Silence. He stares for some moments in the direction from which the milk jug has appeared, then she steps out of the wings, kneels before him and rests her head in his lap.

'How could I forget? I came *here* to try. You know that.' She lifts her face to his. 'Not one of my brightest ideas.'

They gaze at each other for a long moment, then he bends and kisses her slowly, lovingly, on the mouth. A strange mix of jealousy and sexual stirring beneath the bed; I want him to stop, and not to stop.

'Don't stop now,' he tells her as she pulls free and rests her head on his knees again.

'Poor Robbie,' she says. 'I treated him badly last night. Do you think I hurt his feelings?'

A disdainful laugh. 'Oh, I wouldn't be too concerned about him. He's got enough on his hands. Or perhaps in them.'

'What do you mean?'

'Don't play the *ingénue* with me, mouse. What do you think

the boys get up to each night after spending the day in your classroom?'

'More tea?' she says, rising abruptly and moving out of frame.

He grimaces. 'If I must. But pull the blinds if you're planning to tease me again. Your protégé is probably sitting out there in his tree-house, playing with himself.'

My heart skips a beat. The professor knows about my crow's nest?

'That's a coarse thing to say, Geoffrey.'

'That's a *true* thing to say.'

'He has a crush on me. What's the harm in that?'

'We all have a crush on you, country mouse. Who could blame us?' A small bitter laugh. 'The face that launched a billion spermatozoa. The harm is, I don't think you do anything to deter him.'

'He's one of the few people I like down here. One of the few people with any curiosity. Any . . . spark.'

'A fourteen-year-old boy? You're in more trouble in the back-woods than I thought.' He reaches out of frame, brings back the teacup and tries to sip from it. His hand is trembling again, tea sloshes into the saucer. He lowers it to the floor with difficulty. 'I really could use a drink. Just one. To settle me down.'

Here is Miss Peach again, standing behind him, massaging his shoulders as if to calm him. 'He's a special boy, Geoffrey. You've read his stories.'

'He has talent, I'll grant him that. Just be careful. Don't give too much of yourself. I've known kids like that. Blaze early, burnt out by twenty. Break your heart. End up as accountants. Doctors.'

'Country schoolteachers?' she says, bending over him.

He leans his head back, looking straight up at her. 'You *know* I wanted you in the doctoral program. I got down on my knees and begged you to enrol.'

'You pretended to beg. I think you were secretly relieved.'

'I was heartbroken.'

'Some other body part, more like it.'

Her language surprises me, and perhaps even the professor, who gives a snort of amusement. 'Margaret was relieved.'

'Then you know why I couldn't stay in the city,' she says, and wrenches herself abruptly out of my view again, offstage.

He sits forward on the lounge, staring after her, angry for the first time himself. 'You still insist on blaming me for ending up in this fucking *anus mundi*?'

'I blame no one but myself! I blame myself entirely. I was too weak! I had to get away from you.' She appears again in the frame of my small stage, walking rapidly, disappears, reappears. 'Otherwise I don't know what would have happened.'

'Can you stop all that pacing about? You're making me giddy.'

'The booze has made you giddy! You know what I think? Merv was right. When *are* you going to stop playing your little games with me?'

He is on his feet also, shouting into the wings. 'What business is it of his? And *who's* playing games? You say you moved to this shithole to get away from me, but you're back in the city every weekend, giving me come-hither looks. What's *that* about, Miss Virtue? Let alone this? Inviting me down for the weekend.'

'I invited you for *one* night. To give a lecture.'

'And that's all? Bullshit, Pam! Absolute bullshit!' I watch astonished; I hadn't thought this sarcastic, world-weary man capable of such passion. 'Yes, I can't let you go! And yes, of *course* I was going to visit. I'm honest about what I want. Can you say the same? Be honest with yourself, even if you can't be honest with me.'

A sudden pounding on the front door; a hiss from Miss Peach. 'Who the hell could that be?'

'The boy wonder,' the professor scoffs. 'The great white hope of Australian literature come down from his tree. Who else?'

A moment of absurd, giddy possibility: *is* it me at the door? But no – I am here, under the bed. The gruff, muffled voice from outside is unmistakeable: 'Everything all right in there, Pam?'

'*Mea culpa*,' from the professor. 'Your other admirer. Does he usually call at this late hour?'

'He lives next door,' she says, and pads out into the hall. The front door clicks open, Big Merv's voice is clearer now. 'I heard . . . a disturbance. And with the girls away. You on your own. I thought . . .'

'I'm fine, Merv.'

'You sure?' A pair of carpet-slippers steps into frame, striped pyjama pants, the hem of a dressing-gown. 'You sure?'

'I'm fine, Merv. Everything's fine. But thanks for your concern.'

'I'm fine too, Merv,' the professor says, looking out of the lounge with a mocking smile.

'I did hear raised voices . . .'

'I suppose that would depend on how close your ear was to the door,' the professor says.

The slippers take a lurching step into the lounge. 'You've got a smart mouth, sport! I warned you about it last night, I won't warn you again. If you can't keep it shut I'm more than happy to shut it for you.'

'A threat! How quaint! But how true to type.'

'And what type would that be, big-mouth?'

'Plenty of synonyms in the thesaurus, if not enough to do pig-stupidity justice.'

'Merv! Geoffrey! Please!'

But the man in the dressing-gown is standing over the seated man now, fists clenched. 'On your feet, sport! Outside! Now!'

The professor isn't budging. 'Oh, go pick on someone your own mental age.'

'*You* talk about age? You're twice hers! *And* you're a married man!'

'Aren't we all, my friend? Aren't we all?'

'I'm no friend of yours, you ponce! And you're no friend of hers. What's a married man doing in her house at this hour?'

'My question exactly,' the professor says. 'What *are* you doing here? And wearing your best pyjamas as well.' He gives a small, harsh laugh. 'She tells me you're always sniffing around for a fuck.'

Merv looks to Miss Peach, stunned. 'Is that what you think of me, Pam?'

'Of course not! Geoffrey – that's not what I said at all!'

'It's what you meant, blithe spirit. Haven't you got a home to go to, *sport*? A sandpit to play in? Isn't it past your bedtime?'

Big Merv reaches both hands down and yanks the older man to his feet by the shirtfront. Buttons pop; one comes spinning my way, across the hall and under the bed. I flick it out again before someone comes looking for it. Miss Peach steps forward and grabs Merv's arm. 'Merv!'

He looks at her, his face filled with fury, then shoves the professor back down onto the sofa. 'I wouldn't waste a punch on you, you . . . you fucking *pisspot*!'

The professor smoothes his runched shirt and stares back calmly. 'Neither fucking nor pissed at the moment, unfortunately. Not for want of trying both.' He gives his dark laugh. 'But the situation is not unsalvageable either way.' And he rises again, pushes past the other man, heads down the hall in the direction of the kitchen.

Miss Peach turns on her neighbour. 'How could you, Merv?'

His fists have loosened, his hands fallen to his side, his tone is

contrite. 'I'm sorry. I was worried about you. I never intended . . .
well, to make a scene.'

'Just go. Please.'

He steps out into the hall, no more than a pair of slippers and
pyjama trousers again. 'If you need me. If there's ever —'

'Anything you can do? Anything at *all*.' She groans, exasperated.
'It's a stuck record, Merv. Just *go*.' And she follows him out onto
the front porch and screams the words for the whole world to hear:
'And don't worry. My virtue is intact.'

The door closes, her bare feet reappear; she stands in frame for a
moment, breathing heavily. From the kitchen the suck of the fridge
door opening, the soft thud of its closing, a clink of glass.

'Geoffrey – you *promised*!'

Silence.

'You're going to use this as an excuse?'

'I've got a much better excuse,' he says.

'Let me guess. Unrequited love?'

'You got it in one.'

'Men!' she mutters to herself. 'Talk about stuck records.'

Her bare feet are moving restlessly now, treading the spot,
rocking back and forth. 'Shit!' she hisses, then again with each
step. 'Shit! Shit!'

Finally she halts, takes a deep breath and raises her voice. 'Lips
that touch wine!'

A mocking laugh from the kitchen. 'It *is* the fucking Women's
Temperance Union.'

'No, it's not.' A pause, then, 'It's an offer.'

She turns and pads my way, into the bedroom. I hear the strike
of a match, feel, within seconds, the faint tickle of acrid fumes
in my nose. Flickering yellow shadows begin to play here and
there on the skirting-boards. Her ski pants hit the floor, then her

polo-neck jumper. Her feet disappear, the springs creak, the object that next hits the floor looks more like a bikini top than a bra and is a strange colour – black.

I lie there frozen-breathed; Miss Peach is naked only a few inches above me.

The brown brogues are standing in the doorway now, a dandled flagon of wine also in view. 'A *new* game! Prick-tease by candlelight?'

'Only one way to find out.'

For a long time he doesn't move. When he speaks again his tone is far more tender. 'I wish I were in your class, Miss Peach.'

'I have more than enough troublemakers already, Master Barry. Come here.'

Still he doesn't move. 'Can I just stand and look at you first? I mean, *all* of you?'

Movement above me, the quilt slides off the bed and joins her clothes on the floor.

'Thank you,' he says, his voice hoarse. 'Thank you so much.' Silence, then he adds in a whisper, '"She is foremost of those that I would hear praised."'

More silence; still he stands there. Her voice, softly: 'You're making me feel shy, Geoffrey.'

'You're making *me* feel shy.'

'You'd better come here before I change my mind.'

He steps closer, turns and sits on the edge of the bed, his heels a few inches from my nose.

'You won't be needing those,' she says, and her hands appear and deposit the flagon of wine and a half-full glass on the polished floorboards. His feet vanish upwards, the bedsprings press down further against me; I am forced to roll onto my back. An even more pressing problem: the fluff and dust stirred by all this movement.

I try not to think about it lest the fear of sneezing become the thing itself.

Her soft murmur: 'Your hands are trembling.'

His snorted laugh: 'The demon drink.'

More silence, apart from the seismic shifting of the mattress above me.

Her throaty voice again: 'I'll unlace these.'

One brown brogue thuds onto the floor, followed shortly by the other.

'I do love you, Geoffrey.'

'Then why did you run away to the bush?'

'That's why I ran away.'

More slow shiftings of the mattress-continent, more of his clothes hitting the floor, a soft snowfall of garments and under-garments on both sides of me.

'I love you, Geoffrey,' she repeats.

'It's a question?'

'I suppose it is. In a way.'

'And what's the correct answer, Miss? This?'

'Oh, yes, *that*. Your hand feels like silk.'

'Last time I touched you there you asked me to stop.'

She gives a small, muffled gasp, then whispers, 'I didn't *want* you to stop.'

'I don't think you know what you want.'

His words might be aimed at me. That same quandary: part of me wants him to stop, another part wants him to keep going. Another part wants him to drop dead. The strange noises she is making – hoarse whimpers now – electrify me, arouse me, *terrify* me. These are the noises of a language previously unheard, even through my parents' bedroom door – but known all the same, and known deeply. My cock is as stiff as it has ever been, my heart pounds mightily. She gasps again, then groans loudly. What's going on up there? She seems in pain, but oddly wants the pain to continue. Is he hurting her? Should I roll out from under the bed and put a stop to it?

Another hoarse gasp. 'I think I'm – ready.'

'You're more than ready, mouse. You're in flood.'

More slow, geological shifting of the bed-mass. I am still puzzling his last odd words when he speaks again, more impatiently. 'Well, at least one of us is ready.'

Silence again, the bed motionless. 'Take it in your hand,' he says. 'Play with it for a while.'

'Perhaps it's the wine, Geoffrey.'

Disdain in his voice: 'It's not usually such a shy little thing.'

Her tone is soothing, gentle. 'We're both a little shy with each other. We've wanted this for so long – perhaps wanted it too much.'

His harshness is back. 'Bullshit. I *never* have this trouble.'

'Don't worry about it, darling. Give it time. I love you. Let's just lie here together. Hold each other.'

Silence. Time passes. I shift position on the hard floor, stealthily. Have they fallen asleep? If so, can I safely sneak out? Perhaps if they drink more first.

A whisper from Miss Peach: 'You've never had this trouble with Margaret?'

'I've never had this trouble with anyone!'

The silence shorter this time, but somehow deeper – the kind my mother would say you could cut with a knife. My loud breathing is less cutting than sawing at it, but the more I try not to breathe, the more deafening it sounds in my ears.

'Who else has there *been*?' Miss Peach finally asks in a very small voice.

'Does it matter?'

'It shouldn't.' Pause. 'But it seems it does.'

Irritation in his voice. 'You want names, dates, places?'

More silence, apart from my loud, rasping breaths.

Her whisper is barely more audible than a breath itself. 'You do love me, don't you?'

A snort. 'It's worse than love, blithe spirit. More serious than love. Glue might be a better word for it. No, tar. I seem to be stuck to you, my little tar-baby. Stuck on you.'

'Perhaps you were relying on me to say no,' she says eventually. 'Perhaps you can't be unfaithful after all. Your body can't be unfaithful.'

Another snorted laugh. 'Could you light me a cigarette, Dr Freud?'

Some shifting of springs; I sense her leaning out to the candle, hear the sucking, smell the tobacco smoke.

'The first time I've smoked after foreplay,' he mutters.

My breathing hacksaws away at the silence again. I could have made a breadboard by now.

'I know it's not the first time you've been unfaithful, Geoffrey. But I'd like to believe it's the first time you've been deeply unfaithful. Unfaithful with your heart, I mean. Not just with your . . .' Her words trail off.

'Cock?' he finishes the thought. Another sour laugh. 'I want to be unfaithful with my cock most of all!'

'Perhaps it's for the best.'

'Don't be ridiculous, mouse.'

'It's a reminder. Of your – our – situation.'

He laughs wearily. 'What does Stevenson call marriage? A friendship recognised by the police.'

'Your cock seems to recognise it.'

'So you can say the word!'

'It wasn't meant to happen, Geoffrey. Not tonight.'

'We'll try again in a minute. I'll be fine. I just need the right . . . arousal.'

'Let's talk about something else,' she cuts him short.

'What else? I've wanted this – you – for years. Ever since that first morning you walked into English 1. And you want to talk about, what? The weather?'

'You haven't said anything about my poems. It took a lot of courage for me to show them to you, Geoffrey. I was terrified.'

Silence.

'Well?' she prompts.

'They're promising. They show a lot of, um, promise. You have an ashtray?'

'The side table. Which did you like best?'

'I'll need to have another look. A closer reading. Line by line. Do we really have to talk about this now?'

'Did you read them at all?'

'Of course I read them. Might I help myself to another of your smokes?'

The scratch of a match. As he puffs away above I breathe more easily beneath. Terror has become thrill, and thrill is now becoming curiosity.

'If you must know,' he says, 'I liked them. I liked them a lot. Beautiful calligraphy, by the way. And such beautiful floral paper.'

'What did you like?'

'Many things. The use of metaphor. The deft touches here and there.'

'Such as?'

'Is this the time and place for a seminar? We're in bed together for the first time —'

'Did you like the one about the hawk?' she interrupts.

'The hawk?' He sounds vague. 'Oh, yes. The hawk. Look, in all your poems I think you use language intelligently. You avoid cliché.'

A sudden upwards shift of the mattress. 'I didn't *write* a poem about a hawk! You haven't even looked at them, you bastard!'

'Of course I *looked* at them. I just need more time with them.'

'Bullshit.' Her tiny bare feet are dangling in my face now; she is sitting on the edge of the bed.

'We'll go through them together. Tomorrow. Line by line. Now come back here.'

A standoff for several long moments.

'Please?' he whispers, and her feet vanish again. Muffled wet sounds, presumably kissing.

The professor: 'I do believe I'm starting to feel, ah, interested again. Here – take me in your mouth.'

'My *mouth*? I don't know that I'd like that.'

'You *have* led a sheltered life, country mouse. You'll get to like it soon enough.' He gives a small chuckle. 'It's an acquired taste.'

'Did Margaret acquire it?'

'I don't want to talk about Margaret!' he snaps. More silence. Then: 'I'm sorry. I was being selfish. What if I gave you pleasure, but didn't take any myself? Then I wouldn't be unfaithful.'

'A rather technical distinction.'

'I'll put it less technically. Let me make love to you with *my* mouth.'

'That's not how I want our first time to be, Geoffrey. I want it to be . . . perfect. No, not perfect – equal. For now I just want you to hold me. I want to lie here in your arms. And feel . . . safe.'

Quiet descends once more.

'This wasn't a good idea,' she says. 'I don't know what came over me. It was too soon.'

'We could pretend,' he says.

Miss Peach asks the question I want to ask: 'What do you mean?'

'Make the appropriate noises. Think of the ears at the door. The eyes at the keyhole.' He raises his voice a little. 'Robbie Burns! Come out wherever you are! Home free! I know you're hiding somewhere!'

I freeze, but he is laughing again, and even Miss Peach gives a giggle, her first for some time. A shadowy hand reaches down into view, it seems to be one of hers. The wineglass is lifted up first, then the flagon; shortly the flagon is returned to the floor.

'I feel a little guilty,' she says. 'His parents are away this weekend. I think he was hoping to see more of me.'

'Not this much of you, I hope.'

'Stop it. That tickles.'

Her dainty hand reappears, reaching again for the flagon.

'You should go easy on that,' he murmurs. 'You're not used to it.'

'Let's just say it's one taste I am acquiring fast.'

'Lips that touch wine,' he reminds her jokily.

She giggles again, then speaks more seriously. 'You treated him badly – but you can help him. We can help him. We can get him out of this dump.'

'What is he, an orphan? His father is the town *cop*, mouse.'

'Which is part of the reason he's always in trouble. He's a fish out of water. He's bored here. And he's just going to get more bored.'

News to me beneath the bed. I have never felt less bored.

'You're the one who's bored,' he suggests.

'He needs to escape, Geoffrey. Get to the city.'

'What's he going to do in the city? He's fourteen years old, for Christ's sake. Where's he going to live?'

Her hand reaches down for the third time; this time the flagon is not returned.

'With us,' she says eventually, and my sharp intake of breath echoes deafeningly. I hold that breath, alarmed. Have I revealed myself?

The professor's mocking laugh is his harshest yet. 'Is that what this weekend is all about? Make-believe families? You be the mummy, I can be the daddy. We can have a child together – and we don't even have to, dare I say the word, *fuck*!'

'You can be very cruel,' she whispers hoarsely.

'You really should go easy on that paint-stripper, Pamela.'

'I'll drink what I bloody well want, thank you very much. Of course we would have our own baby. One day.'

His tone is contemptuous. 'You're planning that far ahead? Wedding bells, bridesmaids? The whole middle-class catastrophe. What else do you want before we fuck – an engagement ring?'

'What do *you* need before we fuck? Monkey glands?'

'Oh, *touché*. *Touché*. Now I'll never get it up. Might as well get smashed after all.'

'You promised, Geoffrey!'

'I'm doing it for you, blithe spirit. Every mouthful I take is one less for you. You really need to slow down.'

'What's this?' she says. 'The pisspot calling the kettle black?'

'Oh, bravo! Very good indeed. Maybe there's a half-decent poem in you after all. But you might as well toss out the rest. You'd be better off writing science fiction with your precious protégé.'

'Is that what you really think?'

'It takes a lifetime to learn to write poetry. It's a passion, an obsession – it takes every waking moment. It's not a hobby! You don't light up a candle in a fucking chianti bottle and take out some fine lady notepaper and scribble the first thing that comes into your head.'

'But you *encouraged* me.' Her voice choking with tears. 'You said it was something we could share.'

'I must have had other things on my mind.'

She is sobbing now. 'Like what? A naked body? Is *this* all I am to you?'

An earthquake in the bed-mass above me. 'You really want to know what you are to me? You're a fucking prick-teaser! And I've let you tease mine for four fucking years. Sitting in the front row of my lectures mooning at me. Simpering over my poems. But inviting me down here for . . . for what? A lost weekend? That takes the cake! Christ! No wonder I can't get it up.'

His bare feet thump down against the floorboards. The light flicks on, he stoops to gather his clothes from the floor. He is bent low enough to see me, his face inches from mine, but his mind is elsewhere. 'I don't suppose *other* men have this problem with you!' he shouts.

The most intense silence yet. His words might have left a vacuum in their wake, sucking all air from the room.

Her own voice is tiny, racked with sobs. 'How many men do you think I've had?'

He is jumping around on one foot, pulling his trousers on, still shouting. 'I've no bloody idea! But there seems to be a queue! Your suitors must think they can get somewhere, Penelope.' He wrestles furiously with his upper clothes. 'Those two fugitives from the island of Lesbos you live with – what do the three of you get up to at night?'

Her small, shocked voice is getting even smaller. 'How can you say such things?'

'Not to mention the drooling neighbour! And the surgeon-barber who doubles as the village idiot! Charles Bovary, eat your heart out!' He gives his angriest, most explosive snort and shouts on. 'Last but not least, Robbie Burns! Novelist manqué! The Jules Verne of the south! Speaking of whom, he must be around here somewhere. Robbie! Come out from under the bed! Home free!'

I screw my eyes shut, absurdly, automatically. Ostrich magic: if I can't see him he can't see me. I can still hear her sobbing in the darkness.

'I didn't mean what I said, Geoffrey.'

I risk a peep; he is hopping about on one leg in the hall, suitcase in one hand, trying to pull a shoe on with the other.

'Don't go, Geoffrey. Please. It's nothing —'

'Too late for crocodile tears,' he says, and vanishes stage right. The front door opens, slams shut. The noise above me is more muffled now – a face buried in pillows? – but no less wrenching; the mattress convulses with each sob. What to do? I feel a great urge to take her in my arms, console her, soothe her.

The flagon is lifted out of view again; I listen to the dull rising melody of a glass filling with liquid. Her sobs interrupted now by gulping, by more glass-filling music, more sobs, more gulping. Then the bedsprings release her weight, her bare feet pad to the window, I hear her move the blind, her feet pad back to bed. Another drink, and then at last the mattress above me is still, her irregular sobs easing into the rhythmic breathing of sleep.

I give her shoe a firm push, send it skittering a few inches across the floor. No disturbance in her breathing pattern. I give the mattress above me a slight upward jolt with my knees. Still no change.

I worm my way out and crawl on all fours towards the door. I'm not about to look back: the ostrich magic is still working. Having reached the hall, I carefully re-erect myself to full ostrich height, strut by bony cross-strut, and tiptoe to safety.

And yet.

At the back door I halt. I'm home free, the professor is long gone, Miss Peach comatose. But she is also – the thought keeps tugging at me – naked. She is far more to me than a naked body – I despise the professor for his cruel words – but what harm in taking a last look? I retrace my steps stealthily and peek around her bedroom door. She is lying on her side, facing away from me, her body shadowy and indistinct in the candlelight. I take a step into the room, a second step – then freeze as she rolls over to face me. Her eyes flutter open, close; I breathe again. No ostrich magic in reverse: she might not have seen me, but I can see her. For a long time I am unable to see anything *but* her, sprawled across the mattress, small graceful limbs akimbo, hair for once dishevelled. All thought of escape is forgotten as I gaze down at her, study her, swot her. Swot *it*: a naked woman's body, motionless apart from the slow rise and fall of its breathing.

For some time I'm a thing myself, a statue, also motionless apart from my carefully husbanded breathing. Yet more alive inside the marble than I have ever been, awash with feelings so turbulent they have their own rustling life, like parasites of some kind. I feel as if I am being eaten inside out by eels, a seething, squirming mass of eels.

How long do I stand there, restlessly still? Why stand when I can kneel? I reach for 'a fucking chianti bottle', sink to my knees and begin inspecting that spreadeagled body by candlelight, inch by inch, mesmerised by things never imagined before, let alone seen. My dreams of her naked – of it naked – might as well have had her fully clothed, so vague and lacking in detail, so made up, do they now seem. One unimagined detail: body heat. Her cheeks are flushed; I can feel their glow against my own cheeks from a foot away. Sweat is another: her skin glistens in the candlelight as if varnished. But the night is cold: might she be ill? I lean closer, into the shallow give-and-take of her breathing. A hot, stale-wine smell. Uncle Possum breath, but sweeter, if only because it is hers.

I inch the candle downwards. I have no sister; my mother primly guards her whale-body from my gaze. The brassières I occasionally glimpse in magazine ads, or the complicated mechanical constructions hung up to dry on washing day offer no proper clue as to what they hide. Her breasts are barely large enough to be dragged off centre by gravity but their nipples are startlingly large and pink. I stare, they stare back. My eels thrash more dangerously, but they are the eels of forbidden high jinks, of heart-in-mouth outlaw excitement, not outlaw sex.

It's all too strange for sex.

Strangest of all is something else my mind's eye has never brought into even cloudy focus: the bird's nest of dark pubic hair between her spread thighs. And within that nest – what? The pink, gaping mouth of some alien fledgling? What had I imagined? That the silk-stocking smoothness of her thighs went all the way up and across? Not this origami infolding of pink skin, certainly. I might be looking at the sexual organs of a Martian, something dragged from the wreckage of a flying saucer.

A plop of hot wax onto her thigh; I hold my breath as she whimpers in her sleep and shifts position. Her head lolls away from me, exposing the full nape of her neck. She might be offering it up for a bite; I lean closer and plant the softest of kisses instead.

She sleeps on drunkenly, unrouseable, but the kiss wakes me from my trance. Rain is pelting the roof now, sealing me in, sealing the rest of the world out. No one is about to knock on the door, I have nowhere else I need to be. I can do anything I want for as long as I like. Small beer first. Small wine: I reach down for her glass and drain the dregs. I feel recklessly free, safe; nothing will wake her. I lean forward and blow a soft raspberry on her tummy, then laugh out loud at my daring. Idea for a story: the prince wakes his sleeping beauty from her hundred-year sleep with a big, blurty raspberry. I find the flagon once more and drink straight from the mouth. The slow-spreading warmth of wine through my insides reminds me how cold I am on the outside. The naked Miss Peach surely more so. I set down the candle on the bedside table, retrieve the quilt from the floor and spread it gently over her. Still she snores, softly. I kick off my shoes and ease myself fully clothed beneath the quilt, facing her now, but keeping just out of touch.

Her winy breath puffs into my face, her lashes flutter and quiver as she dreams. Of what? Me? I dream of her nightly. A giddy, half-drunken thought: am I dreaming of her now? How could I be sharing her bed otherwise? Unless – another giddy thought – I have travelled even further into the future. Am I still fourteen? Still a schoolboy? Still – giddiest thought of all – unmarried? Was it the rest of the day that was a dream? A tender calm steals over me as I lie warm and snug next to my wife's sleeping body. Is this what stories mean by happy ever after? Is this the aftermath, the end that is the beginning of the best bit? My eyes slide shut. I have never felt less restless, less fidgety.

It's the future, and all is well.

6

By the year 2064 everyone can live for ever. The catch? It turns out that the secret of eternal life is the source of life itself: human ovaries, human testes. Their elixir must be extracted at adolescence, before any of the life force has been spent.

Small price to pay? So it seems at first. But once the last ovary has been juiced, the last ball crushed, no more children can be born into the brave new world of ever-after. Robot surrogates are available. Animated dolls of various shapes and sizes, infant or adolescent, cuddly or cute, charmingly precocious or seen-but-not-heard at the flick of a switch. And while they might not live for ever – what machine does? – they never grow up.

Years pass, centuries pass, the mills of time grind on. Death might have no dominion, but time and gravity wreak their usual havoc on human bodies: all too soon the Eternal Ones are a race of wrinkled, sagging, hairless methuselahs.

Living death? Ashamed of their disgusting physical envelopes, people become more reclusive, more solitary. Marriages break apart; how is marriage possible to a walking corpse? How is sex possible? Or even – after taking a look at the first person you ever had sex with in the mirror – masturbation? Robot surrogates meet these needs also, in the form of Pleasure Units that can expertly stimulate excitement in even the most withered organs.

It's now the year 2164 and all the mirrors have long been smashed. The human population, increasingly frail, has taken to bed, and the streets are filled with flawless humanoids, modelled on the most beautiful human beings of the past. Replicants of Sophia Loren and Audrey Hepburn and Gregory Peck are by far the most popular.

The real thought experiment begins here. Do robot slaves have souls? What are their rights? Can they fall in love? A much-told story in the hands of others, a personal milestone as I discover the bleeding obvious for myself.

7

'Geoffrey?' Her voice is a blurred mumble, less treacle-thick now than stumbling over its own thick tongue. 'You came back.'

She throws an arm over me and nuzzles her face into the nape of my neck. 'I was *so* unhappy,' she whispers, then immediately falls back to sleep.

Nerves jangling, I lie statue-still again. A statue of the professor? A close enough copy, perhaps. The right length. Lacking breadth and depth, but sufficiently dark and handsome if she keeps her eyes closed. I close my own eyes, then reopen them. No chance of sleep with her naked body snuggled against my back. All calm has gone; my thoughts are racing. Possibly my cock has been stiff all along – a statue's marbled cock – but only now do the waves of pleasure washing through my body begin to concentrate there, magnified in that lens of hard flesh.

Once noticed, that pressure becomes increasingly unbearable. Her face is buried in my neck, her breath caresses my skin, I can feel the rise and fall of her breasts against my back. All sense of self disappears into the heavenly warmth of her, the heaven of her. My tight trousers squeeze my cock like a firm hand; almost immediately comes the pulsing gush of orgasm.

Surely she notices this? A statue again, a spent Pleasure Unit, I hold my breath, but still she sleeps. Her breathing is deep and slow; I find its rhythm soothing, hypnotic, and soon enough my eyes slide shut again.

I wake as I have never woken before – into the kiss of an open mouth. A body sits on top of me, straddling me; for a moment, still half asleep, I think it must be Billy's.

'I love you,' it whispers. 'I love you, Geoffrey.'

That name again, but this time no more off-putting than the sour breath that comes from her mouth as two urgent hands fumble at my trouser belt, fumble to liberate the hardness within. That hardness seems to slip into the grip of a different sort of hand, a hot wet fist. Has she spilled something down there? Who cares as the mouth that is bent forward kissing mine moans that name again – 'Geoffrey' – and one arm grips my neck and another my thigh, and I realise, in a kind of slow-motion ecstasy, that it isn't a fist down there at all.

I am rooting Miss Peach. No: she, straddling me, is *rooting* me.

She gives a sudden whimper, as if in pain, and whispers his name again, our name, perhaps, his and mine, or even mostly mine now, as she begins to move up and down above me, still whimpering. The pressure builds in me more slowly this second time, and more agonisingly, as if that wet fist is reaching into the depths of me, trying to drag something to the surface, or even everything, trying to rip my guts out, every shred and nerve.

Her body shudders, tossed about in some inner storm. Who is this? Someone possessed? Then she seems to be in the eye of her storm, stilled, and is staring straight down, wide-eyed, but – most disconcerting of all – I have no idea at whom, or what. No 'Geoffrey' this time, just a final sad, painful moan and her eyes roll up, all whites, and she sinks over me and releases a gush of air that sounds like it must be her last.

I am gutted, and gutted again, the sweet stuff dragged out of me by hooks – cruel, beautiful hooks.

She rolls away onto her back. On cue the candle flickers, goes out. Pitch-dark now, but what did she see in the half-darkness before? Me? Him? She lies statue-still herself now, as if asleep. Too still? She recognised me, surely, at the end, even if she didn't speak my name. I pretend to sleep myself, not wanting to find out if I am wrong. I want to tell her that I love her, that I will always love her, but there is too much to think, let alone say. And too much, even in the enveloping blackness, to notice. The glow of her close-by body, the wrung-out afterglow of mine. The scent-stew of stale

Kool tobacco, stale wine, sweat and perfume, and – is it? – trimethylamine that envelopes us.

Her breathing eases; definitely asleep now. I lie astonished and
exhilarated. For how long? An hour? Two? Who cares – I want to
be nowhere else. Is there anywhere else? The rain starts up on the
roof again; I close my eyes and wish the rains would flood down for
forty nights. And if the house breaks free of its moorings and floats
away, no matter. We have everything we need. Cans of baked beans.
Flagons of red wine. A giraffe-sized bed. Each other. Plus – a more
pressing need as the hours pass – a toilet bowl. I ease carefully out
of bed with a bursting bladder only to trip over my own trousers,
still shackled about my ankles.

I clatter into the door; still she doesn't stir. Heart pounding, I
tug up my trousers, wriggle my toes into unseen desert boots, and
grope my way out of the room.

I sit to piss, less risk of seat-clatter that way. I aim the stream
quietly against the side of the bowl, then curse myself when I've
finished: to flush or not? I should have sneaked outside and used
the garden.

I gently lower the lid and tiptoe towards the back door,
feeling my way by dimly filtered moonlight.

'Geoffrey?'

Her voice is a hoarse whisper but alarmingly close. The light
comes on, blindingly; she is standing no more than a few feet
away, hand on switch, wrapped in a loose dressing-gown, her hair
a magpie's nest.

'Robbie!' Her cheeks are stained with tears and mascara, her
eyes screwed tight against the light. 'What on earth are *you* doing
here?'

Her puzzlement seems genuine. Her body gives a small
heave, like a hiccup; she claps a hand over her mouth, pushes past

me into the toilet and falls to her knees, retching.

My glance slides to the escape-hatch of the back door, but what point in leaving now?

A flush of the cistern; she returns to the kitchen, bends into the sink and splashes water on her face.

'I asked you a question,' she says, wiping her face on a tea-towel. 'What are you doing in my house at four in the morning?'

I lick my dry lips, speechless.

'And where's Geoffrey?'

At last I find my tongue; it has been in my dry mouth all along. 'He's not here.'

Her gaze wanders past me, as if not quite able to see me or acknowledge my presence. 'Geoffrey?' she calls down the hall. 'Geoffrey?'

'He left.'

'How long ago?'

Much seems to depend on my answer. 'I'm not exactly sure.'

A glaze over her eyes; is she still half drunk or half asleep? She moves back to the kitchen tap like a zombie and fills a glass with water.

'How did you get in?'

'The back door was open.'

She takes a mouthful of the water, gasps involuntarily at its coldness. 'You didn't *knock*?'

'There was no answer,' I say, which is true, or was true, a long night-time before.

She watches me, more alert now. 'So you just walked straight in?'

'I wanted to make sure you were all right. You said to keep close to you.'

'On Thursday afternoon,' she says with some force. 'Not the

small hours of Sunday morning!' There is a sudden sharpness in her gaze. 'Have you been here before?'

I keep my mouth shut, wanting neither to lie nor confess – but perhaps that silence is confession enough.

'It *was* you who broke in before!'

'When?'

'Don't play games, Robert.' She shivers, wraps her gown more tightly about her. 'Merv told me it was you and I refused to believe him. I thought . . .' She pauses, her brow knotted. 'I thought he was jealous,' she continues, and stands there open-mouthed, as if struck by the thought for the first time. 'Jealous of a fourteen-year-old boy!'

My 'Nearly fifteen, Miss,' goes unheard as she gulps, as if swallowing that thought in turn, and stares at me angrily. 'You let your *friend* take the blame, Robert!'

'I told you it wasn't him. I told everyone.'

'You didn't try very hard!' She looks away in disgust, looks back. 'Did Billy know it was you?'

'I suppose.'

'And he said nothing! Have you thought about *that*? He was prepared to take the blame. For you! That poor boy! After all he's been through – and you let all of us think it was him. I was *sure* it was him!'

'I told you,' I repeat lamely. 'And the charges were dropped.'

'You've disappointed me, Robert. I can't believe you'd do that to him.' A pause; her gaze slides away, troubled. 'And now *this* to me!'

This meaning exactly what? Perhaps she is wondering the same thing, or trying not to, as she turns her back on me, leaning over the sink.

'What do think your father will say?' she eventually asks, without turning.

'Do we have to tell him?'

'I *trusted* you,' she shouts into the sink.

And I trusted you, I want to say.

'Have you nothing to say for yourself?'

The only words that find their way into my mouth are Big Merv's. 'The professor is old enough to be your father.'

Perhaps they are easier to say to her back. Perhaps her answer comes more easily for the same reason. 'And I'm nearly old enough to be your mother.'

Her anger bewilders me; my glance moves again to the escape-hatch a few steps away. 'Shall I go?'

'No. Sit down.' She pushes away from the sink and opens the fridge. 'Your parents are away, aren't they? I'll make some cocoa.'

I reluctantly sit at the laminex table; she pours milk into a saucepan and lights the gas ring. When she speaks again her tone is gentler, but still she won't look my way. 'You need to find a girl your own age, Robbie. This . . . this thing can't go on.'

'What thing?'

'Following me around. Spying on me. Breaking into my house! Where do you think it can lead?'

More bewilderment. Hasn't it already led there?

'People will talk, Robbie. People *are* talking.' She nods in the direction of Big Merv's house.

'I couldn't care less what he thinks.'

'You don't have to live next door to him.' A faint, wan smile. 'A crush on a teacher is nothing to be ashamed of —'

'A crush! I love you! And I thought, last night —'

She cuts me short, alarmed. 'Your crush will pass. I'm sorry if you think that I might have in any way . . . well, encouraged you.' Her gaze slides away again, then returns, more determined. 'I just wanted to . . . help you. Help your talent. Surely you realise I love someone else, Robbie?'

'Then why did you want me to protect you from him?'

She stirs two teaspoons of cocoa into the heating milk, then sugar. A tear crawls down her cheek and plops into the saucepan; she doesn't seem to notice it. 'Silly boy,' she says hoarsely. 'You want to write novels but you don't understand anything! Your job was to protect *him* from *me*.'

This is as incomprehensible as anything I have heard all night. She passes me a cup, fumbles with a box of Bex on the mantelpiece, shakes one of the powders into her mouth and washes it down. 'Let me put that another way. To protect *me* from me.'

'How can you love him? He's an old man. He's —'

'You don't know much about women, do you Robbie?'

'I'm a quick learner.'

'Perhaps too quick.' She sits opposite me, staring into her cup, refusing again to meet my eye. So *does* she know? Whose face did she see through the clear eye of the storm?

'I'm nearly fifteen,' I exaggerate again. 'You're only twenty.'

A scornful laugh. 'And the rest.'

I open my mouth, she reaches over and presses her fingers against my lips. 'Don't say anything more, Robbie. Don't say anything that can't be taken back. You're a dreamer. You imagine things. You imagine you love me, and that's . . . that's very touching. But life is not a book. A story.'

I imagine nothing, I want to say. We *shagged*. No, you shagged me. I *love* you, I want to say.

'I won't tell your father this time, Robbie – but don't ever come into my house uninvited again. Not *ever*. Understand?'

'But —'

'No buts. And I can't give you any special favours at school. From now on I have to treat you like any other student. I've let myself get too close to you. Far too close. Now, finish your cocoa and go.' She rises abruptly, still without looking at me, and walks out into the hall.

'You can let yourself out,' she calls back. 'You seem to know the way.'

8

It's the year 2064 and androids can no longer be distinguished from human beings. They have looked like us – a more beautiful us – for many years. High cheekbones and firm breasts, or tallness and brooding good looks are standard accessories. Both models even come equipped with navels, as if born of mammal, not machine.

The latest models also act like humans. They blink on cue. They sweat. They talk like us, think like us, mimic our mammal emotions, but in fact they have no consciousness at all. Their actions are those of complicated acting machines, their reactions reflexes, their conversation rote, if subtle and varied rote, and mixed at times with scraps of random rote-nonsense and chitchat.

The old problem: how to tell android from human? Cut it open? Oops, sorry, I'll just put this sloppy wet stuff back. Ask it? A useless exercise: least of all can a robot tell itself from the real thing, its computer brain has no awareness of self at all. Until one saws itself open to find out, an act of suicidal free will that is also the first act of true machine consciousness.

It's 1964 and the world is in darkness. The rain has eased but the streetlights are off, the moon and stars curtained by cloud. I walk to the pepper tree blind, guessing the path of the road, splashing in and out of unseen puddles. Vague, greyish forms appear and disappear in the blackness; they might be houses, trees, cars, or perhaps just my imagination.

It feels like the end of the world. No, the beginning of the world, a new world on which only two beings have thus far been created.

Another vague, looming greyness; I grope in the black ink beneath its boughs for my bike. And find two bikes, tangled together.

'Where the hell you *been*, Robbie?'

I almost jump out of my skin. 'Jesus! You *scared* me, Billy! What're you doing up there?'

'What *you* been doing down there?'

'You were asleep. I went for a ride.'

'Pig's arse! I found your bike hours ago. I saw ya come outa *her* place.'

I glance away into the blackness. He occasionally boasts that Abos are born with night vision, but he's surely guessing tonight.

'You gonna let me take the blame again, Robbie?'

'I was never gonna let that happen. I woulda testified. In court. I told ya.'

'Bullshit!' A thump of feet on the ground nearby, his voice now at ear level. 'Where are ya, fuck ya? I can't *see* ya!'

'Then you didn't see me come outa her place!'

He ignores this. 'I can bloody smell ya. You stink!'

'*You* stink. What ya been smoking up there? Dried dog shit?'

Dog-sniffing noises, close by. 'What *is* that stink? It's like, like some sheila's perfume!'

I take a step away from the direction of the sniffing. 'None of your business,' I say, but as soon as I utter the words I want to make it his business. This is *the* milestone, the biggest of my life; I want to make it the whole world's business.

'You broke in and – what? Put on her perfume?'

I give a scornful laugh. 'I broke into her, Billy.'

'Whatcha mean, ya broke into her?'

The news can be held in no longer. 'What do you think I mean, stupid? I broke into her house and rooted her!' I might have been in school, slamming my pen down on my desk at the end of a test. First again! 'I fucking shagged her!'

Silence. Is that his face, grey and featureless, a few feet away? Is the night so black that even Billy looks pale?

'Bullshit,' he repeats hoarsely. 'You're the *biggest* bullshit artist.'

'I rooted her! I did, Billy!' I am beaming, but only I can tell. He can no more see my face than I his.

'*Who* did you root? Pig's, you did. Who?'

'You can *smell* her.'

'You nicked her perfume. What does that prove?'

'I *shagged* her, Billy.'

'Yeah, in one of your dumb stories.'

'In her *bed*. She *wanted* me to shag her. She started it.'

'Pull the other one, it's got bells on. You wouldn't know how to. You wouldn't even know how to pash.'

'Just cos I wouldn't pash you.'

'What's that supposed to mean?'

'You tried to kiss me, remember?'

'Fucking did *not*.'

'Fucking did! Last night!'

His angry face clearer now, as if rage is making him glow slightly. 'You wanted to kiss *me*, you liar!'

A porch-light blinks on across the street, a silhouette appears in an opened front doorway.

'You gonna deny it?' I say.

'You couldn't have rooted her. She wouldn't let you.'

'She was pissed!' I shout back. 'She thought I was the *professor*. At first.'

'Who would root you, Robbie? You're nothin' but a . . . a bloody *fairy*. You even stink like one.'

A fist arrives out of the darkness, and another, but landing unaimed, glancing from my arms.

'Fucking liar!' he shouts, flailing, but I stand my ground, exultant and invulnerable, and let the flurry peter out.

A gruff shout from across the road. 'What the hell's going on over there?'

The blows stop. Big Merv is standing on his lit porch, playing a torch-beam out across the road, but he can see nothing. 'That you bloody Currie kids again? Billy? Piss off home before you get into more trouble!'

At my shoulder, an angry whisper. 'I can't believe you'd root her! Why would ya?' His hand finds and grips my arm; I shake it off.

'You're the poofter!' I shout.

I throw a fist at the patch of greyness and hit his face. 'You're a fucking curly *worm*!' I scream as loudly as I've screamed anything in my life, and lash out again and miss, then hit an arm and miss again, then keep missing because there's nothing left to hit.

The torch-beam approaches jerkily across the road. 'That *your* voice, Burns? You little perve! What are you doing here at this time of night?'

'It's not me,' I say, absurdly, and untangle the pedals of my bike from Billy's and climb on. 'It's not him either!' I shout as I ride away, whatever that means.

How I navigate those pitch-black streets I've no idea. An unconscious mental map? My conscious mind is back in Miss Peach's bedroom; I can think of nothing else. The conversation in the kitchen, my poofter friend dropping out of the tree, Big Merv on the prowl – everything afterwards is easily forgotten.

I turn into Church Street and a beacon appears: a lit bedroom window, mine, two blocks distant. The world here is less vague, more visible; in no hurry now, I zigzag joyfully across the street, ride up into the blackness of the shop verandahs, jump steps and gutters, glide back onto the greyness of the road. A dark shape flits across low in front of me. Cat? Possum? I brake, straddling my bike. No, fox – the first I've seen in the town. It halts in the shadows and turns to watch me in return, perhaps the first centaur it has seen. Half-night itself already, it turns and becomes one with the blackness.

At home, another first: I lock the back door behind me. My best friendship is over, but the curly worm who was the other half of that friendship might not yet realise it.

9

Night, still, when I wake. Indistinct male voices, arguing, angrily, a closed door or two away. Or is it the after-echo of a dreamworld?

'Robbie!' A distinct voice, my mother's, in my ear. A hand, shaking me; the weight of a heavy body threatening to capsize my bed. 'Robbie! Wake up!'

'Mum? What are you doing back?'

Her tone stern: 'We were always coming back on Sunday night.'

'It's Sunday *night*?'

'Don't act the innocent with me, young man. What have you two been up to this time? Tell me!'

I am still half asleep, time-travelling. 'I must have slept all day.'

'Robbie! Pay attention. Jacko is outside with your father. He's *very* angry. What have you boys been up to?'

My heart lurches into full wakefulness. 'I dunno. You'd better ask him.'

Her face above me, as stern as her tone of voice. 'He said it wasn't for my ears. What's going on, Robbie? I want to hear it from you first.'

'We got drunk,' I say, more the first thing that pops out of my mouth than into my mind.

'Did that Billy Currie bring alcohol into our house?'

A small admission now might lend credence to any larger, later denials. 'I made some.'

'You *made* some?'

'Distilled some. In the shed.'

'Your father locked the shed.'

'I climbed in through the window.'

'Your father specifically *said*. Is this how you repay our trust?'

'I got bored.' If Miss Peach could use the word to defend me, why not borrow it myself?

'Is that all you have to say? You got bored?'

'I was here on my own.'

'You weren't on your own. That's the point. Was making the, the moonshine your idea or your friend Billy's?'

'He's not my friend, Mum. Not any more.'

'And what's that supposed to mean?'

Another pre-emptive strike. 'He started . . . well, doing *things*. Acting stupid.'

'You're acting stupid. Stop making excuses.'

'Mum! He tried to kiss me!'

Her triple chins wobble, startled. 'I beg yours?'

'He tried to bloody *kiss* me!'

'Language, Robbie,' she warns, but more quietly now. 'What's the harm in that?' she eventually asks, or suggests. 'Perhaps it was just a joke. Horsing around.'

'On the *mouth*? He wanted to *pash* me, Mum. Like a girl!'

'People do funny things when they've been drinking. Out-of-character things.'

'He wanted to touch my penis! He cried when I shoved him off!'

This silences her for a long moment. 'Has anything like this ever happened before?'

'Course not!' I say indignantly. 'That's when I jumped on my bike and cleared off. I couldn't stay here.'

'You should have asked *him* to leave.'

'I thought he was going to hit me, Mum. He was as mad as a cut snake.'

Her lips purse, her brow knots as if trying to squeeze some kind of juice from the halves of her brain. 'I always knew there was something about that boy. I *told* your father . . .'

'Robbie!' His angry voice in the hall, on cue. 'Kitchen! Now!'

'Just tell him the truth, Robbie,' she says more calmly. 'There's nothing to worry about if you tell the truth.' She hands me my dressing-gown and pushes me gently ahead of her out the door. 'Don't jump to conclusions,' she tells my father. 'That Billy Currie would say anything to keep out of trouble.'

'Two of a kind,' he snaps. 'Don't know which one is worse.'

'Am I under arrest?' I joke half-heartedly.

'Don't be a smart mouth, sonny-jim. Jacko's made some serious accusations. You'd better have some serious answers.'

We sit facing each other across the big kitchen table; my mother sits at the end. 'Anything you might want to get off your chest first?' he says. 'Your side of the story?'

'Tell him, Robbie. Just like I said. Tell the truth.'

'Stay out of it, Mother. This is your chance, son. But it's your only chance. You'd better tell me everything.'

'We got drunk,' I begin.

'You'll have to do better than that.'

'Billy went completely bonkers. I had to get away. I didn't know where to go.'

'We'll get back to Billy in a minute. *Where* did you go?'

'Around to the pepper tree.' I'm stalling. I've never played poker but have watched the game often enough, in saloons, on ranch night at the drive-in. What cards is he holding?

'Then what?'

'It started raining. I didn't know what to do.'

'What *did* you do?'

'I knocked on Miss Peach's door. It's just across the road.'

'I know where it is.' A slight change in his expression, whether relaxation or tightening, I can't tell. 'Anyone home?'

'She was home. She asked me in. Out of the rain.'

He glances to Mum, back to me. 'Billy told his old man you broke in.'

'Course I didn't break in!'

'He reckons you were the one before. That other time.'

'You going to take that Billy Currie's word over your own son's?' Mum puts in.

'Mother! I said stay out of it.' He turns back to me. 'Jacko is pretty dark on you. Says you called Billy a curly worm.'

'He called me a poofter!'

A faint, suppressed smile. 'Sticks and stones. Upshot is, he wants you to stay away from Billy.'

Mum can't help herself. 'He wants Robbie to stay away from Billy? He's got a nerve! A few weeks back he was saying how wonderful Robbie was! I warned you about those Curries, Jim. Years ago.'

'Miss Peach let you in,' Dad says, ignoring her. 'What time was that?'

'I dunno. Before midnight. She made some cocoa.'

Are the name-calling and the break-in all there is to it? Mention of cocoa triggers an automatic response in my mother; she rises and takes the milk billy from the cool-safe and lifts the lid and spills a little into a saucepan.

'What time did you leave?'

'She let me stay. It was pissing down.'

'Don't use that language in front of your mother, sonny-jim. I asked you what time you left.'

Mum is fiddling with the wick of the kero primus. 'Don't give him the third degree, Jim.'

'Without fear or favour, Mother.'

'Well, I can't see that he did anything wrong.'

'Breaking and entering is a serious charge. I need to be absolutely sure.'

She bites her tongue, but only for a moment. 'Did Jacko tell you what Billy did? Tell him, Robbie. Tell him why you couldn't stay here. Why you ran away.'

'It's no big deal, Mum.'

'That Billy Currie tried to kiss him, Jim.'

He glances, puzzled, from her to me. 'Another one of your cock-and-bull stories, sonny-jim?'

'It's the truth. He wanted to pash me.'

He studies me impassively from across the table. 'Where? Outer space?'

Match-strike behind me, a whiff of kerosene, an excuse to glance over my shoulder to where Mum is placing the saucepan on the primus.

'You avoiding my eyes?'

I turn back to him, indignant. 'You really want the truth?'

'Of course.'

'He wanted to kiss my *cock*.'

A gasp from my mother. 'You didn't tell me that! You think he would make that up, Jim?'

'Don't get your knickers in a knot, Mother. Just a couple of kids fooling around. Experimenting. Had too much to drink. It's not the end of the world.'

'He's a *homo*, Dad!'

'Takes one to know one, according to Jacko.' He gives a dismissive snort. 'I don't reckon the pair of you have got a clue what the word means.'

'Is *that* all you have to say, Jim? You going to let the Curries spread stories like that around town?'

She deals three saucers across the table like cards, plonks a steaming cup of cocoa on each; we sit and stare at them for a time.

'It's easy enough to put this to bed,' he says eventually. 'Pull on some clothes, sonny-jim.'

'Where are we going?'

A glance at his watch. 'Miss Peach vouches for you, you're off the hook.'

'You're talking to him as if he's one of your criminals, Jim.'

'Without fear or favour, Mother. How many times do I have to say it?'

'What's it got to do with Miss Peach?' I say. 'I don't want to drag her into it.'

'Bit late for that now.'

'But why ask her? Why don't you believe me?'

'Get dressed, I said. If she confirms your story, we'll go around to Billy's and set a few things straight.'

'*If* she confirms his story, Jim?'

'All right, *when*. Let's go.'

'But I don't want to go there!' I turn to my mother for help. 'Mum?'

Her face is stern again. 'Your father's right. It's a serious accusation. Your word against his.' She turns to Dad. 'But I'm coming too.'

'It's a police matter, Mother. Pure and simple. You're staying right here.'

I sit tight, hoping for a miracle. A murder in Nangwarry. A fatal on the Naracoorte road. A flash-flood anywhere. But the phone fails to ring, no one comes banging on the door trailing blood.

A warning growl: 'I'm not going to ask again.'

10

By the year 3064 the men and women on planet Earth speak two separate languages. Each can understand the other's but is forbidden to use it. On pain of death . . .

I distract myself as we drive across town by inventing the different vocabularies. The swearwords come easily enough: darn it, fuck it, heck, hell, strewth, shit, bulldust, bullshit. Descriptions of each other likewise: bitch, bastard, cunt, prick . . .

'Sergeant Burns. Missing our company already?'

A Tweedle-twin stands in the doorway wearing a geisha mask of white face-paint, fluffy pink bathrobe, and radar-array of hair-curlers – but which one?

A voice from behind her. 'Who is it, Miss Burke?'

Miss Burke's wired-up head revolves towards the voice as smoothly as a turning antenna. 'The constabulary, Miss Hammond.'

Miss Hammond appears wearing the same fluffy bathrobe, facemask and radar-array. A glass of the same wine in hand. 'Did we leave something on the train, Sergeant?'

'Only our peace of mind, Miss Hammond,' the other smirks.

Dad shifts his feet uneasily. 'Ah, ladies . . . is Miss Peach at home?'

'You found the body then, Sergeant?'

'Body?'

'Figure of speech, Sergeant. But the great poet does seem to have gone missing.'

If he senses even the shape of a joke he gives no sign. 'Miss Peach?' he reminds them.

Both radar-arrays rotate towards her closed bedroom door. 'Pining away, poor creature. Poked our heads in but couldn't get a sensible answer.'

'I rather suspect she spent the weekend in her bedroom, Miss Hammond.'

'The weather was hardly conducive to outdoor activities, Miss Burke. Who could blame her for – how to put this delicately? – taking to her bed with enthusiasm?'

They share a titter, and sip at their separate glasses. Dad glances at me, opens his mouth to speak; Miss Hammond swallows her wine and gets in first.

'Perhaps he hasn't gone missing after all, Miss Burke. Perhaps he's . . .' she gives a theatrical gasp and covers her mouth with her hand, 'still *in* there.'

'I don't quite follow, ladies.'

'Who does, Sergeant? Who ever does? The ways of Miss Peach are a mystery to us all.'

'Especially when it comes to weekend houseguests,' from her twin.

Dad solves the riddle. 'She had a friend staying over the weekend?'

'A man friend,' one tells him. 'An *older* man friend.'

'A *distinguished* older man friend, Miss Burke,' the other adds. 'And don't you forget it!'

'Well, ah, that's neither here nor there. Could one of you ladies knock on her door and tell her I'd like a word?'

They exchange a look of mock horror. 'Taking our lives in our hands.' 'Braver souls than we.'

'It's police business, ladies.'

'Police business! Sergeant, you should have said —'

The bedroom door behind them has opened and here is Miss Peach, pale and drawn, but every hair on her head bunned tightly in place. The unfamiliar clothes take a moment to register: below-knee frock, brown cardigan, plain shoes.

My father is rocking on his heels. 'Sorry to intrude, Miss Peach. I know it's late. I wondered if I might have a quick word.'

Her eyes dart to me. I want to make some reassuring sign, whisper some words. *It's all right. I haven't told. He knows nothing.*

'Has there been some . . . unpleasantness, Sergeant?' Miss Burke asks eagerly.

'Nothing serious, ladies. Perhaps – Miss Peach – somewhere private?'

'I think *we* should be there,' Miss Burke says. 'In fact, we insist. To lend our young companion moral support.'

Miss Hammond wraps a fleshy, protective arm around the younger woman. 'All for one and one for all, Sergeant. Our young ward *needs* us here.'

'Moreover she wants us here,' Miss Burke adds.

My father shrugs. 'You weren't here at the time, but the matter concerns all of you.'

'We have cast-iron alibis. We were on a train under your very nose for most of the weekend.'

Miss Hammond is equally thrilled. 'So *tell* us, Sergeant. Spill the beans.'

'It's the accused who spills the beans, Miss Hammond,' Miss Burke reminds her. 'Not the police. Isn't that right, Sergeant?'

'An, um, accusation has been made,' he begins.

Miss Peach's eyes catch mine again; again I want to shake my head. No beans have been spilled. Or only one small, harmless bean.

'Personally I don't give it much credence. It should take no time at all to clear up the matter. But there are procedures to follow. More so since the allegation involves my son.'

All this spoken with painful slowness. We step into the lounge; the four adults sit, I stay standing near the escape hatch.

Another duet: 'We're all ears, aren't we, Miss Burke.' 'The plot thickens, Miss Hammond.'

'There's been a suggestion that Robbie here broke into your house. Last night.'

No change to Miss Peach's numb expression; the antennae of the older women rotate my way. 'That *is* serious.' 'What does the accused himself say?'

'He claims that Miss Peach invited him in, ladies. Out of the rain. He also claims he stayed overnight.'

Their eyes on me, mine on Miss Peach, hers on the carpet.

'It was raining,' I prompt. 'Remember? I couldn't go home.'

'Objection, your Honour,' Miss Burke pipes up. 'I believe that's what's called leading the witness.' She sips her wine, pleased with herself, as her companion snickers.

'Miss Peach?' from my father.

'He's telling the truth. I said he could stay. Just till the rain stopped.'

'But he said he stayed all night.'

'It didn't stop,' she says simply.

'You haven't been sleeping in *my* bed, I hope, Master Burns,' Miss Burke says.

'You haven't been eating *my* porridge,' from her offsider, and they chortle again.

'He slept on the lounge,' Miss Peach says, still avoiding my eye.

Dad is back on his feet. 'That's that, then. Thank you for helping out. I have to say, Marj and I appreciate everything you've done for the boy. P'raps we shouldn't have left him on his own. P'raps he shouldn't have been out in the rain that late. No need for details, but in sonny-jim's defence, he was fleeing a rather . . . difficult situation.'

Miss Burke arches an eyebrow. Miss Hammond says: 'A glass of wine, Sergeant? Do tell more.'

'Not on duty, ladies. Sorry again to disturb you. It's been a long day – for all of us.'

I seek Miss Peach's eye again at the door, but she is already heading back to her bedroom. Of course the Tweedle-twins follow us out onto the porch.

'Now remember, Master Burns. There's always a bed for you here. Not so, Miss Burke?'

'A bed just the right size, Miss Hammond. And porridge in the morning. Not too hot, not too cold.'

'Couple of queer fish, those two,' Dad mutters as we climb into the car. 'Bit too fond of the turps for my liking.' He starts the engine, then turns my way. 'Sorry to put you through it. I never doubted your story, but it had to be followed up. No hard feelings?'

'I spose.'

'Good. We won't talk about it again.' He shifts into gear and pulls out into the road. 'Your Miss Peach is a decent sort. She's on your side. You be good for her.'

Surplus to the continuing investigation, I am dropped off at home. I am hiding out in the shed when Dad backs into the drive an hour later. A car door slams, then the boot; he appears in the doorway with my old 26-inch Malvern Star and tosses it in a corner.

'Don't ask,' he says, and walks straight out.

I let my mother do the asking; I put my ear to their bedroom door after lights out to hear his answers.

'Never you mind what else was said. I didn't believe Billy and neither did Jacko.'

'Well, then tell me.'

'Not fit to repeat. You were right. A foul mouth and a filthy mind.'

'Ingratitude, I call it. You tried so hard with him, Jim.'

'Gave him the benefit of the doubt once too often.'

'Can't say I didn't warn you.'

'Going to have to keep a close eye on him these next few years.'

'Did Jacko listen to reason?'

'Dragged the little bastard to the sink and washed his mouth out with soap. Right there and then. In front of my eyes.'

'He's a tough man, Jim. But he's fair, I'll say that for him.'

'He's got a good head on his shoulders.'

And a good fist on the end of his arm. Billy's brown face is sporting a black eye at school the next day. Neither that eye nor its undamaged twin gives me so much as a glance; the inky bruise might be some kind of formal stamp, sealing the end of our friendship.

Nor is eye contact offered by Miss Peach as we plough through a paragraph of Seneca that morning. Small consolation that my classmates fare no better; her distracted gaze is mostly out the window. Her voice when she speaks is a flat monotone, that lesson and those of hers that follow little more than rote. Not until Thursday does she gird up her loins, as if having arrived at some deep decision, and force herself to smile. Her set, willed smile barely changes as the hours pass. Her first word to me all week comes later that day when my hand shoots into the air, automatically, to answer one of those questions only I can answer.

'Burns?' she says, after scanning the rest of the class in vain.

That terse surname stabs me like a knife. Anne Hunter looks around, surprised; she too has noticed. 'The Weimar Republic, Miss,' I eventually get out.

'Correct.'

I keep my hand down as she smiles her way grimly through the rest of day, as if hoping that the wind might change and her smile become something fixed and effortless. But the wind outside is a steady south-westerly, the bringer of sleet and frigid showers from the southern ocean. It stays that way the next day, and all through the next week, a wind straight from Antarctica, but her expression becomes warmer and more natural anyway, if erratically, one frown backwards, two smiles forwards. 'Robbie' still fails to emerge from her mouth, however often I curry favour during lessons or dawdle past her desk at their end.

'When's the next club meeting, Miss?'

'I'm not sure the town was ready for the Lyceum Club.'

A rare slip; for a moment we might be friends again, confidants even, then her face stiffens. 'You'd better run along, Burns. Your friends are waiting outside.'

'Have you heard from the professor, Miss?'

'None of your business.'

I proffer an exercise book I happen to have in my hand. 'Can I leave my new story?'

'I'm very busy. Exam marking.'

I set it down on her desk anyway. 'There's no hurry.'

She looks up at me again, more in tiredness than in anger. 'Do you remember a word of what I said to you, Robert? That night?'

I do, and I don't. That is, I remember every word, but that was then and this is now.

'Sort of.'

'Let me remind you. I can't give you any special favours. I have to treat you like any other student. I let you get much too close to me. Too . . .' A pause, while she gropes in her head for the word. 'Attached.'

I remember it the other way around – she let herself get too attached to me – but I am given no chance to argue as she hurries on.

'So I can't read your stories. I hope I've been able to give you some encouragement, and support. You have a special talent, it doesn't need my help. And I have less talented students, with more pressing needs. I've been neglecting them.'

'But Miss —'

'That will be *all*, Burns.'

'But —'

'Not another word. Please.' She rests her face in her cupped hands; I can't see her eyes. Forbidden to speak, I am left with two choices. To reach out and offer some kind of awkward physical comfort is clearly impossible; I make the other choice, the only choice on offer, and turn on my heels and leave.

II

Life gets no easier as the second school term crawls by. The more distant Miss Peach becomes, the more I play up. Am I acting out my anger, or just acting up to get her attention? I have no idea. If unhappiness is my new default setting, it is as unexamined as the happiness that preceded it.

In the schoolyard I am on my own. Unable or unwilling to choose between Billy's lies and mine, our schoolmates cast both of us out. The boys want to believe I rooted Miss Peach; my denials thwart and thereby anger them. And the girls? They don't believe Billy's story for a moment, but turn their backs (and their tightly rolled buns of hair) on me as one, imitating their idol in this as in all else. One small advantage: Anne Hunter stops feeding me the results of her Domestic Science experiments, doughy cupcakes and tooth-breaking Anzac biscuits and meringues as white and crumbly as sun-bleached dog turds.

I can't avoid Billy in the Woodwork block, but we are now assigned to workbenches on opposite sides of the room. We sit with our backs to each other as Big Merv chalks up the plan and the side and front elevations of the next term project – a dowelled magazine rack – on the blackboard. I keep my head down as I copy the measurements, precisely to scale, into my graph book; Merv is clearly on the warpath. When the Woodwork monitors distribute the timber I gratefully set to work with carpenter's pencil and steel carpenter's square and handsaw. I can lose myself in this kind of tinkering, it's in my blood. Time passes; I forget where I am until startled by a gruff voice in my ear: 'I've got my eye on you, Burns. You and your filthy-minded gang.'

Gang? The gang never had more than two members and is now a gang of exactly one. And why is he picking on me? I've spread no filth, I've repeatedly denied it.

I keep clear of the other gang member during recess breaks. Lunchtimes I hole up in the library, furiously writing. This, at least, goes well; goes better, for reasons I don't understand, than ever. The days pass. The weeks. I fail a Latin test for the first time, my History grades plummet. I decide to hate Shakespeare.

'Who would like to read Juliet's part today?'

'Me, Miss!'

'You read yesterday, Anne. Cheryl? Page ninety-two. Act three, scene three. "Wherefore art thou Romeo?"'

Once I might have stuck my hand in the air, but which Juliet would have me now? Miss Peach tosses me scraps from time to time. I am a Second Musician, reluctantly. A Servant, listlessly. Mostly, as the other boys talk tough and flourish imaginary swords and bite their thumbs at each other, and the girls talk of nothing but marriage, I write.

One thing is becoming clear: I need a very special story to win her back, or even to get her attention. And so I scribble on, ever more urgently, as Romeo and Juliet swear true love across my head and Miss Peach gazes absently out through the window, or mumbles distractedly about the legacy of the Treaty of Versailles, and one Friday afternoon I look up from my scribblings and discover it's the last day of term and she is going through the motions of confirming that, yes, she is heading for Adelaide 'to see my mother' for a week. Still no glance in my direction as she speaks, or, two hours later, in the direction of the pepper tree in which I perch, binoculars pressed to my eyes, as she lugs her case up the road to the station, unaccompanied.

The September holidays have begun, but I head straight home to my back-shed cave and open a new lined exercise book and write. Night falls and I put a match to the wick of my spirit burner, and by the light of its faint blueish flame write on. Thought experiments, I call my stories now, but from that time on they will be as violent as any chemical experiment, and no less dangerous.

The long empty days and the blue-lit nights grind past, and still I sit in my dark magician's cave and write. And write.

term three

It's the year 2064 and on planet Earth the women get pregnant by being spat on. A nuclear war has destroyed life as we know it; the surviving humans have mutated into leathery, toadlike bipeds. Male spittle teems with spermatozoa that burrow into a woman's skin and fertilise the eggs, which lie in cysts beneath her thick toad-hides. Pregnancies grow on the skin like warts, or boils; when they reach full term the hatchlings burst out of their mother like pus.

The story is bursting out of me. Love plays no part in this strange mating practice. Nor does sexual desire. Spitting is as taboo in the mutant future as it is in the present, especially spitting – slagging – on a woman. Anger and not lust is the irresistible mating force; husbands need to be in a rage to overcome the taboo and get with child their warty toad-brides.

The men of the future have to be quick-tempered, I realise as I write, or the species will die out. It's in their nature. The women, likewise, are ugly nags, programmed by evolution to provoke their husbands to spitting-point. I scribble on in an excited, angry reverie, my words covering the pages like a kind of inky spittle themselves. There are no love songs in the future, only hate songs. Dancing is more a kind of sparring, or stylised boxing; lovers shout obscenities into each other's ears rather than whisper sweet nothings. The most sought-after husbands are the most short-tempered, the most marriageable wives the most ugly.

A paradox: are the most ugly therefore the most beautiful? This puzzles me, but I am in too much of a rush to finish my thought experiment to linger. As Mum finger-tinkles on the Bechstein inside the house, crooning show tunes to herself, a title pops into my head. I scrawl it across the front of the exercise book in big bold letters. SOME ENSPITTLED EVENING.

A catchy title to bait the hook? Surely this is my best bait yet. I finish the story on the last Sunday afternoon of the school holidays and want to show it to Miss Peach immediately. I throw down my pen and pace restlessly about. Is she back in town yet? The shed is too small to contain my agitation, I need space. I jam the rolled exercise book into a duffle-coat pocket and jump on my bike. Within minutes I am perched in the pepper tree, binoculars in hand. Her scooter hasn't moved from the driveway all week; it sits there still. A painful thought as night falls and no light appears in her bedroom window: might she not come back at all? I abandon my watch, sick at heart, and sleep poorly, but the Vespa is sitting in the teacher's car park when I arrive at school next morning, and soon enough, here she is, walking into the classroom.

'Good morning, 1A.'

'Good morning, Miss Peach.'

'I trust you are all refreshed by your holiday and ready for our last term together.'

Oddly final words, but no need for panic. A school term is near infinite in length, a sizeable chunk of my lifetime so far. There will be plenty of opportunities to wear her down. And if not, there is always next year.

She looks anything but ready herself. Improbably her tiny body has lost weight; her elfin face is pale and drawn, although it might just be the absence – for the first time ever – of lipstick.

'Brian Bell,' she recites from the roll.

'Here, Miss.'

'Robert Burns.'

'Here, Miss.'

Some Enspittled Evening sits on her desk. A frown momentarily ripples the smooth waters of her face; has she noticed it?

'Cheryl Wallace?'

'Here, Miss.'

Progress, of sorts, since last term; my story is not yet in the bin.

'Open *Legamus*,' she says. 'Page forty-five. This is a story from book two of *The Histories*. Tacitus writes about the terrible civil war of 69 AD, as the troops of Otho move north, destroying their own countryside . . .'

All this in that now familiar monotone. She talks on, trying to breathe a little life into the words of the dead language, but half-heartedly. '*Praeclaro exemplo femina Ligus*. Anyone? No? The proper noun might give you trouble. Liga: the province of Liguria. Ligus – case?'

'Genitive, Miss?'

'Correct, Anne. So – *femina Ligus?*'

'A woman of Liguria.'

'Good. Let's move on: *quae filio abdito*. The woman is asked to surrender her son; this makes sense in the context of the next phrase, *cum simul*, "together with" – correct, Brian. *Pecuniam occultari* – yes, "money hidden" – *milites credidissent*, "the soldiers believed". So, the soldiers believe she has hidden her son together with some money. Let's pause at the next interesting word, *cruciatus*.'

'Cross, Miss?' I remember.

The barest nod of acknowledgement. 'Same root, but a more general sense: torture. *Interrogarent ubi filium occuleret.* The soldiers threaten her to make her reveal the whereabouts of her son, and here is one of the finest lines in Tacitus – *uterum ostendens latere respondit* – she points to her womb and answers, he is hidden here.'

She pauses, and stares out the window, clearly moved.

'Was she pregnant, Miss?' Anne Hunter asks.

'Hmm?' Her head swings back, a tired smile. 'No. She is speaking symbolically, Anne. I am his mother, she is saying. He is part of me. I am willing to die to protect my son.'

'They killed her, Miss?'

She takes a deep breath. '*Nec ullis deinde terroribus aut morte constantiam vocis egregiae mutavit.* There are some new words there. Take out your dictionaries and make a literal for the rest of the lesson.'

'Did they find the son anyway, Miss?' I ask. 'After they killed her?'

'Tacitus doesn't mention that.' Still no glance my way.

'It was a waste of her life if they found him,' I say. 'You know what I think, Miss? I think they found him and killed him anyway. *And* took the money.'

Her voice, when she speaks, has the quietness of exhaustion. 'Fortunately Tacitus is not interested in what you think, Burns. And neither am I. Take out your dictionary. One noun in particular you might like to check: *constantum*.'

I have a confused word-string down in seconds – *and not then next terror either death constancy noble words to change.* I watch secretly as she glances again at my story on her desk. So she *is* interested in what I think. How long can she resist the bait? She glances up in my direction; I instantly put my head down, pretending to work. When I next risk a peep she has my story in her hand. Hooked? Perplexed, at least. And – clearly – worried. Her once-smooth face, as perfect as a blank white page, has become more readable over the holidays. Frown-lines across the brow, fine spiderwebs at the corners of her eyes. A downturning of the corners of her unpainted mouth. *Constantum*: neuter, second. Constancy, loyalty. At last she peels open the front cover, but cautiously, leaning back away from it as if it might explode in her face. No sooner has she begun to read than she gives a loud gasp, then another, even louder. Now everyone is watching. She turns another page and her hand flies to cover her open mouth, but not quickly enough to muffle an audible 'No!' She reaches for her fountain pen and begins scribbling as furiously as I had scribbled on the same pages. Then stops abruptly, tosses the pen aside, folds her arms on the desk and sinks her head into their pillow.

Anne Hunter gives me a look of pure hatred; the rest of the class has eyes only for Miss Peach. A minute passes. Three. When she lifts her head she looks ill – more grey now than pale, more green in parts than grey.

'You can all take an early minute,' she says, then holds up her hand to stifle the eruption of puzzled concern. 'Be *very* quiet in the quadrangle. Other classes will still be working.' She gives her first glance of the day in my direction. 'Robert Burns, stay behind.'

I sit at my desk, heart pounding, as the room empties and she rises and closes the door. She paces back and forth without speaking for a time, but it's a slow-moving, weary kind of pacing, lacking the pent-up energy of old. Eventually she stops at the window and stares out.

'I don't know where to begin.'

'Did you like it?'

She turns, incredulous. '*Like* it? Do you have any idea what you've written, Robert?'

'It's just a story, Miss.'

'Nothing is just a story! Have you ever heard a woman called a slag?'

'No,' I say truthfully.

A snort. 'Always the innocent. Is that what you think of me, Robert?'

What on earth is she talking about? 'It's not about you, Miss.'

'I *lied* for you, Robert. I lied to your father.' A small, harsh laugh. 'To the police. You broke into my house – more than once, don't deny it – and I lied to protect you. Well, I'm not going to put myself in that position again. It's time for the truth.' She pauses, swallows hard. 'I'm telling no more lies. Especially to myself. Pack your bag and come with me.'

2

It's the year 2064 and it's compulsory for teachers to have sex with their students. No one makes a fuss; it's just another school rule, like having to wear a blazer and tie, or not turning up late for lessons. If anything, it's a productive rule: good for morale, an incentive for better grades.

I think this through as I sit outside the headmaster's office. A nicely baited hook, but where to now? My fingers itch for pen and paper. A biology lesson seems an obvious place to start. Or English, where we are still thumb-biting and sword-fighting our way through *Romeo and Juliet*; a bedroom scene would add extra passion. Arithmetic, Algebra, Geometry? Might the rhythms of times-tables be coupled with what I know of the rhythms of sex? And what of teacher–student ratios? Easy enough to imagine the wisdom of an older tutor (sexual wisdom not least) being passed down to a much loved student on a one-to-one basis. But ours are big classes, postwar explosions of forty-plus students per teacher. My imagination has wandered freely through any number of possible universes but doesn't yet stretch to group sex. It doesn't even stretch to rooting Miss Hammond or Miss Burke; the thought disgusts me. But a school rule is a school rule. I don't much like wearing a tie either. And the girls? I try to imagine Anne Hunter bouncing up and down on Big Merv Bailey. The idea makes no sense, if only because girls don't do Woodwork. What of Headmaster Bell, then?

His office door is still closed. The prim-mouthed school secretary is watching me; I stare back till she looks away. Then I stare at the door itself. Miss Peach has been in there an awfully long time. Faint murmurings inside, and not much more than the murmuring of faint emotions inside me. What can she be telling him? The truth and nothing but? I hope so. Is hope an emotion? I feel *some*thing as I sit there, but if I can't properly describe it do I really feel it? Faint hope? Faint pride? I felt a definite surge of pride as I followed Miss Peach through the stares of my classmates across the quadrangle. Foreboding followed that, but only briefly. What is left? Relief? Mostly I just feel – ready. Ready for what? For whatever comes next.

Which is the arrival of my father, in peaked cap and sergeant's uniform. He offers only a curt nod my way as he barges into the headmaster's office without knocking and shuts the door behind him.

Raised voices now, his loud among them, but subsiding soon enough. More murmurings. I stare down the secretary again. I've been in trouble before, I'm ready for the consequences. Is fatalism an emotion? A mood? A rational choice? All of the above, perhaps – but at fourteen I haven't even read the word in Tacitus.

My father reappears, impassive, cap under arm. He pulls the door shut after him, jams his cap on his big head and gestures me to follow. Still no glimpse of Miss Peach.

Silence all the way home: a very short drive that takes a very long time. No handcuffs – he never uses them – but I feel a slight thrill as we park next to the holding cells; where exactly am I heading?

He looks my way, gives a perplexed shake of his head. 'You ready for this, sonny-jim? Your mother will have a blue fit. As for the rest of this town . . .' A deep breath, a faint half-smile. 'Before the shit hits the fan, let me say this – can't say I blame you. You've got to lose your cherry sometime.'

The surge of joy I feel is anything but faint; she admitted it! She *does* remember!

'What I do blame you for – you lied. That break-in before. You let Billy take the fall for you.'

'I didn't lie about him wanting to kiss my cock.'

'Well, she's not blaming anyone but herself. Least of all you. You should thank your lucky stars.'

He pushes his door open. 'Ready to face the music?' A grim smile as he clambers out. 'Dunno that I am.'

Difficult to concentrate on the events that follow; my thoughts are back with her, my eyes still trying to stare through that closed office door. What is happening? What is she feeling?

'The . . . the little *tramp*! The hussy! And those airs and graces! More front than John Martin's!'

'It wasn't her fault, Mum.'

'Stay out of it, Robert! In fact, go to your room while your father and I talk. You shouldn't even be here.'

'She was drunk,' I say, 'She didn't know what she was doing.'

'And you did?'

'I love her, Mum.'

'Will you *listen* to your son, Jim Burns? I've never heard such foolishness in all my life. Your room, Robert – now! Tell him, Jim.'

'Do as your mother says. And close the door after you.'

Closing the door fails to keep out my mother's ranting – *hussy, loose woman, tramp, slut*. My father murmurs from time to time; is he defending the tramp? Someone needs to; she stuck up for me.

'It's not her fault!' I repeat, bursting back into the kitchen.

'Stay in your room!' my mother shouts back.

'*I* started it!' I tell her, which is as much a schoolboy's boast as a confession, although I feel schoolboyishly gallant in the saying of it.

'How could *you* start it? I never! In all my days! Where does he get these ideas from? Billy Currie, that's where!'

'Billy's got nothin' to do with it, Mum!'

'I won't hear any more of this nonsense. You hear what's coming out of his mouth, Jim? Are you going to just stand there?'

'Back to your room, sonny-jim.'

'I won't! This is about me.'

'You bloody *will*.' He seizes me by the arm, frog-marches me to my room, slams the door after me, and the kitchen door even more forcefully after that. His placatory murmurings inaudible now, her high-pitched protestations still loud enough – 'Trollop . . . Who does she think she . . .? Painted Jezebel . . . I have news for her . . . This was a nice town . . . Hussy . . . Just a boy' – but slowly diminishing. When she too is inaudible, I creep along the hall and ease the kitchen door open a crack. Neither notices; they are sitting together facing the stove, his meaty arm across her humped shoulders.

'Calm down, Mother. It's not the end of the world.'

'But it *is* a crime, isn't it? Carnal knowledge? Something like that? If she were a man, you'd charge her, Jim. He's just a child. A minor.'

'She's not a man. And he hasn't been a child for some time. In case you hadn't noticed.'

She dabs at her eyes with an apron corner. 'He's fourteen, Jim.'

'Nearly fifteen.' He speaks my thought for me.

'Not till January,' she says.

'For what it's worth, Mother, she does confirm his story. Said she had too much to drink.'

'That changes nothing.'

'Said she'd never drank that much in her life. Can't properly remember what happened. Thought it was . . . um . . . someone else.'

'Who? The darned milkman?'

'Her . . . ah, friend. That professor bloke from the city.'

'That's her excuse? He's a married man himself, Jim!'

'She seemed genuinely upset, Mother.'

She shrugs off his arm violently. 'Oh, turn on the waterworks and you men all melt! The *nerve* of the hussy!'

'Calm down,' he repeats. 'Count to ten. It hasn't done the boy any harm. Can't say the same for her, of course.'

She dabs at her eyes again, sniffs. 'I know men see these things differently. But what about . . . well, disease? She has a reputation, you know. Who knows what Robbie might have caught.'

I push open the door, I can eavesdrop no longer. 'She was a virgin, Mum.'

She turns on me, startled. 'How long have you been there?'

'She's not a tramp. She was a virgin!'

'And you'd be an expert in that! I declare! The filth that comes out of your mouth!'

'Give the boy a hearing, Mother.'

'I *won't* give him hearing. Or you either! For your information, both of you, Rita Bailey told me it was a parade of one man after another through that house. In the front door, out the back!'

He laughs harshly. 'She would say that, wouldn't she?'

'What's that supposed to mean?'

'Merv would love to be first in line.'

'What? How do you know that?'

He glances my way, her eyes follow. 'Back to your room, sonny-jim. I won't ask again.'

I shut the kitchen door after me but of course go no further. Instead I lower myself stealthily to the floor and crouch there, catlike, waiting for their words to squeeze beneath the door like mice.

'Tell me, Jim.'

'Just a few things he let drop. At the club.'

'You talk about that little minx at the footy club?'

'He talks about her. Too much, if you ask me.'

'And I suppose you can't do anything but sit there and listen?'

Frustrated, getting nowhere, he raises his voice for the first time. 'Fair go, Mother! You know as well as I do that Merv Bailey would root a dog on a chain!'

When she speaks again her voice is the quiet one. 'I don't expect to hear language like that in my own home, Jim. This is not the football club.'

'Sorry. But you know what I mean.'

Another lengthy silence. 'If I didn't know you better, I'd think that part of you envies the boy. Part of you might like to stand in the same queue. Oh, the nerve! Prancing around town as though butter wouldn't melt in her mouth.'

I crouch there, still wanting to defend her but content for the moment to let my father do it.

'What about those other two, Jim? Tweedledum and Tweedledee. Where were they? It's supposed to be a teachers' house, not a . . . a house of ill repute!'

'I don't think those two are interested in men.'

'And just what is that supposed to mean?'

I hold my breath, waiting to pounce on the next mice.

'I think they prefer the, ah, sticky-fingered business.'

'Oh, that's choice, Jim Burns. Very choice. You might not say much, but when you do!'

'You asked me. I told you.'

What has he told her? I've caught his words, but have no idea what to do with them. Bat them between my own sticky paws?

'I don't believe it for a minute,' she says. 'And if it's true why haven't you done anything about it?'

'It's not against the law.'

'It's against God's law, Jim.'

'Then God can punish them. If I followed up every shred of rumour that came my way I'd never be done.'

'This used to be a nice town. Now it's . . . it's . . .'

'Sodom and Gomorrah?'

'Are you *grinning*? You are! You do envy the boy, don't you?'

I can hear the grin myself in his tone of voice. 'I like a bit of meat on a woman, meself. You know that, Mother.'

'Keep your hands to yourself, Jim Burns. If you think you can sweet-talk your way out of this, you have another think coming. What does the reverend say about it?'

'I haven't asked.'

'Well, don't you think you'd better? Quick-smart.'

'It was wrong,' he says. 'But worse things happen. It's hardly the end of the world. When I was in Egypt —' He halts, as surprised as I am to hear such a phrase in his mouth, perhaps his first war reminiscence ever. 'Well, ah, in other countries, a father will sometimes take his son to a . . . to an experienced woman. Someone who can teach him the facts of life. Saw it all the time in Cairo.'

'Is that why you were so keen to leave him on his own for the weekend? You wanted him to sow some wild oats?'

'Of course not. Listen to what you're saying, Mother!'

'You were the one who said he'd be all right.'

'We both discussed it, as I remember. We agreed.'

'I remember I didn't want to leave him. You talked me into it. He's just a child, Jim.'

'Have you been listening? He's hardly a child.'

'Then he's old enough to know better. To know it's a sin. Fornication is a sin. I want him to talk to the reverend. And I want him to see the doctor.'

'Which first?'

'This is no time for sarcasm.'

A chair scrapes, heavy footsteps approach the door. I'm on my feet and behind the second door in a flash. I hear the ratchet-click of the phone being dialled.

'Jean? Marj Burns . . . Connect me to the doctor's, please. Yes, I'll wait.' Her voice rises: 'If you won't take him, Jim, I will!' Conversational again: 'Jenny? Marj Burns . . . Yes, Robbie again . . . Not this time, thankfully, but a bit of an emergency all the same . . . Straight around? . . . I'm very grateful.'

Silence after she hangs up. Her tone is agonised when next she speaks. 'She knows, Jim. Al*ready*. I can hear it in her voice. Which means they all know. This is so humiliating. And the policeman's son – I don't know if I can face them.'

'I'll take him, Mother. But it's hardly an emergency.'

'If it isn't I don't know what is!'

'It's been nearly three months. Let's all take a deep breath. If he had, well, caught something, it would have shown up by now.'

'Is that so? You know that for certain, do you Dr Burns? From your Egypt days?'

'Don't start, Mother.'

'How would I know what you all got up to in the army?'

'You know I don't like to talk about it.'

'I'm beginning to understand why.'

A police-rap on my bedroom door, his head pokes through. 'On your feet, sonny-jim. Let's get this over with.'

Her anger is already fading as she sees us to the door; her eyes swim a little as she wraps me into her great bear-bulk. 'Don't worry, Robbie. Everything will be all right.'

She must be reassuring herself; I am the least worried person in town, perhaps in the known universe. I am the opposite of worried, whatever that state of mind might be. All worried out? Content? Pleased, certainly; pleased with myself and pleased it's out in the open. Of course it will be all right. Just ask, well, anybody. Ask the Friday-afternoon shoppers who watch us as we walk along Church Street to the doctor's. Ask the three regulars who spill out of the Oak, beers in hand, fags in mouth, as if to watch a parade go by.

'What you staring at?' Dad glares at them.

'Popped out to say g'day, Sarge.'

'No drinking off the premises. You know the law.'

'Sorry, Sarge. Hot day. Man works up a thirst.'

Their words are aimed at Dad, but the eyes are all on me.

'Your boy looks a bit sweaty, Sarge,' one says, and gives me a broad wink. 'Could use a man's drink himself. Whaddya reckon?'

'I reckon if you're not off the street in three seconds flat you'll be finishing that drink in the lock-up.' He stalks on with me lagging behind. 'Should have driven,' he says out of the corner of his mouth.

I'm glad we didn't. I've never felt so famous, so infamous, so noticed and notorious, so *manly*. School is out; I spot Anne Hunter with her mother outside Dalziel's and watch them with my peripheral vision watching me until they are far behind my back. Plenty more schoolmates, plenty more glances and nudges as we walk on. Has the story spread at light-speed? Of course it has; don't telephone cables operate at the speed of light?

The doctor's ancient receptionist is whispering at light-speed into a telephone herself as we enter; she covers the receiver, nods us through, continues whispering. The waiting room is empty, the doctor's door wide open. His scuffed boots are up on his big desk, a pot of unpoured tea steams near his elbow, he is lost in the latest issue of *Analog* magazine. Dad clears his throat once, twice; the doctor blinks up at us, puzzled, having trouble re-entering Earth's atmosphere.

'Young Lucifer,' he finally says. 'What scientific catastrophe have you got for me today?'

Is he the only person in town who hasn't heard? Dad prods me in the back but I am saying nothing.

'It's, ah, a little embarrassing, Doc.'

Embarrassment, like most other human emotions, is beyond the doctor's tonal range. He sets the magazine aside but leaves his boots resting on the desk. 'Sit.'

I sit in the furthest chair in the room; Dad sits in the hot seat, at a corner of the desk. 'The missus is, ah, worried the boy may have been, well, exposed, ah, to contact . . .'

Doc McKenzie seems mystified by this code. Contact with what? Little green men?

Dad glances uneasily towards the open door and the receptionist still whispering communiqués into her phone. 'You know – down there. With a woman.'

'Coitus!' the doctor says, and reaches for a pen and scribbles the word on my file-card, as if it's the solution to a crossword clue. 'Any sores, young Lucifer?'

I pull up my trouser leg and show him a scab on my knee. 'I came off my bike. Last Saturday.'

'Don't be a smart-aleck,' Dad says.

I'm not, and say so, and he seems to believe me, or is willing to try. 'He means on your old feller, sonny-jim.'

'Any itch? Any discharge?'

'Nocturnal emissions?' I ask the doctor.

'No, no. We all have those. I mean frank pus.'

A shudder at the thought. 'From my penis? Of course not.'

'Stand up and drop your trousers. Let's take a look.'

'You need to look?'

'On your feet,' from Dad. 'We haven't got all day.'

The doctor's chair is on rollers; he skates it around the desk and sits there waiting, at eye level now with my groin, a bearded Sherlock Holmes holding a cartoon-sized magnifying glass. He pulls down my underpants, pinches my penis between thumb and forefinger and lifts it this way and that, peering all the time through his glass. Dad stares fixedly out through the glass of the window; I concentrate on the shelf of glass pickling jars behind the desk, trying not to notice those tickling, intrusive fingers.

'Healthy-looking genitalia. Both testes fully descended. Normal cremasteric reflex.'

Without warning he grips the thin shaft and squeezes it two or three times, as if milking it. I yelp, but thankfully nothing fluid – milk or urine, Frank pus or Bruce pus – emerges. He abruptly drops my penis and scooters his chair backwards in the direction of the corner basin. 'When did coitus take place?'

Dad nudges me, again I stay mute, again he speaks for me. 'Couple of months back. Give or take.'

The doctor mumbles into the porcelain sink as he washes his hands, his words drowned by splashing water. Has he finished the examination? Can I pull up my trousers?

'He's clean?' from Dad.

'Hmm? Yes. Of course. Signs would be evident by now. Primary chancre. Urethral discharge.' He seems disappointed not to have found something. Scootering back to the desk he seems also to have already forgotten our presence; the lurid cover of the magazine on his desk has caught his eye.

'Thanks, Doc. The missus will be very relieved. If there's nothing else?'

There is nothing else, not even an indication that there is nothing else. I pull up my trousers, belt them, and follow my father into the empty waiting room.

'Glad you could squeeze us in, Jenny,' he says to the receptionist in passing. His mood has enlarged, relieved as much perhaps by the doctor's indifference, his refusal to pass judgement, as by the lack of disease. Has this confirmed his own first instincts: it's a storm in a teacup? We've been to confession and found there is nothing to confess. Heads still turn our way as we walk back along Church Street, but his own head is higher; he returns the stares now, stares them down.

'About time we had a talk,' he says as we approach the Oak. 'But not at home. Man to man.' He pushes through the door into the front bar; I follow. 'Might as well face the music full on, sonny-jim. Best thing in my experience. Take it on the chin. Show you don't give a —' He swallows the next word, makes a different choice. 'Rat's.'

The same drinkers stand at the bar who watched us from the street; they lift their beers in our direction, grinning. Harry, behind the bar, is beaming. 'Long time between drinks, Sarge. Lemon squash?'

'Thought I'd have a beer.'

'There's a first time for everything. Drinking on duty?'

'Taking the day off, Harry. Family business.'

Harry lifts a glass to the tap and begins to pull the beer. 'Lemon squash for the big feller?'

'Give him a beer too.'

Harry is as surprised as me. 'You make the rules, Sarge.'

The regulars propping up the bar are less surprised than amused. 'Something to celebrate, Sarge?' 'Reckon you've earnt that beer, young feller?' 'Put some hair on your chest.'

'We'll take 'em at the corner table,' Dad says.

We sit together in awkward silence until the foaming beers are plonked on coasters before us. 'Wet your whistle, sonny-jim.'

I sip, but don't much like the bitter taste. Can I ask for a sweet sherry? He sips his own, sets it down. 'What I'm going to say isn't for your mother's ears.'

I nod.

'I'm not one to beat about the bush. Like I said, I'm not blaming you. Any red-blooded bloke would have done the same. Truth to tell, I was a bit relieved.'

A strange word to use. 'About what?'

He stares into his beer. 'Oh, you know. You and Billy.'

I stare into my own beer.

'Funny customs they have in other countries,' he begins again. 'I was telling your mother about Egypt the other night. I'm not saying I approve of a young boy and an older woman. Not necessarily. But it's their way.'

More separate staring into beer glasses.

'No damage done,' he comes out with next. 'It's happened. Might as well look on the bright side. Maybe you learnt something. You know – about the birds and the bees.' At last he takes a second sip; I follow suit. 'Better than spending an hour with the doc looking at something in a bloody pickle bottle.'

He chuckles; I chuckle with him.

'When you were in Egypt,' I venture, 'did you . . . you know . . .?'

'Plenty of offers,' he says, then seems to remember he is talking to his son and becomes stern-faced again. 'But no. Of course not. Not recommended.' He sips again, buying some extra thinking time. 'So.'

I force down more of my own bitter beer.

'This is the last I'll speak of this, sonny-jim. You've had your fun and games.' A slightly wistful look in his eyes. 'God knows, she's an attractive enough piece. If that's your cup of tea. Bit of a feather in your cap. But you won't be seeing her again.'

A jangle of alarm bells. 'Why not?'

'She can hardly stay at the school, can she?'

'But you just said —'

'Forget what I just said. She won't be teaching anywhere for a while.'

'But why? What will she do? Where will she go?'

'Back to the city, I expect.'

'She had to *leave* the city, Dad.'

This gives him pause. 'She get into trouble there too?'

'Of course not. She had to get away from the, the professor. He's an old perve. Old enough to be her father.'

A slow-widening grin. 'Likes them all shapes and sizes, does she?'

'What do I say to her tomorrow? At school?'

'Have you heard a word I've said? She won't be there tomorrow. She's resigned.' He shakes his head. 'Maybe your mother's right. You are still a child.'

The weight of this is taking time to sink in. 'Where will she go?'

'Her problem, sonny-jim. She'll find another school some-where. Make a fresh start.'

'But I love her, Dad.'

A grunt of derision. 'We all have a soft spot for our first one, son. But love? That's stupid talk. You'll get over her soon enough. Plenty of other fish in the sea.'

'There's none!' I shout. 'And *she* loves me!'

A silent bar. Perhaps it's been silent for some time. Perhaps every face has been staring our way all along. Those faces seem suddenly alien to me, completely unrecognisable. Where am I? On some planet where human life has evolved from reptiles? The proof sur-rounds me: a wall of cracked, sun-reddened cheeks; a scaly mosaic of necks and arms. Sack-bellied bodies balanced on spindly, vestigial skink-legs. And just arm's length away, in Dad's open, astonished mouth, a row of sharp, thinly filed lizard-teeth.

He reaches over and cuffs me across the ear. 'That's enough of that, sonny-jim!'

I hardly notice the blow. I feel trapped, surrounded by lizard-men; a great weight presses on my chest. I seem unable to breathe. 'I *won't* not see her again,' I gasp, using the last of my air. 'I won't.'

And I break free of my father's restraining claw and run out of the bar.

3

Wedged in a fork of the pepper tree, I watch her house and her Vespa for what remains of the afternoon. Hauled up after me with great difficulty, my bike hangs by its handlebars from a nearby branch like a strange metallic fruit, but it's invisible from below. My heavy heart is getting heavier, a dragging weight that might topple me out of the tree. I've felt nothing like this before: a kind of shocked, empty helplessness. Why must she go away? No one goes away, except the very old and very dead.

A white EK Holden crawls past beneath and turns into her drive. A red-faced reptile in a blue policeman's uniform climbs out, knocks on the front door, speaks to someone unseen, climbs back into the car, backs out and drives off. Instinct tells me to stay put. A tree-mammal's instinct in a world of reptiles? Sure enough, the car circles the block and cruises by again, even more slowly, before disappearing for good.

Time passes. The scooter stays put. I take out my story and try to imagine the language intelligent reptiles might speak. Anything to free my mind up, lighten my heart. Billy rides by, checks under the tree for my bike, sees nothing, rides on. A strange thing: his dark face, at least, looks human. I sit there sketching the letters of an ugly reptilian alphabet until the light begins to fail. Night already? Surely not; six o'clock on my watch. A flash of lightning to the north, a lagging rumble of thunder; black-bellied storm clouds have darkened the sky unnoticed. I tuck the exercise book inside my shirt and shimmy down the trunk, concerned less about sitting in a lightning conductor than with the need to get a clearer view. Leaving my bike-fruit unpicked I stroll up the street. The blinds of the house are drawn; would she answer if I knocked? I walk on, turn and make another slow pass before finding the courage to step through the gate.

A loud rap on the door, but the only answer seems to be my heart, knocking inside its cage of ribs as if trying to get out. To get away, perhaps, from its own unbearable excitement. At least that excitement – the excitement of doing something – has cured its unbearable heaviness. What next? Sneak around the side, ease the louvres free, dive in? I knock again, just in case, and this time sense some sort of movement, or faint vibration, inside. Or is it still the vibration inside my chest?

The door opens. 'Master Burns.' Miss Burke's tone is more tired than sarcastic, her plump face flaccid and expressionless. 'What do you think you're doing here?'

'I want to talk to her, Miss.'

Irritation tightens and lifts the jowls of her face. 'As I told your father, she's not here.'

'Why was he here?'

Miss Hammond's face appears next to her friend's. 'Do you think perhaps he might have been looking for you?'

'Her scooter's here.'

'But she's not. And you – *you* of all people – shouldn't be here either. So clear off!'

The door thumps solidly shut in my face. I bang again. I don't believe her for a moment. 'Miss Peach!' I shout. 'Miss Peach! It's me, Robbie.'

This time the door is flung open. Miss Burke barrels out onto the porch like a small locomotive. Miss Hammond follows close behind; they seize me by the arms, engines working in tandem, and shunt me rapidly up the drive and out the gate. Their plump faces are living, quivering things now, red with rage, but at least they are mammal faces, with mammal breasts bouncing around below them like four members of a separate mammal species.

'You think we don't know who broke into our house that first time!' 'If we catch so much as a glimpse of you riding past again we're going to call the . . . ' a glance between them, 'your *father*. Is that clear?'

'Need a hand, ladies?' A loud male voice from the next yard. Big Merv watches from his lit porch. Other front doors are opening up and down the street, other witnesses emerging.

'Thank you for your concern, Mervyn,' Miss Burke calls back. 'But I believe we have the situation under control.'

He steps down from the porch, rolling up his shirt-sleeves. 'I think I heard the ladies ask you to leave, Burns, so I'd p.o.q. if I were you.'

'Merv,' Miss Hammond says. 'Please. This is a private matter. We don't want any *more* scenes.'

He halts, but stands his ground, arms folded; the women turn back to me.

'*Do* we need a hand, Master Burns?' Miss Burke asks, more quietly now.

Another flash of lightning from the north. Automatically I count the seconds to the thunder, make the calculation. 'The storm's three miles away, Miss.'

Incredulity on those puffy faces. 'What's that got to do with the price of eggs?'

'We're going to get wet if we stay out here.'

'You want us to invite you in out of the rain?' They give identical harsh laughs. 'Isn't that how all this trouble started?'

A deep breath. 'I love her.'

'So much that you've ruined her life, Burns.'

'We're not part of the lynch mob that blames *her*, are we Miss Burke?'

'Quite the contrary, Miss Hammond. We think she was taken advantage of.'

Their routine is less playful today than grimly determined, the two locomotives working up steam.

'We think she drank far too much and was . . . interfered with.'

'So piss off, you nasty little boy. Or we *will* call your father.'

Piss off yourselves, I want to tell them. This is her house too. I look past them to Big Merv, hold his menacing gaze for a moment. *You piss off too, big-mouth!* The unsaid words rise in me like gorge, like vomit.

'Burns!' both women growl, reading my mind, or my face.

The street gallery is full, clumps of neighbours crowding the opera boxes of their front porches. I take a last look at her house, hoping for some sign, some curtain-twitch or eye-peep.

'You've done enough damage,' Miss Burke hisses.

'More than enough,' from Miss Hammond.

Damage? To Miss Peach? I would never hurt her, but momentarily I exult in the thought that I might have. My anger eases; there is an affirmation in Miss Burke's words, less of cruelty than of manly action, manly agency. I turn and walk away along the street, but slowly and deliberately, not so much running the gauntlet of nosey-parkers and sticky-beaks as sauntering, head held high, returning their disapproving stares. Yes, they all know, but so what? My chest swells again with pride; the gorge of words that rises in me, that wants to burst out of me, is a sweeter vomit. *Yes, it was me! The town delinquent. I'm the one! I took advantage! I did the damage!* I pluck my bike from the pepper tree and look back up the road.

True twilight now, the witnesses spotlit in their porches. An indistinct Miss Burke and Big Merv are murmuring together across their common fence. As I watch, a third figure joins them. Is it her? I ride stealthily back, watched by every face in the street except theirs. I am within a house of them before realising it's only short, squat Rita Bailey. Her husband spots me at the same time; I brake as he steps out onto the road to block my approach.

'You're a slow learner, Burns. I told you to make yourself scarce.'

'It's a free country. I'm just riding home.'

'Ride the long way round, you insolent bastard!'

I turn my bike but remain stationary, straddling it. 'This is none of your business.'

'It's *every*one's business, thanks to you, you bloody great streak of misery!'

I begin pedalling, but very slowly, still looking back. 'Then everyone should know you were first in the queue,' I shout, parroting my father. 'You wanted to fuck her too! But she wouldn't have you! So piss off yourself, hypocrite!'

He roars with rage and sprints towards me, but I am high on the pedals and pushing down hard. His feet pound the bitumen, his shouting sounds perilously close. Once again I think I've miscalculated, but a centaur will always outstrip a mere mortal. A mortal reptile. At the end of the street, I risk a glance back; he stands with his hands on his knees, his wife behind him, clearly berating him. More manly action on my part, more damage done? Yes, and I glory in it. A momentary anxiety only: will he ring my father? Will his wife? Will he ambush me on the way home, or even be waiting for me at home? I doubt it; my rapidly maturing rat-cunning tells me I have too much on him. Better still: he knows I have too much on him.

Another thunder-crack; the first big fat raindrops begin to spatter the bitumen, but as I pedal on homewards none seem to hit me. Am I still the skinny stripling who needs to run around in a rainshower to get wet? I might lack muscle bulk but I feel filled out with muscular fierceness, with a capacity to cause even greater damage.

I'm not deluded, I will never be a match for Big Merv but I'd happily take a beating if I could land one nose-bloodying punch.

Mum is silhouetted in the kitchen window, sifting flour. Too restless to join her, too grown up for the confines of the kitchen and preparations for baking day, I head into the man's world of the stables instead. Immediately I reach for my chemicals. I spill a cupful of yellow sulphur dust, as fine as sifted flour itself, into a beaker. My stock of ammonium nitrate, untouched for months, has solidified; I pulverise the largest chunks in a mortar and mix the crystalline powder fifty-fifty with the sulphur. Baking day in the back shed. I pack my pungent cake mixture into a jam tin and top it with a wick of twisted, torn newspaper. Big firecracker or small bomb? I've an urge to make a ferocious explosion, a noise-and-light show that will compete with the elements above. Another lightning flash, the thunder-crack instantaneous. No time to lose. I slip on Dad's welding goggles and set my sulphur cake on the back lawn, between the holding cells and the shed. With a bottle of metho I spill a flammable liquid fuse a few yards long, from the tip of the newspaper to the door of the shed. I am striking the match when the heavens open.

Divine intervention? No miracle will thwart me today, even from making another involuntary attempt on my own life. I retrieve the rain-soaked cake-bomb and set it down on the packed-earth floor of the stables instead. After tamping in a dry newspaper wick, I lay another metho trail, this time crouching outside the door and looking back in as the blueish flame crawls at a surprising snail-pace towards the bomb.

The *whoosh* is more volcanic eruption than explosion, a roaring blowtorch of flame and smoke shooting up out of the furiously trembling tin. The fluorescent light above shatters almost immediately; thick, acrid smoke fills the shed. The fierce flame is barely visible as the tin finally flips onto its side and begins spinning and skittering about the floor like an out-of-control rocket sled, spraying exhaust in every direction. Soon only a dull flicker can be seen through the dense smoke; soon it can only be heard – a dull roar – and soon, rocket fuel exhausted, there is nothing but silence. Smoke is still pouring as thickly as ever out of the door and windows and beneath the eaves, an acrid sulphurous stink which stings my throat and clogs my breathing.

'Fire!' a hoarse voice shouts from a holding cell. 'Hey! Missus! Fire!'

I stagger backwards from the shed, bent double, coughing and gasping, but the eerily silent fog pursues me, envelops me. I slump onto my knees on the lawn, dizzy and wheezing. Raindrops spatter my head and neck, but it's a far-off rain, as far as the repeated calls of 'Fire!' and 'Missus!' I am fighting for breath, or perhaps fighting against breath, fighting to get the breath out. The dark shape of Uncle Possum is bent over me, coughing itself.

'You gotta get up, Robbie!'

I can no more move than breathe. I seem to be suffocating in air – able to suck the stuff in but unable to push it out, each breath leaving even less room for the next. Then I am being hoisted up and carried inside to bed. My mother's voice: 'Find Doc McKenzie, Possum!' She wants me to lie flat. I can't, I need to sit up, bent forwards, gasping for breath. After what seems like five hours but is probably no more than the same number of minutes, the doc waddles through the bedroom door. I am dying but he is as languid and unconcerned as ever as he sits on the edge of the bed and peers at me over his half-moons.

'Don't worry, young Lucifer. No one ever dies of asthma. Unless they panic.'

I panic. *Do something!* I want to scream, but haven't the breath even to whisper. He bends closer and sniffs as if he were, after all, the whiskered, tuft-browed Scottie dog he most resembles. 'A bit on the sulphurous side. What hellfire have you been cooking up tonight?'

He presses a cold stethoscope about my chest, then fishes a horse needle from his battered kitbag of vet tools. 'You've been to the very gates tonight, Lazarus – but this will bring you back. A little cocktail of my own devising. Adrenaline. Phenobarb.'

The sting of the needle is nothing more than a sharper, colder raindrop. Somewhere the doctor repeats his refrain: 'The important thing is not to panic.'

This time the surge of panic that follows is short-lived; my breathing begins rapidly to ease, and with it comes a flood of relief. My heart pounds mightily, but the act of breathing, usually as invisible as the lungfuls of air it moves in and out, has become a source of great pleasure. That pleasure might be nothing more than the absence of pain, but is also nothing less. I lie there luxuriating in my own breathing, slowly in, even more slowly out. I might be ejaculating air, molecule by sexual molecule. Which reminds me. If Miss Peach is leaving on tonight's train, is there still time to intercept her?

'You've sniffed the brimstone tonight,' the doctor mumbles, per-haps to me, perhaps not. 'Could be there's a lesson to be learnt.'

I shut my eyes, open them. The doctor is standing now, my mother is sitting on the bed.

'Got up to larks like this myself once,' he mumbles on. 'Had my own little backyard laboratory —'

'So you've said,' Mum interrupts, unconvinced.

'Distilled ether once. Found a recipe in Towler. Six drachmas of potassa, four pints alcohol, one pint sulphuric acid —'

'Don't you go giving the boy any more ideas!'

'Dangerous stuff, ether. Maintaining the correct temperature is the problem. Below 260 degrees, alcohol distills across. Greater than 310 degrees, olefiant gas. Very explosive, either way. Still, I survived.'

'You mentioned that last time too, Doctor. When he spilt the acid in his eyes. Now, if that's all . . .?'

His voice grumbles on soothingly. What is he telling her? Don't panic? No one ever died from a bomb explosion? I open my eyes; she has got him out into the hall now, but still he mumbles.

'Medical school funnelled my, ah, boyish energy. Robert might spend some time with me during the holidays. Get the feel of the work.'

Somehow the drugs have split mind from body: my adrenaline-drugged heart rattles the bars of its bony cage but my sedated brain has slipped into some clear, tranquil zone. I feel at a great distance from the world, no longer a subjective part of it and its myriad objects. Among which are its inhabitants. One of those – the doctor – has apparently left. Another – the hero – is eating his reward in the kitchen: lemon delicious pudding by the delicious smell of it. The mother – mine? – is fussing around him, perhaps plying him with sweet milky tea in lieu of sweet sherry. No sign yet of the police sergeant, who is driving back from a pub brawl in Kalangadoo. And the teacher? Miss Peach is her name, and hopefully she will be leaving on the morning train instead. If at all. No panic, definitely. Plenty of time. I close my eyes again, or perhaps my heavy lids, heavier than my heart has ever been, close themselves.

What wakes me? The far-off blast of the Bluebird's air-horn? The frame of narrow bright light around the drawn blind? Have the clouds cleared outside? Has the evening train left yet? The air-horn sounds again, more urgently, then again, this time a continuous blast. Livestock on the track? Fully awake now, I glance at the clock: 8.35. But the night train comes through at seven. And how can it still be light this late? I jackknife out of bed but the walls of the room close in on me immediately. I slump back on the mattress and let my giddy head fall between my knees.

Mum's faint voice somewhere in this faded, unfocused world: 'Feeling better this morning, Robbie? You've slept like a log.'

Sensory information of all kinds not making sense. A creaking of springs, her weight lowering my mattress, tilting it her way, her arm resting on my shoulders. 'Breakfast might perk you up.'

The world swims back into focus, alarmingly. I've slept all night? The air-horn belongs to the morning train? Which morning, for that matter? Which year – 2064?

The phone jangles, the tread of police-issue boots in the hall, a police-issue voice. 'Sergeant Burns speaking . . . Bluey? Slow down, mate . . . *What?* Lying on the tracks? Oh, bugger me! . . . Who? Possum? . . . Get onto the doc. I'm on my way.'

The mattress rights itself as Mum heads out the door and into an urgently whispered conversation. Her muffled gasp is followed by rapid boot-steps, the clatter of the back door, the *creak*-open and *thunk*-shut of the car door.

Stable on my feet now, I shuffle into the hall. 'What's going on?'

Her face is ashen. 'There's been an accident.' Outside, the tyre-crunch of the EK reversing out of the gravel drive, fast; inside, her anxious glance to the window. 'Someone's been hit by the Bluebird.'

'Possum?'

'It doesn't bear thinking about, Robbie.' She clamps a big arm around my shoulders and steers me back to bed. 'Doctor's orders. No excitement. I'll bring some breakfast.'

I can lie still for a few seconds only before jackknifing up again and following her into the kitchen. 'Was he drunk?'

'I don't want to talk about it, Robbie.' She butters the jaffle-iron, then decides to talk about it anyway. 'He was sitting right there last night. Drank nothing but tea, bless him.' She jams bread and bacon into the iron and trims it to size, then turns my way, agitated. 'This is *exactly* why I tell you to keep away from the line! And your father. He's just a big kid sometimes, standing so close. The pair of you! A pair of stupid kids!'

The words seem to burst out of her; I sit there astonished as she lifts a metal plate from the stove top and rests the jaffle-iron above the crackling inferno. 'Now, back to bed this instant. I'll bring you a tray.'

My mind is jumping. I imagine Uncle Possum, released early last night for heroic behaviour, sleeping on the line with a belly full of sweet tea and lemon delicious pudding. Has Billy heard the news? But maybe it's not Possum. Maybe it's Big Merv Bailey, chased into the path of the Bluebird by his shrew wife. A better possibility, but I can't make it stick. I raise my blind, jerk up the window, and sit on the edge of the bed straining to hear any clues – tooting cars, shouted voices – above the light patter of rain against the roof. The most thrilling thing to happen in the town for years and I might as well be locked in a holding cell.

'*In* bed, I said.' Mum has materialised behind me, holding a tray.

I climb into bed; she sets the tray on my knees, repeats her 'Doctor's orders' instruction, and leaves, closing the door behind her. Phone-dialling noises in the hall; I wolf down the jaffle and am out of bed and dressed and duffle-coated by the time the connection is made: 'Jean? Marj Burns. Any news?'

I ease up the window, unhook the flyscreen and lower it carefully to the ground outside. The steady drizzle of rain is of no account as

I squeeze out. Which direction? The old Kalangadoo road crossing? The station?

The station. I pedal hard, riding up under the eaves and braking hard on an empty platform within minutes. Bluey's cave behind the ticket grille is also empty. I look south along the tracks: nothing. North: a small flock of people, perhaps fifty yards distant, trudging towards the station through misty rain. Most are carrying luggage; bringing up the rear is the bobbing carrot-top of Bluey McPherson, as bright as ever in the gloom, keeping the stragglers bunched and moving, looking like nothing so much as a red-haired kelpie-cross. A couple of hundred yards beyond him are the orange chin and dull square eyes of the Bluebird.

I fling down my bike, jump onto the tracks and head north, walking as quickly as possible on the slippery wet sleepers. Hurrying with their heads down, none of the passengers notice me until I'm among them; I am through the flock before the red kelpie barks. 'Where do you think you're going, young Burns?'

I keep moving, more quickly, jumping two slippery sleepers at a time. 'I need to see Dad.'

'He won't want to see you!' he barks after me, but his charges are eager for shelter, for cocoa and blankets, and he can do nothing but turn and trot on in their wake.

The rain heavier now, blurring the world, blurring me in the eyes of the world. Is that a police sergeant's navy uniform further up, bent almost double, peering beneath a coupling? A face glances my way through the filmy mist, but only briefly; clad in my heavy duffle coat, and some distance off, I am everyman. Clumps of bystanders have gathered here and there along the track. I stop at the first and peer over the shield-wall of umbrellas, unnoticed. Constable Hicks is standing guard over something between the tracks, but what? An empty wheat sack spread across a small mound. The victim? Surely not, the mound is no larger than a rabbit, the spots of blood that soak the coarse wet hessian are rabbit-sized.

'Kneeling there when the train came around the bend,' someone is murmuring. 'Must have heard the horn but didn't move. Just sort of leant forward . . .'

'What, with their neck on the track?'

'Like a guillotine.'

'Like a chook.'

'Like she was praying.'

She. I step back, still unnoticed. Uncle Possum sits watching from the shelter of a tree on the far side of the line, bemused but safe and sound, and male. He waves a paper-bagged bottle my way. I look about; no sign of Billy. No one else recognises me. More clumps of umbrellas and more scraps of wet sacking lie between me and the train, still fifty yards distant. I walk on, fascinated rather than repelled by the thought of what might lie beneath. Doc McKenzie is on his hands and knees at another smallish mound; stout Mrs Dalziel holds an umbrella over him while staring steadfastly away. Wanting steadfastly to do the opposite, I ease my way through the press of bodies and umbrellas.

'Look at that,' the doctor mutters, lifting a corner of hessian. 'That's something you don't see every day. Just look at that.' He glances up over the top of his rain-spattered half-moons; his eyes seem to seize on me. 'Young Lucifer. Just in time for your first anatomy tutorial. Just in time.'

Mrs Dalziel turns on him, incredulous. 'Doctor, what *are* you saying? You can't possibly allow a boy to see such things!'

His muttering seems a little driven, and repetitive. 'Do him good. Not much here that he hasn't seen stuck in a rabbit trap – isn't that so, young Burns? Give him a taste of the dissecting room. Yes, do him good.'

She leans closer to him. 'Doctor! Hedley! *He's* the one . . .' The rest of the sentence is hissed in his ear.

But now he tugs the sacking aside. Gasps behind us; Mrs Dalziel lowers her umbrella to obstruct my view. 'Go away,' she tells me sternly, and then more loudly, 'you should all go away. What are you doing here?'

Uneasy glances among the bystanders, but no one is leaving. I shove the protective umbrella aside and squat at the doctor's side. The light is dim; he has a shoe of some kind in his hand. A woman's ballet slipper, with something stuffed inside it, some sort of thick sock, barely protruding. He plucks a pocket torch from some-where with his free hand, plays it across the sock, turns his wet face to mine. 'Surprisingly clean dissection of an ankle joint, young Lucifer.' What is he talking about? I'm not sure he knows himself. His expression is strained, he mumbles on automatically. 'Can't let a little rain spoil an opportunity like this. Look here – talar cartilage. And here – Achilles insertion.'

Mrs Dalziel steps away, taking her umbrella with her. 'I'm fetch-ing the boy's father. You hear me, Hedley? I said I'm fetching his father!'

Frigid raindrops splatter my head and neck but I can see every-thing on the track clearly enough. Can both see and not see: the severed foot registers less than the undamaged perfection of the shoe that contains it. My eyes cling to that, as if finding reassurance in its intactness. For a time it seems less the missing piece of a weird puzzle than the only piece that fits. Where are the others? I don't know. I know nothing as the doctor mutters on; I feel nothing. Is numbness an emotion in its own right, or the absence of emotion? The terrible thrill in my limbs is more physical than mental, as if my body is doing the thinking that my mind can't manage. My mind can barely manage one stray thought: why would this foot have borrowed one of Miss Peach's ballet slippers? And where is the other one? At her house? She'll want it back. She needs a complete pair.

Two plump hands seize my shoulders, raise me to my feet, spin me round. Now those same two hands cup my face like blinkers, allowing me to see nothing but another face, my mother's. 'Oh, Robbie, Robbie! Darling boy, what are you *doing* here?'

I twist free. Her umbrella lies on the ground behind her, a black, one-legged beetle on its back.

'What are *you* doing here?'

Her expression agonised. 'Looking for *you*, of course.'

The unbearable pressure in my body – the painful fizzing of its veins, the restless numbness of its limbs – finds a way out at last. 'Bullshit! That's not why you came. You came for the same reason everyone else came. The whole bloody town's here. You're no better than the rest of them!'

She stares at me, speechless.

'The rest of *us*!' I shout.

'What are we going to do with you, Robbie?' she finally asks, but quietly now, almost to herself. She steps towards me again, trying to enfold me in the vast, soft butter of her arms.

The cold rain feels hot on my cheeks, tastes salty on my lips. 'Fuck off,' I scream. 'You were too late! You were *all* too late!' I shove her away, or rather shove myself away from her massive gravity, and turn and sprint towards the Bluebird. It watches me all the way; I could take an axe to the big square face with its ridiculous chin, its empty, stupid eyes that have seen everything and nothing. A dark uniform steps out of the blur of rain between me and the train, I dodge past, seize the door handle of the first carriage and hoist myself up.

My father's voice: 'Robbie! Get down! There's nothing you can do.'

There is everything to do. The seats first, I need to check every seat. Then check under every seat. The luggage racks. The toilets at the far end; half a dozen people could hide in there. I yank open the doors of the Ladies. Empty. The Gents. Empty. The driver's cubicle, likewise. I shoulder on through the communicating doors into the next carriage, with Dad somewhere behind. 'It's okay, son. I understand.'

More empty seats, more empty toilet cubicles. Miss Peach must be further up the tracks, trudging homewards, or at home already, snuggled in her big double bed with a mug of cocoa. I leap from the last door, land on my feet in a spray of wet ballast, and sprint away, Dad's shouts fading behind. 'It's okay, Robbie. It'll be all right.'

Rain beats against the outside of my head, a dull roar inside. The rushing world – faces, fences, trees, shops – closes around me, like the walls of a tunnel. Where am I? Still dreaming? Outside Dalziel's store at the end of the dream-tunnel, yes – but where really? Lying drugged in bed listening to the doctor mumble on about the boiling point of ether, last time I noticed. The parallel world makes consistent sense: Dalziel's is empty because Mrs Dalziel is at the accident. I step through the dream-door, yank open the ice chest and peer in. Which flavour Slippery Sam? Pineapple? I grab six. Spoils of a dream-crime only, but frost-bitingly cold in my hands as I flee the scene.

Safe home within minutes, I bolt the cave door and set to work. Erlenmeyer flask. Asbestos tripod. Double-holed, red rubber bung, thermometer in one hole, angled glass tubing in the other. This equipment all solid to handle and suspiciously real. *Maintaining the correct temperature is the problem.* Jury-rigged Liebig condenser. Water isn't an adequate coolant for what I have in mind; I pound the stolen goods against the bench, slit the plastic sheaths open, and pack the glass outer sleeve of the apparatus with crushed pineapple-ice. The still is ready, now for the ingredients. Into the flask goes – what was the doctor's recipe? *Four parts alcohol. One part sulphuric acid . . .*

Have I forgotten anything? The chemistry is simple enough, and beautiful in its simplicity. $2C_2H_5OH - H_2O = (C_2H_5)_2O$. Alcohol minus water equals ether.

Highly explosive either way. I desperately hope so. I light the lamp beneath the tripod, then sit with one eye on the creeping rise of the mercury, one on the slowly heating mixture. A watched Erlenmeyer flask never boils? The first tiny frog-spawn of bubbles take for ever to cluster against the inside of the glass, but here at last are the big aggregating bubbles, breaking free, rising. A smoky vapour swirls through the flask then inches up the tube, rounds the acute bend, creeps down into the condenser. The smell comes first – sickly sweet, a little nauseating, the smell of the dentist's waiting room – then, at last, a drop of distillate at the end of the tube, gathering, gathering, then falling, only to vanish smokily before it hits the base of the beaker.

I stick my thumb beneath the spout and catch the second; it vaporises from my fingertip, leaving a white frost-stain and a feeling of intense cold, sharp as a burn. I like the feeling, and want more. Anything but numbness. I kneel and put my mouth to the glass tip; a hot sweetness on my tongue this time, but just as intense. My head is already spinning, I feel drunk. Have I got the temperature wrong? Is alcohol distilling, rather than the ether? My eyes swim, the thermometer won't come into proper focus. A delicious weight in my head, a heaviness in my limbs. I lie down on the floor; perhaps I'll just shut my eyes for a moment.

Loud knocking somewhere in outer space. A voice, either my father's or the galactic emperor's. 'Robbie? You in there?' Thoughts swirling like vapour in the flask of my head now; actions, including my own, taking place at a distance, although more in time than space, as if I'm a little ahead of myself, as if I've travelled a second or two into the future and am looking back at my just-past self lying on the hard-packed floor. Numb limbs still, but this numbness also delicious, not terrible at all. The apparatus on the bench silent, the spirit burner dead.

I, or he, the person separated fractionally from me in time, struggles to his knees and strikes a match, and the great *whoomf* of flame that follows also seems already in the past even as it happens. The distant, prickling pain is not unpleasant, nor the new tunnel I find myself in, dark and closed-in again but lit in a different way by those invisible, prickling sparklers in the skin.

4

Darkness still, although the pounding on the tunnel walls has stopped. The only noise is Doc McKenzie's low rumble. 'Something for the pain.' What pain? I yelp; the only pain is a needle being pushed into my arm. Also a vague grittiness in my eyes; I am back in the present, but which present? I try to force my lids open, they stay shut. I lift my hands to rub them and touch – what? Some kind of mask? And what am I touching with? Boxing gloves? My hands feel swollen and heavy, my fingers trapped.

A second voice, my mother's: 'Keep still, Robbie.'

Two hands, also hers, take my wrists and place them by my side. 'Lie still, darling boy.'

'Where am I?' I speak like a ventriloquist, unable to move my lips and jaw.

'Hospital.'

I wave those heavy, unseen mitts. 'Was I knocked out?'

'Your hands are bandaged, Robbie. And your face. There were some burns. And glass splinters. From the explosion.'

The doctor's rumble again. 'Lucky you were already under your own anaesthetic, young Lucifer. Made my job easy.' It might be a joke, but his tone is flat, mechanical.

My mother's hands cradle my head, a soft pillow is slipped beneath. The movement stirs a little nausea, but I seem to be floating beyond its full reach.

'Your eyes will be fine. Isn't that right, Doctor?'

A barely audible reply, possibly: 'Bit early to tell.'

'You can come home tomorrow, Robbie. But the bandages stay on. Doctor?'

A longer mumble, in the midst of which: 'Need to rest the eyes,' and 'a week or so.'

'I've got to lie here a week? What will I do?'

'Nothing in the back shed,' she says with some force.

More rumbling from the doctor, but at least my mother's voice is clear. 'Isn't that thoughtful, Robbie? The latest issue. I can read to you.'

'What about school? What about Miss Peach?'

Silence. I lie in my railway tunnel, unable to see or touch. The room might be empty – empty also of me, floating in darkness, disembodied, apart from the faint grittiness of my eyes.

The doctor clears his throat, and for the first time there is some life in his voice. 'Had a scholarship when I was his age. Adelaide Grammar. Think I mentioned it before.'

'Many times, Doctor,' my mother says.

'Boarding and tuition for bright country boys. First-rate Science teaching. Fresh start. I've got the paperwork somewhere. Sent away for it a few months back.'

'Are we keeping you from your other patients?'

'Hmm? No. Not at all. Plenty of time. Nothing pressing . . .'

A rustling of pages. 'Perhaps I'll read you something from the *Weekly*, Robbie,' she announces, and begins immediately, singsong. '*First and Last Love*, by Georgette Heyer. "In the year 1776, Prudence Hayes left her comfortable home in Surrey to . . ."'

Perhaps the doctor stays to the bitter end, but I leave almost immediately, fast asleep within seconds. I sense that I'm alone when I wake. Bandaged darkness still, but bright sparkles of pain again, more insistently, plus other, different sense-colours. Nose-colours: a nauseous mix of frying bacon, floor ammonia and – what? Shit? Not mine, I hope, but how can I tell? I would bandage my nostrils if I could. Sparkles of sound also in the darkness, bird noises mostly. Bacon and early birds – it must be morning. The clatter of metal instruments somewhere. Surgical, or kitchen? Not so loud, please! The pain-sparkles now a migrainous throb. A door-creak, footsteps, firm hands rolling me over: the quick, sharp jab of a needle; the slow, spreading ache of its freight. More slowly, the ebbing of pain, and in its wake the rising tide of a story, washing over my mind's empty beach.

It's the year 9064 and the burnt-out sun has become a dark star, a galactic cinder, plunging the Earth into perpetual night. Human beings are now as blind as bats, as moles, as earthworms. What use eyes? Instead we have evolved enormous, complex noses, dog-noses that allow us to navigate a sense-world rich in smell-textures and scent-colours.

Formulaic? Another single-issue world, another single-issue thought experiment going nowhere? My head aches, my face throbs. Lying in the darkness, I imagine a future world in which all six senses are variations of one: pain. No, I imaginatively inhabit that world, a planet so filled with acid oceans, toxic rains, lava rivers and poisonous carnivores that only the hair-trigger responses of pain allow its inhabitants to survive. These inhabitants wear the wiring of their nervous system on the outside of their skin; their surface is nothing but a woven mat of exposed nerve-endings. A spectrum of seven pain-colours fleshes out their perceptual world: burning pain, aching pain, throbbing pain, gnawing pain, cramping pain, knifelike pain, vicelike pain. Other senses have evolved their own versions of pain: deafening noise, and especially those stinks – fresh shit, week-dead sheep – which seem as much evil as painful.

Sudden, more extreme pain in the non-imagined world. The bandages on my face are being lifted. Has there been a warning? Doc McKenzie's burble in the background. 'Lights off, Sister. Open slowly, young Lucifer. Warm saline, Sister. How many fingers?'

A dazzle of light; I can't even see an arm.

'So how is he, Doc?' My father's low rumble. How long has he been there?

'On track,' the doctor murmurs, which I know means exactly that, for he never says anything merely to reassure a patient. 'Need to wrap him up again for a few days.'

'I can take him home?'

My eyes are already being rebandaged. Re-blinded. The answer sounds like it begins with yes and ends with a promise of a house call tomorrow to change the bandages. 'Might bring the new *Analog*,' he says. 'Could read you a few chapters.'

Perhaps no one hears him except me. My father's firm hand is on my elbow. 'On your feet, sonny-jim. Right hand on my left shoulder. I'm your guide-dog.'

5

A week of darkness and wireless follows. News bulletins interrupted by commercials. Commercials interrupted by top-forty songs, of which the top thirty-odd are the Beatles. The top forty meals of my life interrupting everything else. I might have been eating those same meals for years, week in, week out, but never with such wolf-ish immersion. Eating, I soon discover, is the ecstasy of the blind. Playing with my dick also, but that must be done with caution. Anyone might be watching, especially my mother, who pads quietly about the house all day, surprisingly soft-footed for one so large. After tea each night she sits uninvited on the end of my bed and reads aloud to me.

'I don't enjoy those magazines the doctor left, Robbie. I've brought in one of my favourite novels, *The Robe*.'

The doctor visits daily, my yelps and groans through each re-bandaging ignored, or more likely unnoticed. His offer of reading science fiction has been fended off – 'I'm sure you're far too busy, Doctor' – but I sense him lingering in the doorway each day, as if wanting to speak, to say something more clearly, before mumbling goodbye and shuffling off. After work my father looks in; not much is said, but there are raised voices in the next room later, behind closed doors. No need to eavesdrop; blindness has sharpened hearing as well as taste and sexual sensitivity. One thing is soon clear: I'm not going back to school for the rest of the final term. Next year's schooling is the issue. They argue back and forth every night for a week before my mother capitulates.

'We're not saying you have to go, Robbie,' she tells me. 'Not if you don't want to.'

I can't see her face, I ignore the catch in her throat. Boarding school – the city! If Miss Peach is anywhere, she is in the city.

And then the bandages are off for the last time and I am out of the tunnel. The dazzle of the dull bedroom light bulb blinds me in a different way, but slowly the faces of the people who surround me – anxious mother, expectant father, distracted doctor – swim into focus, the room beyond rebuilds itself, brick by perceptual brick, and the thoughts that have hidden themselves in the darkness of my head are held up to the light.

'It's all right, son,' Dad mutters awkwardly as I lie on my back shocked, seeing everything.

But it isn't; it wasn't.

AFTER

I

Universe, Milky Way, Solar System, Earth, Australia, South
Australia, Penola. It's the year 2007 and I have given up booze
and cigarettes and unprotected sex, my prostate gland is 'soft and
unremarkable to palpation', and my serum cholesterol has broken
the four-millimol-per-litre barrier.

Science fiction? With a little bad luck I might live for ever.

Forty years ago my parents also seemed immortal to me, and
therefore – at some deep, unconsidered level – I was more immortal.
Miss Peach would have scratched purple ink through that sentence,
but the sums were simple: If Mum and Dad were going to live for
ever, I would live at least for ever and a day.

Forty-odd years later that day has come, and its open-
endedness, once so full of promise, now seems merely empty.
I can't say I feel lonely without them – we've lived mostly apart
since that year – but I do feel alone, a state of mind at once less
painful and more difficult to come to grips with. Another

milestone? Two, at least. Mum died of heart failure a month back; Dad followed her a week ago, heartbroken, although he refused to acknowledge it, especially to himself. Her hearse was a lovingly restored black-and-chrome, left-hand-drive '48 Chevy he hired from Mount Gambier for the occasion; he spent a few quiet moments before the service with the bonnet popped, meditating upon the antique, finely engineered machinery beneath, then took a deep breath, marched up the steps into St Andrew's and gave one of his briefest policeman's speeches.

Back from exile, I recognised almost no one. Did anyone recognise me? Doc McKenzie's nose was buried in what might have been a hymn book or a copy of *Galaxy* magazine; did he even notice I was there? He looked no older than the last time I'd seen him, forty years before, but also no younger. His beeper went off during the benediction; he looked up from his reading, startled, glanced about as if there might be another doctor in the church, then realised that the pesky gadget was his. He read another page, folded down a dog-ear, then rose and hurried out as fast as his walking cane would carry him.

I was left to do the talking at Dad's funeral. I booked the same hearse and the same Presbyterian hymns; the same scones and date loaf and lamingtons and jubilee cake covered the trestle table in the Caledonian Hall afterwards. The same faces filled the pews – widows, mostly, plus the odd Eagles stalwart, and a few retired colleagues from the force, gamely wedged into the faded dress uniforms of their fitter, younger selves. Doc McKenzie's nose was stuck in another book. There were a few new faces. Possum and Jacko Currie showed up, silver-haired and silver-bearded and sitting straight-backed in their pew like a pair of distinguished Easter Island statues. They knew I was there, but looked away as I spoke. Their wives sat each side of them, plumper, softer statues, also avoiding my gaze. For the first time it struck me as odd how little I knew of Billy's mum and Auntie Dulcie, how little I had seen of them; it was even odder that while Billy had half lived at my house, I was never allowed to stay at his. I spotted his older brother Neville sitting among the footballers at the back, but there was no sign of Billy himself. He had sent one letter to me at boarding school, a page of wood-work paper covered with mispellings and crossings-out. Miss Peach wasn't mentioned, just my move to the city. He was still pissed off I had gone, he wrote. He wondered if I'd be home for the holidays. Rabbiting wasn't the same without me.

I was done with the past, even if this letter wasn't the past that I remembered. It was too incomprehensible to answer.

Rumours of his doings reached my ears from time to time in the years that followed. I never sought them out; perhaps they sought me for that reason. His face jumped out of the sports pages when he first came up to play football in the city – Did they have the name right? Surely they meant Neville? – and again a year later when a knee injury ended his short career. Next I heard he'd married, had a child, done time in jail – a cell with locked doors – after belting a cop, got unmarried, had another child, done time in rehab, joined AA, done some sort of social-work course. I hoped he was well on the way to silver-haired, wise-elder status himself.

I gave the speech Dad hadn't given the month before, the rest of his speech, and then some. Standard-version noises for the most part, but the congregation of friends needed to hear them. *They would have wanted to go together. A part of him died when she died. He loved her very much.*

Rest in peace? If only it were that easy. Having seen him off with due ceremony I felt a growing urge, or inner pressure, to say more. But to whom? Jacko? Possum? Mrs Currie? The wise-looking but stone-faced elders looked unapproachable. Doc McKenzie? Again his beeper went off, again he looked bemused, again he rose and hurried out.

I pushed my way through the throng on the steps afterwards as quickly as I could. By the time I reached the footpath he was at the corner of Church Street, moving quickly for an old man with a stick; I took off after him.

'Robbie! Hey, Robbie! Hang on!'

I turned to find Neville waving from the steps. No escape; I waited, a little apprehensive, as he limped towards me. He looked like he needed a stick as well.

'Where you going in such a hurry?'

I hadn't heard the voice since it was a boy's, unbroken and high-pitched; it took time to see the rest of the dark, skinny boy who owned it in this thickset, middle-aged man with a flabby, pock-marked face.

'Billy?' I was guessing. It could still just as easily have been Neville.

'Been a long time, Robbie.'

2

Year's end, 1964. Summertime outside, the rabbits jumping and the wheat high, but I spend my last weeks in town hidden inside the stables, writing. Shelves of magical chemicals surround me, but I am lost in the alchemy of ink on paper. Is Billy out there somewhere, setting traps and drinking sweet brown sherry and playing with his dick by campfire light? I have no idea, and even less interest. Imploding stars, exploding planets, galactic plagues, intergalactic wars – the dark materials of words are all I need as I scribble violently on through the season of Festive Cheer and Good Will to Men.

Uncle Possum sees in the new year inside a holding cell, and doesn't emerge all day. He has nothing to say to me. I have nothing to say to him. I have nothing to say to anyone. I have no interest in anyone. I climb no roofs or trees; what else is there to observe? I am fourteen, going on fifteen, and I know more than enough about life on Earth. Mixed nitrogen-oxygen atmosphere, water-cycle climate, carbon-based life forms. Intelligent life forms? Scant evidence, now that Miss Peach has gone. The doctor? My anxious mother summons him weekly, as if fearing my thought experiments might physically damage me. He tries in his bumbling, obvious way to bring me out of myself. 'Ever sublimated iodine, young Lucifer? First-class laboratories at your boarding school.' I half listen only; I am doing fine inside myself. Being inside the town is the problem.

January creeps by, February takes for ever to arrive, but at last I am leaving for the city. I refuse to take the Bluebird; Mum fusses in the background, fighting tears, as Dad loads my bags into the Holden at dawn. Another new school year, another new school uniform; he aims the box Brownie at me and presses the shutter. Nothing happens: it has spent time recently on his bench being fixed. It's too dark for photography anyway, the sun still hidden, no colour in the empty streets, no sound but a few early birds and, somewhere, a block away, the clop of the milkie's horse and the bright metallic clatter of a billy on a stone doorstep.

'Better get moving, sonny-jim,' Dad says, which is fine by me. I don't even want to face the milkie.

Is Billy perched in the old pepper tree as we drive past the Arthur Street corner? Too dark to tell. Goodbye and good riddance, I whisper to this foreign country as we slip out of it, unseen.

3

It's the year 2007 and here I am alone at the beginning of my long remaining day, both parents gone up in smoke. The accumulated ballast of their two lifetimes remains, a vast clutter of possessions, a great asteroid belt of *stuff* that orbits me as I sit at the big familiar kitchen table in a small unfamiliar house.

If I had married successfully – success measured on the scale of standard grandchild-units – the grandmother might have cajoled the grandfather to move closer to the city when he retired from the force. Instead they moved a few doors closer to the Penola District Hospital. Everything that once filled the big station house was crammed into this cottage; everything that once filled the stables was jam-packed into a compact green Colorbond garden shed out back. Nothing was left behind. Even the old oil drum, held together now by soot and rust, somehow survived the move.

It might come in useful later; there is plenty more to send up in smoke. I have a skip dumpster parked in the drive for non-inflammables, and rolls of colour-coded stickers at my elbow for anything salvageable. Red for the things I'll keep, green for go; the estate auctioneers are sending a truck from the Mount next week.

Where to start? I've stuck a red sticker on the kitchen table. If my sheath-knife turns up in the back shed I might even carve my galactic address into the wood beneath. A survivor of two divorces and thirty-plus years of teacher's pay, I'm not about to look gift furniture in the mouth, especially the quadruped from which I ate the seven best meals of my life, week in, week out.

The rest of the furniture? A green sticker for Mum's old Bechstein – I never got past *Für Elise*. Another green on Dad's single bed; even safe, middle-aged sex requires something with more knee room. Mum's queen-sized mattress, in better nick than mine, cries out for red. Her big, scrubbed-pine chest likewise. The contents of its deep drawers – vast, square-rigged undergarments, folded cubic cardigans – I spill out over her bed, the better to separate wheat from chaff. Except it is all chaff, pungent chaff smelling of lavender and the naphtha of mothballs. More chaff follows from the built-in wardrobe: circus-tent frocks, her comfortable barge-shoes.

The linen press next. I tug open the doors and naphtha fumes roll down over me like a breaking wave. She threw nothing out, I throw out everything. Stacks of neatly folded pillowslips; yellowed bed linen, endlessly patched and re-hemmed; spare, darned-together blankets; faded quilts. Up on a stepladder now, I sweep more chaff out of the topmost shelves: towels and tea-towels; balls of yarn skewered with knitting needles; two big, feather-light paper bags bulging with Christmas decorations; yet more towels.

The deepest recesses are packed with identical cardboard cartons. Each is sealed with masking tape, each also has a jam-jar label fixed to its outward-facing side. It's dark back there; my mother's tiny, neat handwriting is indecipherable. I reach in and drag the nearest box closer to the light. *Robbie, 1956*.

For some time I stand there on the ladder, paralysed. I haven't expected this; I don't know what to make of it. I drag the next box to the edge of the shelf. *Robbie, 1957*.

One by one, I shoulder the heavy boxes down the ladder and lug them into the kitchen. Lined up on the tabletop they resemble nothing so much as a train – a train of box-cars eight years long.

I make a cheese sandwich (my default school lunch, the foil-wrapped plastic cheddar weeks old but still tasteless), then sit and munch and ponder those sealed time-capsules. A roll of amber-coloured stickers – *Caution! Hazard ahead!* – might be useful. These days I don't care to get too close to trains. The caboose especially – *Robbie, 1964* – doesn't bear thinking about.

I finish the sandwich slowly – those wads of white bread and cheese were never easily swallowed – then brew another pot of tea. And sit and sip.

The past is a foreign country. Meaningless the day Miss Peach first chalked them across the blackboard, those words nevertheless stuck in my head like pearl grit, accumulating layers as the years passed.

They do things differently there. How many times have I chalked up those same words myself since? Cast the same grit before swine? Was teaching History a perverse career choice for me or entirely predictable? If the past is a foreign country then its inhabitants must be foreigners, and none seem more foreign to me here, today, sipping tea, than the inhabitant who kept turning into me, who keeps turning into me, the inhabitant who once was me.

Another paradox: the student who won the Latin prize at Adelaide Grammar School, and majored in Classics and History at university, turned his back on his own past completely.

4

It's the year 1965 and the physical country of the past is not so easy for that student to avoid. On exeat weekends he invites day-boy friends to invite him to stay over. Term holidays he can always find a refresher course to keep him in the city, or school sporting trips interstate. Tennis, hockey, cricket, football – he can play none of them competently, but any will do. His parents are patient, and understanding; at the end of his first year of boarding school they take the Police Union beach house at Robe for the duration of the summer holidays, and book it again every Christmas after that.

It's the year 1969, his first at university. He hasn't been back to Penola since he left for boarding school, and no longer gives it much thought, at least during daylight. He keeps his life stuck fast in the glue of the present. Exams and term assignments help; deadlines of any kind offer useful end-stops to past anxieties, a firewall against absurd hopes. He is determined to never again find himself getting too far ahead of himself; getting through the given day is more than enough challenge. Getting through the nights proves difficult at times, especially the small, tight, heart-squeezing hours, when the hell of memory threatens to break loose – but there is always sweet wine to drink, dope to smoke, music loud enough to impede thinking.

In the years to come there is also sex. His tallness and prettiness help. He still looks harmlessly unmasculine to himself, but perhaps women are attracted because of that, because he looks safe. There is no shortage of demand. If at the beginning of the sixties he looked like a girlish Paul McCartney, by the seventies he is David Bowie, slim, androgynous, and for the first time learning to exploit the resemblance. He avoids the subject of English at university without really thinking about it. He hears that the professor has retired through ill health – like news of Billy, news of the professor also seems to seek him out – but he pays little attention. Slim volumes with a certain name on their spine find his eyes in bookshops from time to time, but he leaves them on the shelf. He writes his honours dissertation on Juvenal, and the poets of the Silver Age; he reads no poetry written after the second century AD. Poetry also belongs to the past.

And what of the future? For many years he allows it to take care of itself; it firms up soon enough. Tomorrow always arrives on time, or at least when it is ready, whichever comes first. And the day after tomorrow? He still writes science fiction in his spare time. Whatever hopes or dreams he harbours for the future are pinned vaguely to the success of this, and are about as likely to happen as the outlandish plots themselves. History is his day job, he jokes to friends, his cover job. His night job – his real work – is the future.

Marriage arrives on time, or perhaps ahead of time, firming up a little more quickly than expected, but proves the most reliable and efficient way yet of getting through the nights. It's the year 1975 and for the first time the World Science Fiction Congress comes to a city near him. He hitchhikes across the small corner of the galaxy between Adelaide and Melbourne carrying a rucksack packed with unpublished stories, a heart bursting with excited ambition, and a head full of long-suppressed ideas, manifestos, one-sided conversations.

Of course he is the first on his feet when questions are invited after the guest of honour's keynote address. 'Miss Le Guin, I enjoyed your novel, but since your androgynous beings have no fixed gender, isn't it rather old-fashioned to still use the male pronouns "he" and "him" for them?'

Seeking attention, he gets more than he bargains for in a hostile auditorium. His next words, 'In my short story on a similar theme —' are drowned out by hissing. More trouble follows in the foyer of the Southern Cross Hotel from the attractive red-head he's had his eye on since registration.

'Who the hell do you think you are? You – a *man* – presume to speak for women?'

'No, only for androgynous beings.'

His checkmate smile infuriates her more. 'You're not fit to lick her boots. I've never heard anything so arrogant!'

They are married in five months. Five years later, when Susan asks him if he ever loved her, he replies that he thought so at the time, and therefore (he can't help logically adding) must have, by definition.

Another five-year relationship with another Susan – a fellow History teacher this time – follows closely on the heels of the first. One Susan from the future and one from the past, he jokes, but each time she is less amused. The second relationship, like the first, has to be lived in the present, and it is very much in the present that it founders, when he finally admits he isn't ready for the children she so keenly wants.

He publishes his first two stories in *Analog* during this time. One appears towards the end of each marriage, the timing of which both Susans take to heart.

'You milked my life for your stupid stories!'

'They're set on other planets, Susan. They're about aliens.'

He mentions as little as possible of his life to either. He never – a trivial instance, but perhaps more revealing because of it – mentions his brief comical fling at age thirteen with Miss Loren. He tells no stories against himself, or against any of his foreign selves, no matter how funny or charming or self-deprecating they can be made to sound.

The past is another planet, in a galaxy far, far away. To hell with it, he thinks, when he thinks about it at all. To hell with foreign lands. To hell with childhood and its bullshit innocence. To hell with nostalgia.

He is as fine and pretty as David Bowie but he drives those intelligent, loving, decent women crazy.

He? I. It's time to face the music. I could wince remembering his self-importance, his self-absorption, and if nothing else, perhaps that wince still connects us, me to him – an umbilical cord of shame, stretched to breaking point at times, but somehow holding intact.

So, one more time, with feeling.

5

A swirl of mixed feelings blows through me: surprise, curiosity, apprehension, a twinge of guilt. 'Forty years, Billy,' I say. 'Hard to believe.'

It's his flattened nose all right, and sun-visor brow, but the face is less dark than I remember. Has the boy grown blacker in memory? He watches me cautiously in return, his expression hard to read.

'How you been, Robbie?'

'Getting by. You living back here how?'

'Nah. The Coorong.'

'The mission?'

'We call it a community these days.'

A rebuke? A joke? Watching his impassive face I still can't tell.

'We drove down for the day. Mum, Dad, Poss, Auntie Dulcie – the whole mob. To pay our respects.'

'I appreciate it,' I say.

His face is still expressionless. 'It wasn't for you we come.'

'Dad would appreciate it.'

At last a small, tight smile. 'Dunno bout that. I gave him a hard time. But he always looked out for me. Got me playing footy.'

'Saw you in the paper once. Couldn't believe it. You were such a skinny bugger. Like me.'

'I filled out.' He pats his ample paunch, his smile also more ample. 'My old man woulda disowned me if I didn't play footy. Wonder yours didn't you.'

I disowned myself, I think, but the point doesn't seem worth making aloud.

'Got me boxing too, your old man. Remember the police boxing club?'

'I remember him talking about it.'

A baffled look. 'The Caledonian Hall, remember? Friday nights. We was always sparring. You and me. Going at it hell for leather. Smoke?' He produces a crumpled pack; I take one of two remaining cigarettes, he takes the other, we bend our heads together over a match. Beyond him, clumps of mourners are moving off in the direction of the hall. No one seems interested in us, least of all his family.

'You bullshitting me, Robbie? Your old man started the club for you. You had the better reach but was weak as piss close in.'

'Your memory's playing tricks. I didn't like getting hit. Neither did you.'

He doesn't believe me, but shrugs it off. 'Why'd you let them send you away anyway?'

'I had a scholarship, remember?'

'You always was a brain.' He looks up at me, narrow-eyed through the smoke. 'I wouldn't have gone. Left me friends. Me family.'

You nearly did, I think. You nearly had to. But I don't want to open that can of worms, especially since he doesn't seem to remember my part in it.

'School wasn't the same when you left, Robbie.'

'I needed to get away.'

He puzzles at this, his big brow furrowed. 'You wrote to me that time. Don't remember if I wrote back. Sorry. Never one for sending letters.' He glances over his shoulder. 'Coming to the hall for a cuppa? Say hullo to my old man. Auntie Dulcie brought some scones.'

'They still talking to me?'

Another baffled look. 'Course. They always talk about you.' A nod in the direction of the church. 'And your old man. The old days. Been years now since they moved back to the Coorong. When the sawmill closed.'

I turn and look up Arthur Street. The doctor has vanished. 'Be there in a minute. I need some fresh air.'

He follows my gaze and a grin breaks out across his face. 'What you gonna do? Climb the old pepper tree?'

It hadn't crossed my mind. I haven't noticed the tree until now; it's leaning into the street a couple of blocks away. 'Why not? Say hullo to your dad from me. It's been good to see you, Billy.'

'Hang on.' He flicks his butt away and limps after me. 'I'd better tag along. You might kill yourself.'

We walk a block in silence.

'So what you been doing all these years?' he asks eventually. 'Been teaching, I hear. And writing kids' stories.'

'Adult stories. Speculative fiction.'

He isn't listening. 'I used to like them stories you told. Round the fire. Any kids yourself?'

'None.'

'Lucky feller. Mine are nothing but trouble. Cars. Plonk. Nicking stuff. Funny thing – been doing a bit of teaching myself, sort of. Helping out at the mission school.' A smile, he checks himself. 'The community school. The old culture. Nunga history.' He chuckles again. 'Who'd have thought it back then? The two of us, respectable teachers. Married.'

'What happened to the Tweedle-twins?' I change the subject.

'Moved on somewhere. Strange birds, them two.'

The giant tree looms above us, seemingly unchanged from forty years before. We push through the creaking gate and circumnavigate the great bole of the trunk.

'You coming up, Billy?'

He pats his thigh, grins. 'Trick knee.'

The handholds and footholds feel in exactly the same positions; perhaps the tree has grown at the same rate as me. I clamber up a little creakily, but soon enough am settled into the high, familiar fork.

'Don't expect me to catch you,' Billy calls up.

Of course the old teachers' house, four doors down, draws my gaze first, and holds it for some time. Tiles on the roof now, the woodwork more brightly painted. Better kept lawn; unfamiliar, manicured shrubs. No scooters in sight. And no VW Beetles: a boat with an outboard is parked in Big Merv's drive.

'Anything in the snake hole?' from Billy.

'You think I'm going to stick my arm in and find out?'

'Yep,' he says, and chuckles. 'You always was a crazy bastard.'

I peer into the dark mouth of the hole cautiously, from various angles. It looks safe enough – no snakes, no man-eating possums. Nothing but a cellophane glint deep in the darkness. I reach in and retrieve a pack of Camel. For one absurd moment I think it might be forty years old, then flip open the top and find a disposable lighter inside.

'Billy,' I shout, and drop the modest treasure down through the foliage.

Footballer's reflexes: he catches it effortlessly, chuckles again. 'Fair go, Robbie! You stealing from kids now?'

A kid myself again, I plunge in my arm to the hilt, recklessly. Nothing bites back. Least of all does the past bite back: no boxes of rusting slugs, no forgotten sweet-sherry bottles.

'You better put these back,' Billy says. 'Before you get down.'

I drop out of the tree next to him. 'Finders keepers,' I tell him.

'Maybe just two,' he says, and we bend our heads together again and light up.

'I remember you did a shit out of the tree once,' he says, exhaling.

'*You* did the shit.'

'Pig's arse. It was you, Robbie. You was always horsing around.'
He shakes his head in disbelief. 'I nearly fell out of the tree laughing.
Jesus, they was great times. You could be a prick, but it wasn't the
same without you, after. Everyone missed you. Remember Anne
Hunter?'

'You remember Miss Peach?' I interrupt.

'Course. Everyone remembers. Chucked herself under the
train.' Another drag on his cigarette, a pursed-mouth grimace. 'Jeez,
these must have been up there a while.' He spits out a few loose
tobacco strands. 'Everyone reckoned Big Merv was fucking her.'

'Bullshit,' I say.

'No. Fair dinkum, that's what they reckoned.'

I take a large lungful of smoke, try to calm myself. 'What
happened to him?'

'Dunno. A real bastard at school, but a good bloke when you
got to know him. Played footy with him a couple of seasons. Course
he was a bit past it by then.' Another puff. 'You told everyone you
shagged her,' he suddenly remembers. 'Created a stink, that did.
Jeez, you got yourself into some scrapes.' A wistful shake of the
head. 'We both did. Remember that time they wanted to lock me
up in Colebrooke House?' He looks directly at me, grins. 'But you
told everyone I wasn't with you.'

I keep my lips clamped about my cigarette. If that's how he
wants to remember it, so be it. I'd like to be able to remember it
like that too.

That wistful look again. 'Best time of my life,' he says.

'And mine,' I say, and wonder for the first time if it was. I also
wonder, briefly, if my memory of those good times is as faulty as
his.

A car toots up the road. He glances away, turns back. 'Me old
man. Never one for standing about on his hind legs yakking. He'll

be wanting to look around. The sawmill. The footy club. Sacred sites, eh?' A self-mocking laugh. 'Mine too, I suppose.'

'Ours,' I say, and his face lights up, and for a moment it's the smaller, darker Billy of forty years ago standing there, made sentimental by sweet sherry, forever wishing he'd never left the last place he'd left.

'Been good to catch up,' I say, before anything else sentimental leaks out of my mouth. I offer my hand; he pumps it warmly.

'You too,' he says, then surprises me by stepping in and wrapping his arms around me. 'You too, brother.'

Touched, I press my lips briefly to his temple – a peck of brotherly affection, nothing more, but he steps back, startled, and eyes me suspiciously. Then grins and shakes his head. 'You was always a funny one, Robbie.'

He tosses me the pack of Camels. 'Make sure you put them back.'

'You don't trust me?'

His grin widens; the car toots once more. 'Come and see us on the Coorong sometime, Robbie. I'm chairman of the school council now. You could read some of your stories to the kids.'

6

It's the year 2064 and I have been proved wrong. Time-tourism is now possible, speed-of-light constraints have been circumvented. But the more things change, the more things stay the same. Tourists have been taking economy-class trips into space for years, but the cost of travel back into the past is prohibitive: a billion Earth-credits return – history-neutral, butterfly-effect tax not included. I need to rescue a butterfly from a railway line. If I've learnt one lesson in any of my hundred and fourteen years it's this: if you don't do things yourself, they don't get done. But how to pay for the trip? Win a lottery? Rob a bank? I reach for the phone instead. I have some urgent long-distance phone calls to make, very urgent and very long, at the speed of light.

I lift my head from my mother's kitchen table, force open my eyes. The loud knocking at the back door reaches me on some kind of delay loop, the sound registering only after the squeak of the door that in real time must have surely followed it.

'Young Lucifer?'

He has aged a little after all, close up. Gnarled knuckles. Red, rheumy eyes. Further signs are no doubt hidden under the dense facial shrubbery.

'Couldn't stay for the wake yesterday. Urgent call.'

My glance falls on the battered black bag in his hand. 'You're still practising?'

'Can't get the graduates out of the city. Someone has to hold the fort. Bit disappointed you didn't follow in my footsteps.'

I think: Perhaps I should have. This old but unageing man will outlive us all. What's his secret? That legendary emotional detachment? One thing is certain, he will never worry himself to death.

He eases his bulk into a chair, lifts the lid of the teapot and peers in.

'I'll make a fresh pot,' I say, rising.

'Odd line of work for a science-fiction writer,' he mutters as I fill the kettle.

'What is?'

'Teaching History.'

'The future is just the past repeated,' I tell him.

'Hmm?' He has his black bag of doctor-tools open and is

rummaging about inside. Glass phials spill out, a stethoscope tangled up with tongue depressors. I watch, amused. Does he plan to examine me for old time's sake? Both his hands are inside the bag now, up to the elbows; with difficulty he eases out a battered paperback – probably, it occurs to me, much as he once delivered me.

'Bought a copy of your book,' he says.

'So *you're* my reader.'

He blinks, uncomprehending, and slides the book across the table. *DNA AND DNA. Robert Burns.* 'Clever title.'

'Too clever by half. The publishers didn't get it. Then the sales department didn't think it would work.'

'A whole book of DNA stories?' He's still not listening.

'It's a selfish gene,' I say.

This joke is less over his head than beneath his notice. 'The first story is the best.'

I always bristle at such judgements. 'Oranges and apples,' I say.

He stares at me across his half-moons, baffled. 'Nice first line,' he says, opening the book. '"Once upon a time there will be a world . . ."'

Is he mumbling at me or just talking to himself? Perhaps it is the best story. Cleverest, best – in the world of sci-fi the words are largely interchangeable.

'Is the science correct, young Lucifer? Most DNA in our genes is, what, junk DNA? It doesn't do anything?'

'According to the boffins. Can't quite see it myself. Evolution doesn't waste resources. Which is my starting point.'

It's the year 2064 and a scientist mapping the human genome discovers a repeating sequence on a strand of DNA, the prime numbers 1, 2, 3, 5, 7, 11 counted out in base pairs. At first he can't believe the printouts. A sequence of primes can't happen accidentally.

'Fred Hoyle did something similar,' the doctor mumbles on. 'Didn't I once lend you *The Black Cloud*? Beaming prime numbers from outer space? As proof of intelligent life?'

'This is different,' I tell him. 'This is proof of a Creator. Of the hand of a Creator. His thumbprint on our genes. His trademark. Or so the world wants to believe. We *are* special after all. The churches are full again, sinners repent . . .'

He's reading the story himself now, lost to conversation. Has he got to the part where the scientist makes another discovery? A higher code is found, an ur-code, which is a modulation, a harmonic, of the original code, and the world's spiritual hopes come crashing down. *Made on Sirius IV* is the final message inscribed on human DNA. *Copyright. All Rights Reserved.*

He looks up from under his eyebrow thickets. 'You had me worried for a moment. Never took you for the superstitious sort.'

'It's just the warm-up story. A five-finger exercise.' At five-finger discount. For I can't fault his memory. I did borrow the Hoyle, forty years back.

'The next story is the best,' I tell him, but he no more registers contradictions than jokes.

'Your mission, *Homo sapiens*, should you decide to accept it,' I prompt. Same premise, different message. This time the junk DNA contains a code that will cause automatic self-destruction of the species after a trillion replications.

'Not sure about *this* ending,' he mutters.

'What do you mean?'

'Not quite finished, is it.'

'Of course it's finished.'

His watches me blankly, waiting.

'It's as if evolution is some kind of exam,' I explain. 'With a time limit. What answers will it come up with?' I'm beginning to enjoy talking about my work; I've had precious few opportunities.

'Doesn't that depend on the questions?'

'There's only one question.'

He waits again. This time I keep him waiting. The tea is stewed; I pour out two steaming cups. 'Milk?'

'And three sugars. What's the question?'

'Why?' I tell him.

'Why what?'

'Why *anything*? Why is there anything?'

'So what's the answer in your story?'

'It takes too long to work out. Time's up. Exam's over. Hand in your DNA.'

He sips thoughtfully at his tea. 'Did we pass or fail?'

'I let readers make up their own minds. My stories don't spell things out. Think of them as philosophical hypotheticals.'

He doesn't appear convinced.

'They are how I interrogate the assumptions of our culture,' I add grandly. A phrase nicked from Susan the First, who probably nicked it from Ursula K. Le Guin. It impresses the doctor far less than it impressed me all those years back.

'So what's next? New book in the pipeline?'

'My memory isn't good enough for writing science fiction any more,' I tell him. A more original line – one of my best – but still beneath his notice. The doctor is reading the last story, *The Second Coming of Santa*. It's the year 2064 and a scientist in Bari, Italy, clones St Nicholas from DNA remnants found on his sacred relics in the ossuary of the local cathedral.

'Ever thought of bringing back dinosaurs, young Lucifer? T. Rex?'

'Can't be done. No DNA. Just eggshells and bone.'

The clone of Santa Claus is reared in great secrecy, on a military base near the North Pole, until on Christmas Day . . .

The doctor's beeper startles both of us; once again the source of the sound seems to mystify him. He finds it in the third pocket he searches, reads a message, shrugs and puts it back.

'Santa Claus the best choice? Would have thought Jesus Christ.' He is on his feet now, closing his bag, 'Fragments of the Cross,' he mutters, preoccupied. 'Shroud of Turin . . . Plenty of DNA.' He is still muttering to himself as he hobbles out the door.

7

It's the year 1975 and I am twenty-four and teaching Latin and Ancient History in my first school posting, just married, just breakfasted, and staring down at the morning paper when a familiar face staring back from page three arrests my gaze. I'd know it anywhere: the dumb, impassive eyes, the recessed silver nose, the orange, square-jawed chin. *End of an Era: Last Bluebirds Decommissioned.*

A gorge of anger rises in my throat; I rear to my feet, scattering newspaper and cereal. 'About time!' I shout. 'About fucking time!' A woman called Susan comes running from the bathroom, alarmed – 'What's the matter, darling?' – and for a moment I wonder who the hell she is, and where the hell I am.

It's the year 1964 and I open my eyes. I have missed the evening train, but hopefully Miss Peach will leave in the morning instead. If at all. No panic. Plenty of time. I close my eyes again – or perhaps my heavy lids, heavier than my heart has ever been, close themselves.

What wakes me? The thumping of my heart? The phone ringing

in the hall? I hear the tread of police-issue bootsteps. My father's voice.

'Robbie's in bed. Who is this? You, Billy-boy? Some kind of joke? Who is it then? No, you can't talk to him. He's not well. Nearly burnt the stables down last night . . . What? What kind of cock-and-bull story is that? No? If this is a joke, I don't think it's funny.'

More heavy steps, my bedroom door opening. 'What have you been up to now, sonny-jim?'

My mother's face appears in the door behind him. 'Who was it?'

'Some drunken idiot. Wanted to talk to Robbie. Kept saying there'll be an accident in the morning. Some nonsense about having to stop the Bluebird.'

'Possum? He only drank tea last night.'

'Sounded long-distance. You know anything about this, sonny-jim?'

I am half conscious only. The conscious half knows nothing, the dreaming half thinks it's a dream; I close my heavy eyes again, and sleep.

It's 1964 and my parents are in Adelaide for the weekend and my former best friend is snoring on the floor. What time is it? I stick my head out the door. Ten to nine on the hall clock.

The phone rings; I lift it to my ear. Nothing but hiss and static at first, the sound of great distances across time and space. Then a faint, echoey word: 'Robert?'

'Who is it?'

'You don't recognise your own voice?'

That voice is not unlike my father's, made hoarse and less firm with age. 'Dad? Is that you?'

'Never mind who. I'm ringing from the future. I need to tell you something.'

'Are you drunk, Dad?'

'It's not Dad. Listen. I can prove it. Billy has just tried to kiss you. How could Dad know that?'

I splutter, laughing. I like this game. 'Billy – where the fuck *are* you?' I shout, then remember he is snoring on the floor in the room behind me.

'I need you to pay attention,' the voice whispers in its great echo chamber. 'It's very important you listen carefully to everything I say.'

A quick glance up and down the hall. Is someone spying on me?

'In a few hours you will be in Miss Peach's bed. You will have sex with her.'

More laughter bursts out of me. Am I dreaming? Still high on distilled ether and sweet sherry?

'You mustn't do it. *We* mustn't do it. She'll get pregnant.'

The dream voice fades back into hiss and static. I hang up the phone, then head for the dream door and my dream bike, planning to stay asleep as long as possible, to make use of the dream, to see if there is a place for Miss Peach in it, and if so, what might follow. There are no rules in dreams. No one can be hurt, nothing is against the law. Anything is possible, any alternative future. Ideas for such futures fill my head as I ride, a swarm of futures.

It's the year 2064 and human beings have become a pampered leisure class. Robot workers assemble the cars and homes and planes, robot farmers till the fields and fish the seas, robot soldiers fight the wars. Robot maids make the beds each morning, robot Pleasure Units unmake them each night, with a little help from their human companions.

Life is wonderful. Time passes. But by the year 3064 the computers that run the world have begun to show signs of age. Slowly the machines forget how to look after us, and we – their basket-weaving, wet-brain dependants, their soft toys – are left helpless, having long ago forgotten how to look after ourselves.

'Another TEOTWAWKI story,' Miss Peach says as she hands it back after school.

'Teot-what, Miss?'

It's the year 1964 and her smile is the only sunny thing in a wintry afternoon. 'The End Of The World As We Know It. Where *do* you get your ideas from, Robbie?'

They surprise me too, I might have said. They still do. It's the year 2007 and here's a more depressing one, arriving even as I write: might senior moments offer creative opportunities? Might forgetfulness somehow free up the brain by emptying it out, thereby allowing it to go on surprising itself for ever? But how to forget here, now? I turn my attention back to the train of boxes. No sheath-knife has come to light; I scrounge a tomato knife from the oddments drawer and slit the binding of the first in line, *Robbie, 1957.*

I lift the lid and even after all these years the mothball fumes fill my nose so powerfully I am forced to lean back. A string-tied stack of Dick and Dora readers on top. *This is Spot. See Spot Run.* Bundled artworks come next, in two distinct styles – expressionist finger-paintings, and representational watercolours of stick-figures under half-inch blue bands of sky. Another string-tied stack: exercise books, filled with mostly correct spelling and always correct sums. In the bottom of the box, my Grade One report. *Having arrived at school already able to read and write, Robert has a tendency to be a little restless in class . . .*

I reach for the knife and release the fumes of the next year. More of the same books. My handwriting has become flowingly cursive, but the sky on the artworks is still that same half-inch blue strip across the top of the page. Did I see nothing as it was? Did I not even look out the window?

Robbie, 1959. A sky-blue background all the way down at last. A white sailboat perched on a sea-blue horizon. New perspectives in reading also; I lift out a small stack of *Wide Range Readers* and thumb my way in. Old favourites catch my eye. *The Boy Who Liked Stories*, a four-page life of Robert Louis Stevenson. *The Girl Who Liked Science* – Madame Curie, who had her own backyard laboratory as a girl. *Horatio at the Bridge. Leonidas and the Three Hundred.* Pungent memories all of them, mixed with the pungent naphtha of the mothballs. *Traveller, tell the Spartans that here we lie, obedient to their Law.* I am reading slowly, infinitely more slowly than the speed of light, but I am travelling back through time surely enough; the goosebumps that spider-walk up my backbone feel exactly the same as those of half a century ago.

Actual time moves onwards in the other direction. Afternoon becomes evening as I browse through the box-cars – *1960, 1961* – dipping in and out and back and forth and taking all the time in the world, drinking all the tea in the caddy and not thinking about the caboose waiting at the end. It's the year 1963 and here is my final primary-school report, with Miss Burke's praise that surprised and pleased me at the time, but which now reads as faint and formal and pursed-lipped, the very minimum that a top boy could be given. *I can't recall ever teaching a boy as quick as Robert, which hasn't been easy at times. If he can learn to temper his cleverness with self-discipline . . .*

Her voice rises from the fumes, with Miss Hammond's not far behind. I amuse myself by channelling them aloud, like a medium. 'Faint praise, Miss Hammond. Do I speak the truth?' 'The whole truth and nothing but, Miss Burke. As always.' 'The boy has talent, Miss Hammond. But can it be properly harnessed?'

I take a last deep gulp of tea, an even deeper breath of air, and reach for the knife again; the final box can be shirked no longer.

The 1964 high-school magazine sits on top. I open it calmly enough, even a little eagerly, wanting suddenly to look at her again, to see her face. Of course she isn't in the staff photo. She was dust and ashes long before the end-of-year photo. Miss Hammond is there, breasting into the camera; Big Merv, grim-faced, arms folded; Jingle Bell, front and centre, hand in pocket. Miss P. Peach isn't even listed in the *Absents*. Nor does her name appear in the *Class IA Report*, written by Anne Hunter. Neither does mine, but my surge of indignation is for her alone. How seamlessly she has been purged from the official history of that year. A second-term lesson on the Russian Revolution comes back to me. *We know the future with absolute certainty*, she clacked across the board, *it's the past that keeps changing*. 'Does anyone know the source of that quote? Anyone?'

Not me, then or now. I lift out a stack of textbooks. *Romeo and Juliet. Intermediate Latin Grammar. Australian Poets Speak.* This last I remember. *Down in that poor country no pauper was I . . .*

Beneath the text books – what? Exercise books. Exercise books all the way down, smelling of mothballs. *Destination Pluto* on the topmost cover. *By Robert James Burns.* Is this foreigner's handwriting an earlier, neater version of mine? Only an expert could tell.

It was five o'clock, on the morning of December 3, 2064. The two-seater G-class space-fighter, was rocketing through the Magellan dust-cloud at a steady fifty thousand miles, per second. Then, suddenly, the navigator turned to shout, to the pilot. 'Bandits at three o'clock, skipper. Coming in fast.'

'Got 'em, Billy,' Squadron Leader Robbie Burns replied, coolly. 'They're coming out of the supernova, the bastards. Hold on tight.'

He banked right, and put the G-class through an Immelman turn, an old fighter pilot's trick he had learnt in the Sirian Wars . . .

I laugh out loud. Interrogations of the assumptions of the culture? Not back then, it seems. Was I really that bad? Purple-ink corrections everywhere – crossed-out commas, colons mutated into semicolons, endless margin comments. *Why exactly this day and month, Robbie?* I imagine her amusement, although there is no sign of amusement, or even condescension, in her words.

Her words? *Yours*, surely, as I read on, and your voice begins to rise from the page, a perfume far more powerful than naphtha. *Would anything be visible in a dust-cloud, Robbie?* For a moment you might be sitting on the far side of the table; I smile, as I smiled forty years before, at your ignorance of cosmic lore. *Do you need to explain what you mean by an Immelman turn?* Likewise your ignorance of Biggles lore.

I riffle the pages with my thumb, and the purple markings that flicker in the margins come to a kind of jerky, animated life. Novels, I liked to call these stories at the time, but they were never more than one standard, lined, 48-page exercise book in length. And never less: the words poured out of me in a scribbled reverie until I found myself on the last page, still a million light years from home and with any number of loose narrative threads to tie up.

I became good at endings. Too good, you often teased me. Too neat. *Traveller tell the Earthlings that here we lie disintegrated, obedient to their Law. The End.*

The final word is yours: a large purple tick, a mark – *17/20* – and a line of encouragement: *Very imaginative, Robbie – although you left the best line till last. Have you read* Brave New World *yet?*

Green or red sticker? Amber. Too early to say. It's only been forty years. My nose prickles, my eyes mist over. Too much moth-naphtha? I reach for the next book. *The Sands of Mars.* This time I read only your purple-ink comments, wishing you had written more and I had written less. Wishing I had written nothing. These Boy's Own stories are nothing like the clever hypotheticals I remember. *Expand, expand . . . Remind me to talk to you about this bit,*

Robert . . . Nicely put . . . One too many adjectives, a bad habit of yours . . . 19/20. Olaf Stapledon did something similar in First and Last Men, *which I will lend to you if you like. Have you finished* Anna Karenina?

No, I haven't, Miss – still – and yes, I would like. Right now I would like. I reach for the next book. *Once Upon a Time There Will be a World . . .*

'Young Lucifer?' The voice startles me; he is framed in the kitchen door again, propped on his stick. 'Getting absent-minded in my old age.' He steps through and sets his black bag on the table. 'Had something else to show you this morning.'

'Another book?'

'Hmm? No. Well, the same book, in a way.' He is up to his elbows in the bag again. 'It got me thinking.'

A more difficult delivery: he struggles to ease out a specimen jar, which he plonks down on the table before me. 'I think you should have this.'

For a time the pale, amoebic shape inside the bottle doesn't register. It might be anything from his collection of wacky pickles. Fish? Fowl? Mutant vegetable?

The doctor's low rumble in the background. 'She came to see me that last week. Worried sick. Couldn't keep anything down.' He looks away, pensive. 'Wouldn't let me examine her.'

My hairline begins to prickle. I peer at the thing in the jar: three or four inches long, small bird-body, big pale head, bulging eyelids fused shut. Animal, certainly. Not quite a bird – where's the beak? – but also not quite human.

'Found this little feller at the postmortem. This a fresh pot?'

No, more than human: a more intelligent species in which the head has grown as large as the body, and the vestigial limbs have shrunk to bent matchsticks. It might be an ancient homunculus, a creature that has lived for ever – except for the baby thumb stuck in its baby mouth.

I can't seem to move; he pours himself a cup of cold tea, sits at my side.

'Ten weeks,' he says. 'Eleven at the outside. Male of the species. Nice lesson in embryology. Testes undescended. Chorda neurona still cartilaginous, not yet ossified.'

I could be sitting in the Caledonian Hall with my father, forty years before, listening to the Facts of Life in Latin. The numbness rises in me, my throat is clogged, my breathing fast; this time the facts are far too late.

'Did Dad know?' I get out.

The doctor blinks at me, switches back into English. 'Of course. It was a suicide. Coroner's case. Full autopsy report. He was the first to know.'

And the last, I realise immediately, with the certainty of revelation. He told no one, not even my mother. Especially not my mother. There were no late-night chats behind the bedroom door, no front-bar celebrations. The report ended up in the backyard incinerator, doused in kerosene.

The doctor begins mumbling again. 'The unmarried ones thought it was the end of the world back then.' He shakes his shaggy head, incredulous. 'Never could understand the fuss.'

I find my tongue. 'No greater shame in those days.'

'But to put your neck on a railway track. Completely irrational.'

Is that an irrational tear in his rheumy eye? He wipes it away with his grubby coat-sleeve, takes a gulp of tea. Cold, and surely bitter, but he doesn't seem to notice.

'Always liked delivering babies myself. Sponging them down, weighing them. Best part of the job, weighing babies. You would have enjoyed it, young Lucifer. Like weighing butter.' He tugs a crumpled handkerchief from a pocket, blows his nose, then nods towards the pickle bottle. 'Could have found a good family for it.'

My own eyes are prickling. 'She could have brought it up herself,' I say.

'You and I might think so. Makes sense. But we'd have been the only ones. A single mother. By herself —'

'I would have helped,' I interrupt.

'At fourteen?'

'Nearly fifteen!' I shout, as childishly as ever. 'We could have brought it up together.'

He thinks for a moment, always the rationalist. 'It's possible. She told me it was yours. Don't know how she knew for certain.'

'What's that supposed to mean?'

'She had plenty of admirers.'

Including one I never suspected, but that is of no account as we stare into the bottle and the bird-fish floating inside.

'It was mine,' I eventually say. 'It is mine.'

'You're the DNA expert,' he mumbles. He blinks at me again, then closes his bag and rises, leaving the jar on the table. And as though the tears in his eyes are due merely to naphthalene, he adds brightly: 'Read something about Asimov the other day. Apparently has books in every Dewey Decimal section of the library – except Philosophy 802.'

It's 1964, term two, the afterglow of the second meeting of your precious Lyceum Club. A large crowd again; the professor's visit is still only a rumour for next time. I have lingered late, finding things to do, chipped blue china to rinse, cake dishes to de-crumb, cutlery to wash. I have outlasted the Tweedle-twins, and both Bells, and the doctor, and the entire flock of your teenage replicants and their cyborg mothers. I have outlasted my own mother – 'Miss Peach asked me to stay and clean up.' I have even outlasted Big Merv.

It is me, and me alone, who walks you to the staff car park.

'I though a symposium on Plato might be asking a bit much, but it went well, Robbie. Don't you think?'

Was the subject Plato? It might as well have been Pluto; I have been watching more than listening. 'Everyone loved it, Miss.'

As always your smile is the warmest part of the evening, a radiant, all-encompassing warmth. 'Do you think so? Really?' The question needs no answer from me. 'It was a triumph, I think. Are you riding home, Robbie?'

'Walking tonight, Miss.' An unthinking lie, but inspired.

'Jump on. I'll give you a lift.'

'Me?' Unthinking again, but this time uninspired.

'Can't see anyone else.' You laugh, glowing, exultant, and pat the pillion seat behind you. 'Hold on tight. Can't have you falling off.'

I reach my long clumsy arms around your wasp-waist and hold you far more carefully than I have held anything before. Your neck is an inch from my mouth, your scented hair an inch from my nose. Banished for life from the country of childhood, its exiles, who are all of us, are determined to believe they did things more innocently there – but your buttocks are definitely an inch from my stiff cock. I can barely breathe for the thrill of it, I can barely think for happiness – a new, non-default happiness that is off any previously known scale.

We putter slowly home, the engine straining beneath an extra passenger, but who wants speed? I want this to last for ever, and when it is over, all too soon, and I watch you wave happily and ride away into the night, I want the memory of it to last for ever, which I suppose it has, losing none of its magic through a thousand messy late-night or early morning re-enactments.

It might be the last thing I remember. You will certainly be the last thing I forget. And I would have that ride home in bliss the last of all, the last thing I see when the last light is turned out and I too go up in smoke.

It's the year 600 billion AD and everything has gone up in smoke. Planets, worlds, stars – all going, going, gone, all spun into galactic ash, intergalactic dust, cosmic wind. Traveller, tell thermodynamic entropy that here we lie, obedient to its Law, all of us and all our stuff, our present selves and our foreign selves, students and teachers, poets and footballers, war heroes and war comics, clag-sperm and pickle-jars, bicycle thieves and bicycle centaurs and baked-bean thieves, all vaporised in the great swirling flask of the universe. Mr and Mrs Carlo Ponti are here, and Misses Tweedledum and Tweedledee, and Mum and Dad, and Billy and Uncle Possum, and the once immortal doctor, the finally mortal me, the already mortal you. My last astounding story – this story – is here, and the desk I slap it down on, which is always yours. Look at me, Miss! I've finished! It's the future and all's well, all of us together again, all mixed and dispersed, reduced to our elements, carbon and hydrogen, lead and gold, sulphur and brimstone, and they to their elements, to protons and neutrons and quarks, all of us and all of them blowing with the wind, the unsentimental cosmic wind that blows through Church Street, Penola, the stiff galactic wind that blows us all away, every wisp and speck of us, blows on across South Australia, Australia, Earth, Solar System, Milky Way, Universe . . .

Acknowledgements

I owe a huge debt to my wife Lisa Temple and my daughter Anna
Goldsworthy for their patient reading and rereading of numerous
drafts, and their judicious criticism and encouragement. Thanks also to
Meredith Rose of the astonishing eidetic memory, and for her endless
necessary editorial cruelties; and to Ben Ball for useful early advice.

My Penola researchers, Margaret Muller and Peter Rymill, provided
painstaking background checking; from my parents, Jan and Reuben,
came additional period detail.

A large debt is also owed to my late friends and patients, Veronica Brodie
and Doug Milera, who shared their memories of mission childhoods with
me, and later with the rest of the world through their memoirs: Veronica's
My Side of the Bridge (Wakefield Press), and Doug's *Walkabout to Nowhere*
(Australian Foundation on Alcoholism and Drug Dependence).

Thanks also to another of my patients, retired Police Sergeant Len
White, for useful backgrounding, and to various members of the South
Australia Police Historical Society.